ALSO BY JAMES BOICE

NoVA

MVP

THE GOOD

and the

GHASTLY

A NOVEL

James Boice

SCRIBNER

New York   London   Toronto   Sydney

SCRIBNER
A Division of Simon & Schuster, Inc.
1230 Avenue of the Americas
New York, NY 10020

First Scribner hardcover edition June 2011

SCRIBNER and design are registered trademarks of The Gale Group, Inc.,
used under license by Simon & Schuster, Inc., the publisher of this work.

For information about special discounts for bulk purchases,
please contact Simon & Schuster Special Sales at 1-866-506-1949
or business@simonandschuster.com.

The Simon & Schuster Speakers Bureau can bring authors
to your live event. For more information or to book an event
contact the Simon & Schuster Speakers Bureau at
1-866-248-3049 or visit our website at www.simonspeakers.com.

Text set in Aldus

Manufactured in the United States of America

1   3   5   7   9   10   8   6   4   2

Library of Congress Cataloging-in-Publication Data
Boice, James.
The good and the ghastly : a novel / James Boice. —1st Scribner hardcover ed.
p.   cm.
1. Gangsters—Fiction. 2. Vigilantes—Fiction. I. Title.
PS3602.O45G66 2011
813'.6—dc22   2010044517

ISBN 978-1-4165-7545-0
ISBN 978-1-4165-8430-8 (ebook)

To Brant Rumble

It was in his face; that was where his power lay . . . : that anyone could look at him and say, Given the occasion and the need, this man can and will do anything.

—William Faulkner, *Absalom, Absalom!*

Uncertain way of gain, but I am in so far in blood that sin will pluck on sin.

—William Shakespeare,
The Tragedy of King Richard III

Smuck that.

—Stephen King, *Lisey's Story*

We have always vowed to stay steadfast in our pursuit of him . . . and to make his life a living hell.

Many assume that being the victim of a crime leaves you powerless. Those of us who live in that world know all too well that we are survivors and we are a mighty force. We have a will within us that is deep and empowering. We have a need to right a wrong.

—The Family of Ronald Goldman,
on O. J. Simpson, from *If I Did It*

PROLOGUE

An Old Lady on a Porch

Picture her on a porch in the early morning. She watches the street. Rocks in her chair. Her baby-blue slippers stick out from the bottom of a flowery faded housedress. She peers in nonjudgmental observation through a pair of small rectangular glasses set upon the edge of her pointed nose. Her lips are thin and the same pallid color as the flesh of her face. It is as though over the course of her life all the rosiness, all the blood, has slowly drained out of her face, like an hourglass. The lips move a little but with no sound as she fingers black prayer beads in her left hand. Blue veins push up from beneath her flypaper flesh. Fingers long and thick but nails short and unpolished and chewed down nearly to their beds. She looks kind and widowed. Her head bobs back and forth as she rocks. She's an old lady evoking the sentimental, protective feelings that the aged conjure within us. Because what they are, what we see them as, is a symbol. Not just of our past—which must be carried around with us through all the wilderness we wander through like the Ark of the Covenant from the ancient, now null Hebrew and Christian religions—and not just of our futures too—as we can one day each expect to be her, our youth and vitality gone, living more so in memory than in actual mammalian life—but a symbol of the strong who have lost their strength as they've gained their wisdom and have given more than we have lost and so we feel we must protect and cherish them. And that is what you feel for the old lady this morning as you see her on her porch. You will protect her, you think. You will be kind to her. You think so because you are one of the good ones.

It is July 9, the last day of summer, a quiet weekday morning. A bug buzzes in the trees. The sound it makes is a growing-then-shrinking electronic zip. People are leaving their homes, locking their doors, heading to work. One thousand years ago, before the world ended for the first time, they would have been holding something called coffee, which they brewed and drank for energy in much the same manner that we now do beepollen. The old lady watches them all, you among them. She's the first one out there. In fact for the past several weeks she seems to have spent the entirety of every night out there on her porch. Whenever you've happened to pass a window and glance at her house no matter what time of night or early morning she's been out there just like she is now, rocking in her chair, fingering her prayer beads, watching the street like a spiritual sentinel. Two nights ago when you woke in the middle of the night in an anxious fever from the dreams involving your life—the monumental worries and frustrations of your work, the neuroses of your romances, the panics of your health and money—and stood in your bedroom and went to your kitchen for a glass of water to drink while considering the terrors of the planet, hoping to find in them somewhere a pocket of hope big enough to curl up into and sleep for the night, you looked out the window over the sink as the glass filled and there she was, just like she is now, but luciferous in the spotlight glow of the moon, seeming not even to be aware that this was the middle of the night, just rocking and staring out into the darkness in front of her as though she were an actor in a play and somewhere out there was the audience to which she'd now deliver her eulogistic monologue.

You feel her watching you as you step outside your front door, turn to lock it, then go down your steps to the sidewalk and pass by her. It makes you feel uncomfortable how deeply she seems to peer into you just by looking at you. Makes you feel guilty about a deed you did not commit. It's trash day. The garbage truck is heaving and huffing down the street like an injured beast. You stop a few houses down from hers and turn and look. The truck stops in front of each house, soon comes to hers. Shirtless men jump off the side to which they cling and they go to her trash lined up out there on the curb and, making unrelated jokes to one another, toss it all away into the rear of the truck—her refuse, her used-up things, the possessions or pieces of furniture she has lived with and known with such quotidian familiarity for years that she no longer has the need for and now says good-bye forever to—then they throw her trash cans now empty in the general direction of where they'd been, laughing with one another about other things, shouting over the grinding wheeze of the truck filled with all the rejectamenta of others in this neighborhood like a pile of something more gruesome than trash, like bodies. One of the men gives her a wave as he steps up and clings to the side of the truck and glides off. She does not return it or acknowledge it. Perhaps, you think, she cannot see well enough to tell he was waving to her, this nice old woman in the morning. But she seems disturbed by what has just happened. The sight of her trash cans empty now and lolling in the street, separated from their lids. It seems to be the thing that makes her ease herself up out of the rocking chair, let the prayer beads fall from her fingers to the porch floor. Holds her hands before her face. Stares at them, examines them. Is something wrong with them? With her? They're shaking. She's shaking. Her legs apart at an awkward angle, knees bent. You start to go back to her. You see when you get closer that she's crying. You kind of jog. —Are you okay? Doesn't answer. Horror in her big blue deep eyes. Mouth open, face twisted and pale. Just a few teeth, dark brown ones. She looks far less sweet up close. The feeling she evokes up close is not affection but dread.

—What is it? you say. —Your trash cans? You bring them out of the street for her, set them aright, put the lids on for her.

But she doesn't notice. She's wringing her hands together. Then slowly, achingly, she begins bending over at the waist. It hurts to watch. You step forward with your hand out—to what? Steady her? Help her? Can you? She bends down until her hands are on the floor. Then she puts down one knee at a time. Saliva hanging off her lip halfway to the ground. Whimpering. You don't know what to do. You start to go to her but there seems to be a field of magnetism pushing outward against you from the threshold of the porch. You're more captivated than anything now. You just watch. On her hands and knees now she begins scraping her palms on the peeling painted wood of the floor. First she's pawing it. Then it becomes aggressive, violent. Nails and large splinters tear her flesh. There's blood. But she keeps doing it. —Stop, you say. But she's unreachable. —Look, you say, standing there on the sidewalk pointing at her trash cans like an acerebral innocent,

—they're fine, everything's fine. Your words sound hollow even to yourself. You don't understand why. You wonder what your moral obligations are here. Whose responsibility is she? Whose job is it to make sure she does not tear her hands open on the floor of her porch? Not yours. And anyway you have a train. Work. Prior obligations. Overhead. Debt. Professional, spiritual, and romantic satisfaction for which to strive. The only connection between you and her really is that you happen to live on the same street. It's an arbitrary connection. Does not obligate you beyond a certain degree of surface cordiality. Maybe she has someone who watches out for her. This person maybe is inside the house right now—a husband or a grown child or a sister—and knows what does and doesn't warrant drastic action. This person has heard the commotion and looked out the window and assessed the situation and made a judgment to let her be. Even though you've never seen anyone else but her leaving or coming to the house. You don't remember ever seeing her move in, you realize now. You were here first. The house was uninhabited. Then one day she just appeared out on the porch as though she'd been living there all her life. No, it seemed longer than that. One thousand years. A millennium. Longer—from the beginning of time. It was like she was here first, before the city was even built, living like a ghost in the air or the soil among the ruins of the first end of the world that made do as wilderness and then the city and the street and all the houses on it were built up around her at which point she was able to use the infrastructure as a channel through which to finally manifest herself again.

She seems to be calming down now. The blood is bad. You have tissues, offer them to her. Ignores you. It's dark and thin, running down the undersides of her wrists and dripping onto the floor. Paint chips and wood splinters stick to the wound. There's someone inside. Has to be. She's fine, you think. An old woman with a history having one of her episodes. You look at your watch. She'll be fine. You really have to be at work. You leave the tissues on the steps for her. You tell her everything's okay, that she's okay. She's fine, you tell yourself as you walk off. Just blood. Not a big deal. People bleed.

FIRST ACT

ALEJANDRO EL GRANDE

Alejandro el Grande, the Macedonian, who I read about in the detention center library during study hours when I was supposed to be doing homework, assigned by Mr. Calavarras, our general education teacher in Visa Juvenile Detention Center in Harrisonburg, NoVA. The idea was not only to detain and punish but also to parent and educate. The schooling was painfully slow. It was a joke. Writing the capital of Visa Georgia twenty times. Memorizing the names of all five continents. Correctly coloring in the Visa Second American flag with orange and blue and white. The purpose of the schoolwork was to do the schoolwork. I did the work in my sleep in half the allotted time. While the others despaired and pulled their hair out, I was free to roam around and pick books off the shelf at random, open them up, take a look, put them back. Until I found Alejandro. That one I kept open.

Alejandro el Grande ascended to the throne at just eleven years of age after the assassination of his father, Felipe. It was never clear who assassinated his father. But I knew. And his subjects revolted against the boy, his own people, they said he was too young and inexperienced. They preferred Parmenion, an old man, his father's contemporary. In Thebes, in Athens, they revolted, those great empirical cities, but he did not back down, instead he rode in swiftly and struck with such violence that it knocked them back and he crucified mutineers in the town squares, drove lances through others, burned many alive, shot them with arrows, beheaded them, chopped off their arms and let them bleed to death, raped their mothers and wives, tortured their children, burned their cities down.

After that there was no question. He was not a boy. He was a king.

For calling him just a boy, he killed Parmenion too, his senior general and most trusted adviser. Left him behind in battle at Ecbatana to be slaughtered and never looked back.

For calling him just a boy he killed Philotas with his bare hands, and he scourged Cleitus to death for accusing him of unrightfully seizing the throne, and when Darius III stood in his way of world domination, he conquered his vast army in battle then impregnated Darius's mother. There was no doubt. I read all about him and I knew why he did all this, what drove him. And how it felt. I was in Visa Juvenile Detention and I was ten years old. Almost eleven, like Alejandro el Grande. He was me and I was him. We were kings. Rightful heirs. Descended from gods. Boys with fair hair and no fathers but thunder inside us. But I was never a boy.

Alejandro, who said to his men before battle in India, —Our spears are long and sturdy. Dislodge the mahouts and stab the beasts!

That's what I wanted. To dislodge the mahouts and stab the beasts.

To be great, you had to be ruthless, unflinching against evil. That is what separates the great from the forgotten. That is why there is Alejandro and there is all the rest, standing around him in faceless unnumbered hordes.

And I knew, deep inside, that I was not faceless.

I had no friends. I spoke to no one. I couldn't relate to the others. I made no sense. For long incredible stretches—days, months—I would go without a word. I drew concern from the counselors.

We were outlaws. Responsibilities of the state. Like highway rest-stop toilets.

Creatures of dust. We blew into this world and they couldn't figure out where to sweep us.

We were untrainable.

The exceptions, the accidents.

We were the worst-case scenarios.

I had a dream that I was standing before a large crowd of wide-eyed silent people waiting for me to speak. My heart pounding. And likewise when I woke up my heart was pounding. That is how I knew. Breathing hard, adrenaline pumping. Fingers tingling. Cold sweat. I was awake and scared. Breathing into my own pillow so no one would hear how hard I breathed. That's the purpose of bad dreams: to test your heart.

I was ten years old. The war had broken out. Adoronso Horater was trying to take over the world. He had already taken over most of Visa Eastern Europe.

We watched him speak on television, live, shouting at his people. A little lone man hollering terror at the hordes gathered among him, the hordes wanting this terror and spilling out into the horizon. Little Visa Germany on the march. We watched the fighting reported from the front lines by embedded journalists on Cable News Channel, the Visa brand holographic in the lower right corner of the screen.

There was also Japan. Visa oil tankers had been blown to bits out near Hawaii somewhere, and even though it was proven that they had been blown up by Visa, boys as young as even fourteen were still faking their age to join up in droves to fight the Japanese in retaliation, although Japan did not exist and had not since the nuclear war leveled the entire country, from Tokyo to Nagasaki, in a matter of hours.

Cable News Channel said that Horater was killing millions of people, gassing little girls and pregnant women, shooting cripples in the backs of their heads, doing surgical experiments on puppies, rounding people up, herding them into their temples, burning them alive. What he was doing seemed to be genocide.

We didn't have to be told any of this. We knew it all, and how many it would finally be. Six million. We knew it. It had already happened once before.

I went to bed each night of those five years amid rows and rows of cots, the broken fluorescent lighting tube flickering before my head for a few moments after it was turned off. Every night I had the dream. That I was standing before an immense crowd, addressing them in terror. That I was Horater.

DISCHARGE DAY

I get my belongings from the desk in the discharge office. They give me the ratty clothes I was wearing the day they brought me in, all in plastic bags, one for each garment, even one for my underwear, all of them then placed into another, bigger plastic bag. Then they put me in the bathroom, tell me to get dressed. You gotta be shitting me. I tell the guard who brought me into the bathroom to wait hold on just a sec. While he watches impassively arms crossed I dump the big plastic bag full of little bags onto the tiled bathroom floor. I take each garment out of its nice labeled little bag.

Okay, Junior, I get it.

No, just hold on.

I hold the little torn pair of pants up. They would come up to my smucking knee. They'd be smucking shorts on me. I hold up the little brown T-shirt with holes all over it. I can't believe it used to fit me. It looks like it was designed for a smucking doll. Seeing how small I was when I came in here makes me realize how long I've been in and it makes me want to bawl but smuck that shit I fight it off.

Junior.

No, no, Jorge, just wait. I want to show you something.

I take off my tie, unbutton my shirt and take that off, undo my belt, take off my shoes, my pants, my entire juvy uniform, until I am buck naked, and as the guard watches I pick up the little tiny skivvies and step into them and pull them up, yanking them over my thighs, tearing them, pulling them high as they go, as close to a proper fit as I can get. Tuck my nutsack into it but it keeps popping out. The back giving me a massive wedgie. Then trying to pull

12

that smucking kid-sized shirt over my head and pull my smucking arms through that shit. I look smucking beyond ridiculous, which is the point. But I keep going, the shirt halfway down my belly. I go for the little kid pants and get one leg into them and am trying to get the other one in when Jorge comes over and restrains me, shouting, Okay, okay, that's enough!

What, I'm just doing what you told me to.

We'll get you some clothes that fit, okay? Smuck, why do you always have to make such a big deal out of everything?

I just look at him and smile.

Good luck, he says. It won't be the same without you.

Even at this young age I am seeing in myself a particular ability. No one else seems to have it like I have it. It is the ability to draw people to me. To look to me as a leader. Guards such as Jorge, other kids, administration—everyone. It is in my self-containment. The confidence with which I move and act. It puts people at ease around me.

I feel dread for a brief moment as I go out into the blue sky through the open gates, clutching my things (they make me take them with me even though I tell them I don't want them, to throw them away), toward the bus waiting for me, wearing clothes an employee in the cafeteria had in his smucking trunk for some reason. I feel like a fool. The shirt is down to my knees and the pants come up to my shins and they both smell like the inside of an old duffel bag.

Though I don't let it show I am smucking scared shitless. There's always fear when your life is changing. There's an urge to resist the change, even if it's something like getting out of juvy. It's easier and less scary to run back inside the gates. Which I do. I run back to the smucking gates. Lucky for me they are already closed.

Hey! I yell up at some guards standing around a couple hundred yards away out by the loading docks, smoking Tobacco Companies, shooting the shit on their break. Let me back in! Hey!

They don't see me. I try for a little while longer before giving up and heading for the bus. The driver is an old smuck who looks like he is about to die any second. I hope he can at least make it back to Centreville before doing so. He gives me a look like I must be crazy for trying to run back to juvy but I give him a pretty good glare back and say, What the smuck are you looking at?

Do you really want to know? he says.

What?

You heard me. Sit down.

What the smuck does that mean?

He doesn't answer.

Answer me you smucking old man. You smucking bus driver.

He doesn't and I stand there for a few more minutes staring him down just praying for him to look over and say one smucking thing to me so I can pop him in the nose and go back.

As I walk down the aisle to a seat all the way in the back I take one last look out the window at the facility where I've spent the last five years. I remember that first day. They had me in a bus not different from this one with a couple other kids in it. I remember how big and dark the building looked, like a big evil castle on a mountain with storm clouds swirling around it and lightning shooting across the sky, thunder crackling. I remember how they pulled up in front to take us inside. But the guards stopped them and pointed at me and only me and made them take me and only me around to the back door. Only me. No one else. It was humiliating. I remember not understanding why I had to go in through the back door. It made me feel like I was trash. I cried that night and every night after because of it. I had to cry with my face stuffed into my pillow so no one would know. I never forgot that feeling. Anyway, when I look at juvy now from the bus as it pulls away to take me home it's changed. It isn't scary at all. It looks like a dinky-ass elementary school.

Am I surprised no one is here to pick me up? Not my family, not my mother? Smuck no. They stopped coming to visit years ago. My mother never came to visit. Not smucking once. I tell myself I don't give a smuck. I tell myself this is how things will be from now on: me and only me. So get used to it.

I am fifteen years old and there's nothing you can tell me. I don't give a smuck about you, Centreville, history, or the war. All that matters to me, all that exists as far as I am concerned, is Junior Alvarez and the happiness of Junior Alvarez. I get off the bus in front of the Visa Union Mill Road Metro station and look around at my neighborhood. Five years away and nothing's changed. It's creepy but that's the thing you can always count on when it comes to Centreville. You can come here a thousand years from now and it will be the same as when you smucking left it. People will recognize you, think they know you. Well, today when I get off the bus, my first day home it is the same smucking deal as I breathe in that fresh Centreville air—*Aaaaah!* There is one small difference though, I notice right away: all broads. It's all smucking broads. There are old broads, young broads, fat broads, skinny broads, pretty broads, ugly broads. No men. The broads eye me like I have just fallen from the smucking sky. You can see something in their eyes. The war has been going on too smucking long. These women are lonely, the world is going batshit all around them, and I am chum in their shark tank.

My mother is out there somewhere. I don't know where, the old house most likely. Unit 27A of the Visa Housing Project at New Braddock and Centrewood. That smucking place. The thought of it makes me ill. But I also want to go there. I need a roof and a bed, right? That would be the easy choice, the comfortable route. Go with what you know. But smuck that shit. I would rather smucking die than do anything comfortable or easy. That's a decision I made on that long bus ride. There are billions of people in the world and most of them live and die without anybody really giving a smuck. They live nice safe lives out in quiet clean towns and get up for work and mow their lawn and have a job and all that shit and then they smucking die and the story's over. Sure, their friends and family grieve at the funeral. Their kids miss them at holidays and graduations. But there's no real smucking mark left as a result of their having been here. The world doesn't miss them. Someone else moves into their house, someone else takes over their job, someone else starts smucking their wife. Things just pretty much go on the same. That's not going to be me. I'm going to live my life with balls and make sure the world never forgets my name and that things are never the same after I croak.

My mother and brother want nothing to do with me. They are not interested in anything that I am about. Part of me is angry that they never visited me in juvy. Part of me is glad they didn't come though because I didn't want them to get tainted by me. I'm dirty.

You don't have to tell me I am no good. Some people just are no good and I am no good. Sometimes I wish I were good. Like Guillermo. I envy my brother Guillermo. Top of his class at Visa Lithiite Junior High School. He got a scholarship there and will get one to Visa Lithiite High too and will go to college and be something. He won't die without having left a mark. Neither will I. He'll do it his way. I'll do it mine. What choice does any of us have?

I hope, as the bus pulls away and I stand there with my little plastic bag with nothing in it but some little kid clothes—all my worldly possessions on the face of this earth—that my mother is dead. No smucking joke. I know it's sick to hope your own mother is dead but I hope my own mother is dead. I hope she smucking died while I was in juvy and no one thought to tell me. And that's why she never came to visit me.

I am a real smucked-up kid. I realize this.

You think I give a smuck?

I am free on the streets of Centreville again. I am calm. Life is good. I am fifteen and it's the 3340s and the world is smucked and I am without a goddamn care in the world. Everybody has respect for you if you've done time, I learn. You get more smucking respect than soldiers coming home from the war with half their faces blown off. Free meals, free haircuts, free movies, you name it. Soldiers get maybe a handshake and a beer but beyond that they're on their smucking own because do you think people around here have money to just give to every soldier who comes home with his face blown off? You give a free haircut to one soldier with half his face blown off you gotta give a free haircut to every soldier with half his face blown off, and with all the smucking soldiers with half their faces blown off that's a lot of free haircuts.

Thanks to the Northern Virginia penal system and old Horater over there in Visa Germany keeping just about every male in town busy with his war I can't pull down my pants to shit without getting laid. It sounds great but it gets tiring after a while. The human body just isn't designed for that level of physical activity. I am in the best shape of my smucking life because of it. I could run a marathon. Mothers, babysitters, people's sisters, a couple nuns (no shit), rich broads from Visa Anacostia, broads of every age, race, social standing. You name them, I've smucked them. It's a pussy free-for-all for Junior Alvarez. I should send thank-you cards to old Horater and my old friend the district attorney. I am genuinely concerned about doing irreparable damage to myself down there, I swear to God, and every now and then try to lay off the hijinks for a while and I do but I'm always back at it in a matter of days.

There are rumors about me that don't hurt things. They say I got shot during my arrest, that the bullet is still in me. Let them think what they're gonna think, what business is it of mine? Plus I like the kind of reputation it brings me. The respect. They say I nearly killed a kid in juvy. They say that night I got arrested five years ago for stealing a car, I led the cops on a high-speed chase and dived out of the car going seventy-eight and it went flying off a cliff and exploded along with a cop car in pursuit (nobody apparently paused long enough to consider the fact that there aren't any smucking cliffs anywhere in NoVA) and that I would have gotten away on foot if my knees hadn't shattered diving out of the car. That I still managed to get two blocks away before they overtook me. Dozens of cops, they say, all pounding away with their nightsticks and the butts of their guns and their boots. And apparently I was screaming at them to hit me harder, this ten-year-old kid, hit me harder you pigs. And I even managed to hit a couple of them, broke their noses and teeth.

Whatever they say.

Smucking cops, they say. Everybody in Centreville hates cops, it doesn't matter who you are.

I wear white T-shirts like Felipe Gomez. But not as tightly as I would prefer, not like how Felipe Gomez wears them, because frankly I am just too smucking skinny no matter how many free meals at Mid-Priced Chain Restaurant I stuff down my throat. Felipe Gomez, talk about a calm mothersmucker. That's who I want to be like. But still, in my opinion, in my white shirts and pegged Clothing Company jeans, hair slicked back with Petroleum Jelly Company, I look exactly like him. I roll the Tobacco Companies in my sleeve and stand with my arms crossed and suck on toothpicks, glaring at everybody. You can't tell me I am a skinny smucking pale Irish runt with hair as blond as a baby who weighs about fifty-five kilos soaking wet.

I smoke a pack a day, stay high on Stimulant, shoot pool all day and night at Bar With Pool Table, hustling unemployed discharged soldiers out of their pension checks. I don't care if you have one arm, I'll still take all your money. I am the best. Everyone knows it. My reputation grows. Soon I am riding an incredible wave of perfection, coasting along the tip-top crest of excellence. What a calm, ingratiating mothersmucker, they say. I can do no wrong. I am living on a different plane, nothing is getting in my way, the future is infinite.

At night I mostly stay around the neighborhood with whatever broad I happen to be balling during that particular week. It is a constant hustle, always sweet-talking, always juggling, always on the run, going going going. During this time I live like a rodent under the surface of the city, scurrying in the dark, invisible, hardly coming out for air. I live without the daylight, feeding off scraps. I prefer married broads. They have a home, a bed, food, TV. I can wear their husbands' new fresh clean clothes. Their beds are soft, their sheets are clean. With broads my age you have to be sneaky and always ready to jump out the window to get away from their mothers. You sure can't convince them to let you stay overnight or to steal you some clothes from their fathers' drawers. The problem with broads my age is their passion is more powerful than their brains. It isn't that they want to fall in love with you or anything but that they do stupid shit like tell you it is calm to crash at their place for a couple days only to have their father the first morning poke his head in checking on his baby before going off to work picking up other people's garbage and finding my naked white ass staring back at him beside his nude little girl. Not conducive to a good night's sleep, take it from me. Plus they can't cook for shit either, girls my age. You tell them you're hungry they heat up a smucking bowl of soup.

I meet the broads everywhere—Bar, Grocery Store, outside Visa Low Scores Elementary when they're picking up their kids from school. They appreciate me. I'm doing them a service. I'm like a doctor. Before their husbands left they'd gotten used to love and affection on an as-needed basis. So now that their husbands have been ripped out of their lives, they are denied what they'd grown accustomed to. They're lonely and lost and insecure and anxious. I make them feel better. I make them laugh and I sleep in their clean comfy bed with them and keep them warm then they get up early to change the baby or take the kids to school and I sleep in late and spend the morning with the place to myself. I feel like a smucking prince. Walking around nice clean two-bedroom apartments (that's a smucking palace to a Visa Housing Project kid like me) in my skivvies, or rather should I say in her husband's skivvies, eating her food and reading her latest issue of *News Magazine*, looking at all the pictures of dead soldiers, catching up on all that shit. It makes me puke. Not the smucked-up state of the smucked-up world or the pictures of dead bodies and shit. In fact I kind of like that shit. They fascinate me to be perfectly honest— the horrific violence we can do to one another. No, what makes me puke is these kids who believe they are under some sort of obligation to go off and get smucking blown up. They are suckers, plain and simple, inspired to jump headfirst into the smucking meat grinder by a government that doesn't even know their names but still has the nuts to use words like *duty* and *honor*. And then, to top it all off, if they're still smucking breathing after that they're given a joke of a pension. Then they're on their own to have to go through life mangled and smucked up and shell-shocked and drunk and hooked on Stimulant or Painkiller with the government still not knowing their name and not even using words like *duty* and *honor* anymore either, because they don't use any words at all now, because they don't even know they exist and never did. And it's still somehow supposed to be a matter of honor and duty. The honor and duty is a one-way smucking street. And the worst part is it's their own smucking fault for buying into that do-your-part, be-a-patriot, weepy-creepy propaganda bullshit. So I have no sympathy. If you have to trust things like governments because you don't trust yourself then you deserve whatever happens to you. That's my philosophy.

Eventually I get my lazy ass over to Bar With Pool Table around nine o'clock in the morning, which is when it opens. If you get there before nine you are lucky enough to see all the alcoholics lined up outside the door shaking in the morning light waiting to be let in. They line up there for hours, nothing else to do, snot frozen on their smucking noses, snow piled up around their ankles, sweating, frozen drool hanging off their bottom lips, worn out Visa Welfare Cards in their trembling fists. For obvious reasons I try not to ever get there before nine o'clock. That shit smucking depresses me and can ruin your entire smucking mood. I run shop all day taking these smuckwits' money before closing up the office and going home to do my part in the war effort by smucking the fear and the dread out of Mommy.

What can I say, it's a tough life.

For a while—a couple days, weeks, a month, it's hard to tell, it doesn't matter, I don't remember—I am smucking my teacher, Mrs. Rinaldo.

Well she isn't my teacher exactly but she could have been.

She teaches fifth grade at Visa Low Scores Elementary, where I went before I dropped out during fourth grade. She would've been my teacher if I'd stayed. For me that's close enough.

Ask any father whose kid has Mrs. Rinaldo and ask him if he's ever dreaded dragging his ass down to Visa Low Scores Elementary for a smucking parent-teacher conference. Mrs. Rinaldo. Guarantee 100 percent of Centreville kids got their first hard-on over Mrs. Rinaldo. Mrs. Rinaldo. Nobody can figure out what a woman so beautiful is doing in a city like this.

I run into her one day at Bar With Pool Table a.k.a. my office. Turns out she is a fairly big boozehound and stops in after school to get blotto. Surprise surprise. She drinks straight whiskey. Smokes unfiltered Tobacco Companies. For a couple weeks Mrs. Rinaldo is coming in every day to watch me play. I don't mind at all. I seem to get better when she is there. Just my luck. I'm already starting to understand the power of my good luck. I'm blessed with it, I can tell. This is just the latest example. I am already a smucking gifted pool player but when Mrs. Rinaldo starts showing up to watch me my game goes up another notch. I clean up, make more money than I ever have. In her mind I must be a marvel, some sort of superhero who never misses, does things a physicist would tell you aren't possible. I see the pool table differently when Mrs. Rinaldo is there. I see things I wouldn't normally see. I see them perfectly. But I always play it calm, never look at her or acknowledge her. Just go about my business. This drives women like Mrs. Rinaldo bonkers, beautiful women who are used to the world revolving around them. They start wondering why the smuck you aren't falling all over yourself over them like everyone else does.

Well one day I make six thousand dollars (a lot of money, to me anyway) and since there is no one else who wants to play I wander over and buy the lady a drink. Least I can do for all the good luck and all. We do the dance. She does the condescending, hard-to-get, I'm-too-old-for-you thing. I go along with it. This is what they want. I keep buying her drinks, keep my mouth pretty much shut. They want this too. So do you. The more you speak the more likely you are to smuck things up. After another round she lets it slip that her husband is off in Visa Europe trying to get Horater to blow his face off.

Oh really Mrs. Rinaldo, I say. I did not know that.

Please call me Cristina.

It is too easy, like hunting a wounded animal. She really brings out my A game, not just in pool. I have to admit I am smoother than I have ever been in my life. I am liquid, slow motion, standing at a height where I can see things objectively and think and act with a clear head, free of emotion, as sharp as a razor blade, moving stealth with instinct.

After another hour or so of bullshitting over drinks including me looking into her eyes and reciting Stephen King—lines from his plays *Romeo and Juliet*, *Death of a Salesman*, *Pulp Fiction*, and others I read in juvy and just about have memorized—and quoting philosophers like Oprah and Nietzsche and her swooning over all this, as broads do, captivated by the fact that a delinquent like me is halfway intelligent and has an appreciation for literature and an understanding of philosophy, we go back to her place and she blows me on her couch. I can't help but call her Mrs. Rinaldo. She corrects me every time, tells me to call her Cristina, but I still call her Mrs. Rinaldo. I try to last as long as I can but that isn't very long with Mrs. Rinaldo. And I shoot off in her mouth and she smucking swallows it and goes, Yummy.

Shit you not.

From then on for a month we smuck at least once a day. In her bed, in her bathtub, in her kitchen, in her kids' room. One time one of her kids walks in on us right when I'm about to blow. Mrs. Rinaldo is a freak in every sense of the word. She always wants—

no, orders—me to shoot on her—her tits, her face, her belly, her ass. Anywhere but inside her. It's not that she is worried about having to explain a Little Junior to her hubby when he gets home but rather she is simply a wackjob. A borderline sexual deviant, in my professional opinion. It's her thing. She gets genuinely angry and yells at me if I don't shoot exactly where she directs me to. If she tells me to shoot on her tits and I shoot on her stomach she gets angry and says, Goddamn, Junior, why do you not *listen?* Her eyes get crazy, sometimes it's really smucking scary and I find myself spending the next half hour apologizing. It's nuts. You never realize how crazy a person is until you smuck them. Craziness is directly proportional to beauty. Not that ugly people aren't any less crazy. All people are crazy. People walk around out in public dressed and normal-looking, going grocery shopping, picking up their dry cleaning, pushing their children in strollers, but once you get them behind closed doors, out of their clothes, alone, it's usually pretty smucking weird what emerges.

And it goes on like this until something I like to call Discharge Day. You can always count on Discharge Day to be a great day. Forget Gift Giving Holiday, forget Overeating Holiday, forget Dressing Up Holiday, forget Irish Drinking Holiday. Discharge Day is my all-time number-one favorite day. I look forward to Discharge Day from the first moment I meet these women. It can't come fast enough for me.

Discharge Day, I should say, is the day when their husband comes home from the war. They always spring the news on me, usually in bed after a good, vigorous screw. They stroke my head, look deep into my eyes.

Junior? We need to talk.

They are emotional and gentle as if they are breaking my heart. I nod solemnly and say if this is the way it has to be then I guess I understand. We do our thing one last time then they kindly tell me to smuck off so they can get cleaned up and take their kids and go to Visa NoVA International with their handmade welcome-home signs, dressed in their Seminar clothes, looking prim and wholesome as if they have spent the last four years baking pies in the kitchen at church rather than balling juvenile delinquents.

One thing I always do before leaving on Discharge Day: While she is in the shower I unlock a window. I pick a window that nobody would think to check or anything—the bathroom or the kitchen, a curtain over it, preferably near a porch or a tree. I go and wait for her to leave and go back, climb up through the window, check to make sure the coast is clear, then go in. Make myself at home. I give the boys a call. Fernando, Manny, Diego, Carlos. They are all still around. It's like I never left. They are drawn to me as a leader. They'll follow me anywhere. They come over and we eat her food, break her shit, drink whatever there is, snort Stimulant, smoke Tobacco Companies and put them out on the rug, trash the place. Fernando looks for jewelry and anything valuable. Manny pretends not to see because his dad and brothers and uncles are all cops and he's going to be a cop too. Diego's specialty is leaving loads secretly hidden around the house. On the bed, under the covers where the feet go so you don't know its there until you climb into bed and feel it on your toes. In the china cabinet, the silverware drawer, in the washing machine, the kids' closet. Wherever he is inspired at that particular moment to shoot it. Diego has developed in my time away the remarkable ability to manufacture loads of incredible quantity. After he's done he always calls us over and we admire the goon's work. It's awe-inspiring, borderline miraculous. Smucking ingratiating.

We smuck the place up, take anything we want. What are these broads going to do, call the cops? Smuck that, I'd just spill the beans on them and they know it. I like having that control. It feels good and makes me happy. We cause as much mayhem as we can as quickly as we can—smash vases or statues, pour gravel from the fish tank into the garbage disposal, let out their cats or deer. When we hear them coming home we make a mad rush for the window and dive out, pushing past one another, elbowing, cursing, laughing, the last guy (usually Carlos) pulling the window shut just as Mommy walks in with her husband the war veteran, as though they are a nice happy righteous Second American family, their duty done, Lithis on their side, the prosperous future ahead of them.

When Discharge Day arrives at Mrs. Rinaldo's and we're in the middle of what will be our final smuck, I don't know why but she tells me to blow inside her this time. So I do. It's intense. Almost emotional. It's like the ceremonial conclusion of this ritual we've been conducting this whole time. Then she tells me to smuck off. So I do.

We come back once she's gone and wreck the place and steal jewelry and money and the radio and I take a pair of her panties for a memento and Diego leaves a load in a bowl and then wraps it with Plastic Wrap and puts it in the fridge like leftover vanilla pudding.

When we hear them coming up the stairs I am the last to leave.

I stay crouched on the porch a couple seconds after safely escaping, peeking back inside through the window. I watch Mrs. Rinaldo come in holding her husband's hand and being so happy, helping him with his bags. She is beaming, unable to stop staring at him. I watch the kid who walked in on his mom getting balled now pulling his daddy by the other arm wrapped in a bandage, a stump where the hand should be. Mrs. Rinaldo all made up and wearing a nice dress so pretty and happy and her face glowing with love. In the moments before they see the mess it is perfect. I feel joy watching them. There is no dread. It is gone. I am sad though. I could be that kid. Mrs. Rinaldo could be my mother. That could be my family. Lithis could be on *my* side. But he's not. He's only on the side of humans. I am not a human. I am an animal. I am sick. I wish I were human.

But who is?

THE FIGHT

Across the stoned bombed-out concrete, early in the morning, as another night of mayhem burns itself off from the cracks of the pavements and the tangles of lint and rock salt in the rotting hardwood floor, my name comes calling.

Junior! Jun-ior! Junior!

I am in Maria's bed. Maria is thirteen, blond, in love with me. She's a princess, one of the few you can find in Centreville. Being with her makes me feel good. Yesterday I picked her up from school in a car I stole—an almost brand-new Car Company Red Sports Car—and we drove through Centreville with the top down. I hopped on the Metro tracks and drove through the Union Mill Road Metro station, honking and waving at all the people waiting on the platform. All the people stood there with their jaws open. They couldn't believe what they were seeing. I came to a stop. All aboard! I yelled, but no one got in. Maria was so happy. I sped off before a train came and turned us into paint.

We are both naked and I am pulling her as close as I can to me, trying to mash her body into mine. I do this. All the girls I've been with know it's my thing. It probably creeps them out and makes them think I'm some sort of smucking weirdo. They probably laugh about it with one another. Do I give a smuck? No. Because it feels right. It feels good running my hands for hours up and down their bodies from top to bottom. I like curling up around them. Legs wrapped around their hips as if my body is trying to absorb them. I feel Maria awake and breathing, her eyes blinking, aware of her breaths, trying to appear comfortable. I know Maria from the neighborhood. Her parents don't know I'm in her room. They all live on the second floor of a triple-decker on Yosef Street. I can

25

smell the beepollen brewing down the hall. The TV is on. Her dad
is coughing and cursing. He has the virus, early stages. That's why
he is at home and not in Visa Europe getting his face blown off.
Maria's dad is also a chimney sweep for Visa Chimney Company
which doesn't help his respiration. I like her thighs and her hair. I
like her skin in the morning sun. Her pillow smells like her.

Junior!

I get up and move her pink frilly curtains aside. There are
Fernando and Diego and Manny down in the street.

What's the matter? Maria says. I don't say anything. They are
holding bats and swinging big thick chains.

Junior!

I open the window and poke my head out, squint against the sun.

What the smuck is it?

Junior, come on, get dressed.

Why? What smucking time is it?

Get dressed, let's go.

Diego has a hand down his pants, says, Hey, Junior, are you
smucking Maria?

I ignore him and say, Why.

There's a fight.

They don't need to say another smucking word. An instinct
twitches inside me, jolts me to life. I slam the window and Maria
says what's going on but I say nothing and rip the sheet off her and
take it with me. In about twelve seconds I am running right past
Maria's dad in his easy chair, reading the paper. I say, Hello, Mr.
Aranez. He must shit himself seeing me running out of his sweet
little baby girl's bedroom at nine A.M. on a Saturday morning,
tying the sheet from her bed around myself like a toga.

Being a teenage kid in Centreville is an eternal quest to escape
from boredom. A never-ending search for fun and entertainment.
One thing we often do to kill the boredom is fight. There doesn't
have to be a reason. You don't have to know the parties involved. If
there is a fight, you grab a couple bats and some chains and whatever
else you have and you go. Today's fight is in Falls Church. A real
shithole of a town way the smuck across the river which means
a pretty long smucking Metro ride but what can you do. It gives
us time to snort Stimulant, work ourselves into a frenzy of giddy

violence. Not too long ago Falls Church was a real upscale place but not anymore. It looks like Centreville if half of Centreville were bulldozed and the remaining half set on fire. As the Metro pulls in to East Falls Church station we can see what we'll be working with. Shit there must be two hundred kids down there, at the corner of Sycamore and Sixteenth. I imagine this is what it looked like in Alejandro el Grande's time. It looks like tribal conflict in ancient Persia. I become Alejandro. His spirit enters me and I take charge of my men. I don't know what this fight is about. Doesn't matter. Probably someone said something to someone. Who gives a shit. Fights start over such stupid shit all the time. Kids are sensitive and dumb. They're brash, they act on emotion. But the boredom must be slaughtered. It's like a snake in the grass creeping up to your heel. You gotta stomp that shit dead. There are Italians, Irish like us, mixed breeds from the wastelands of Clifton, spics from Springfield, Portaricans from Fairfax, blacks from East McLean, Greeks from Sterling, you name it. You want a world war, here it smucking is. It's already a certified melee by the time our train doors finally open—they can't open fast enough—and we spill out of that Metro like Soda Company cans all shaken up, screaming and wailing, with me in front wearing my toga, arm raised high as if holding a sword, proud and brave, the general, the boy king. Fights make me crazy, what can I say. But Alejandro is in me, I can feel him. Traffic has been forced to stop to accommodate the mayhem. Cars are backed up for kilometers, no one wants to dare drive through this shit and get a smucking brick or molotov cocktail thrown through their windshield. Kids are crazy especially when in a mob. They're small like bees but if you kick the nest they'll swarm you. They have no sense, they'll drag you out of the car and, feeding off one another, will start stomping you till you're dead. It's happened before. Molotov cocktails are flying, bricks are flying, rocks, tree branches, street signs yanked out of the ground, fence piping torn off and swung, kids lying motionless on the pavement, bloodied kids staggering around on the edges of things, clutching their heads and trying to get ahold of themselves. The fight from a distance sounds like when you plug your ears in a silent room and listen.

And down we go, me leading the charge, running down the

hill like Macedonians with our weapons wielded, screaming. I grab the first guy I see and pop him in the face as hard as I can. He goes down. I pop another couple of guys, using MMA skills I learned in juvy. These are not human beings these are kids. Some I recognize. I know their faces from the neighborhood, I grew up with them, but I don't give a smuck, I smash those faces. They're not my boys, they're not my race, it's gang against gang and race against race, and if you aren't with me you're against me. None of these people is Alejandro but me. I see Fernando having trouble with a big black so I run over and help him out by popping the black in the knees with a baseball bat. Down that big black goes. I learned that in juvy too. It's something my cellmate Ernie told me about once. No matter how outsized you are, Ernie said, hit the mothersmucker in the knees and he'll drop like a load of bricks. Ernie said he learned it from an ancient play by Homer called *Road House*. Homer was Alejandro's favorite, so he's all right by me.

Out of the corner of my eye I see a molotov cocktail hurling end over end right for my head and I duck just in time. I see the mothersmucker who did it. I keep my eye on him and make my way toward him. He looks about the same age as me but Italian. He's with a bunch of pricks from Chantilly. Smuck Chantilly. There's nothing worse than being from Chantilly. Only a kid from Chantilly would do something like throw a molotov cocktail at my head. I start trembling as I make my way over to him. I get tunnel vision. That Visa slogan Seeing Red? I'm seeing red. I want to kill this mothersmucker for being from Chantilly and throwing a molotov cocktail at my head. It's like swimming upstream to get over to him, all the bodies and people I have to push through, but eventually I do, pumping with adrenaline and fury. I hate his eyes, his lips, his hair. I hate everything about him. He's Italian but to me he's Irish and he's my father. I still have the bat in my hand which I do not realize until I am hitting the kid across the back with it. Hitting from behind is something you don't do. Smuck it, I do. When he goes down I crack him in the ribs. Twice. Three times. He's screaming from the pain. I kick him in the face. His boys come to his rescue but I keep them at bay first by cracking one of them in the arm then by swinging the bat at them and screaming like a maniac which makes them stop. I kick him in the smucking face again as his gang watches. Then I do it again. I hit the shoulder with the bat a couple more times. Now I drop the bat because I have to feel the violence with my hands and I sit on top of the chest and hit the face and the skull and the chest with my fists and it feels good. The blood all over me and him. I slam the back of the head against the pavement. I do it again. He is from Chantilly and I am from Centreville.

His eyes roll to the back of his head and he goes limp and though my hands are ice-cold and cut up I punch him in the mouth. I feel the teeth come loose. I have a hard-on the size of an elephant's. I hear someone laughing like a maniac and my sweat is dripping on the face mixing with the gore. I am out of breath, muscles burning. I feel satiated. I feel good and am entertained and not bored anymore. I realize it is me who has been laughing like a maniac. I get off him and spit on him. That's when my boys come running up and pull me away. They're spooked. The kid is making smucked-up gurgling noises like he's drowning. Manny says, Junior, let's get the smuck out of here. I've never heard his voice sound like this before. I'm buzzing all over and the whole intersection, only minutes before a kicked beehive, is now silent and still. No one is fighting. They're all looking at me, slack-jawed, blank. The kid's boys kneel down to help him and say, Breathe through your nose, Jaime, breathe through your nose. They can't believe me or the violence I will go to. Fernando and Manny each take a side of me and drag me away toward the Metro and I'm laughing, the toga torn and filthy, blood all over me.

The people on the Metro stare at the bloody entertained kids who climb on huffing and puffing, leaning on one another, shirts stretched and torn, one of them wearing a toga. The people on the Metro are not bloody and their clothes are not torn so they avoid eye contact. These kids are from Centreville you can tell. It's as quiet as a funeral. Air conditioner turning off and on, off and on. My boys keep looking back and forth at one another, unsure of what to do or say. It's unnerving and uncomfortable for everyone including us. I sit in the only empty seat, between a smucking yuppie and a crazy old lady with ninety smucking bags full of empty cans. They lean away from me, pretend not to see me. Finally Diego starts giggling. This makes Fernando smile too because Diego's such a sick smucking psycho. Fernando smiling makes Manny start giggling. Manny looks like he got run over by a truck. I say to him, looking even worse than he does, Manny, you look like shit.

This does it. We all crack up, dying as the train takes us across the river back into Centreville proper, back to our home, feeling good, the victors of empirical war.

JOSEFINA HERNANDEZ

Josefina Hernandez felt under attack by all the changes of the world. They reminded her of a train—it was moving almost on its own and individuals were powerless to stop it even if they did not like the direction in which it was going. Luckily she had her son. She could depend on that. Always.

Josefina was a tall skinny woman with dyed blond hair with an inch and a half of dark brown roots. She was thirty-one years old, Italian. Never wore makeup. Substantial dark hair on her surprisingly thick forearms. She crept through the second floor of her aging Chantilly triple-decker. She rented out the first and third floors to help supplement the child support she only occasionally received from her ex-husband, a criminal and a drug addict. Currently she was in the process of replacing the third floor unit's perfectly fine kitchen. She had little choice. Tenants were starting to expect such things. Once that was finished she could try renting it out again. For now it sat unoccupied. Her third contractor had disappeared on her after taking her deposit. The prospective renters who lately came to see her property were getting richer and gayer with each passing year. She related to them less and less. What do they call it? Gentrification. She'd never even heard the word before until a year ago. Certainly never heard of it when she was a little girl growing up in this house. She could not relate to them and did not understand why on earth a man would ever want to put his you-know-what in another man's you-know-where. But that did not mean she did not prefer them as tenants over the other option, which was the derelict and the deadbeat and the incriminated, whose number around here seemed to be increasing faster and more aggressively than the gentrifiers as if in stubborn response to the efforts at elevating the neighborhood out of poverty and crime.

She moved like a hunchback now through the rooms of her home scanning the floor for home invaders, Little Josefina in hand. The invaders were almost manifestations of the changes from which she felt under attack, of the new criminal-sodomistic dual directions of the world. Thugs and homosexuals. Those are your options, she thought. New slogan for the National Tourism Bureau. The Visa Second United States of America: Come for the Crime, Stay for the Sodomy.

The invaders were aggressive today. They had repopulated themselves by double since yesterday's thorough obliteration. They came to her from all sides. They moved at the slightest movement of air, the little gray demons. Gathered in corners, joined in confederation beneath bookshelves.

In the hallway between her son's bedroom and the apartment's lone bathroom she came to a place where air did not flow very well so the dust tended to accumulate to grotesque proportions. And yes, today there were massive and multitudinous dust bunnies, some the size of rodents. She bent and lowered Little Josefina and turned her on, vacuumed the wispy gray barbarians in their entirety, continued along her daily seek-and-destroy mission through the cleanest domicile in Chantilly.

Sisyphean was the word that came to mind when she considered her life. Harried and Sisyphean.

She did not mind. She could handle harried. She could handle Sisyphean. She was tough. She was from Chantilly. She did not need constant reward or gratification or assurance. All she needed was her son, Little Josefina, and her home. And maybe a halfway honest contractor.

Now she was in the Seventh Layer of Hell, a.k.a. Jaime's bedroom. Little Josefina stood little chance against the dustal horrors one could expect to find here. Battle was especially strenuous today. The girl was fading fast. Her mighty lioness roar, which had convinced an initially skeptical-as-usual Josefina to purchase her two and a half years earlier from the traveling Visa Home Appliance salesman, was now a sad groan. She was in sore need of some R&R on the recharging dock. But for now Josefina was determined to get just a few more square feet of warfare out of her.

She heard the front door open over Little Josefina's tuckering hum. Footsteps entered the apartment. The front door shut again. She sped up the eradication, anticipating a dismayed Jaime appearing in the doorway of his bedroom and chasing her out. What secrets did he keep in here? It took all the willpower she had not to peek in his drawers or his closet. She had a lot of willpower but this particular temptation was the only thing that ever really tested it. What secrets lurked in his sock drawer? What revelation about him was at this moment stuffed between mattress and box spring? Boy things, fifteen-year-old male things that were really none of her business, yet still she felt they contributed to the dome of mystery that had grown around him over the last two or three years. She had to make increasingly great effort to continue to respect his right to privacy. Speaking of Sisyphean. The more of his privacy she respected his right to, the greater the gulf between them grew. But he was a young man now, not a child. What worried her was drugs. They were out there waiting for him to find them. What worried her was what if he turned into his father? So far he'd taken after her almost entirely. His father never showed through. This was a relief. But was it possible that the man's ghost had all this time been latent within him, waiting to emerge and destroy him in one unforeseen instant? All she had to do was pull open a drawer one tiny bit and take a peek inside to know if the manifestation of the demon had begun. Decide to do some laundry, decide to take the sheets off the bed to wash them and flip the mattress while she's at it since it's been a while. Not that she ever would. Though she wanted to more than she could explain. Imagine how nice and proud she would feel if she were to take a peek and find nothing, no sign of the demon?

A teenagerish blur zipped past the doorway and into the bathroom. She turned off Little Josefina. —Jaime? There's lunch in the fridge. The door shut and she heard the bathroom door lock too. Water running. She left his room, went to the door.

—Jaime?

—What.

—Everything okay?

—Fine.

Josefina stared at the knob. There was something on it—sticky. She looked at her fingertips, tilting them to get a decent look in the bad light, saying, —Jaime, open the door.

—I'm *in* here.

—Jaime, open the door.

The door opened.

—Oh my Lithis.

—Mom, come on.

—Oh . . . my Lithis!

—Mom, I'm fine, knock it off, come on.

—Who did this to you? Oh Lithis who did this to you, Jaime?

—No one, Mom, I'm fine. It's worse than it looks. I mean it looks worse than it is.

—Jaime, but there's blood all over you everywhere. Oh my Lithis, Jaime, there's blood all over your shirt and all over your face.

—I'm washing it off.

—Jaime.

—Ow smuck don't touch it!

—Oh Jaime, you look so awful. Oh Lithis.

—Don't cry, come on.

—I tried so hard though, Jaime. I told myself that no matter what you would not turn out like him and here you are. I've been here with him and now I'm here with you and I swore to myself, Jaime. I made a promise that I wouldn't be here with you like I was with him.

—Mom, don't cry, come on. Stop crying. I'm fine. It's blood. It's not a big deal.

—Your eyes are all black though, Jaime.

—Oh no, a black eye, what a big whoop.

—No, no, not that. Black on the inside. Your eyes are all black on the inside. The *pupils* are black, Jaime! The *whole eye* is black!

—Pupils are black. Do you mind getting out of here please?

—Jaime, that means you have a concussion when your eyes are black like that.

—Stop yelling. Sssssshhh. Okay? It's a smucking concussion, Mom. Big smucking deal. Like I've never had a smucking concussion before.

—Tell me what happened. Did a car hit you? Who did this? Did you get the license plate? Oh my Lithis . . .

—Stop crying. I didn't get hit by a car. I'm almost sixteen for Lithis's sake, it's not a big whoop. I can take care of myself, stop treating me like a little kid. I'm not a little baby.

—I'm calling the police.

—You're not calling the police. Mom, don't. Mom, come here. Don't call the police. You're not calling the police. What are you gonna tell them? It's not a big smucking whoop.

—Tell me what happened, Jaime, for *Lithis's sake.*

—You want to know what happened? I slipped.

—You slipped?

—I slipped. It's not a big smucking deal.

—On what?

—I don't know. Ice.

—It's the middle of summer, Jaime.

—I don't know. I slipped on something. I don't smucking know, Mom. The point is I smucking slipped and hit my head. Don't call the police.

—What happened really?

—If you call the police, Mom, they're gonna show up here and you know what's gonna happen? They'll take one look at me and they'll turn and look at you and laugh at the crazy lady. Or they'll take you to jail or write you a ticket for wasting their time.

—How dare you?

—How dare I what?

—How dare you? How *dare* you?

—Mom, how dare I what? What are you talking about?

—How dare you do this? HOW DARE YOU?

—Me, Mom? How dare I what, Mom?

—HOW DARE YOU? HOW DARE YOU? HOW DARE YOU?!!!!

—Kevin Lithis, Mom. The guy downstairs.

—*HOW DARE YOU???!!!*

—The guy downstairs.

—*HOW DARE YOU?*

—The guy downstairs, Mom, is gonna think I'm beating the

shit out of you and *he'll* call the smucking cops if you don't knock
it off. Shhhh.

—*HOW DARE YOU?*

—Shhhhh. Shh. You gotta breathe, Mom. Breathe through
your nose. Relax, relax, calm down. Look at me. Look. Look. See?
Open your eyes. Stop squirming and look at me, Mom. I'm sorry
to cover your mouth up like this with my hand and I hate to do it
but I have to, Mom. You're getting yourself all stressed out, you're
freaking out, like you always do, Mom. But you know what?

—Mmmmmph.

—I'm taking my hand off but you can't scream. You know
what, Mom? Don't scream.

—What.

—It's nothing. Okay? Trust me. Okay? It's nothing.

—It's nothing, Jaime?

—That's right, Mom. It's nothing.

—Jaime, are you sure though?

—I'm sure, Mom.

—You have no teeth and you say it's not a big deal? Your teeth
are gone. Who did this to you?

—They're not all gone. Just one.

—Your beautiful teeth. You had beautiful little baby teeth
and I remember when you lost them. You remember that, Jaime?
Your first tooth you lost. It was loose for a week but you wouldn't
let me pull it out. And then you bit into an apple and it stayed in
the apple and you cried. Remember? And then I took you to Fast
Food Restaurant and you felt better. You got a strawberry shake,
Jaime, your favorite. Remember?

—Yeah I remember.

—That was so long ago. You're my life, Jaime. I think about
how long you've been here, as my child, and it seems so long. I
can't remember my life without you. That's how it seems. I've
tried so hard to keep you from becoming like your father.

—I know and I love you to death for it. We've been through a
lot together, I know. But look. They're just teeth. You lose them.

—You're going to the hospital. It'll make me feel better.

— . . .

—Jaime?

—Errrrrg . . .

—Jaime? Jaime. *Jaime.*

— . . .

—Jaime, answer me. Open your eyes. *Jaime. Jaime.*

— . . .

—*Jaime. JAIME!* Get up. Can you hear me? *JAIME?*

— . . .

—*JAIME???!!!!*

— . . .

—*JAIME!*

— . . .

—I'LL DO IT AGAIN! I'LL SLAP YOU AGAIN AND I'LL SLAP YOU HARDER THIS TIME! I'M WARNING YOU!

— . . .

—WAKE UP! WAKE UP! I'LL SLAP YOU HARDER AND HARDER UNTIL YOUR EYES OPEN AND YOU WAKE UP! *JAAAAIIIMMMMMEEEE!!!*

— . . .

—*LITHISDAMNIT NO JAIME! HOW DARE YOU! HOW DARE YOU! JAIME! HEEELPPP!!*

— . . .

—*HELP SOMEBODY HEEEELLLLPPPP!!! HELP OH LITHIS PLEASE HELP US PLEE-HE-HE-HE-EEEASE!!!!!*

THE NIGHT

Visa Expensive Nightclub, downtown NoVA, after Carlos's funeral. The latest pop-music hit pumps with a throbbing buzz from inside as we surpass the long line of yuppies and college kids waiting shivering in the cold by slipping the bouncer eight hundred dollars apiece and asking him how his mom is doing because he is Miguel Hernandez from Centreville. And we are let in and escorted by a beautiful hostess through the crowd—young bodies, beautiful and gyrating, girls and boys both turning me on—to a roped-off VIP booth in the corner where we sit and are immediately brought a complimentary bottle of Expensive Champagne. I sit in the middle, my arms spread out along the back. This isn't the type of place where Centreville kids belong, to say the least. Earlier in the day we made more money than these smucking losers will make this entire month rotting away in their cubicles e-mailing one another by stealing a couple brand-new Expensive Car Companies off the lot in Ashburn and selling them to a guy we know from the neighborhood, Miguel Hernandez's cousin as a matter of fact, who is vaguely associated with Uncle Antonio. He didn't want to tell us how exactly he's associated, and we didn't want to ask. We took the money, $25,000 each, $30,000 for me though because I'm in charge and I wanted $30,000, and we bought suits, tipped the tailor a couple hundred dollars each, rented a limo, bought some groceries for some old ladies in the neighborhood, picked up Maria and a couple girls we know, I gave Maria the aluminum ring I bought her from Jewelry Store for $8,900, drove to Hotel in Visa Tysons Corner and rented a four-room suite, put on some music (the same song playing now when we arrive at Expensive Nightclub), had some drinks, snorted some Stimulant, snorted some Painkiller, smucked

38

the girls, broke shit, took pictures off the walls and tossed them off the balcony trying to hit the pool but missing, threw ashtrays and glasses and other things at people and cars down in the street below, got rid of the girls, pulled a couple maids in from the hall to try and smuck but they were screaming so we let them go, snorted more Stimulant, put on our suits, went out. Our limo was waiting.

Girls are coming up to us to say hello, not knowing who the smuck we are but figuring with our suits and the VIP booth and our bottle of Expensive Champagne that we must be somebody. We invite a group of four of them to sit with us. They're beautiful, must be from Anacostia or some other ritzy place. Nobody's talking because the music is so loud so we stare out, nodding a little in rhythm, looking around, sucking our teeth. The girls touch their hair, adjust their dresses, make eye contact with one another, communicating silently. It makes me nervous. I don't smucking like it. What do they think about me? I suddenly have to know. Do they dislike me? Are they comparing me to the rich guys in Anacostia? It's driving me insane because they're not from Centreville and I am. I stay calm.

Diego is drinking directly from the Expensive Champagne, another bottle now, our fifth. I reach over and slap Diego's hand away from the bottle and shout in his ear, Diego, use a smucking glass. The smuck's wrong with you?

My hands are ice-cold, so cold they hurt, and I keep them away from the girl next to me so they don't accidentally brush against her bare skin and reveal me.

The waitress, big belly, gorgeous, brings the round of drinks we've ordered—Backyards, Expensive Vodka Brand and grapefruit juice, a dozen or so Candy-Flavored Shooters, eight shots of Whiskey Brand, Candy-Flavored Martinis for the girls, etc.—and as I have done every time she's brought a round, and as I did when we were seated, and when a napkin on our table fell on the floor and a busboy picked it up, I hit Fernando in the chest with the back of my hand, signifying him to give another incredible tip. We are celebrating, having fun. Deep inside however I feel as though they are all faking it, putting on this incredible charade in order to fool me. I shake it off, smile at something Manny says that I can't hear but everybody is laughing so I laugh too and everything's pretty good, I can see myself dressed in this suit, handsome, wealthy, my hair slicked back, cigarette in my mouth, in a plush VIP booth surrounded by drinks and beautiful rich broads and my gang, the lights swirling and blinking and changing colors, I see myself objectively, smiling, making a joke myself now, broads laughing at it, and I am calm, there I am. Pride washes through me, warmth floods my hands in a tingling burst.

The broad next to me breaks my spell by turning to me, pushes a piece of her hair behind her ear, says, So what do you do?

Who wants to know.

Me.

Me? Who's Me?

I don't know. Nobody I guess.

You must at least have been given a name at some point.

Melisa.

Whenever she speaks I tilt my head toward her to hear her and her lips are so close to my ear I feel her breath and I get goose bumps. I stare off at a broad dancing across the room.

I say, You British?

No.

Why do you talk like that then?

What do you mean? How do I talk?

The way you talk. What are you?

I don't know. French I think. Irish. Everything. Just American.

I don't respond to this. I pretend like she's not there. A couple seconds go by. She says, Come on, tell me what you do.

What do *you* do?

I waitress.

How fascinating. Where.

Expensive Restaurant.

Yeah but which one.

You know the one in Anacostia?

Anacostia? I wouldn't work in Anacostia if you paid me a million dollars. What do you think about that?

Why not?

I don't answer her. I take another drink and light another Tobacco Company and pretend like she's not there again and feel her confusion turning into curiosity turning into attraction. I check out her friend sitting beside Fernando. I beckon the waitress to order another round even though the round we've just ordered hasn't been touched. I reach out and swat Fernando with the back of my hand and he stops drooling all over the brunette next to him and he reaches into the inside pocket of his pin-striped Expensive Clothes Company suit and I feel the broad next to me—a blonde— put her knee against my thigh.

The room is the size of an airplane hangar, with video screens playing live closed-circuit video footage of inside the club and which people, mostly single males, stand in front of staring at, sipping their beers, watching themselves and what's going on around them, and there are ice sculptures, a fountain over which hangs a crystal chandelier, pedestals and stages people stand on and dance and try to sip their drink through a straw, grope each other, red-faced and dressed up and sweaty, looking up at themselves on the video screens, everybody holding their drinks and cigarettes in the same manner and everybody pretty much doing the exact same thing and saying the same words, take pictures of one another out at Expensive Nightclub with their phones, take pictures of themselves taking pictures, pictures of their friends taking pictures of them taking pictures. And it all revolves around me. In fact it becomes me, the name of the club becomes Junior Alvarez, there is no purpose or pattern aside from me. The people populating the space since they are not me are objects with no faces and no emotions. The music is my name. The perfume the broads wear smells like me. I am what pours into tall skinny glasses and what is sprayed from pressurized nozzles behind the bars. Ice cubes clink into me. I am the ice cubes. The hostess leads people to me, sits them in me. I am on the video screens, I am walked on by Expensive Clothes Company shoes, I am raised to painted feminine lips and I'm lit and I am burned into smoke that goes down girl throats and into girl lungs, circulates through endless networks of girl veins. I enter blood and bodies.

The bill comes dropped off by the hostess who smiles and gives me a look as she puts it down on the table encased by a small leather book. I hit Fernando with the back of my hand and motion at it with my head and look away and he reaches into his coat to pay. We take the girls back to our suite at Expensive Hotel in the

limo and in the limo we snort more Stimulant and get them to
kiss each other and in the room I smuck the blonde for a while
but even though we try every position I still get bored and can't
come so I get off her and get a Tobacco Company and light it and
she puts her arms around me from behind and kisses my neck and
asks what's wrong, am I too high, and I look at her like she's crazy
and irritating (which she is) and say nothing is wrong, I just want
to smuck her friend now, the brunette, whatever her name is, the
one Fernando is currently smucking in the next room, go in there
and send her over to me. When she comes I smuck her hard from
behind for a while, bent over the desk, but it's not enough for me,
I still can't come and soon lose my hard-on. I lie down with her
on the bed and wrap my arms around her then my legs too, try
to mesh with her or to consume her with my body, knowing that
even though she pretends to be asleep that she's not because I can
feel the way she's breathing, and I stay this way until morning,
saying nothing, trying to stay calm and pretty much succeeding.

OUR BEGINNINGS

Over a millennium ago, in the near extinction that followed the Visa Nuclear War, all progress we had ever made—from discovering fire to locating extraterrestrial life—was nullified overnight to quick black cigarette ash nothing. Most records of our historical, scientific, and social achievements were lost. They'd been long ago digitized and stored on computer servers, the hard copies allowed to fall apart or be lost. If the servers we relied on were not melted by the bombs they were erased by all the magnetism from the bombs. Ancient Egyptian papyrus texts, the Declaration of Independence, the Magna Carta, the Bible, census records, the *Mona Lisa*, *The Odyssey*—all gone, gone, gone. If not for the small number of survivors it would have been like none of it had ever existed. All the footprints we'd left over tens of thousands of years would have been vanquished. As we had guessed about the dinosaurs, the future rulers of the earth would guess about us. What would it be next time after those lizards, after us monkeys: Cockroaches? Mollusks? We survivors sat distraught around desert campfires in the aftermath of the war, eating what mangled retarded vermin or old leather apparel we could, keeping our spirits up by singing pop songs and telling one another plotlines from movies and television shows. These became our folktales, our literature. We told our children whatever we could remember from history class or Sunday school or cable television documentaries or the Internet or books about the history of man. It was mostly inaccurate. But because it was repeated enough times by enough generations it became fact. Thus we began the rebuilding of civilization.

We were in a hurry. Without realizing it we were putting things back together the same way they had been before. We wanted our automobiles and our indoor plumbing and our social networking applications back as soon as possible. We wanted to re-create what we had lost, what we had known, even if it had almost destroyed us. So history began to repeat itself. A second cycle began that was almost identical to what had led to the nuclear war. There was oceanic exploration, innovation in food production, medical advancement. But you cannot re-create something that could not have been built by design in the first place. So things were a little off. For example, Northern Virginia was a bland, desolate suburb the first time. But this time NoVA was not only its own state but a dense vast blighted urban epicenter. Yet it was somehow just as desolate. And you cannot avoid repeating the mistakes of your past. So this time just as last time there was wretchedness in the name of God, there was exploitation of the weak and the impoverished, there was murder for money, there was injustice for no reason, there was bigotry disguised as other things, hatred disguised as other things, fear disguised as other things. There was death. There was war.

And so on.

What happened was that the majority of us mourned and buried the dead and gathered the strength to pick ourselves up and soldier on. But there was a small group of exceptional men, men of greatness and power who saw life as a constant state of war with no rules except what can be gotten away with, and while the majority of us were sharing food and replenishing the species these men swooped in and capitalized. The end of the world was a fantastic financial opportunity. These men explained that they were making things better, that they were helping. They were smart, charismatic. They seemed to speak right to us. They seemed to be extensions of ourselves. They bit their lower lips and delivered captivating speeches among rubbled sites of mass death. They sang "God Bless America" on a pile of shattered stone that was once the steps of the United States Capitol. To the rest of us too distracted by obtaining food and shelter for ourselves and our children, these men appeared to be good. They struck pleasant-feeling nerves in us. Made us angry about things we felt we should be angry about and then made us feel as though they were the only ones we could trust to do something about what made us angry. So we trusted them. They ruled us by our emotions. They thrived on the susceptibility of the human imagination. They distracted us. Thus they were successful.

And so we proceeded.

As poets and prophets had forever sworn he would, man had endured.

For better and for worse.

THE RIDE

I am sixteen, I am seventeen, I am eighteen. The year is 3348 A.W. and it is fall. After a pretty boring night we find a bum under the Bridge and smuck with him. Then we go down Union Mill Road to Bar With Pool Table. It's a pretty normal night, nothing special. All the Internet terminals are occupied, men pounding away on the keyboards and staring, drooling, looking at porn, clicking, jerking off through their pockets thinking no one notices. When I buy my own Bar franchise, no smucking computers allowed. If you don't like it, you can take it up with me and I'll give you a kick in the ass. Manny is mimicking the bum. These high, whining drunken yelps. Uncle Antonio is here. He owns the place. He's never here but tonight he's here. Everybody knows about Uncle Antonio. Even if you don't know what he looks like you sure as smuck know the name. You have nightmares about the name. He runs Centreville. There are stories about him knocking guys off, paying off cops, going quail hunting with the mayor, running rackets, charging bank robbers and drug dealers fees for working on his turf, throwing people into vats of boiling oil until the skin burns off their bones. That kind of thing. He's a guy you don't ever want to deal with if you have the choice. I respect his power but I envy him. I want to be him. He has what I believe is mine and I want it. I want to tell him, Do you know I'm out here and I'm coming for you? He's walking around patting people on the backs, chatting, wearing an Expensive Clothes Company suit, hair slicked back, clean-shaven and put together, a real nice piece of ass (blond, big fake belly) at his side. There's a chill in the place with Uncle Antonio here. Sure, we smile and carry on as if we're oblivious, but the place is tense, like we're all sitting on a bus dangling off

THE GOOD AND THE GHASTLY

the edge of a bridge—one wrong move and we all go over. I'm listening to Fernando now talking about how Manny emptied a smucking full can of trash on top of the bum. Fernando is laughing about how the bum had trash all over him, a cantaloupe rind on top of his head like a soldier's helmet, making a mockery of him and his lack of dignity and honor.

I feel a hand on my shoulder. I look up. Uncle Antonio's nostrils are so big I can see into his brain. His face looks like an old tire. An aluminum the size of my head on his ring finger, which looks like it's been broken, burned, gnawed on, and dislocated about fifteen times. In a brief moment I see all the evil this man has done. It plays like a movie in the blackness of his eyes.

Hello, boys.

I think he's going to tell us to please kindly smuck off because Fernando is being so smucking loud. Uncle Antonio hates drunks. He also hates drugs, dipshits, debt. The four Ds. The table goes ice-cold, and Uncle Antonio is kneading my shoulder, giving me a smucking massage. I have chills, I'll admit it. I start to apologize for Fernando, but Uncle Antonio just looks at me with that glazed frozen smile, cutting me off.

Junior, I need a ride. Mind giving me a ride?

Lithis, judging from the look on everyone's face you'd think he's pulled out his dick and stuck it in my ear. The fear in the room is smucking palpable. When Uncle Antonio asks you for a ride, you don't come back. Things are running through my head about a trillion kilometers an hour, trying to figure out what I've done. The bum? Is the bum related to Uncle Antonio somehow? I run through the girls I've smucked recently, maybe they're tied in to him somehow. I don't know, everybody's smucking related in Centreville. You can't jerk off without squirting on somebody's cousin.

Uncle Antonio's grip tightens on my shoulder and I stay calm and get up and go with him.

Word to the wise: Never get in a car with anyone named Uncle Antonio.

His big black Expensive Car Company is parked in the alley around back right under a No Parking Sign. Think there's a ticket on that windshield? He tosses me the keys. Take 66 toward Orange, he says.

Orange, so I'll die in Orange. I'll drive this car to Orange so I can die. And I'll probably have to dig the grave first too.

My hands are sweaty. My heart hasn't beat in about forty seconds. In my extreme anxiety though, I still appreciate the man's style. I'm even at this point observing, learning.

We drive through the night. It's so quiet I can't stand it. I try to put on the radio but he hits my hand away and says, No radio. From my point of view, I'm the one who's about to die, so if I want to listen to the smucking radio I should be able to. But I just keep driving. It seems like we're driving for hours in this unnerving silence before he finally speaks. He clears his throat and says, You like my car?

I'm thinking, Who? What car? What the smuck are you talking about?

Junior.

Yeah, yeah I do. It's really ingratiating, Mr.—

You can call me Uncle Antonio, Junior. But, Junior?

Yeah? Yes sir?

Don't say those words around me. Okay? I hate those words. Ingratiating. Calm. All those slang words. They're words you kids use to give yourselves a false sense of individuality. You're not individuals. You're clowns. Know how I know this? Because you use clown words. Use tried-and-true words. And don't curse. It only shows how powerless you are. Once more: Do you like my car?

I do, Uncle Antonio. It's . . . it's really something.

Thank you. Guess how much I paid for it.

I don't know.

Participate, Junior. Engage in the discourse. How much did I pay?

Nothing?

He puts his head back and laughs. No, Junior, unfortunately that is an impossibility. Only a slang-using, vulgar clown such as yourself would ever expect to pay nothing for anything. You have a lot to learn about the nature of the universe. Here's an introductory lesson: Making up the universe are four elements. There is matter, there is light, there is energy, and there is money. And that's all. Nothing else. But actually you were close, Junior. I paid about as near to nothing for a car like this as one can. I paid six hundred and fifty thousand for it.

Calm.

Junior. Did you not hear a word I said? If you can't speak correctly to me, don't speak at all. Put some effort into your life, starting with your vocabulary. I can't tolerate mediocrity. Understood?

I'm thinking, Why? What difference does it make, if I'm going to die tonight? I hear myself say, No. He looks at me. I don't care. What am I scared of?

What did you say?

I said no, I don't understand. Why do you have to talk my ear off? If you're gonna kill me, shut the smuck up and put the smucking bullet in my head.

He doesn't say anything. He's just staring at me in the darkness of the car, his face obscured. I'm imagining the feeling of a bullet entering my head and ripping apart my brain, exiting on the other side. I can almost feel it. What is it like to die? I can hear him breathing through his nose, staring at me, his face shadowed by the darkness.

Take this exit, he says.

He directs me through a few rights and lefts. We end up on some street somewhere, some neighborhood. It doesn't look much different from Centreville. Rows of triple-deckers all smashed together with hardly any room between them for driveways. Turn off the lights, he says. Drive slowly.

I'm feeling defiant. It's all I have left at this point. I say, I'll drive how I want.

Shut your goddamn mouth, Junior, and go slow. Turn the lights off.

Halfway down the street he has me stop the car. Keep it running, he says, getting out and heading toward the porch of a house. He goes up to the door and rings the bell and steps away to the edge of the porch and waits. Ding-dong, I'm here with our guest of honor, boys. Come on out and drag him inside. Shoot him. Wrap him in plastic. Toss him in the Visa Potomac. I light a Tobacco Company. Smuck him. Smuck his car too. I use the cigarette to put a burn hole into the passenger seat. Why? Because I want to. I don't even think about it first, just do it. It's satisfying. I do it a few more times. Make a bunch of holes in that beautiful leather upholstery. I take the key out of the ignition and start stabbing the seat with it, ripping it up. In-smucking-gratiating. I carve CALM into the dashboard. Who's a clown now? On the porch, he's straightening his tie and testing his breath against his palm and ringing the bell again. What's he doing, picking up a date? Hey baby, I'm gonna kill some kid, wanna come watch and suck my dick after? I have to piss. I whip it out and piss all over the floor and pedals. Why? Same reason I put burn holes in his seat and carved up the dash. I'm shouting as I do it, Six hundred and fifty grand for this torn-up, pee-smelling piece of shit? He doesn't hear me. I start screaming, Calm! Ingratiating! Calm calm calm! Ingratiating ingratiating ingratiating! I look through the glove compartment to see if by chance there's a gun in there. Blow my own smucking head off. Speed things up a bit.

The porch light comes on and the door opens. I can't see who it is, it's too dark. Uncle Antonio gives a friendly hello and goes inside. The door closes behind him. About half a minute later I'm reaching back to burn holes into the rear seats too when the front door opens and a little pasty guy in his underwear comes out, Uncle Antonio behind him holding a gun to the back of his head. The guy has a hard-on poking through his underwear. Uncle Antonio is laughing. It looks like some kind of smucking fraternity prank. The other guy's not laughing. Uncle Antonio walks the guy down the porch stairs and down the front walk and to the car. Knocks on the window. Trunk, he's saying through the glass, still laughing. Then he pistol-whips the guy a couple times. He taps on the window with his aluminum ring and says again, Trunk, Junior. I pop the trunk. Uncle Antonio knocks again, motioning me out of the car. I get out. The guy's on the ground unconscious. Give me a hand, Junior, will you please. I get the guy's feet. Uncle Antonio gets him under the arms. We put him in the trunk, fold him and stuff him until he fits. As I close the lid Uncle Antonio says, Easy, easy, watch his head. Then he goes back inside the house, still chuckling to himself about whatever the smuck's so hilarious. I hear two dull gunshots. In the house next door and the one across the street, I see people in windows peeking through their blinds. A baby crying somewhere. Uncle Antonio comes back out, laughing, his face red, wiping tears from his eyes. We get in the car and drive off. That's a first for me, he's saying as he gasps for air from laughing so hard. He wipes his eyes with the edge of his thumb. He says, Holy cow. He was in the middle of screwing. Talk about timing. I almost apologized. I mean, what do I do? Let them finish? No, no, it's okay, I'll wait, take your time, I'll just be outside. He laughs, wheezing, coughing into his hand. Holy cow. Junior, you should have seen this woman. I have never seen a fatter human being. You should have seen all that flesh. I thought it was a giant mound of tapioca pudding on the bed! He laughs and laughs. When he finally gets ahold of himself he sighs and sees what I carved into the dash. What's this? he says. Then he sees all the burn holes. What the smuck did you do? He sniffs the air. Smells the piss. Junior, what the smuck happened to my car?

We drive. Get on the interstate. I'm in a much better mood now because I'm not going to die. The clock on the dashboard has stopped. Uncle Antonio pushes several buttons but nothing makes it start again. He thinks I did it, but I didn't.

It's actually kind of peaceful out here this far out of the city. All the stars. I guess we're probably an hour and a half southwest. Juvy was out here somewhere. I don't know where exactly. I don't want to think about juvy. That's all a black hole of dark, wasted years. How can it be possible to waste so much of your life like that? It's not only possible but pretty smucking easy. Sometimes I think it's the most natural thing to waste your life considering how easy it is to do it. You have to be rigorous at all times, otherwise you wake up one day and realize you've been wasting your life without even realizing it.

I don't want to think about juvy. I want to think about the stars. I want to think about the lights of the small towns spread out in valleys below us when we're driving on a high winding part of road. And the wildfires you can see off hundreds of kilometers in the distance like a bunch of little match flames. And the green steam shooting up in the road here and there. And the headlights of Uncle Antonio's car flashing on the eyes of the wild deer on the shoulders. Now and again one will wander out into the middle of the road. They'll just appear in front of you and you have to

swerve. They're hideous. Sinister. Goiters and oozing open sores
all over them, milky unseeing eyes, some with three legs, others
with a fifth one that started growing out of their rib or neck or
something but never fully developed. Every time I swerve to avoid
one of these nasty things, Uncle Antonio grabs the handle above
his window and there's a thump in the trunk as the guy is thrown
around and Uncle Antonio says under his breath, Easy, easy . . .
There are no human beings out here, no other cars. No signs of
life except for the horrible deer and the wildfires and the lights
way down below us in the valleys. Uncle Antonio keeps hitting the
broken clock with his hand. Come on you stupid thing, he says.
He asks me if I broke it. I tell him the truth: I didn't touch it. It
just stopped. He keeps hitting it, pushing buttons, hitting it. First
it annoys me but then it starts driving me crazy, his hitting it and
hitting it and obsessing over it. I try to turn on the radio to distract
myself but he hits my hand away and mumbles, No radio. Then
he keeps hitting the clock. I try to focus on what's out the window
instead of on him hitting the clock. But it's all blackness out there.
It gets blacker and blacker the farther we drive. The wildfires in
the distance never getting closer. And he keeps hitting it. I want to
grab his wrist to make him stop. I'm chewing the side of my tongue
because of how crazy his hitting the clock is making me. And every
once in a while punctuating the silence there's a series of thumps
from the trunk. It's unnerving. Each time scares the shit out of me.
Uncle Antonio doesn't even seem to notice.

Now we're off the highway and on an unpaved service road
driving through the woods. It's basically a hiking trail. There are
no lights except for the car's. I can't see shit. It's bumpy as smuck.
I think I'm going to run us into a tree or gack all over the smucking
steering wheel.

Finally Uncle Antonio has me stop. We're in the middle of
the woods. No signs of civilization. There's nothing creepier than
a night in the boonies. You could set off a wheelbarrow full of
dynamite out here and no one would know. I don't like that. If I set
off a wheelbarrow full of dynamite I want someone to hear it. But
that's just me.

As if reading my mind, Uncle Antonio goes, Let's get this over
with, this place gives me the heebie-jeebies. Pop the trunk, will you

please? I reach down and pop the trunk. In the rearview mirror as soon as the trunk opens we see the guy jump out shrieking and take off into the night.

Oh smuck, I say. Uncle Antonio does not seem interested. He's only interested in the clock. He mutters, hitting it, Go get him, Junior, will you please?

I get out, leaving Uncle Antonio to his clock. Take off after the guy. Thank Lithis he's so pale otherwise I'd never be able to see him. He's a slow runner. Has a limp or something wrong with his leg. I feel good as I chase him. Shivers up my spine—good ones. I imagine Uncle Antonio is my father and I am his son, obeying my father. For the first time in my life I feel like someone's son. It feels good to obey your father.

The guy tries to cut off the service road and into the trees but I overtake him, tackle him. He hits his face on a tree on the way down. His lip splits. Big gash on his forehead. I'm on top of him, have him in a nelson. Blood on his mouth, black bits of dirt and little sticks stuck to it. He's real smucking skinny. Skinnier than me. He's at least twenty years older than me but has the body of a child. And I have the shivers of a son. He's crying and whimpering. Please let me go, please let me go. He smells hot but feels cold. The blood on his mouth sprays and bubbles when he talks. Please let me go. Please. There's snot on his nose and another big cut I didn't see before on his chin starting to bleed a lot. Eyes darting around. Please, he'll kill me. Tell him I got away. I'll give you anything. Please. He's going to kill me. I don't want to die. Don't let me die. I try to pull him to his feet but can't. He's just lying there unmoving and limp. I pull him by the waistband of his underwear but it rips. So I take him by the feet and start dragging him, walking backward. His fingers claw the dirt the whole way, leaving a meandering track. It wears me out. I have to stop a couple times to take a break and plead with him to get up and walk but he refuses. When we finally get back to the car, I'm about spent. My father is smoking a Tobacco Company and leaning against the car. He looks up.

Clock's still not working, he says, as if that's even remotely smucking relevant.

I let the guy's legs drop. They thump to the ground. We both look down at him.

He's got a bum leg, Uncle Antonio says. It got crushed in the war. A jeep ran over it. One of his own guys. He's a cripple. Aren't you, you goddamn cripple?

My father has me, the son, drag the guy out into the headlights several yards from the car. He's shaking and crying. His chest and hands and face all torn up. There's piss all over his legs. I've never seen anyone so afraid. I look to my father who stands beside me. He tells me to get the guy on his knees. The guy obeys now. Just the slightest push on his shoulders and he kneels. He's kneeling facing away from the headlights of the car, into the night and the wilderness. He's looking at me, his face in globes of cold sweat, his eyes red. So much dirt clinging to the blood. Please, he's saying. My father pulls a gun from the inside pocket of his jacket and hands it to me. It's heavy, feels good in my hand. It is the metal that conducts the electricity that creates the shivers on my spine and I am breathing, sweating. I cock the gun. My hand is shaking. I have no control over it. No matter how much I try to stop it, it still shakes. The guy is crying, begging for his life. He looks tiny. Cold and wet and helpless. I don't want to do this. Everything in me is telling me not to. But I know that I can will these voices out of me, I can will myself to do it. I try not to think about anything that makes me feel guilty—the guy's eyes, the guy's mother. My own mother. We are predisposed toward guilt. Just like we are predisposed to wasting our lives. Both are part of our nature. But so is will. And I have that. It is the only thing I have. So I will the guilty thoughts out of my mind. I will the good out of me. I am not good. I am just a son.

You're gonna want to take about one and a half steps back. If you're that close to him you'll have a real mess.

I take one and a half steps back.

This place used to be all ashes. Can you believe that? All these trees weren't here. There were no trees anywhere in the world actually. It was all flat and covered in ash. This was a thousand years ago.

I point the gun at the back of his head.

This used to be a town called Charlottesville. There was a college right here, right here where we're standing. A big prestigious university founded by Thomas Jefferson. Know who Thomas Jefferson was?

I don't answer. My finger on the trigger.

He discovered electricity. Invented the lightbulb too. And movies. Want my advice? Study history. It's important.

I can feel the heat of the wildfires though I cannot see them and I can feel the shivers and hear the breathing of the deer in my fingers.

Quit drinking too. Altogether. Not even a cocktail at the end of the day. No drinking, no Stimulant, no Painkiller even with a prescription. I know about you. You need to knock it off. If you're an alcoholic or a drug addict, which I suspect you are, go into Visa Rehab Program first thing. It's just going to destroy you otherwise. No sex too if you can help it. Know what sex leads to? Lots of things. And you don't want any of them. But the main thing is babies. If they want to destroy you, your babies are the easiest way to do it. So don't make any. Sex and drugs and alcohol are all things that warp our perceptions and influence us. They make us vulnerable. You don't want to be vulnerable. You want to be invulnerable. You don't want to be influenced. You want to be uninfluenced. Let the rest of them be vulnerable. Let the rest of them be influenced. Be the only one who is neither. That is how one becomes mighty. Do you want to become mighty, Junior?

At a distance, from somewhere deep inside my own body, I feel myself saying yes but I do not nod because I cannot move other than the gun in my shaking hand.

Please. Please don't. Please.

Aim for right here, Junior. He taps a spot on the back of the head, right behind his right ear.

He stands back, wiping the man's sweat off on his pant leg.

It becomes silent.

I pull the trigger. The head explodes out of its center.

He falls forward, facedown. The shot echoes into the night. No one hears it.

I turn away, scream at the ground, puke, scream at myself to stop puking, to feel okay. To will out the guilt and the good and to keep the shivers on my spine and the wildfires in the hills of my deer-breathing fingers.

Digging the hole and filling it back up take three hours. I dig the whole thing myself because Uncle Antonio did something to his back, he says. The whole time I'm digging it, he sits in the car tinkering with the clock.

Afterward I can't turn my head from side to side. Everything hurts. I can't even think. I don't want to. I just want to sleep.

I get back in the car and drive out of those awful smucking woods. We get back on the interstate. Out of the blue, Uncle Antonio, who has not touched the clock for a while, now points at it and says, Look at that. It's working again.

He's right, it is.

I didn't even do anything to it and it works, he says.

It's a struggle to stay awake. I have to bite my tongue as hard as I can. It hurts to touch the steering wheel, my hands are so ripped up from the shovel.

After a while Uncle Antonio is dozing in the passenger seat. I say, What'd he do to you?

Who? he says not even opening his eyes, as if there were some confusion over who exactly I'm referring to.

You know. Him.

Oh him. He called me a dickhole.

I start laughing. I can't help it, can't stop. I laugh and laugh. It all comes out. Uncle Antonio cracks open an eye. Watch the road, he says.

That's the first time I ever killed somebody. Uncle Antonio paid me a hundred thousand dollars for it, minus the price of fixing his car. I have no idea how many more there will be. I'll forget a lot of them, but I'll never forget that one.

THE FRONT DOOR

The young man leaves his apartment. It's the new one, paid for with the proceeds of his recent work for Uncle Antonio. Making deliveries, collecting money. He's one of a myriad of young Irish enforcers. He's nineteen years old, locking his door. The apartment is a symbol. It delineates the threshold between Life and Death. Death after Life. Every morning he wakes up in silence staring at the white walls of the unadorned bedroom of his own apartment. He sees in the whiteness the walls of Before: The little black fingerprints on pale gray that were the walls of his childhood home. The paint-caked cinder-block walls antibacterialized by the flickering tubes of state light in the ceiling panels—juvenile detention. The faux-wood paneling of Maria's bedroom with sweetheart cutouts of hunks from magazines and curling year-old photographs of herself with friends and family in which she seems not a year but a decade younger. He lies there blinking watching the Before walls transposed by the After walls, white uncracked walls still smelling of sawdust and caulk and the alcohol sweat and cigarette breath of the workers who put them up. The Before walls seeming to sink beneath the After walls, like the new ones are ocean water and the old ones are beach sand and the new ones are rising up in the advent of a high tide to conceal the sand inch by inch until only a few odd islets are visible then those too are consumed and washed away by the rhythms of the sea.

He walks down Union Mill Road. It's quiet at this hour. Everybody is at work or in court or breast-feeding a baby or lying on their couch watching television. It's the offbeat hour of the marginal. Old newspapers stamped with shoeprints flap like windblown wings of dead gulls in vestibules and alleys. Harrowed degenerates emerge from Convenience Store with no money and no purchase, their shoes untied. Missing children lie sleeping under benches covered in leaves. He passes Deli, Chewey the schizophrenic sitting in the chair they put out there for him eating a cheese sandwich and calling out to Junior in an indecipherable yawn. He keeps close to the buildings and the shadows. It's overcast and April, the threat, or is it the promise, of snow in the taste and heft and grayness of the air. He walks. He moves through the city. Hands in the pockets of his jacket like he has a gun and is on his way to rob a Bank. Passes a cop, Manny's uncle, parked idle in his cruiser in a handicap spot idly flirting with a young girl whore. Each corner, each sidewalk square, seemingly stamped with the name of a child and the manner of his or her death. Overdose, murder, murder, suicide, overdose, suicide. He can't believe how many kids have died. People he never would have imagined. It was like his release from juvenile detention triggered a transformational quaking of the earth that sent everyone on a new trajectory skewed toward tragedy. Carlos's throat cut in this building in an argument over a negligible sum of money. Jose Marques shooting Eva Gardoza in the head on this stoop here while their friends waiting for the school bus watched because she had taken his virginity the week before and the power this gave her over him humiliated him, drove him to insanity. They were fourteen years old. The owner of the building to this day unwilling to spend the money to replace the front door so the bullet hole remains there as a reminder, like Eva's eye still watching us. Marco Lopes one night climbing drunk up the scaffolding of this building here and falling off. Alicia Rodriguez overdosing on Painkiller she was shooting in an apartment on the third floor of this building. And on and on. Every step he takes seems to bring another name and another fading face that then dissolves before his own. He passes the Visa Housing Project where he grew up. A dreary unadorned single square brown-gray tower reaching up and up forever into the gray sky until it seems to disappear among the storm clouds there. Humans packed in like factory goods. Living ratty noisy lives. Smelling one another's breath and shit. The window of unit 27A above his head, up there somewhere among all those other windows, all those other floors. His childhood home. His mother still there. She could be in the window now, looking down, watching the beady top of her son's head as he passes. He doesn't care.

The reason it looks like he's holding a gun in his pocket is because he's holding a gun in his pocket. It's wrapped in a thin rag and is to be taken to an executive suite at Expensive Hotel in Reston. Not to be used but to be delivered. As though it were lunch.

He moves through the city with a job thinking about all the people he's known who have died, carrying a probably stolen gun given to him by Uncle Antonio to deliver, most likely to be used to etch another name into the sidewalk squares, to drill another shattered glass eye into the front door of a bloodied stoop in this doomed town.

He is recognized by people in cars, men driving delivery trucks and taxicabs and vans rattling with the tools of carpentry and plumbing. There he goes, they say. He can hear them. Ol' Whatshisname, there he goes. Uncle Antonio's bitch boy. On his way to suck his cock. He has a gun but he's not tough. Must be sixty kilos max. What's he done in his life that would make him tough? Execute an unarmed and terrified man for a reason that had nothing to do with him? What a big man. What difficult decisions has he made? What risks has he taken? Look how much of a hurry he's in to get it in his mouth. He can't wait. Bet he gets a phone call as soon as it pops up—Junior, get over here immediately, my dick's hard—and he goes running. Yes sir, Uncle Antonio sir, right away sir. Part of his job. Spelled out explicitly in his job description. If he weren't connected to Uncle Antonio and I saw him in my neighborhood I'd kick the shit out of him. It'd be easy. Because I have something he does not have: character. I've earned it grinding away every day of my life, making tough decisions, taking risks. I'm a man. He's a boy, doing what he's told. Used to think he was Alejandro el Grande. What a joke. Think Alejandro would be running across town to the train to go all the way out to Reston to deliver something to some man he does not know in a hotel room bigger than any room he himself has ever set foot in in his life, excluding courtrooms? What a smucking joke. Thinks he's a hotshot but he's just a lackey. Just another stooge. One of a long line. I don't even know his name. I'll forget his face in a month, as soon as he's knocked off or picked up for something Uncle Antonio put him up to and will let him take the fall for. I'll forget him. How long will it take him to realize that he'll be forgotten? That he's just another forgettable boy as kept and anonymous and meaningless and small and not free and harried and Sisyphean as the rest of us?

He can hear them.

He can feel the world pulling him down by the ankles sometimes. Covering him with a fat layer of wet heavy mud. Maybe this is the biggest change of all since he did what he did on that black-night service road where no one could hear anything no matter how hard you screamed.

Do this, do that. That's all he ever hears anymore. Be here, be there. This time, that time. Say these words. Live in this apartment. Wear these clothes. Don't curse. Don't drink. Don't smuck. Be this way. Do what I say. Make me money. Keep a little for yourself. Not too much, just a teeny-tiny bit. To me it's chump change but to you it's a fortune. Risk your life for me. Risk prison. Thank me for the opportunity.

He can feel it pulling him down, he can hear them saying it.

Takes the train out to Reston, gets off, stands outside the station for half an hour waiting for a bus, gets on it, pays. Four others on the bus. All of them old or derelict or disabled or heavily medicated. He sits among these spent, unfortunate people who have nowhere to be. They are not their own masters. Their bodies are. The ones they depend on are. They all look so miserable. Why are they alive? They smell like doctors' offices.

And here I am on the same bus as they are.

Transfers to another line for which he waits on a quiet corner in a residential area for fifteen or twenty minutes. This bus drops him eight blocks from the Expensive Hotel, the closest stop to it, a distance he walks. He'll walk eight blocks, deliver the gun, then turn around and do it all over again in reverse to get back to Centreville. Like the nobody that he is.

When he rounds the corner and first lays eyes on the Expensive Hotel, he stops dead in the middle of the street. His stomach flips.

—Kevin smucking Lithis.

He stands there in the middle of the street just looking up at it. First time he's ever seen one in real life. He feels dwarfed by it. It's something else. It looks like a Persian palace in Alejandro's time. He feels full of swirling emotions: beauty, ambition, despair, hope, lust.

A car honks behind him. He moves aside for it, a black Expensive Car Company. Watches it go past him and up the long driveway past the fountain to the circular drive at the door. He walks up to the wrought-iron fence at the edge of the property, grabs hold of it, puts his face between two bars, and observes. What he sees amazes him. A man standing outside the front doors approaches the car and opens the rear passenger door and a man steps out. The guest. The driver of the guest's car hands the keys to the other man who takes the guest's car and drives it off to park it for him. Another man meanwhile has come out and taken the guest's luggage out of the trunk of the car and carries it inside, the guest following concerned with winding his wristwatch as though he is not even halfway aware of the opulence around him nor of the men driving his car and parking his car and carrying his bags for him. And there is yet another man. He is waiting inside the vestibule. His single and entire purpose is to open the door for the guest and to continue holding it while the guest enters through the door and once the guest is finished with his entering to close it again. That is the only reason whatsoever for this man. The guest never once looks up from winding his watch. Junior stands there impaled by this scene, this display of whatever it is—greatness, success, wealth, leisure, masculinity—his hands hot and wet against the cold of the wrought-iron fencing, seeming to be made hot and wet by the great, successful, wealthy, leisurely, masculine guest himself, this person, this man—just like the driver and the valet and the doorman and the bellhop are men biologically, and just like Junior too is biologically a man—this man who has bought an Expensive Car Company he does not even have to drive himself, let alone park it, who owns luggage he does not even have to carry himself, who has a room at Expensive Hotel into which he does not even have to open his own doors, all things which he is perfectly capable of doing himself, this man who does not even feel compelled to break from his small self-occupations to appreciate the lavish opulent exterior of the Expensive Hotel that looks like a palace and which he has paid so much money to stay in, staying in it maybe not even an entire twenty-four-hour day, maybe staying in it for only ten or eleven hours, enough time to eat and sleep and wake and dress and eat again so as to be off to whatever business brings him to town—all nothing warranting such lavishness. Yet still here he is, and yet still there they are, the men driving and parking his car and carrying his bags and opening and closing the door for him. Junior's eyes are big and he has a nervous grin as he stands there, his knuckles white around the twisted bars of the wrought-iron fence watching from a hundred yards away this magnificent scene with the obsession of a pervert. This is it! he wants to scream. This is what I want!

The guest is inside now. The valet has returned from parking the car. Junior comes around from behind the fence and makes his approach up the long driveway. He moves in sideways skittering starts and stops, like a rat finding itself one minute in an alleyway feasting on garbage in peace and privacy and the next minute having somehow entered through a hole and is now inside a restaurant exposed out in the open in the middle of a dining room floor causing a commotion of screaming women and busboys trying to crush him with brooms. The men are waiting now for more cars to park, more bags to carry, more doors to open. These are men so low that they are here only as unnecessary servants for other men who are just as much men as they are, a luxurious appendage merely accenting the overall experience of the hotel, unnecessary because they are doing nothing that cannot be done by the guest himself, and still these men on just another day of unnecessary appendageship are wearing blazers and bow ties and shiny black shoes, clothes that are more expensive and fancy than the most flamboyant article Junior has ever tried on in his life while Junior wears merely a pair of old Clothes Company jeans and a Clothes Company T-shirt and his only jacket which is one he did not even pay for but received from Fernando who stole a box of them off a truck—the clothes not even of an appendage as the men are but of a mental patient or a parolee. His hand is still on the gun in his pocket. He approaches past the valet who gazes at him with no expression, more just glancing at him and his outfit as though he were a vehicle passing by out on the street. He steps to the door. Waits for the doorman inside to open it for him as was done for the guest. The door is glass. He can see the doorman just on the other side, in his blazer and bow tie and shiny black shoes, chatting with the bellhop, two unremarkable men whose only skills are their self-restraint and pleasurable temperament and who are mere ornaments to someone else's success yet who still make more money and are more of a man than he is. They don't even see him. So he does it himself, he opens the door himself. As he starts to enter, the doorman stops talking and not even looking at him puts his white-gloved hand on Junior's chest to stop him at the threshold before his foot can come down on the first few inches of carpet within. The doorman says, eyes not even flickering toward him, —Back door.

Junior recognizes the accent from Centreville's lowest-born, squints at him. —Get your smucking hand off me.

The man finally looks at him though not to acknowledge him as a human but as if to reaffirm the measure he's already taken of him as far back as his approach up the driveway.

—Back door.

Junior doesn't want to make a scene considering what's in his pocket. He wants to say something but doesn't. Can't think of anything. Even if he could his mouth would not be able to say it. Because it's frozen. He is frozen. It's not humiliation. It's something else. The doorman reaches out, pulls the door closed again, continues his conversation with the bellhop as though it were never interrupted. Junior stands there for a second with a disbelieving smile on his face that he cannot get rid of. Soon he finds himself turning and considering things but still frozen even though he is moving as he heads around the corner toward the back, toward the back door. He does not even decide to do so, it's more like his body automatically goes. He's in a kind of quietly frantic spell. He'll never have a name for it but he'll never forget it either. He passes the valet who does not look at him. It's not that the valet is ashamed at the discrimination or uncomfortable for standing by at this parade of fraudulence and pretension. It's that he's as uninterested in Junior and in Junior's being refused as he would be in a flower in one of the big beige pots out here being browned and drooped.

On the side of the building, halfway to the back, he stops. The spell breaks. It is replaced by fear. It is cold, calm fear. There are no other emotions in it, it's just fear. He stands there coldly and calmly terrified. He stares straight ahead. The memory of juvenile hall is there. A holographic replay in cinematic clarity hovering between him and the end of the wall around the corner from which is the back door. Is it here, in this moment that is so short but seems to last hours, that the design first etches itself into his will where it will not just stay indelibly but grow and grow and etch itself deeper and spread monstrously like a tumor whose appetite has no limit and who wants only death and horror yet still must be fed? The design that will dictate the rest of his life and the lives of all those in Northern Virginia for decades and decades? Is this the moment that changes everything?

The back door. The back door.

Out front the valet when he catches a movement out of the corner of his eye turns his head to see the young man walking out from the side of the building where he's just gone, his face pointed straight ahead and all the muscles in it tightened to such a degree that the valet feels the muscles in his own face ache. He walks past the valet and down the driveway, not looking at the valet, not looking back at the hotel or the men within the vestibule, his one hand still stuffed into the pocket of his jacket. He's walking hard, almost stomping, as though everything within him wants to sprint and never stop until his heart bursts but the only reason he does not is the self-restraint exerted by the incredible force of his will.

MIMES

Ruben Ortero Lopez stands in a low-ceilinged unfinished basement in a wooden triple-decker on a street of similar, same-colored triple-deckers in East NoVA, a gritty working-class enclave out across the bridge by Visa NoVA International Airport, before a small gathering of people sitting in tan metal folding chairs, as he does every Wednesday evening, which is when the city- and Visa-sanctioned support group Organized Crime Violence Victims Non-Anonymous meets. It used to be Organized Crime Violence Victims *Anonymous*, but everyone knows one another—especially the members from Centreville, who make up the majority of the support group—and, citizens of NoVA nowadays being legendarily impatient, they decided it was silly to continue pretending otherwise. Eight-twelfths of OCVV Non-Anon in fact are from Centreville. Two-twelfths are from Falls Church. Two more twelfths are from Fairfax. Tonight there are two new members.

Ruben Ortero Lopez, who has no tongue, is miming, doing his best via a sort of game of Visa Charades to give his testimony of renting the second-floor unit of a triple-decker much like this one but in Fairfax, and, when it came time to mail his first rent check to his landlord, he—not having the address or a phone number for the landlord, he realized, having gone through Real Estate Agency and never met his landlord face-to-face—looked on his lease and found an address that he assumed was it and wrote it on the envelope and stamped the envelope and put it in the mail. What he didn't know was that (a) the address on the lease for his landlord was out of date, and (b) his landlord was a high-midlevel henchman in Uncle Antonio's gambit. Though the check did eventually find its way to the landlord and was debited from Ruben's account, it got there

65

late, unbeknownst to Ruben Ortero Lopez, who went about his business in good conscience, having no reason to think anything was wrong.

Rent had to be in by the fifth of the month. That month, as soon as it turned one minute past midnight on the morning of the sixth, there was a knock on his door. Ruben was in bed. He woke up and went to the door. He had no reservations about answering it, assumed nothing sinister, was more concerned that a neighbor might be in trouble and needed help. He opened the door. There stood a man. A big man. He was huge. Ruben couldn't see the man's face in the blackness of the hallway.

The shadow said, —Have you met your landlord yet? His voice was gravelly and strangled, as though his trachea and lungs had once been crushed and he'd been unable to get a full breath ever since.

—No, Ruben said.

—Well, then allow me to introduce myself. Hello, I'm your mothersmucking landlord.

Long story short, Ruben Ortero Lopez—all his life a fitness aficionado, participating in many physical activities like Visa Triathlons and Visa Adult League Amateur Baseball, etc.—and spending almost a pathological amount of time at Gym—spent the rest of his night getting both kneecaps shattered, his face broken in several places, a couple fingers broken, six ribs cracked, four teeth knocked out, his own trachea crushed, and ultimately paying rent twice that month. He tried to explain in the midst of the assault what must have happened and that it was an honest misunderstanding, that he was an honest and good person. His landlord didn't care. Ruben was screaming for help. Even though he could hear his neighbors above him moving around, nobody called the cops or otherwise did a thing.

Ruben was off his feet for the next four months, bedridden due to his injuries. The sudden end of physical activity caused his metabolism to slow down drastically. (Ruben unfortunately was born before ob-gyns began the routine practice of performing gastric bypasses on newborns.) With nothing to do all day but stare at the ceiling or the TV he became very unhappy. Then he discovered food. He ate and ate and ate. He discovered in food an escape from the torment of significant injuries and the crazy-making boredom of having to lie in bed all day. So he ate a lot and due to his new slow metabolism that he was not accustomed to he got very fat. The fatter he got, the worse he felt, so he had to eat more to feel good. Once he healed enough to get back on his feet he was huge and his metabolism would not speed up again, and, because his knees were still not even 80 percent nor would they ever be again, he found little success in losing the weight via exercise. So he got gastric bypass. It worked well at first, and in the first few weeks he lost almost nine kilos. But then he went on a spectacularly decadent binge in which he lost all control and remembers very little beyond dark blurry snippets of weirdness all culminating in him coming to one morning two weeks later on a beach in Visa Acapulco naked and eighteen kilos heavier than when he began the binge, with a terrible incapacitating pain in his belly. The staples in his stomach, a typically impressive Mexican emergency room doctor confirmed, had burst. In the emergency room, Ruben made the emotional decision, while he was in such a medically advanced place as Acapulco, to go ahead and do it, to take control of his life before he lost it for good, *to get dumbed down.* The latest trend in both men's and women's weight-loss surgery has been the practice of removing the tongue—actually going in by hand and pulling the tongue taut and snipping it as far back as possible with a pair of sanitized shears manufactured explicitly for this purpose, referred to in the medical community as *despeakers.* The process is half-jokingly referred to by surgeons as *dumbing down the patient,* or, alternately, *dumbing things down,* etc. The idea is that without the ability to taste, the overweight patient will lose a lot of the desire to eat. The procedure is considered a semiexperimental last hope after even gastric bypass has failed. It costs $980,000. A Visa Health Insurance Standard Plan pays 60 percent. It was a tough decision for Ruben but he figured his face was already damaged beyond repair from his landlord's assault, so what difference did it make if he lost his tongue too if it would make him thin again?

Watching all this, kind of shaking her head blankly, taking it all in and not knowing what to do with any of it, is Josefina Hernandez, the outsider, sitting with legs crossed in a bent folding chair, Little

Josefina in one hand, the other hand idly stroking Jaime's head. Jaime is the only one not in one of the beige metal folding chairs. Jaime is lying down, on a gurney. An upside-down bag drips clear fluid through a tube and into his arm. A heart monitor quietly beeps. His eyes are open but rolled back into his head. They are gray-colored. Every once in a while they come forward but only stare sightlessly up at the ceiling before spasming then rolling back again. He is coated in beads of sweat. He is covered up to his chin with a sheet, so no one can see how grotesquely cramped his hands and feet are. They look badly broken, double-jointed. It's a matter of public decency, putting a sheet over them. Drool oozes thick down both sides of his face. His mouth involuntarily opens and closes a little, like he's trying to will himself to speak. Lips crooked and permanently twitched. He does not look like a human, he looks like a wax dummy. Without looking, Josefina wipes the drool off his lips and face with a towel that she keeps on his belly when not in use, adds a couple drops of rewetting solution into his eyes. As for the group, they don't look at Jaime. They are glad he is in the back, in the corner. Their hearts go out to him but it's so hard to look at him.

This is Josefina Hernandez's first time attending the weekly OCVV Non-Anon meeting. It's taken her years to get to this point, to be able to do this. After her son, Jaime, was released from the hospital after his attack four years ago, and after it became clear that the police would never devote the manpower or cognitive energy necessary to locate the savages who did this to her son, and when the prospect of Jaime waking up anytime soon became more and more dim, and after two weeks of sixteen-hour days going door-to-door in Chantilly, Centreville, and other NoVA cities with a picture of Jaime asking the residents if they knew anything about who put this boy into a coma, two weeks of ironlike reticence and silence, Josefina sat down at her Computer Company and Search-Engined the phrase *Gang Violence Victims–fans*. She needed to find others like her and Jaime. They had to kill the isolation. That was the worst of it all—Jaime was alone in his coma, and Josefina was alone in her loss, because all she ever had was Jaime. They had to kill the loneliness. The loneliness was as much the enemy as any miscreant or thug. There was strength in numbers. She had gone door-to-door in Centreville in order to find the cretin who did this and to get him off the streets but also to meet others who had lost like she had, to reach out beyond the isolation of violence so they could see one another's faces. But they shut the door on her as soon as they figured out what she wanted. Out of fear. First it disappointed her. Then it disgusted her. Then it just enraged her. The reason for the –*fans* in her Search Engine query was that there turned out to be a tremendous array of celebratory sites made by *fans* of gruesome organized-crime violence. Apparently there existed *fans,* there existed *people* out there who were so warped and deranged that they felt *fondness* toward these monsters. The sites featured photos and homemade video tributes and collections of news articles and fawning biographies of local mob luminaries like Uncle Antonio and Emilio Gustava, and old-time revered crooked politicians like 3320s sinner-saint Miguel Curletos. The sites also had breathless information about up-and-comers like Junior Alvarez and suggested ways of torturing and killing people. One site had pictures of suspected snitches, with an X through the ones who had been killed so far. Josefina's heart stopped as she scrolled through, expecting to maybe see her face on there. Or Jaime's. There were also crime-scene photos of dead snitches, the colors livid, the resolution crisp, red and flesh sprawled everywhere on nighttime riverbanks and oil-spot black pavement under overpasses, the shoes and cuffs of suit pants of detectives and beat reporters standing around, alive.

Her heart stopped also when she saw that name on the list of criminals: Junior Alvarez. The name stuck to her bones. That name, that name. What a cold ugly name. She knew she didn't recognize it but it felt like she did. She wrote the cold ugly name down and stared at it. Then she put it in a drawer of her desk, closed it. Didn't know what else to do with a name that horrid.

There were so many of these sites that it made it impossible to filter through them and get to any that could help her reach out through the isolation. These sites—the sheer volume and magnitude of them—never failed to fill her with despair. Is this *people?* she can remember thinking. Is this human nature, is this what people *are?* Is this *truth?* Is this what man *is* if you just remove his conscience?

She found at last the Organized Crime Violence Victims Non-Anonymous site. It was less than encouraging. A vacant lot of a site. Dinky and neglected. Comically out-of-date. The phone number listed was answered by a Visa Barber Shop in Fredericksburg. No mailing address. There was an e-mail address though and Josefina wrote several times to ask about when the group met and how she could get involved but never got a response. She could see her messages sitting in a long forgotten inbox somewhere deep in an electronic netherhole, among spam, forwarded chain letters, and other flotsam. She gave up on the group entirely until one day when she was at Grocery Store in Centreville. She believes that the produce is fresher there than it is at Grocery Store in Chantilly, even though she knows that both stores carry the same stock, supplied by the same laboratories in Nebrasklahoma. She happened to overhear a produce stocker and a customer talking in low voices next to the lettuce—a gray rubbery ball one peels layers off with a peeler. She casually moved a bit closer to eavesdrop on the conversation. It looked secretive and interesting. She made the pretense of looking at the eggplants—yellow glass balls of perpetually bubbling liquid that, when the ball is cracked over a bowl, comes out and solidifies into a crunchy off-white object that is edible. What they were talking about in such paranoid, low voices turned out to be OCVV Non-Anon.

She approached them. They clammed up. Wouldn't tell her where the group met. Wouldn't even confirm that they were talking about what they were talking about. It could have been a reaction to how alarming she was, this sudden, excited woman in a supermarket demanding answers. But she knew that was not what it was. So the next day she went down to Visa Public Library where they keep pamphlets and literature for every Visa-sanctioned organization that exists. She had to vigorously, devotedly dig. Her search led her to the basement, way in the far corner, in a box that apparently—judging from the cobwebs and dust nearly half an inch thick—had not been touched in decades. But she eventually found the OCVV Non-Anon pamphlet. There was only one copy, and it was folded up and squooshed by binders full of old city documents and reports and other records of some sort. But she found it. And there was an address on it. And so here she is at last. The isolation breaking.

When Ruben Ortero Lopez is done, the group applauds with aplomb. He bows, smiles, goes around shaking hands, kissing the women on the cheek, face flushed and dotted with beads of perspiration, before finally squeezing his way through the rows of metal folding chairs and plopping onto his seat which bends and creaks under his weight. As they applaud, the heavyset woman next to Josefina leans over to the man next to her—the produce stocker—and mouths, —Wow.

The produce stocker says, —Subpar.

—Come the smuck on.

—It was not his best performance.

—Strong ending though you gotta admit.

—First of all I *have* to admit nothing. In fact, I must *do* nothing but breathe and pay taxes. Second of all, the ending was derivative and unconvincing.

—You're out of your mind.

—I am not. You must be out of yours, if you disagree.

—Derivative of *what*?

—Many things but if I have to name one, it would be Stefan Gonzalez's testimony three weeks ago.

—I disagree. I completely disagree.

—You would.

OCVV Non-Anon's Statement of Purpose, as laid out in the pamphlet Josefina picked up, strictly expresses that OCVV Non-Anon has no leader. The only true leader, the literature states, besides the understood one of Kevin Lithis, is one's self. But then, later, before the profound vapidness of that has settled, the flowery and ill-grammatized Statement of Purpose says that there actually cannot be a leader because the only leader is organized crime and the thugs who hijack their neighborhoods, poison the ballot boxes, etc. The only leader of OCVV Non-Anon, it says at the end, the last sentence of the Statement of Purpose, is evil. Josefina was confused by and skeptical of the contradiction when she sat at home that night reading it, found herself scribbling on the pamphlet with red pen, underlining, madly scratching retorts to things in the margins, correcting grammar mistakes, getting more enraged the more Visa Red Wine she drank.

The applause has now stopped and Ruben Ortero Lopez is in

his chair huffing and puffing and wiping his red sweaty brow with a hankie like a preacher, smiling to those around him offering their congratulations for yet another spellbinding performance. The produce stocker sits with his arms crossed, proudly standing by his opinions. A hunchbacked elderly man with red pants and ears two different shapes hands Ruben a bouquet of roses, pats him on the shoulder. A woman who seems to be the leader that the pamphlet insisted does not exist stands up and faces the group. Her eyes are so lively and positive and blue. She wears a name tag that says DEBORA. She stands up, a spry woman in her midthirties maybe, still clapping, says, —Wow! Just, wow! She's exhilarated, a little flushed. Puts a hand on her chest as though to steady her fluttering heart. She seems almost postcoital. She says, fanning her red face with her hand, —Thank you, Ruben! Would anybody else like to give their testimony tonight?

Josefina Hernandez raises Little Josefina high in the air and says, —I would.

And a dozen metal folding chairs scrape and shuffle the concrete floor as suddenly a gang of suspicious, unfriendly faces turn and look at her. In so doing they all see Jaime, cannot pretend now that he is not there, as Josefina gets up and clears her throat and tries to smile, squeezes her way between chairs and bodies up to the front, excusing herself.

Once at the front, she turns and faces them all. —Four years ago, she begins, voice wavering, clutching Little Josefina before her with both hands, —my son Jaime was attacked. He was assaulted, violently, by a mob of thugs. He was beaten with fists, and a bat, and maybe heavy chains, the doctor said. He was nearly beaten to death. He suffered permanent liver, kidney, spleen, and trachea damage as well as internal-bleeding injuries and brain contusions. No one came to his aid, not even his so-called friends. After the attack he did not know how bad his injuries were. Bravely, he thought he felt good enough to come home, all the way from Falls Church. We live in Chantilly. To this day I do not know how he got home all the way from Falls Church. If he rode the bus in this condition or what. He was a mere child of fifteen at the time and was covered significantly in blood and severely injured. If he rode the bus, why did no one help him? Why didn't the bus driver call an ambulance? Where were his so-called friends? Where were the police? I ask myself this every day. Was everyone blind? They must have been. But I'm not. My son came home that day and I saw what they'd done. I saw the blood. It was everywhere. It was clumped in his hair. He told me he was fine, that I was being crazy. Maybe I believed him. He wouldn't tell me who did it. I thought, Maybe leave him alone. Then he collapsed. We were in the bathroom and he collapsed on the floor. I thought he was making fun of me. I laughed, sarcastic, ho ho. Ho ho. I told him get up. I realized he was not faking when I heard sirens. They were right outside. Oh good, I thought, somebody called or somehow they knew. Then I realized it wasn't sirens I was hearing, it was my screaming. My own screaming. I started slapping his face so hard I thought I'd break his jaw, if it wasn't broken already. They beat my son Jaime to knock him out, I beat my son Jaime to wake him up. He didn't wake up then and he still hasn't woken up four years later. His injuries, the doctors say, are irreversible. He'll never speak another word. He'll never converse. He'll never comprehend. He'll never regain functionality. I was screaming so loud. Four years now he has been like this and his attacker is still at large. Why does no one do anything? Why does no one see that we've got to wake up and break this culture of fear? Why does no one see how the violence isolates us? We've got to break the isolation. We've got to take back our community and our lives. And the lives of our children. Jaime's life is slipping away from him. These are supposed to be his good years. He is supposed to be enjoying his youth. He is just nineteen years old. He should be out meeting girls and learning a job. As a mother, seeing my son's life going by without him, it breaks my heart. It kills me. I am a good woman. I've devoted my life to giving my son, Jaime, a good foundation for his life. They not only took away Jaime's best years from him, but they took the nineteen years I spent building him his foundation. I am a good law-abiding woman. I do not do drugs. I do not cheat welfare and only seldom play the lottery. I keep a home. I am a good mother. I work as a landlord, renting my property of one three-family home in Chantilly. I've had to move into the smallest unit because I need the money for the medical bills. I maintain the property. I spray down the sidewalk and pick up trash. I respond to maintenance issues right away. I keep a garden out front. I adhere to the standards I myself would expect as a tenant. I keep the rent stable. I do not extort. I do not screw my tenants over. I could raise rent. I could charge much more than I do. I could scam them out of their security deposits. But I do not. Never once have I evicted, not even when my tenant was one of those hoarders. Not even when another one was eight months behind on rent. I could have legally evicted that one but I chose compassion. I sat down with him and helped him organize his finances. And it worked. It took time, but eventually he caught up on the rent. I do not make a big deal of pets. Some landlords will make you give the deer to a pound or find another place to live. Not me. I know what happens in those pounds. I have a heart. I value life more than the condition of my property or anything else at all for that matter. All life, *especially* the lives of animals. Because they are innocent. And I value innocent life the most. Apparently in NoVA I am in the minority in that department. So why do I deserve this? I ask myself this every night in bed and every morning waking up and every afternoon, all hours of the day, for four years. I'm in prison, psychologically and physically. An innocent woman in prison. I cannot leave my house because Jaime needs to be cared for at all times. You have to put drops in his eyes constantly because he can't blink. I think of things in my past that I did to deserve this. Is this my punishment for getting a divorce? Even though my husband domestically abused me in front of my child and was an alcoholic and drug addict and eventual convicted felon? Did I mention my hair has begun falling out? Did I mention I can't sleep more than two and a half hours a night without waking up in the middle of a nightmare? Did I mention I go into fits of rage where I smash things like dishes onto the floor, because it's the only way to feel right? Did I mention I have to wipe my son's rear and empty his bedpan three, four, five times a day? Imagine you have a son. You give birth to him, raise him, feed him, protect him. You sacrifice everything to raising him right and good. You potty-train him. You teach him how to ride a bike and to look both ways. You tell him why the sky is blue, why the grass is green. You devote your life to making him a man who is prepared to live a man's life in the world. And then, when he is almost grown and ready to use all these things you gave him through your sacrifice, it happens that because of someone else's hatred of life that none of any of what you gave him means a goddamn thing because you still have to wipe his rear for him like he's still an infant. Is that fair? You have to ask your nineteen-year-old son, Do you have to go poopoo, Jaime? Even though you know he will not answer. The doctor recommends a diaper. But Jaime is not a baby, I told him. Jaime is a man. Men don't wear diapers. I raised him to be a man because his father couldn't. I told the doctor this. No man deserves to have his mother see him move his bowels. And no man deserves to have his mother see his genitals, when she bathes him with a rag every day. Do you get it? Do you understand what I'm saying to you? Do you understand that sometimes the act of washing that area of a young adult male, by a foreign hand that is not his, creates an erection in him involuntarily? Can you wrap your head around what I'm saying right now? Because of what this so-called person who is still out there tonight did to Jaime, he has to suffer the indignity of getting erections from his mother. It's not funny, whoever laughed. It's a humiliation for him. It's a terrible, sick, horrific indignity. For both of us. I talk to Jaime. Who knows if he can hear me. But I talk to him. I believe he can hear me. I tell him, Jaime, soon you will wake up. You will find a girl to love, Jaime. You will have a baby with her and you'll work, Jaime, to support your family. Every day I tell my son, Jaime, this. Every morning my first thought is, I pray. I say, Dear Lithis, make today be the last day he has to have his mother wash him with a rag, the last day he has to have his mother wipe his rear for him. It's the only thing that gets me out of bed, believing that maybe this will be the day Lithis will decide to answer. I've tried everything else. But nothing works. Telling myself this is the only thing that keeps me from shattering into pieces.

The weight of her words hums in the air before the silent group for a long moment in which no one moves or blinks. Josefina is a little nervous and embarrassed. She got a little carried away, she knows. The words took on a life of their own. She is about to say, So anyway thanks . . . and go sit down with Jaime (she can see a tremendous buildup of glistening drool that needs to be wiped off his face), but she is interrupted by Ruben Ortero Lopez who stands with tears in his eyes slapping his doughy paws together, intermittently stopping his applause to do the sign language for *bravo*. Debora stands with tears in her eyes, clapping hard, saying, —Wow! Wow! The rest of the group joins in. The applause is intense. They come forward and embrace her and she is smothered in their hugs and teary whispered words of strength.

—So captivating, Debora says.

The produce stocker, weeping, says to her as he embraces her, —Heartbreaking, really just truly devastating. You are so strong. Kevin Lithis bless you.

Josefina, tearing up too, hugs them back. It is clear they all share the same pain. Maybe she misjudged them. Maybe, she thinks, I have at last found people like me. Perhaps the isolation has been broken at last.

After a minute of this, the group hug ends and everyone returns to their seats. Josefina says, —Gosh I'm glad I found all of you. I was beginning to think I was all alone. But I see now that I'm not. Together we have the power to do something about what they have done to our city. We can stand up as one and make our voices heard as one voice and create peace in our communities for our children. Once and for all. Together, we can bring an end to this nightmare. We can fight to drive these monsters out. Together, *we can take our lives back*!

She looks around for a reaction—a thumbs-up, a fist pump, anything—but finds none. They're returning to their seats. Debora smiles inanely and says, —Okay, thank you. Who's next?

Josefina says, —What the smuck do you mean, who's next? What are we gonna do? Aren't we gonna do something? What's the plan? What's first? Maybe a protest outside City Hall? A march through the city? Some sort of neighborhood watch? What?

But her words hit the insulated walls and die there in the rotten wood studs and she can't believe what she's seeing. *They're not interested.*

Nobody answers or looks up. Someone clears his or her throat.

Josefina's dismayed. She finds herself up there shrieking, —What the hell is the matter with everybody?

Debora says, —It's a very nuanced issue.

—What's so nuanced about it?

—There are particular . . . *ways* to approach this sort of thing.

—What ways.

—Particular methods.

—What does that mean? That means nothing.

—You have to work with the system.

—This person is out there tonight. Right now. The mutant who did that to that poor man over there is out there tonight. Right now. Where is the system right now? Is the system here tonight? Hello? System? You here? Hello? System? No. The system couldn't make it tonight, I guess.

Debora only sighs, mutters something about Josefina oversimplifying the issue. Everyone else shifting impatiently in their seats.

Later the meeting devolves into a casual social gathering. Backyards and Tobacco Companies appear. The members all stand around Ruben who is miming jokes in a weird silent stand-up-comedy routine. Josefina stands off to the side with Jaime and Little Josefina watching in disgust at them all laughing so hard they're pink. Not a care in the world. Debora sees how aghast she is and comes over. She glances quickly down at Jaime then away and touches Josefina's arm and says to her, smiling, —You're not Irish so maybe you don't understand. Our sense of humor is how we endure tragedy.

—You're right, I'm not Irish. I'm Italian. We don't endure shit. We fix it.

She squeezes Josefina's arm and smiles with what's supposed to be compassion. —Poor, poor thing, she says. —You're in all our prayers. I hope you know that.

Josefina just looks down at the hand on her arm like its contact is soaking something through her flesh and into her bloodstream. Debora turns and goes to join the others. The meeting clearly over now. Music is playing—a Bob Dylan song called "Happy Birthday." Everyone laughs, endures. Josefina watches them, holding Jaime's cold twisted corpselike hand.

THE ROAD TRIP

He left that afternoon. Didn't tell Uncle Antonio or Maria or anybody other than Diego and Fernando, who went with him. Just left. Fernando and Diego did not need much convincing. They'd follow him anywhere.

When they got on the road the day had become bright and sunny and good. Junior floored the Car Company Red Sports Car he stole from the overnight parking garage at the airport and fueled with ethanol paid for with the sale of the gun he was supposed to deliver to Expensive Hotel. The car ate up the entrance ramp and spat them out onto the Visa Angelina Jolie Beltway, three born-bad souls in a shiny red slingshot. It was the perfect day for this. The sun was out in white-hot splendor. Cars upon cars skimmed down the Beltway's beaten asphalt like water bugs. The wind cooled over their scalps which flared hot with badness and moved their hair around and they were bad and pounding on the side of the car hooting and screaming at the terrified other motorists, darting in and out of traffic high on the tails of the cars in front of them, honking the horn, the drivers glancing into their rearview mirrors and seeing this vehicle with three wild-eyed teenage goons hanging out of it smiling and cackling like they did not give a damn who lived and who died, themselves included, life to them not anything worth cherishing or even thinking too much about because it could vanish so easily. Which to them made it not precious but cheap, just something occurring in the moment for the time being due to factors aligned by the hand of no one in particular, something that in time will be replaced by other occurrences caused by the aligning of other factors, those too by no hand. The drivers seeing them in their rearview mirrors swerving on their bumpers and, intimidated and scared, moving out of their way so they could pass, receiving for their trouble a glob of discolored spit on the windshield or a view of hairy ass, the owner's hands opening and closing the cheeks like a sideways feculent mouth, or a still-lit cigarette butt hurtling end over end in through the window and obscene insults and gestures as the maniac car passed and disappeared to do the same to somebody else.

He did not know where he was going, only that he was going. But as he drove—only he drove, no one else—he felt the energy and excitement of being young and raging and driving. Time was endless, the world was without edges. He was driving west. It was as he sped along the breakdown lane at more than twice the speed limit, nearly clipping the concrete barriers there, the warm wind, the old city of Centreville burning first on all sides of them then behind them for good, car horns honking and tires squealing from other cars driven by nobodies, that a plan began to formulate itself in his will: He was going to see Second America. He was going to find Second America, stamp his feet on Second America, stab the staff of his white flittering flag into Second America, look out over the Second American valley below him and claim it all as his own. As is the way in Second America. He'd even claim the wildfires breathing in his fingers. He would scope out what would be the empire of Junior Alvarez. Rob Visa Banks along the way to make the money necessary to raise a ragtag army of men whom he would lead back to Visa Centreville so that he might topple Uncle Antonio, the mighty Prussian, and seize the underworld of Visa Northern Virginia as his own. As Alejandro would have done. And he would then have so much money and power that he would have a man not only to drive his car for him but a second man to park it for him as well. A man not only to carry his luggage for him but another man to pack it as well. And he would enter through the front door wherever he went for the rest of his life. They would insist he do so. He would never lay eyes on a back door again. He would not only have power and money but also respectability. But he would not be satisfied with Visa Northern Virginia. From there he would move into Visa Baltimore and take over that city as well. From Visa Baltimore, Visa Wilkes-Barre, capital of Visa Pennsylvania. From Visa Wilkes-Barre, Visa New York. From Visa New York, Visa

Chicago. From Visa Chicago, Visa Butte, that western epicenter. Then south to vast glamorous Visa Provo, mighty Visa Phoenix Island, Visa Chihuahua. Then east again. Visa Alberkirkie, Visa Dallas, Visa Jackson, Tennessee. And all the rest along the way. It would not be easy. It would not be quick. It would not be clean. It would take years of relentless slow-burning war. But he would do it. Inch by inch he'd creep. When it was over he would rule the nation. He'd go down in history. One of history's great leaders. There were no limits once you decided to stop being ordinary.

This goal, this single purpose, etched itself into his will here on this day and it never left.

His old life and all the humiliations and fears and compromises its future held were all off and burning away. He could feel the ashes on his nose and the heat of the wildfires on his face from the burning as he lit a Tobacco Company and turned the radio up and looked over at Fernando in the passenger seat who was shouting something and turning in his seat with his pants down to show his brown-black asshole to the motorists in the next lane.

They'd follow him anywhere. Especially if money and violence were involved.

Burn baby burn.

Forever and ever into the future and the magic.

He took Visa Interstate 66 west. Just beyond the state line he exited and pulled into the first Bank branch he saw. They all hopped out and ran inside screeching in the silence of a Bank in a small town in the middle of a weekday afternoon. They had no guns. He put his hand in his jacket pocket the way he had it that morning on his way up the long opulent driveway to Expensive Hotel. He now wished he had not sold the gun. Fernando and Diego assaulted the security guard while Junior approached the teller, a pregnant woman, greeted her, and told her in a calm voice that he had a gun and to give him a big bag filled to the top with money or he'd execute her. She obeyed. They left with $110,000. It took forty-three seconds. He could not believe how easy it was. How good it felt. How right.

They continued west for an hour or so before pulling off again and robbing another one. They ditched the car and stole a late-year Car Company Blue Sedan. Bought shotguns and ski masks at a Huge Retail Store somewhere then used them to rob a Bank on the other side of town. As he drove off after that he could feel himself being consumed by a dangerous impulse. He saw himself objectively. Knew he was not thinking, was only feeling, perhaps so that he would not feel the fear that he knew was inside him and was only increasing with every mile he drove.

The Plan over these last wild hours had taken almost physical form in his will. It seemed to project out in front of him on the other side of the windshield as he drove on the interstate—there it was, a creature that now and again crawled out from beneath the car's hood to perch atop it like a gargoyle presenting itself for Junior's examination if for no other reason than to let him put on a parade of rational thinking for himself. But he could not slow down. He could not stop. Even though he knew how reckless he was being. He could only ride this groove. No matter what the outcome. Being a young man. And being strong-willed. And being afraid.

Drove all that night, all the way through it in its entirety. No Banks were open so they robbed Visa 24-Hour Gas Stations and All-Night Diners to fulfill his raging impulses. He drove and robbed in a good-feeling admixture of crime and hurt and dutiful ambition. The new design of his will which had created itself hours earlier on the Beltway was still there before his eyes. It was there the entire time. As it would be for the rest of his life.

He stuck to Visa I-66 which was also called—according to the Visa Highway Commission signs on the roadsides—the Mother Road. The Mother Road stretched from the magnificent oceania of the Visa Nevada coast all the way east across the country to Visa Easton, Visa Maryland, where the road trickled out at a Visa Roller-Skating Rink. They robbed Banks along it headed west over the course of the following three days. It was a spree of amphetaminic crime. He knew Uncle Antonio was looking for him. He knew the police were looking for him. He tried to make himself slow down and think clearly, fearing that if he did not he would lose control and destroy himself if he had not already. But he could not. Maybe he did not want to. Maybe he wanted only to rob and drive no matter what the outcome until he had revenged the world for the hurt he felt so that the hurt would leave him and be replaced by the physicality of the designs in his will having come to fruition.

The only time they stopped and it was not to rob a Bank or to feed themselves at a Fast Food Restaurant on the side of the interstate was in the town of Walmart, Ohio. They were intrigued by an enormous stone cat in the distance. They pulled off at something called Visa Garfield National Historic Site. Some kind of ruins. The tour guide explained that the cat was eight stories high and that it dated back to the Information Revolution Era, maybe even earlier— they could not be sure because damage caused by the world's near annihilation had affected the substance such that it tainted science's ability to measure its age. There was some disagreement among historians over what it was built for or what it represented. Was it a god? All they knew was that its name was Garfield. This was etched in English at the base of the statue. The tour guide said it was most likely a religious shrine, the central location of a bizarre Christian ritual. Humans were sacrificed here, the guide said. It happened in a peculiar, brutal manner. A citizen was made to stand in the shadow of the Garfield. It was a man or a woman or a child. A horde of his or her fellow Christians was then amassed before him or her. Then coveted objects such as computers, televisions, microwaves, and other valuable, usually entertainment-related merchandise were piled on the other side of the person so that the person stood between the horde and the merchandise. At the command of the priest conducting the ritual, the horde then stampeded toward the pile of merchandise. Each wanted very much to be the first to the pile because they were allowed to buy at a discount whatever they could take. The result was mayhem. The sacrificee was trampled to death. The horde paid no attention as they fought and bit and clawed one another over the marked-down merchandise. Then the dead, trampled body was dragged off somewhere and another sacrificee was brought out. A fresh pile of merchandise was arranged. A new horde was amassed. The ritual was repeated. Junior asked what this ritual was called. The tour guide said, —Christmas.

Junior repeated the word to himself.

—Historians believe it is where our present-day Visa Gift Giving Holiday originated. Though that theory has its skeptics. Lithiite executives and Lithiite faithful, mostly.

Junior found all this pretty interesting.

SENATOR TAVAREZ

How many tears have I cried, in my entire life, up until this point? thought Josefina Hernandez as she walked through Georgetown, the tears on her face mixing with the rain. It was the thirteenth day in a row that it had rained, without a break. How many buckets could all the tears I've cried over these last several years fill up? Thousands? Tens of thousands? Is my life any more than a sum total of tears? Little Josefina was safely beneath her custom-made plastic water-resistant carrying case—kind of a clear poncho Josefina created with a sewing machine out of a cheap four-hundred-dollar poncho you can buy from the racks at the register of Drug Store. Then she embroidered flowers and a couple little suns on it and LITTLE JOSEFINA in cursive purple lettering. She had not remembered to bring an umbrella for herself though and was now paying the price for it. Above her head a soggy *Visa Times*. Her forehead and upper face were streaked with gray from the running ink. Her hair clung to her skull. She passed an Expensive Restaurant with its particular pocket of air lingering around it that smelled of cooking meat. She looked straight down, hunched, cowering from the rain. Cars whooshed, splashing pedestrians. Smokers stood under canopies in their own pockets of air, frowning, looking desolate. She didn't know why she forgot to bring an umbrella today, because she tends to bring an umbrella every time she leaves the house whether or not rain is in the forecast. But she was too focused on her meeting, which was the reason why she was all the way down in Georgetown today. Her meeting was with an aging ex-senator named Senator Tavarez. Senator Tavarez was recently retired from NoVA politics after serving the people for nearly sixty years. He had been the old-school kind of politician. Eighth-grade education, stump speeches in Visa VFW bars and Visa Mason Halls, deals, relationships, understandings. Senator Tavarez had been the first Irish state senator in NoVA. A politician truly of the people and for the people, from the days back when that meant something. Josefina would like to tell you that it was a difficult process to get a personal meeting with Senator Tavarez, especially at his home, but that would not be true. All she did was go to his door and knock. She couldn't believe she hadn't done this sooner. A maid or personal secretary opened the door and asked what she could do for her and Josefina told her she would like to speak to Senator Tavarez, please, a great man, a noble, kind politician of ethics and principles the type of which there are none anymore, because since Senator Tavarez's retirement from the Senate the quality of life in NoVA has gone utterly downhill and her son, Jaime, is an embodiment of this, as he is right now at home comatose trapped within his body under the care of a PCA Josefina hired for the day even though she can't afford it because someone has to be there to apply his eyedrops because he can't blink and to be at the ready with a little pair of metal tongs in case he has a seizure and chokes on his own tongue and she must then make such an arrangement every time she needs to leave the house for any reason at all, for any length of time. The maid or personal assistant—a girl who looked to Josefina to be around age nine and who wore a shirt that was inappropriately, unsenatorially tight around her belly, in Josefina's opinion—glanced down at Little Josefina, dripping, and back at Josefina, dripping, probably wondering as Josefina gave her this spiel if Josefina was perhaps one of those frustrated, unwell types who hover around the spectacle and theater of politics. After Josefina got to the point of why she was here the maid or personal assistant or whatever she was, who was pretty and pouty, said hold on and shut the door rudely on Josefina's face. Josefina stood there wondering if she had just been blown off. She felt her rage swell. Blue bloods wandered up and down the street staring at her, walking shampooed froufrou deer. But then the door opened and the girl told Josefina to come in. She was holding a towel and made Josefina dry off first, took Little Josefina from her. Josefina told her to be careful with that please before deciding, you know what, she'd better just hold on to it. The girl led Josefina up a flight of ornate wood stairs lined with royal-looking family portraits. Josefina didn't want to touch even the banister. The house was quiet and cold and smelled rich. There were antique things everywhere. Josefina didn't know much about such things but if she did she would have recognized them as Ikea end tables, Craten Barrel candle holders, Martha Stewart Collection chandeliers—all incredibly old, incredibly rare, incredibly valuable late-period Information Revolution Era pieces. Josefina had to suppress the urge to give this girl, if she was indeed responsible for cleaning, much-needed advice on dust prevention. Lying in a large, open-doored room that they passed there was a beautiful antique Target rug. It was worth more than Josefina. The girl stopped and yanked the door shut, cursing somebody for leaving the deer's bathroom door open again. As they approached the end of the hall there was the smell of cigar smoke and the sound of a television turned up too loud. Without knocking, the girl opened a door and went in. Josefina followed her. And there he was, former Second United States Senator from Northern Virginia Sebastian Tavarez, sitting in bed in pajamas with a flannel blanket up to his chin, one withered little hand reaching up from the covers to yank the fat stogie from his mouth and hide it beneath the blanket. The girl clicked her tongue and scolded him in a way that made Josefina wonder if she was maybe his daughter. The girl pulled the blanket down to confiscate the stogie and the old senator fixed his eyes on Josefina, looking her over, lingering a little too long at her belly. Josefina crossed her arms to cover it as the senator licked his lips and raised his eyebrows. The girl saw this and lightly slapped him, saying, —Sebastian! The senator made naughty cute fawn eyes at the girl who, with a huff, spun on her heels, sneering at Josefina as she passed, and left the room.

—Never marry someone younger than your cat, the senator said to Josefina as he reached for the remote and turned the television off. He thought better of it then turned it back on, with the volume muted. He asked Josefina what he could do for her. And he said thanks for visiting because he didn't get a lot of visitors these days. He said the best part about retiring from politics was you didn't have to worry about never having a moment to yourself. And he said another thing about it was that you didn't have to wonder who your true friends were anymore because now you didn't have any friends at all.

Josefina said, —Sometimes it's best to not have any friends.

—Why would you say that? I can't imagine any circumstance where that would be true.

—If someone's interested in actually changing anything.

He looked at her with his sparkling eyes that had not diminished since his glory days, when every morning it seemed like those very eyes would be looking out at her from the cover of *Visa Times* beneath a headline such as TAVAREZ WRITES HEALTH CARE LEGISLATION or TAVAREZ WANTS COLLEGE TUITION FREE or TAVAREZ SAYS "NO MAN WITHOUT A JOB." Those were the days. Well Josefina had a chance for the senator to return to those days, she said. If he ever wanted to help people, here was his chance. She told him the whole story—the fight, the blood, the hospital, the brain scans that looked like pictures taken of a forest at night. She told him how she had gone to a victims support group and found little help. She paused briefly at one point to kneel down and use Little Josefina to suck up a humongous dust bunny peeking out from under the bed. And she said how she had gone to the state house to lobby lawmakers but had been treated like she was selling magazine subscriptions. So she'd gone to police headquarters. When they wouldn't let her in to speak to the chief she'd pled her case to the receptionist there and a couple beat officers who happened to be in the lobby drinking beepollen before being escorted out and tossed in the street where she continued pleading her case to the passersby on the sidewalk who all ignored her as though she were just another crazy lady staggering around absorbed by her own psychosomatic nightmares. She had set up shop in front of the Visa NoVA Public Library and stood on a milk crate there wearing sandwich boards and orating her grievances into a bullhorn to the nil results one could expect from going about change in that way. And then she found out Senator Tavarez was still alive. She had thought he was dead, she was a bit ashamed to say. He found that funny. She told him how much she admired him and how she considered him to be the bastion of all that was good and noble about politics and people in general. How the government—all of it, the entire Second

United States Federal and Local Government—long ago farmed itself to private enterprise—of which there is now but one and it is foreign-owned—and so now all lawmakers are Visa executives promoted from inside, usually after failing disastrously in their previous position at the expense of the public, if they are not just Visa-hired actors playing politicians anyway, if they are not overt criminals. She mentioned as an example the current governor of NoVA, the intellectually incurious scion of a corporate-political dynasty—the current Visa CEO's younger brother and the son of a former CEO—who so far in office had been convicted of manslaughter, obstruction of justice, possession of a stolen firearm, possession of a controlled substance with intent to distribute (forty-three kilos of Stimulant), parole violation, and funneling money to extremist Seussian terrorist organizations to fund massive attacks against Second America in the name of their god, Horton, all of which by the grace of God were thwarted. And yet still he remained in office. Because Visa is a private company that does not have to answer to the people. Essentially, she told the aging noble senator, no one within the system could help her do anything about the culture of immorality in this city. She told him that these criminals were the kings. That these people were literally getting away with murder out there, especially people like Uncle Antonio, and that nobody in any position of power seemed especially interested in doing anything about it. Because they were all in cahoots. Officials were receiving kickbacks. Law enforcement agents were receiving gifts—money, crates of Expensive Wine, vacations, houses, women, personal feelings of prestige and respect and excitement. Uncle Antonio and the chief of the Northern Virginia bureau of the Visa FBI had grown up together in Centreville. This was standard—they'd all grown up together. They were all childhood friends. When the time came, when they reached a certain age, some went to one side of the law, some went to the other. No side was the right side, no side was the wrong side. They were just sides. Like of a coin. Any difference was arbitrary. It just depended on what face it happened to fall on. And they were seriously supposed to be trusted to safeguard our well-being? They—the cops—were even digging up personal information on people who owed Uncle Antonio money so he could find them, were being paid by Uncle Antonio to look the other way on Uncle Antonio's gambling rackets, were sometimes helping with framing their cronies' rivals to get them out of the way or even enabling hits by providing untraceable weapons and tainting crime scenes, Josefina had learned in her investigation. She told State Senator Tavarez that it wasn't right for fear to have power. That fear was not power. That Uncle Antonio had Centreville kids working for him, teenagers her son's age, she had learned in the course of her investigations, one of whom could very likely be the one responsible for her son's coma and if so he needed to be brought to justice for it. That no matter what this was still a country founded on democratic principles and that as long as some people were living above the law then those principles were a sham and this country was not free.

The senator said, —When people hurt other people they should pay. This is Second America dammit. We are the good guys. It's time NoVA got its head on straight and started putting these people in jail. The power lies with the people. Only we the people can reject this trash from our city. It will require a change of culture in the shared mentality of the citizenry. Here is what we are going to do. To begin with, we'll do an ad campaign. We'll arrange little moral messages to be subliminally planted in *Television Show*. He rattled off some names of people he could call—high-level execs and advertising people who owed him favors. —Lithis I'm glad you came to me with this. We'll put the pressure on the Visa House to raise mandatory sentences. We'll put the heat on them. We'll scald them, we'll burn them alive until they do it. We're going to clean this state up. He was sitting up in bed now, his face red from anger and excitement, spittle flying off his lips, the ideas about to really start pouring out. And then he stopped, tensed, grabbed his chest, and dropped onto his back. He exhaled. He lay still. His eyes open.

—Senator? Josefina approached him. —Senator? Senator?

Touched him. Shook him gently. Then harder. Checked for a pulse. She began crying, called in the girl. —He . . . The girl looked at the senator and then at Josefina. Her face narrowed and she ran to him and did all the same things Josefina had just done.

Josefina stood there watching. —He was . . . I . . . We were . . . He just . . . Right in the middle of a sentence . . .

The girl grew frantic, called an ambulance. Josefina stood there not knowing what to do. She found herself leaving. She went out into the rain. Her tears mixed in with the rain. This was her life now, a series of moments in which she staggered in rain toward Metro stations, alone and crying, thwarted, let down.

Right in front of her, right in the middle of a sentence.

How much water could the body produce out of the tear ducts? How many tears had she produced in her life? Where did they go after she cried them? Were all old ones now in buckets somewhere, in heaven or underground? Did they drop out down her face and off the edge of her chin and seep into the dirt and go down, down, down into the earth, where they waited and changed and came back to her later as something else? How could she know? How many gallons of tears had she cried over the entire course of her life? Thousands probably. More like hundreds. Dozens at least. Thinking about this was the best thing to think about because if she didn't she might have allowed herself to fall off the train platform as the train came. It would have been easy, magnificent. And final. It would not be selfish, it would not be surrender. It would be an act of martyrdom that sends a profound unforgettable revolutionary statement echoing into the future.

But she could never do that to Jaime.

She was tired of crying. It's all she ever did anymore.

This was the last time.

SOUTH BEND

South Bend, Visa Indiana. They pulled off the highway in the latest stolen car, a brand-new Car Company Black Convertible they lifted off a sales lot in the middle of a business day. It was covered in ash. Caked on the windshield were the splattered remnants of a cicada storm they had driven through on the Mother Road. Small plastic wings glued to the car by thoraxes cracked open on the glass, their guts spilled and hardened in the wind. Inside the car the gang was unwashed and ill-fed and exhilarated to delirium by three days of sleep deprivation and relentless crime. They looked like something from hell. Like demons who had driven this car out of the fires of hell and that is where all the ashes on it and all over them too had come from.

They pulled off a town highway into a Visa Shopping Center. There was a Bank branch here. They cruised through the crowded parking lot. The people of the town pushed carts up and down the aisles of parked cars. Often a child or children rode inside the cart. Grocery Store employees sat on benches outside smoking and staring and talking. They all observed the filthy black ash-covered car from hell. There was bird shit all over it too, the crusted remnants of a dead bat pinned beneath a wiper. It was sinister the way it cruised through the lot slowly and icily like a shark, the ash arms of the occupants hanging out the open windows resting on the side panels, their hypervigilant faces peering out like burrowed baby predators. The people knew right away that this car and the demons inside it were from a place they themselves had never imagined existed and were headed somewhere they would never want to go and that their paths were not meant to cross but here they were crossing paths sure enough on this midmorning, one of them on the way from hell and the other just going about the errands necessary to maintain their families and lives and peace. They knew it. It was impossible not to know it. But what they did not know was that the ash and the feculence and bits of wild corpse in part created a veneer to conceal Junior's cold calm fear that had not gone away over these three wild days of doomed conquest and recklessness. The heists and the driving and The Plan and the running from the law and from Uncle Antonio were all a sport that caused the fear to abate for scattered temporary durations. But it came back. It always did. And when it did it came back stronger. He had more fear than these people would ever have. What was their fear? Of loss? Of pain? Of death? He had those fears. Everyone does. But he had others too, ones that they did not and never would have because they had not seen those things that he had seen—those truths, those unanswerable questions. And when you see them once you cannot unsee them.

In the car, in the passenger seat as Junior cruised through the lot observing the scene, Fernando said, —Nuh-uh. No way. Too crowded.

Junior ignored him, pointed the car toward the Bank sitting there at the end of the strip of businesses—Pharmacy, Video Store, Restaurant, Beepollen Shop, and so on—like a young virgin so oblivious to being the object of a pervert's lust that she is naïve even to the existence of perversion at all.

Fernando said, —Smuck this, Junior. Everyone's looking at us.

Junior just turned the wheel like a sea captain and muttered absently, —Don't curse, it just shows how powerless you are. He pulled the car up to the front door of the Bank. He took in the frame of the front door, the perfect clarity of the recently cleaned glass, the sun catching in it and splattering as though captured in a prism. He wanted nothing more than to go in through it, through this front door. It was an almost sexual urge. Looked up and down the strip of stores. More than a dozen front doors. He felt the fear abating. The coldness was replenished with warmth. He felt calm for the first time since entering the front door of the Bank at the previous robbery which was that morning. He wanted to enter each front door, rob whomever and whatever was inside it. The entering through the front door and taking something and leaving, entering and taking and leaving. It was a pantomime of intercourse. An erotic and primal trespassing.

—Masks, he said. He put his on. Fernando was trying to sway Diego in the backseat to his side of the argument but Diego was as unreachable as Junior though not out of fear and desire and rage and humiliation but out of simple untamable iniquity.

These people in the lot fascinated Junior. They were like another species. What was wrong with them? These ducks sitting unafraid, lacking the ability to see the things that they should be afraid of. These small people scrambling to balance the dissonant elements of their lives. He couldn't understand what they were alive for. To breed? To work? Weren't they terrified of that? Didn't they stay awake at night wondering if the things they put faith in regarding their meaning as individuals were imaginary? Their insufficient fear made them powerless, vulnerable to the exploitations of the powerful and the afraid and the enraged and the humiliated. They were harried and Sisyphean and they did not even seem to be bothered by that or even aware of it at all. Why not?

Fernando was loading his shotgun. —For the record, this is something I think is smucking retarded.

—What you think doesn't matter, Junior said.

—Okay well, pumping the shotgun, —just let the record show.

Junior was opening the car door and stepping out before the eyes of the people of South Bend who stopped pushing their carts full of purchases and babies to watch this person wearing a mask and carrying a shotgun run inside the Bank through the front door. Diego, masked and armed, jumped out of the backseat like a gorilla, knocking over a woman who happened to be passing by from one store to another along the awning-covered sidewalk. He ignored her, let her remain fallen, even obliviously stepping on her hand on his way to follow Junior inside, this 135-kilo teenage brute crushing all the small brittle bones of this fallen old woman's hand. Fernando had no choice at this point but to follow too, muttering a string of vulgarities as he pulled on his mask and exited the vehicle and took another uncertain look at all the people who were standing there staring, unable to believe what they were seeing, frozen wherever they happened to be, Fernando not knowing what to do about them or what to say other than, pointing his shotgun at them for emphasis, —You didn't see shit, and going inside through the front door.

To him it was just another door.

Inside there were complications. The first complication was with the teller. She was a middle-aged woman as conventional as all those out in the parking lot and she was refusing to give them money. —Get out of here, she was saying. —Go back to where you came from. Fernando pointed his shotgun at her, told her to shut up, told her again to fill two bags all the way to the top with money. They had now begun demanding two bags, no longer just one. —You're only doing this because you're unprincipled, incompetent people. Do you know that? *Incompetent*. You think you're men? You're not men. Think you're tough? You're not tough. You're just scared. And stupid. I can see it. Why don't you go out and work real jobs like real men? Why don't you go do something to benefit society like real men instead of going around taking other people's hard-earned money and pointing guns at people just trying to make a living for themselves and their families?

All the customers were on the floor. Junior and Diego were standing above them pointing their guns at the backs of their heads. Junior called over to Fernando, —What's the matter?

—I don't know, she won't give me the money.

—Why not.

—Your mothers must be real proud to have given birth to such *incompetent* people.

—Because she won't smucking shut up long enough to.

—Kill her.

—Yeah kill me. Kill me. Be a big man and kill me, you big tough man.

Fernando pushed the barrel of the shotgun into her throat. He said, —I'm gonna. She was still trying to speak but her voice was now choked by the barrel. This did not stop her. Her mouth still moved though no voice came out of it. Her insults were still in her eyes. She did not need to speak them.

Junior had had enough. He walked over and pumped his shotgun and raised it at her and was about to fire it—Fernando seeing this and taking a fast jump back to get out of the way, the woman closing her eyes and raising her hands up to shield herself from the muzzle blast and turning her wincing face, bracing herself for her death—when a customer to whom Diego had his back turned took advantage of the distraction by climbing to his feet and engaging Diego from behind. They began struggling over his shotgun. Junior turned and saw it. —Hey! he shouted. It was a foolish thing to shout. He went over. The teller opening her eyes and seeing that her life was still intact, resumed her insults. —Why don't you learn a trade? Ever consider that? Why don't you go back to school and learn a trade and get some *competence*? Fernando ignored her and climbed over the counter to help himself to the cash. Once back there, she attacked him, screeching like a feral cat and tearing at his face, biting whatever flesh she could get between her teeth. —Ah! Smuck! Bitch! He fought her off, took a fistful of her hair in his hand, used it to slam her face down onto the counter. She staggered backward dazed and bloodied and fell against the wall and just slouched there staring at him silently. He was sore and cursing her as he used his other hand to fill a bag with money. She was staring at him with no expression, saying nothing, like a furious and pouting child.

Meanwhile Junior struck the customer wrestling with Diego in the back of the head with the butt of his shotgun, which stunned him long enough for Diego to break away and punch him in the chin which sent him crumbling semiconscious to the floor. The customer was big and strong—maybe he was the biggest and strongest man in South Bend and maybe this had given him a dangerous belief in himself: that he could be a hero, that he could protect the good from the ghastly. But neither he nor anybody in South Bend had ever seen anyone like these people before. Diego had a tawdry grin on his face as he followed the hero down, falling atop him and pummeling him with his tremendous hairy fists. The hero was not responding. He was just bleeding. It was like punching a side of beef. Diego reached for his shotgun and used it to bash the hero's face. Junior watched. Customers were screaming, especially one young woman. She was screaming and crying. There was nothing anyone could do. Diego was so big and so strong that no one was capable of restraining him but himself. But he had no capacity for self-restraint in his will. He hardly had any will, for that matter. He was a goldfish of violence—if given the opportunity he would just feed and feed until he destroyed himself. If he had been wired only a little differently he could have been the greatest MMA fighter in the history of the state. But he was too savage. When he was twelve years old a trainer, seeing the awesome potential in his raw physical ability, tried to take him in off the streets and raise him as the son he never had, to groom him not only into a fighter but into a respectable man as well. But Diego could not grasp the concept of MMA. Violence made sense to him. It came naturally. But the idea of controlled violence was incomprehensible. In his first sparring session he ignored the trainer's explanations that this was just practice and to just take it easy. He exploded out of his corner and just went after that kid—Huego Gartinuestro—like it was a street fight. He almost killed him. He paid no attention to his trainer screaming at him to stop. It took the trainer, three assistant trainers, several Visa Gym employees, a Visa Gym district manager who happened to be dropping in for a visit, and half a dozen other fighters working out there that day to pull him off. By then Huego was an abortion. He was in the hospital for weeks. Due to irreparable damage to the neural region of his brain once he healed from his injuries his personality was altered. He looked the same but his friends and family no longer recognized him as the Huego they had known. Before the incident he'd been a polite, measured fourteen-year-old boy, a diligent student on track to one day get himself out of Centreville for good. But now he was brash, vulgar, impulsive. He suffered weeklong bouts of severe, debilitating depression. He became nauseous and dazed in bright light. He could not remember the fight or the hospital at all. He sometimes forgot where he lived and ended up on the other end of the city, scared and lost. He couldn't remember anything for more than a couple minutes. So he failed out of school. All day he wandered around the city lost. The balance between his rational self-restraint and his body's primal urges had been upset. He started committing crimes. He was unable to restrain himself first from committing sexual assaults and fights, then from committing armed robberies for the purpose of obtaining money to buy the Stimulant to which he had grown dependent to get him out of bed and keep him awake and functional. He was in juvenile detention now. Once he turned eighteen he'd be moved to a Visa Maximum

Security Adult Penitentiary franchise to serve out the remaining eleven years of his sentence. The ways he had sexually assaulted his victims were horrific. It could be described as torture. Diego had turned him into a monster. Diego would have been banned from fighting for life and would have faced charges of his own but Uncle Antonio, his eyes huge with the marketing possibilities of such a fighter, used his influence and money to dissuade the Visa District Attorney, with whom he had grown up in Centreville, from bringing charges. He paid Huego's family several million dollars to go about their lives rather than filing a civil suit. He took over as Diego's manager from the trainer who had taken him under his wing to groom him into a good fighter and an even better man (the trainer with a broken heart having already forfeited his claim to Diego after what he did to Huego, not that he had any say in the matter), and in one of his nefarious unclear ways convinced Visa Amateur Fighting Commission to reinstate Diego. But Uncle Antonio's influence had limits: He could not influence the people. That is where the extent of Uncle Antonio's power stopped. No one would allow their fighter to step into the ring with Diego. Not even any referees were comfortable being in the ring with him. So Diego never fought. Uncle Antonio never made a dollar. There were serious talks with Visa Circus about having him fight a bear but nothing ever materialized.

Diego was using both his hands now to hold the hero's head on either side of it to lift it and bash the back of it over and over again onto the floor. The hero seemed dead. The other customers were sobbing and praying into the tile floor, which they faced down into trying to shut their ears off from the sick sound of the repeated impact. The young woman was screaming, —Stop it! Stop it! Stop it!

Fernando was climbing back over the counter now with three bags filled with money and more stuffed into his pants and shirt and mouth and clutched in his fists between the flesh of his palms and the handles of the bags. He stopped halfway, one fat leg lifted in the air. He seemed to be listening to something. Junior saw him and listened too. He couldn't hear over the sound of skull on floor so he screamed at Diego to stop which at last he did for some reason and sat there on top of the hero holding the hero's concussed and

battered head. He stared at Junior, watching him listen. The Bank was silent. Only the young woman's choking heaving sobs. Then they all heard it. The hero opened his eyes at the sound, blood spilling out of his mouth over his broken teeth and down the sides of his face as he smiled and muttered from between Diego's hands,
—Cops.

It was as though the speaking of that word made them all hear it now with undeniable clarity and volume. Sirens. It sounded like ninety of them, not approaching from a distance but instead crammed within each of their heads and blaring from there.

—No! Fernando shouted. He went to the door to look out.
—No! The customers began clapping from their stomachs, drumming the floor and kicking their feet against it. They were cheering, whooping. The hero beneath Diego laughing. Fernando screaming at them to shut up kicked a few but it did not silence them. It could not. He was powerless to stop them. There was nothing he could do.

Junior was now at the door, the front door, watching the dozen or so cop cars pulling through the parking lot in a line like a parade. The parade stretched all the way down the highway as far as he could see, a line of light that never broke. He was thinking about things. He was running his hand along the frame of the front door in an almost wistful manner like it was the nude body of a last-time lover. But he did not accept that. This was not the end. No it was not. It was not. Fernando was advocating a shoot-out. He wanted to fight his way out. They could fight their way through. Look at all this money, they'd be set for years. Junior just looked at him, his hand still running along the door frame. Fernando saw the hand and watched it, confused. He started to open his mouth to ask Junior what the smuck he was doing running his hand along the door frame like that with an army of police outside but stopped because the cops were now opening their doors and kneeling behind them with their guns atop the window frames pointed at the front door.

—Look at that, Junior said. —They have the same shotguns we have. His voice detached, dreamlike.

—Why the smuck are we just standing here? *Why aren't we smucking doing something?*

Junior ignored him. A bullhorn was squawking. Couldn't hear

over the sirens and the helicopters and the maddening taunting cheering of the customers on the floor what it was saying. There were ambulances on the perimeter of the parking lot, more coming down the highway in the unbroken line of light. Two, three helicopters. Maybe more. Police helicopters, news helicopters. Out there beyond the line of light he could see the Mother Road. He ran his fingertips along the cream-white hips of the door frame. They had wildfires in them. He closed his eyes. He parted his lips. His tongue emerged and touched the glass of the front door and spread against it like something alive and moved upward in a slow silent lick. Then it went back within carrying on it the tastes that it now began to spread around within the inside of his lips and cheeks and on his gums. He swallowed the tastes, eyes still closed. The tastes went into his blood, coursed through his veins, filled his limbs and extremities. It was like he was concentrating so as to store fully and forever into his memory every sensation of the moment. He opened his eyes to see slipping away the design that had etched itself into his will. Good-bye. He pondered the flaws of his vision and of his self. He pondered them with regard not to his morality or lack thereof but to his inability to give manifestation to the design to the degree he needed to, which was the utter and total degree. He would chase it. It could not get far. He'd hunt it down. However long that took. Because it was in his will. Always would be. Today was just today, right now just right now. And no matter how long it took or how far he had to go, he would just hunt and hunt and one day he would catch it and when that happened he would hold on to it and give manifestation to it.

The front door opened. Either he was opening it or someone else was.

He stepped through it, dropping the gun.

SECOND ACT

THE VIGILANTE

She was unrecognizable. Her face had grown weathered. It looked scorched. Deep lines in it like the paw of an extinct mammoth. Her gray hair—the dye once maintained so religiously allowed to grow out—standing in a misshapen frizz more like a desert plant than the hair of a human being. At its top it was abrupt and unlevel from trimming it herself with a pair of kitchen scissors on her back porch. She did this because she needed the money to put toward Jaime. Her body had changed to resemble that of a feline predator. She was now lithe, her muscles lean yet bulging beneath her flesh which was drawn tight around her bones. She looked athletic and lethal. Her eyes seemed to have grown. Big white things staring out unblinking in skittish alarm like something nocturnal and scrappy.

Ten years. It had been ten years.

She'd had a choice: spend money for a caretaker so she could go out and earn a living or spend money for a caretaker so she could go out and give manifestation to the design that had etched itself into her will like names and dates and prayers on a tombstone. Which was the fixing of things. The righting of wrongs.

So far she'd eliminated seven of them. It was the beginning of a phantom wave of unforeseen retribution. Something eternal and sprawling had been awoken within her. The victims so far were low-level fringe types. Contract muscle, hangers-on. They were the most easily accessible. Plus she had to develop her skills and shed her inhibitions before moving up to the bigger fish at the top. Her first foray was the execution of a street-level Stimulant dealer. She bought a stolen Gun Company Semiautomatic .50-Caliber Revolver after hours at the back door of a Bakery in Gainesville, used it to shoot the man as he stopped for a red light at Union Mill and Seventeenth at four in the morning. This was the fourth time she had ever fired a gun. The first three were at Shooting Range in the weeks of preparation leading up to this. She dressed herself in black and waited for him and stepped out from the sidewalk into the beam of his headlights and closed her eyes and fired a single round. She hit the fender. She panicked. Couldn't see him inside his car because of the headlights. She was scared, wanted to run, didn't for some reason, stayed where she was and raised the gun again and fired over and over, expecting to be killed at any moment by return fire, leaving her son abandoned by his mother, hating herself for putting Jaime at such risk like this. Then the gun stopped firing so she went around to the driver's side window. Her head was ringing. She buzzed all over. All she could hear was her own heart beating in her throat. Through the window the guy was staring straight ahead. He was fine. He looked like he was still driving. He turned to look at her. The left third of his head was gone. He was crying. He rolled down the window. —Why did you do that? he said. There were sirens. She needed to vomit. She swallowed it. She found herself fishing in her pocket for something. Putting it in the gun. Raising the gun again. Closed her eyes, turned her head away. Fired. The crying stopped. There was a duffel bag on the passenger seat. She leaned in, reached over him, took it. Turns out it was filled with hundreds of thousands of dollars, which she and Jaime lived on for some time, allowing her to keep going.

The next time she used the gun, which was a month later on a seldom-used money launderer loosely connected to the Italians, she made sure to get closer first and to approach from behind, to aim for the base of the skull, where the brain meets the spine, a reliably lethal location as she'd since learned on the Visa Internet. It took only two shots this time. Efficient. Effective. She felt the blast of pleasure that comes with quantifiable self-improvement.

The Visa Internet was a vital tool. She learned how to make a small ugly remote-controlled incendiary device using easily accessible mostly household items such as Nail Polish Remover, Screws, and Cell Phone. She brought the thing without testing it first to the apartment of a sociopath who she had evidence had manufactured and sold child pornography for Uncle Antonio. She jimmied open a window on the fire escape while he was out. She tied the bomb beneath the bed frame and left. She waited on a rooftop a block away with binoculars, monitoring the apartment, and when she observed the man come home and get into bed and turn off the lights she took out her phone and dialed the number and watched the bed burst into flames. His screams were audible even at that distance. He appeared at the window aflame, moving in slow motion as though under water. He broke the glass with his hands. The flames shot out of the broken window like arms reaching into the night. She could hear their popping and static and roaring and his womanlike screaming. The waxy chemical stink of a burning home. He jumped out onto the fire escape and, shrieking, dived headfirst over the rail to his death on the pavement eight stories below. Josefina packed up her things and went home to relieve the caretaker, who had agreed to stay late. She thanked him, said, —Sweetie, you're a lifesaver.

One night in Centreville she came upon a scene in which a teenager was stepping out of a vacant lot with a particular sinister air about him as though the guilt of something he had done had turned into a stink and was now wafting off him. Josefina upon investigation discovered that he was leaving behind a girl, a teenager, a child, intoxicated and unconscious and naked from the waist down. She called an ambulance for the child and followed the boy, who reminded her of the sort who had given her son a living death. She followed him to the Metro station where she pushed him off the platform down into the path of an oncoming train which destroyed him beneath its grinding electric metal as though he were nothing more than a pigeon. After this, inspired, she began studying the Centreville youth gangs, becoming an expert on the subject. She targeted their leaders. She killed several of them. She considered this preventive care.

There was the Chantilly man who for years had been shaking down the innocent owners of local businesses, whom she bound, gagged, stripped naked, and hanged to death from a tree branch in Visa Park to be discovered by morning joggers with his immense criminal record taped to his forehead and the words REFORMED AT LAST scrawled on his chest with a marker.

There was the bookie she shot to death on his back deck while he grilled a steak.

The Italian election fixer she left behind the wheel of his own Expensive Car Company parked in front of the Laundromat that served as the Italians' headquarters, his throat cut ear to ear.

At first it felt horrid to kill. It came with the vertiginous sensation of an irreparable severance. But she believed in nothing anymore beyond manifesting the design that had etched itself into her will. As she kept doing it, the repulsion vanished. Killing became easy. She became excellent at it. You enjoy things you are good at. And it was right. The message had to be sent. The culture of NoVA had to be revolutionized. It felt good. That none of her victims so far were responsible to a direct degree for what had been done to her son—what *had been allowed* to be done to her son—did not matter to her. Neither did the fact that they had been denied the opportunity to defend themselves against the charges brought against them. They had chosen to operate in lawlessness, so lawlessness was the arena in which they would be dealt with.

She killed both Italians and Irish. She displayed neither prejudice nor tolerance. Even managed to eliminate a few Portaricans. Moved up the hierarchies. The bodies that began appearing like the morning paper in their own green front yards with sprinklers drizzling water over their death-mask faces—or in the otherwise uninhabited nosebleed seats at Visa Professional Baseball Stadium—NoVA like an early arrival to that night's game, or facedown in swimming pools, or stuffed into Car Company trunks, or left on the front walk outside businesses leased by criminals—were the bodies of increasingly significant men. People began to notice. It sent waves when the brother of one of Uncle Antonio's favored Painkiller distributors—a real moneymaker—was found bobbing in the Visa Potomac with the words BROTHER'S KEEPER etched with a blade of some kind into his back and six days later in the same waters not half a mile away was discovered by the same fisherman the body of a man who had incriminated himself in exchange for a small fortune in order to exonerate of conspiracy charges a brutal Italian lieutenant named Gomes Freitas who was known to target the wives and children of his nemeses. The Irish assumed it was the Italians who were killing them. The Italians assumed it was the Irish who were killing them. Hell broke loose. A vicious cycle of prideful revenge murders followed. These were emotional, heartbroken slayings. Both sides believed it was a war, that a war had developed somehow before their eyes, that they were suddenly now engaged in war. With each murder they hoped that it would be the one that ended the war and ended it in their favor. It was almost as though they believed it was true that if they were to kill one another with enough theater and conviction it would settle the dispute and satisfy the sorrow in their souls. They were wrong. And so the imagined war became a real war. The rate and magnitude at which they killed one another intensified. Josefina was surprised but thrilled. It was as though she'd had only to flip the switch and now the whole foul machine was off on its own suicidal trajectory.

THE HARDEST PART ABOUT PRISON

Probably shitting in front of other people.

OUT OF PRISON
BUT NEVER LESS FREE

The first few months out I wander in a stupor from this day to that day. There is no particular point to my life, no reason for the days I drift through. But I drift through them anyway. I do so with dull eyes and absent speech. I show up where I must and perform duties I should. I wake up in and return each evening to an inconveniently located apartment for which I pay too much. I stay away from the old neighborhood and out of sight of the people I used to know and listen to the birds in the distance at dusk faced with the fact that I have become just another powerless, harried person scrambling to balance the dissonant elements of my Sisyphean life.

I visit a prostitute my first night out but cannot even get a hard-on. As I leave, humiliated, I make the vow to myself to abstain from all sexual activity, drug use, alcohol consumption, poor dietary habits, and all other aspects of unhealthy living. To show the utmost rational self-restraint from this night forward.

These are the months of the spells. I walk into Grocery Store and put a few things into a handbasket but start to sweat and feel great doom descending upon me and so leave the handbasket wherever I happen to be and walk out of Grocery Store with my face down, privately hysterical.

My brother Guillermo has become the youngest state senator in NoVA history. He wants nothing to do with me, publicly denies we've even spoken since we were kids. But nonetheless he's given me some cash to get back on my feet and pulled some strings to get me a job as a maintenance worker at City Hall. I wear a uniform and push a mop and get paid by the hour. I pay union dues. I sometimes make distant eye contact with prestigious men with power. I decide I want to be a prestigious man with power. I begin putting five hundred dollars a week from my paycheck into a savings account at Bank for the purposes of college. My entire life occurs in the moments of either going to work or returning from work. I drink beepollen to gain the physical energy and sufficiently upbeat attitude required to go to my job and spend nine hours a day doing my job which consists of picking up wads of tissue containing the mucus of prestigious men with power that have missed the trash receptacles. Carefully I remember to write my account number on my check when I pay the electric bill which I feel is too high. Using small magnets I put new bills that arrive on the refrigerator door so that I remember to pay them. Sometimes I circle the due date. I do the dishes. I do my laundry.

There are times at night when I close my eyes and scream and scream in my head trying to figure out if the world, if human life, is really as hollow as it feels.

And this is my life as a corrected felon and productive member of civilized society.

When beepollen stops being enough to kill the unignorable sense of loss I feel for some reason every morning as I make my lunch before work, I buy the gun. It is a small cheap revolver. The guy at the gun show can't guarantee it still functions and can't promise it won't blow my hand off. But it's the only one I can afford. I feel good moving with a gun among the herd of exhausted meaningless humans pouring off the train. I feel good exiting the station and walking home with a gun. I come home from work and sit at the kitchen table with my gun before me, put a bullet in my gun, whirl the chamber, put my gun into my mouth, pull the trigger. When the hammer clicks and I am not dead I feel light shoot up inside me. This becomes something I do every day. I carry my gun with me everywhere. Where some men stand at the sink with the towel around their waist shaving, I load a round into my gun, cock my gun, stick my gun into my mouth, watch myself in the mirror as I pull the trigger. It never fails, it never fails. I keep my gun on the back of the toilet when I shower. I pull the shower curtain back in the middle of my shower and stick my wet head out and see my gun sitting there loaded on top of the toilet tank and I reach my hand out dripping water all over the bathroom floor and grab my gun and stick my gun against the side of my head with shampoo on it and squeeze.

Quick. No thinking. Pure electricity.

I am in the boiler room on a hot summer afternoon, sweat dripping off my nose. I am removing the filters from the central air system and I am using a shop vac to suck all the dust and dirt and lint off the filters. Then I am putting the filters back where they were. This is the way we change the filters at City Hall. And I am alone with the rats. And I am sucking new pure streaks into the thick hairy filters, thinking about how to become one of those prestigious men with power. For months, ever since I started this job, I have been thinking about that. So far I've come up with nothing, despite all the books about such men and about philosophy of warfare that I've spent the last decade reading in prison, writing essays on them to incorporate them to memory. I used to hand my cellmate a book, tell him to open it up to any page and read a sentence, and I'd be able to tell him the number of the page he was reading from. But this is when it hits me. All of a sudden I stop changing the filters and I am saying out loud to the rats over the whirring of the shop vac, —Oh my Lithis! Oh my Lithis!

Alejandro el Grande has come to me yet again and given me a new, better Plan to rise myself out of this low life and seize the mantle of history so that I will never be forgotten. The greatness inside me has manifested itself like I knew it would. It's there, right in front of me.

I leave the shop vac still running and leave work and go home and all afternoon and all through the night with a chair wedged under the doorknob I sit cross-legged on the floor against the wall since I don't have a desk, scribbling madly on a yellow legal pad, not moving, not taking breaks, not taking a piss, going through two, three, four yellow legal pads that I stole from a supplies closet at City Hall, writing so fast and out of control that my hand cramps up, but I keep going despite the pain, and the pen hardly keeps up with the words pouring out of my brain—the ideas and logistics and precedents and strategies for modern political domination— resulting in a glorious mess, the kind that makes the most sense. I follow the pinpricks of lights of new ideas piping up unexpectedly through dark halls leading to dark holes twisting lost so deep and low you can hear water rushing—the bottom of the ocean—roaring over rocks and the blind white furry creatures that are down there with no lights . . . *and beyond* . . . And I see NoVA spreading out and up and west and south and I see NoVA on plateaus and gulf coasts and cornfield flatlands in broken empirical mayhem. Where others see impossibility I see possibility. And when I am done the stack of yellow legal pads stands nearly three feet high and birds are chirping outside because it's morning. But despite the fact that I am so hungry that my jaw is quivering and despite the fact that my hand is so cramped that I must fasten the pen to it with a rubber band, I still, with what vaporous reserves of strengths I have left, rewrite the entire Plan in neat handwriting—not owning a computer—so that it is legible for the governor, to whom I will present it.

Exciting, endless days until I get the opportunity. When I do, when the governor has at last returned from traveling, I go to the maintenance office for the last time and change out of my jumpsuit for the last time and smell all the chemicals soaked into my jumpsuit for the last time and for some reason I punch out for the last time and I crumple the jumpsuit into a ball and toss it in the trash. I tuck The Plan under my arm. I go to the library. It is in the library that I wait for the governor. The way City Hall is laid out, from the library you can see the side entrance, which is where the governor enters. Aside from me, a librarian compulsively scrolling through Visa Social Networking Application, and a security guard whose only purpose it seems is to see to it that you enter on his right and leave on his left, the library is vacant. I am in there for fifteen minutes when I see a tall, imposing, deeply tanned creature in a suit come through the side entrance, flanked by his staff and security. And I am leaving the library and I am holding my hand out and approaching the governor and I am pushed back by his security agents but I am saying, —Mr. Governor, hello, remember me? When you dropped your phone in the toilet?

The governor is smiling lifelessly at me and muttering something to his security guards. The security guards stop pushing me. I recognize a couple of them from growing up in Centreville. They think they're someone else because they're wearing suits and follow the governor around but I know them, I know who they really are. I remember who they were. They know that I know too. You can see it in their eyes. I say, holding up The Plan in its clear plastic binder, —Sir, my name is Jose Alvarez Jr. and I have been working on a Plan, sir. A political strategy. This is a paradigm that I think you may find very interesting. I have put forth a great deal of effort regarding this. In short, I am prepared to make myself available as your special adviser and confidant, sir. With me by your side, I promise you will not only achieve the Presidency of the Second United States but more. You'll see what I mean by reading my Plan. I'll be honest. I have lived a life often checkered with troubles of a legal nature, sir. My rough-and-tumble youth on the streets I believe has given me a certain experience heretofore foreign to the political realm, sir. I bring a fresh, unique perspective. I am untainted by politics-as-usual. Where I come from is Centreville, sir. Thus I unfortunately have had little in the way of privilege and formal education. I am Irish. I grew up very impoverished. My father abandoned the family when I was a very young age. He was abusive and alcoholic. I was forced to be the man of the family. I won't tell you my entire life story. I know you're busy. But the point is none of this has stopped me. I am a lifelong student of history and have recently become a student of politics as well. For a great number of years now I have studied the political strategies of the great leaders of man. I read prolifically is the word. I have written a document containing all of my applied knowledge. This is that document. This is my Plan. It contains my heart and soul. I can't explain in words how hard I have worked on this. I hope you will see in it evidence of a rare mind and that you will then be interested in discussing the possibility of working closely together to implement my ideas in the great state of Northern Virginia. My cause will be to establish you as president. I will then enter politics myself so as to work at reinforcing and advancing at the state level the legislation, ideas, and dogmas established by your federal administration, sir, with the long-term objective of becoming governor myself or president even. That is, of course, after you've retired, sir. I don't intend on becoming your rival, sir. Rather I will be your loyal successor and champion, the devoted caretaker of your legacy. My ideas are available, sir, free of charge. My name is Jose Alvarez Jr., sir.

The governor is still smiling and blinking. His teeth white. His eyes without life. He takes The Plan and flips through it and says, —It's handwritten?

—It is, sir. Yes.

The governor turns to his aides, who look bored. The governor says, —Did I tell you about this? So I'm taking a shit and talking with Francisco at Metro, right?

An aide says, —And you dropped the phone.

—Yeah, no, I did. I totally dropped the phone. Went right between my knees. Plop.

—Lithis, that's like, what, the ninetieth time?

—Right into the toilet. It's sticking out of a pile of my shit like Excalibur. Halfway in, it's lodged. The call's still connected. I can hear Francisco still talking my ear off about his goddamn whatever he's worked up about. This is like four days after the last time it happened. Once a week this happens, right? What I need on my staff is a guy whose job it is to go get my phone after I drop it in the toilet.

One of the aides makes a note of this.

—Anyway, this gentleman here was kind enough to retrieve it for me. I would have myself but, you know. Thanks again for that, by the way. Wish I could tell you it would be the last time.

His security are smirking at me. I know who they really are. I know you, you mothersmuckers. I'll be president, I'll be emperor one day, and I'll remember your sneering. I say, —It was my pleasure, sir. That, I believe, demonstrates my loyalty to you, sir, and the lengths I will go to in order to serve you. I am not averse to getting my hands dirty.

—Apparently not.

—It would mean everything in the world to me, sir, if you consider my Plan.

—No, yeah, certainly, the governor says, looking at it. —Definitely. Totally.

—I've had a hard life. I've made mistakes.

—Who hasn't?

—I believe I can make more of myself than I have. I believe that I am destined for great things. And I hope you will agree after you have had the chance to read my Plan. And I hope you will decide to give me the opportunity to work for Centreville and to help Centreville, which is the city I love. And to work for NoVA and to help NoVA, which is the state I love. And eventually the Second United States of America, which is the country I love. I've never been given many opportunities. I hope you will give me one now to change my life and become the great man I can become. A man like yourself, sir.

The governor says, —I look forward to reading it, Jose. It looks like a fine plan. It really does.

—Thank you, sir.

The governor says, —Is your contact information in here? A phone number or something?

—It is. I've put it right there on the cover.

The governor, who will go over my fine Plan and who asked if there was a phone number with which to contact me in order to offer me a position as his special adviser and confidant, reaches out his hand and I shake it with the same hand I used to touch his shit and to then on his orders lift the shit-covered phone to my ear to tell the prestigious man with power on the other end that the governor would call him back, getting his shit on my cheek and ear, the same hand I used then to wipe his shit off the phone and clean it and give it back to the governor with his shit on my hands, cheek, and ear. I shake his hand even though my hand is sweaty because I am desperate but I squeeze firmly to show him that I am a man who deserves an opportunity to become great despite having a sweaty hand that has had his shit on it. And the governor smiles and looks me in the eye and I thank him, truly, I thank him very much, and I thank his aides and I thank his security, I thank them for pushing me away and for sneering, because that pushing and that sneering are what will make me great. And I am glowing inside, shivers going up and down my spine, because I feel good. I feel like big events are happening in my life. They will last forever. I can feel my history being written as my life happens.

And I'm walking tall through the lobby nodding at the guard who looks up at me from behind the front desk and it is Miguel

Hernandez from Centreville who doesn't recognize me from a long time ago, and there are artificial plants and sunlight pouring in from the skylights forty feet up on the ceiling and there are elevators with golden doors dinging and the clacking of high heels and women in business suits holding manila folders and men with a finger in one ear yelling into the phone and a small group of tourists videotaping a water fountain and I am heading past them—the future governor—unbeknownst to any of them I am the future anonymous genius mastermind, the future governor, the future president—they will see me on TV and my name will become more than a name and my face will become more than a face and they will develop visceral reactions to me, because I will have ascended from human to icon, I will hold strings to their emotions and imaginations and I will pull them according to my whims and desires and judgments, and I will lead them by those strings, and they will trust me and depend on me because I will be powerful and they will be powerless, I will have meaning and they will be meaningless—and I go toward the big glass doors on the other side of which is a wide-open white day with the skyless brick plaza and hot dog carts and pigeons and boys and women and never-ending traffic. But as the future governor nears the revolving doors he finds himself stopping beside the trash bin by the elevators and the trash bin is overflowing and the future governor's attention is caught by an object in it among newspapers and orange juice bottles and the future governor gets closer and the future governor looks and the future governor sees that it is the future governor's Plan in its clear plastic binder with beepollen spilled all over it and other waste on it and crumpled and the future governor takes The Plan out and lets the beepollen drip off the crushed and crinkled clear plastic cover and he is no longer an icon and no longer the future governor but just a man. And he carries The Plan outside into the skyless plaza but he doesn't know why he does this because once he goes through the great big revolving door he just throws it away into another trash bin and then he has to sit down because he feels bottomless, he feels awful, and he sits on the ground against a newspaper dispenser and he puts his face into his hands and smells the piss-soaked concrete and watches all the feet and knees passing by him until everything becomes so blurry that it just goes black.

RIDGERO

We walk across the Visa Nixon Bridge to break into a house on the other side. It is the Alvarez Gang reunited after more than a decade. Fernando rings the doorbell and he and Diego wait to charge in as soon as someone opens the door. It is dark and I am looking at the backs of Fernando's and Diego's heads and thinking, Just like old times. We hear a TV inside, we hear a woman's voice and then a man's voice, and there is sweat on the backs of Diego's and Fernando's necks from the walk across the bridge. Footsteps approach the door. As soon as they open it Fernando will put his gun in the man's face and he and Diego will barge in. I will go in behind them and I will close the door and take control. Just like old times.

I found Diego after I quit my job. He was sitting on somebody's front stoop on Battle Rock in Centreville letting a stray deer lick his mouth. We went to Bar With Pool Table where we used to go and found Fernando there. Diego and Fernando have been out on parole and living with their parents. Aside from the fact that they are older, bigger, more vicious, and more desperate from their time in prison, Fernando and Diego are the same as I remember them. And it feels good to be reunited. Fernando called Manny from Bar With Pool Table and told him guess who's here. Manny came down. He's a cop now, lives with his wife and four children in Newgate. I drank Soda Company only while Manny and Fernando and Diego drank Backyards. And we talked about work and about the good old days, laughing about our wild youth. And we felt good looking at one another and we felt right hearing one another speak while sitting in Bar With Pool Table in the neighborhood where we are from, talking about our childhood.

Soon it occurred to me from the way he was laughing and the way he was talking that Manny was drunk. So I said, —Any interesting cases lately, Manny?

—Nothing.

—Nothing at all?

—Same shit, different toilet. Blacks killing each other. Portaricans raping each other. He looked at us. He could see we were disappointed, that we had been expecting stories. We wanted to be awed and dismayed by stories of the law's efforts at curtailing man's natural skew toward wretchedness. We wanted to share his disdain toward clueless citizens expecting impossible things. He wanted to be admired by us. Looked up to. He wanted to hold court among his old friends having become in all the years in exile from them a more impressive man than they were. He wanted us to see how apparent, how inarguable, this fact was. He wanted us to see that we were still boys but he was a man. That is why he then said, —Well, there is this one thing.

I studied his face.

—I can't say too much about it. It's still an active investigation. He cleared his throat, pausing dramatically. Leaned forward over the table. —There's this particular piece of shit. I can't tell you his name. But he's been going around NoVA the last few years recruiting investors to fund the recovery of a sunken pirate ship somewhere in the middle of the Visa Caribbean Sea, somewhere near Taco Bell Island. The ship is full of treasure. It will net at least a couple billion. The guy's got photographs and video footage of the ship under water, full of treasure, just waiting to be excavated so it can make them all rich. He has data. He has quotes and estimates, buyers lined up, contractors down there just waiting for him to raise the money so he can give them his go-ahead to dive on in.

—Sign me up, I said.

—Well yeah, but one small hiccup.

—No pirate ship.

—The guy's a smucking fraud. The evidence is doctored. What is real though is the three million dollars he's scammed from investors. So now he's busted. Everyone knows he's a con. The jig's up. But Ridgero refuses to return the money. He won't admit he's a fraud. He won't even admit the ship doesn't exist. He's just a piece-of-shit criminal. Dollar a dozen piece of shit. One of a million that fill up the city. So now we have to go around cleaning up after him. As smucking usual. And it's a pain in the smucking ass. All because he decided to be a piece of shit rather than go get a smucking job. We met eyes. —I shouldn't have said his name just then. Oops. He finished his Backyard. —Anyway so now Mr. Dollar a Dozen Piece of Shit's smucked. And not just because the cops know there's no pirate ship. No, he's smucked because he wasn't scamming little old ladies. He was scamming people you don't scam. Unless you're a very stupid piece of shit interested in demonstrating how Palin's Theory of Natural Selection works. We've told him, out of the kindness of our hearts, that if he's not going to give the money back to those he stole it from then he needs to leave the country—better yet, get the smuck off Visa Planet Earth—by yesterday. We've told him that we've got a pool going at the station over which body of water we're going to fish his dead bloated corpse out of. But he acts like we're crazy. He insists there's no reason to do either, that the ship is real.

—He still swears it's damn real? Fernando said.

—That it's all going to pay off. That this is all just a misunderstanding.

—You really have a damn pool? Fernando said.

—A grand a pick.

—What's your damn bet?

—The reservoir down in Blacksburg.

It was quiet. Like we were weighing the likelihood of that being the winner. But Manny was glancing at me over and over out of the corner of his eye. He'd glance at me then look straight ahead then glance at me then straight ahead. After a while I said to him, —Where does Ridgero live, out of curiosity?

—Can't tell you that.

—Just out of curiosity.

—Active investigation.

—Where does he live?

—Can't tell you. But like I was telling my wife: That money's up for grabs. Someone's going to get it. Someone is. That's someone's kids' college money. That's someone's girlfriend's

117

belly job. Someone will get it. It's like I was telling her: If I were a different kind of man . . .

He kind of laughed and he and I met eyes. Something meaningful was exchanged. It was enough.

I leaned closer toward him and said calmly and quietly, —Manny, where does he live?

As his laughter died I was already seeing that the whole time I have been out of prison—nearly two years—has been a waste. My inconveniently located apartment has been a waste. My job has been a waste. The bills I've paid have been a waste. The weekly trips to Grocery Store have been a waste. All the hours spent in Laundromat have been a waste. The Plan has been a waste. My dreams, my aspirations. Every thought I've had since prison. Every word I've said and thing I've done. All a lie.

Fernando sticks his gun into Ridgero's face and we push our way in. There are two people in the house: Ridgero and a woman who is on a couch watching TV with a magazine in her lap. She is screaming with her feet on the coffee table crossed at the ankles during a commercial. Fernando forces Ridgero who has his hands up backward to the couch and makes him fall onto the couch next to the woman. Boxes everywhere. Their things packed up. Ready to make a run for it. Caught in the nick of time. The woman still screams and Ridgero is stammering that it's okay baby, that they're cops baby, they're the police baby, that it's okay baby. Fernando puts his gun into Ridgero's mouth and Ridgero stops saying it's okay baby and Fernando says, —We're not the damn cops.

And I say, looking by habit through a box filled with books, —Yes, we are. We're the cops.

Fernando says, —I mean, yeah, we're the damn cops.

Since prison, Fernando has begun saying the word *damn* in every sentence.

I say, —Where is it, Ridgero?

Ridgero shakes his head back and forth and grunts with the gun in his mouth. The woman is still screaming so I turn to Diego to tell him to please put duct tape over the woman's mouth, which he does. I also tell him to please turn off the TV while he is at it.

Then it is quiet and orderly.

Then I feel better about things.

Ridgero still has Fernando's gun in his mouth and I sit down on the chair that matches the couch and say, —Where is it, Ridgero?

Ridgero looks confused and is shaking his head no, drooling on the gun in his mouth, gagging on it. Fernando takes the gun out of Ridgero's mouth in order to use it to hit Ridgero in the mouth. Ridgero says with a bloody mouth, —Let me show you something. Can I show you something?

Fernando and I look at each other and I decide to let Ridgero show us something. I let him off the couch and still holding his mouth with blood in it he shows me a stack of mail on the desk in the den that is addressed to Raul Ridgero. He says, —See? We've been getting his mail. He lived here before us I guess. We just moved in on Tuesday.

Fernando and I look at each other.

And I let Ridgero show me more things. I let Ridgero show me his ID in his wallet that has his picture and the name Tomas Palmero. And I let Ridgero show me the lease that started two days ago on Tuesday and is in the name Tomas and Raquel Palmero. And I let Ridgero show me his Visa Health Insurance Standard Plan card which is under the name Tomas Palmero and I let Ridgero show me one thing after another including a birth certificate all of which are under the name Tomas Palmero. Fernando and I just look at each other.

Fernando gets an idea and on Ridgero's phone Fernando calls the number listed under MOM and he puts it on speaker. A woman answers. —Hi! How's the move?

Fernando asks her what her damn son's name is and the woman is quiet, confused. She says, —Tomas Palmero, why?

Fernando hangs up and looks at me and I look at Ridgero and Fernando says, —Well this is damn interesting.

I duct-tape Ridgero's mouth. And he looks up at me with big white eyes as I then duct-tape his hands behind his back. Fernando and I take Ridgero out of the bedroom and walk him back into the living room where Diego is sitting next to the woman, watching TV again, magazine still on her lap. —Turn it off, I say.

Ridgero starts flailing and going nuts, so Fernando takes him down by bear-hugging him and kicking at the backs of his knees until he's kneeling on the floor, then Fernando gets Ridgero onto his stomach and ties his feet with duct tape too and pins him down with a knee in his back. And the woman is crying. And we didn't wear masks. Masks weren't supposed to be necessary. And I tell Diego to tie the woman's hands and feet with duct tape too please, which he does. And I tell Diego to please put the woman on the floor next to Ridgero, facedown, which he does. And Ridgero and the woman have their faces turned to each other and look at each other with their big white eyes.

We go through every box. We cut open the mattress. We rip up the floorboards. We smash the TV open. We use hammers to smash up the walls. We spend hours tearing the place apart looking for it. We're sweaty and exhausted and we don't find it. So we wash the dust and sweat off our hands and face and on my orders we go back to the living room and Fernando and Diego stand over Ridgero and the woman and point their guns at the backs of their heads and I sit on the couch and pick up the magazine the woman was reading and it is *Visa New York Arts and Politics Magazine* which doesn't matter and it doesn't matter that Fernando and Diego shoot Ridgero and the woman in the backs of their heads and it doesn't matter that their big white eyes are wide-open looking into each other's as they die still pumping dark blood from their heads and it doesn't matter that it is not Ridgero, that these are innocent people, because what matters is that nobody's innocent. What matters is that I am a person of great will but no spirituality and even less remorse and that is what makes me who I am which is Junior Alvarez and that feels good to finally come to terms with. An important moment in my life.

THE PERFECT SPOT TO STRIKE

Four, five hours every morning in the predawn darkness she ran through Chantilly and Centreville and other cities of eastern NoVA pushing Jaime in a wheelchair. She never felt tired. Her corporal being seemed to have become a motor for motivation and accomplishment. Her body a simple network of muscles all stemming from the heart which felt so clean and new now. She ate only things that could fuel her blood with productive nutrients. Her physical activities consisted only of those that could contribute to her strength. She felt amazed most of the time. She was a passenger within her body which was now capable of any physical feat. She felt reborn. Amorphous. Superhuman—not due to her physical endurance but to her will. Her will was something she'd always had and always would no matter what happened. It could never be taken from her.

It occurred to her that, considering the impossible intertwinement of the criminals with law enforcement in NoVA, ballistics and makeshift incendiary devices and the other methods she had been employing were leaving behind too much forensic evidence. So she took a three-week welding course at Visa Community College then brought Little Josefina down to her basement one night, petting her and murmuring soothing things to her, and welded onto her a heavy cast-iron casing. Began taking her along on hunts, using her to bash in the heads of these men who could hardly be called men because what separated men from beasts whose lives come down to a mere series of eating, procreating, and doing what is necessary to survive? Self-restraint. The ability to exhibit rational self-restraint. That is one thing animals do not have but man does and these people do not have

121

it. She bashed in their Faustus nonman skulls with Little Josefina with such coiled rage that at times the blow went clear through the back of the head all the way to the face and she'd find herself with her forearm resting atop their lower jaw and tongue. In time she improved, learned the perfect spot to strike from behind so the skull would shatter like cheap glass with just one blow. They'd drop like stunned livestock before even realizing they were under assault and she'd move on, leaving no trace.

She spent the first two years after making her choice of vengeance over the disappearance into grief and the rejoining of society and the forging of a livelihood creating a list. For two years she immersed herself in the study and investigation of the Northern Virginia criminal underworld. Two years. This was a woman who once not long ago was a landlady in a middle-class neighborhood, a local character, almost a shut-in who hardly left her property unless it was to procure scrapbooking materials. The information she gathered any agent of the law could have collected in the course of even halfhearted consistent daily work if they had really wanted to put these people behind bars, which they did not, it was clear, Josefina believed. Any partially competent prosecutor could have built a strong case on her evidence. But she knew that turning it over to the state would have been akin to throwing it away. Taking it and throwing it away into the trash. Because the only result would be probations, plea deals, suspended sentences, acquittals, and so on. Changing nothing. All of which would have been second assaults on Jaime and more spit in her face and in the face of anyone else who'd been wronged or worse by these nonpeople. So now she had a list. It was a list of several hundred names written in pencil so she could erase and add and rearrange as needed in order to accommodate the constant personnel shifts inherent in organized crime but accelerated now by her actions and by the gang wars. It would take years to work her way through it. But she was ready for that. She would get them all in time. If the law would not imprison them then she would exterminate them. She would be patient and she would be meticulous. She would maintain her training always and her prowling even when the temptations of a normal life were strong so she could always be ready for any opportunity to erase a name. She would exhibit rational self-restraint. She would be human.

It was not an act of obsession. She was not compulsive. Nor was she emotional. If it was her fury alone that was driving her she would not have made it ten years because emotions burn out as quickly as they enflame. She was hardly single-minded. There were so many temptations working on her trying to make her choose the easier, more pleasurable life that was waiting for her and Jaime if she would just quit and forgive her trespassors and come to terms with what had happened and enjoy what time she and Jaime had left together on earth. No, by now she was driven by something far more powerful than anger or even hurt. Every morning she had to work to rouse it again as though it slept in the bed beside her under a heavy narcotic. Every night when she crept out the basement door to hunt she had to stand there in the shadows and wake it up all over again. Then she had to drag it drowsy and lethargic, almost half-dead, down the street. But soon once its heart began to beat its lethargy would go away and it would take charge and would now be the one doing the dragging. And once it got going it pulled like a train.

EASTON

One Saturday night he sat outside one of the several Gay Bars in Visa Easton, a cozy and isolated beach town on the extreme tip of the Visa Eastern Shore of Maryland also known as a seasonal homosexual village where he'd sometimes find himself as though a giant hand had reached down from the sky and plucked him up off the Centreville streets and set him down there. Here he was not Junior. He was Cristofo. It was not merely a changing of his name. It was fact. Junior was in Centreville, going about his night. At the same time Cristofo was here, going about his.

Tony Be Right Back was a cabdriver with a shamrock tattoo on his left upper arm that had the words I SMUCKING LOVE CENTREVILLE underneath it. Tony Be Right Back was heavy, had a meaty face that wobbled when he talked. Tony Be Right Back didn't drink, he said. He ate an ice cream cone and smoked a cigarette at the same time. His girth took up three-quarters of the bench's available sitting surface. He wore high denim shorts and kicked his pudgy white legs in a bored, childlike way, a flesh-colored knee brace on his left knee that didn't fit right and kept slipping halfway down his shin. An old and big man, bald head, deep booming voice that seemed strained from years of smoking and shouting over the noise of city streets. Cristofo sat next to him drinking a Soda Company that Tony Be Right Back bought him, both of them watching the traffic and the boys strutting up and down the sidewalk before them.

—Know how I got my name, Cristofo? Know how I got my name? All my life ever since I'm a kid I'm always going somewhere. What's the Visa slogan? Places to Go, People to See. I've always got a million smucking things to do. So I'm always saying, Be right back, Be right back. I say the phrase Be right back probably more than anybody else says anything on this smucking planet. Part of the reason is my profession.

Cristofo could blush on command. Cristofo was shy and sweet. He needed to be taken care of, was a bit dumb, had to have things explained to him a couple of times. By acting dumb and naïve Cristofo could pass as younger. Tony Be Right Back—Cristofo saw from thinking his way inside his head—wanted to feel like a father to someone, to feel needed, looked up to. Cristofo remembered reading this in prison in one of Stephen King's plays—*Hamlet*—something about acting naïve in order to pass for young. Tony Be Right Back held the cigarette in his lips as he needed the hand to reach down and tug the knee brace back up. He now licked the ice cream cone with the cigarette still in his mouth, pointed to a gleaming yellow cab parked halfway down the block. —Cleanest cab in the smucking fleet.

—It looks really good, Tony Be Right Back.

—It looks okay. I'm not gonna be driving that smucking thing forever.

—No?

—Whattya smucking think.

—Why?

—You could say I have something up my smucking sleeve.

—What?

—That's a secret, Cristofo. Tony Be Right Back waved to a passing car then said, —Okay smuck it I'll tell you. You're a smucking kid. What are you, seventeen? Eighteen?

Cristofo nodded. He was thirty-one.

—You tell anybody what I'm about to tell you and I'll give you a kick in the ass. I'm serious. No smucking whore's gonna smuck this up for me. No offense. It was quiet for a moment then Tony Be Right Back looked around and said, —Okay I'll trust you. He motioned for Cristofo to lean toward him. He muttered into his ear like they were two undercover intelligence agents, —I'm opening a Liquor Store.

—Yeah?

—It's nearly smucking official. I've spent a lot of time studying this shit, Cristofo. You want to invest in a business, you want to open a smucking Liquor Store. Listen to me. I've spent half my life driving cabs, being around people, overhearing things, watching people. Think I don't soak shit up? Twenty years I've been soaking shit up. Twenty years. I have a mind like a trap. And Cristofo I'll tell you, if I have learned anything in twenty years driving a cab soaking shit up with my mind that's like a trap, it is that there are plenty of hard times in that smucking city and that's not gonna change anytime soon. And what do people do in hard times? Same thing they do in good ones. They drink.

Cristofo crossed his legs and leaned back and said, —The only problem though must be getting the license.

—My cousin's a city councillor. He told me about this auction at City Hall where they were going to auction a license. It was real inside. You had to know somebody to even know about it. I've never won anything in my life but I won this. Happiest day of my life. I can't describe it. I even got the smucking location of the store secured and everything. Put down the deposit yesterday.

—Where?

Tony Be Right Back motioned for Cristofo to lean toward him again and he lowered his voice again and muttered, —There's a smucking Visa Housing Project. Big hideous smucking thing right there on smucking New Braddock and Centrewood? You know it?

It was the one he had grown up in, the one his mother still lived in.

—I think so, yeah.

—It's coming down. And it's about smucking time. That place has been a festering shithole for decades. Nothing but a smucking barn for the worst kind of bottom-feeding refuse-to-work scum. But they're finally getting rid of it and putting businesses there instead. Imagine that. And one of those businesses, lo and smucking behold, is going to be a Liquor Store. No other smucking Liquor Store within eight blocks. And in a neighborhood just smucking lousy with alcoholics. It's a slam smucking dunk. And the franchisee of that smucking Liquor Store shall be none other than Mr. Tony Smucking Be Right Back. Slam smucking dunk. I've been saving for twenty smucking years for this. This is smucking perfect. This is my smucking opportunity to own something for once. Like a real man. This is gonna be something that will be in the family for generations. I'll pass it on to my nephews when I go.

I'm going to give jobs to local kids who have no positive male role models in their lives, take them under my wing, treat them like my own sons. Be a person to look up to. My life is going to change. I'm going to become somebody—a smucking pillar of the community. Be in a position of influence. I'm going to do good things. Help people out when they need it. Give back. This is all top-secret shit though, Cristofo. Don't go blabbing about this. I'm serious. No one even knows they're demolishing that Housing Project yet. Not even the people who live there.

—What's going to happen to them you think?

—Who cares. Smuck them. Maybe now they'll try working for a living like the rest of us. But this is everything to me. This is everything.

Eventually Tony Be Right Back was done with his cigarette and Cristofo led him back inside, back to the bathrooms, where they waited for a stall. Two men came out of one buckling their belts and chatting. Cristofo and Tony Be Right Back went in. A condom was floating in the toilet which Tony Be Right Back flushed. Tony Be Right Back paid Cristofo three hundred dollars and Cristofo fellated Tony Be Right Back who continued to eat his ice cream and didn't notice Cristofo slip Tony Be Right Back's wallet out of his back pocket.

THE BUSINESS MEETING

Junior went to the address on the driver's license in the wallet. It was in Centreville. As he walked up the street he felt himself go dark. Black wet things crawling through his veins. He could feel them. This was familiar by now. He was a wretched individual. It felt right to be. With him were Fernando and Diego. These were two people he'd known all his life but felt as though he didn't. He was all alone, it occurred to him as he walked up the street. He did not only fail to know Fernando and Diego but he also failed to understand them. Their bodies had been in close physical proximity for years and years—minus the time apart in prison and then as a respectable citizen—and that was the extent of things. The address was every address in Centreville. A triple-decker in which the families lived piled on top of one another, listening to one another's lives. The address was the first floor. It was nighttime. The three walked up onto the porch, rang the doorbell, waited. A woman opened the door. She was short, fat, thick glasses, brown hair in a short perm, maroon sweatsuit, Tobacco Company, lots of makeup, looking out the side of her face at them, eyeing them, a middle-aged woman with yellow crooked teeth.

—Is Tony Be Right Back here? Junior said.

—Who's asking? She leaned out and spat a yellow gob of phlegm at their feet.

—My name's Cristofo.

—Who gives a shit. He can't talk to you.

—Why not?

—He's doing shit.

—What's he doing?

—He's sleeping.

—I don't believe you.

—He's tired from working.

—I think you're not being honest with me.

—He smucking works for a living.

Tony Be Right Back appeared behind the woman and went white when he saw who it was. —Lora, make some beepollen.

—Beepollen? It's smucking nine o'clock at night, Tony Be Right Back. It's too smucking late for beepollen.

—Make some beepollen, Lora.

—You gotta get up at smucking four-thirty in the morning.

—Lora, will you make some smucking beepollen? Smuck.

—You want it so bad, you make it.

—Kevin Smucking Lithis, just please make some smucking beepollen, please, Lora.

—Don't use Kevin's name. I don't want all these people in the house. Who the smuck are these people? I don't want all these people in the house at nine o'clock at night drinking all our beepollen and blaspheming Our Savior.

Tony Be Right Back put his hands on Lora's shoulders and turned her around and pushed her not so gently in the direction of the kitchen saying, —Shut your piehole and make some smucking beepollen. He turned to Junior and Fernando and Diego. For a while they stared at one another. Tony Be Right Back said nothing. He blinked and breathed and shook his head like he couldn't believe this and he said softly, —You stole my wallet.

—I got it. It's right here in my pocket. You want it? Tony Be Right Back put his hand out. Junior just looked at it. —May I come in?

—Please?

—We'll discuss it. May I come in?

—I don't wanna discuss it. I just want my wallet. And I want you to go away. And I never want to see you again.

—That's not going to happen. May I come in?

Tony Be Right Back looked out past them like he was sizing up the distance from himself to the moon. He sighed and made a whimpering noise and turned and walked inside. They followed him. He led them to the living room, TV on loud. The place smelled like stale smoke. The furniture was old. Trashy decor such as a porcelain rooster on a hallway table. Family portraits on the wall. Flowery, yellowing wallpaper. Shag carpeting, a ratty old deer padding around. Lora yelling from the kitchen that she's making tea and if they don't like it they're welcome to go to the smucking Beepollen Shop down the smucking street. Tony Be Right Back stared at Junior and muttered to have a seat on the floral print sofa with several cigarette burn holes in it and he sat down on a recliner and they stared at each other for a couple of seconds, listening to Lora now talking about the deer being constipated but how it might break up and he might suddenly just shit all over the floor so they had to look out. That's when Fernando and Diego sprung up and took a single step over the coffee table dividing them and Tony Be Right Back didn't say anything but he started to get up and Fernando and Diego pushed him back down in the chair and pinned him down and Fernando put him in a choke hold while Junior pulled a pair of pliers from his pocket and went over to him and while Fernando pried his mouth open with his hands Junior grabbed a front tooth with the pliers and squeezed and this made Tony Be Right Back stop resisting. Junior watched the sweat appear on Tony Be Right Back's wrinkly forehead and the saliva pooling around his tongue which was littered with little gobs of dried white spittle and twitched and swelled and shrank back, listening to Tony Be Right Back's breath and to Lora's voice in the kitchen. Junior was watching for something in his eyes to break. He enjoyed knowing that Tony Be Right Back was wondering if at any second Junior would twist the pliers and rip the tooth out of his head. And he knew he was thinking about what that would feel like. Junior liked to watch the breaking eyeballs dart around, crackling with red, face flushing, pupils dilating and contracting. He liked to smell the man's breath on his face as he waited for something in the man's eyes to break.

They heard Lora coming. Junior and Fernando and Diego all let go of Tony Be Right Back and went back to the couch. She came in holding a tray of teas in brandy snifters and freebie Visa Professional Football Franchise–NoVA glasses from Gas Station. The three guests smiled up at her. Tony Be Right Back looked glum and touched his mouth. Lora muttered to him that if his tooth hurt so bad he should go to the smucking dentist. She had a fresh cigarette in her mouth and the deer was at her heels. She dropped the tray of teas on the coffee table and explained that these cups were all they had because the only mugs they had were the ones Tony Be Right Back and she used for their morning beepollens and she wasn't about to wash them right now because she works all day for a living and if they didn't like that then, again, pointing, there was the door through which they could leave to go to the Beepollen Shop down the smucking street. She ashed into the ashtray on the coffee table and stared them down. Junior said, —This is fine. Thank you. She opened her jaws and let out a loud harsh belch and left the room. As soon as she was gone Junior was up and Fernando was up and Diego was up and they were on top of Tony Be Right Back again.

The thing in Tony Be Right Back's big white eyeballs had almost broken but Junior hit Tony Be Right Back a couple of times on the side of the face with an open hand to make sure because he knew how hard it was to separate a man from his dreams and he was scared of that. Tony Be Right Back made a face while being hit—scrunching up his face and squeezing his eyes shut like a baby, no choice but to sit there and take it without flinching because one flinch and there goes his tooth. Then Junior stopped hitting Tony Be Right Back and told him to open his big white broken eyeballs and Junior looked into them and told him that the reason he was here was to propose a business deal. He told him that the deal he was proposing was this: that instead of Tony Be Right Back being the franchisee of the Visa Liquor Store, Junior would now be the franchisee of the Visa Liquor Store. And that this would happen by Junior using all the groundwork Tony Be Right Back had been laying including the license that Junior could never hope to obtain himself due to being an ex-felon. And that Tony Be Right Back would do all the day-to-day running of the store such as the ordering and the banking and the stocking, things which Junior had neither the interest in nor the know-how. But the business and all the money it made would be Junior's. In other words, Tony Be Right Back would do all the work and Junior would reap the bounty. That was the business deal he was here today to propose. And also Tony Be Right Back would answer to Junior and be paid an hourly wage decidedly higher than what he made now at Cab

Company however the wage would be withheld or reduced based on how Junior judged Tony Be Right Back's work and attitude and anything else he might feel like judging him on.

And Junior said, —How's that sound? Not that you have a choice.

And Junior said that if Tony Be Right Back didn't like any of this well then Junior would go ahead and pull the tooth out as slowly as possible. And then he would do the next tooth and the next tooth and so on until there were no more teeth to pull out. At which point if an agreement had still not been reached Junior would take the knife from his pocket and move on to the rest of Tony Be Right Back's body. Then he'd tell his wife what Tony Be Right Back liked to pay boys to do out in Easton. Also he'd likely sic Diego on her. Make Tony Be Right Back watch. He made it clear that Diego was very deranged. One just had to look at Diego to understand this. So Tony Be Right Back agreed. Junior released him, shook his hand, gave him his wallet back. —Pleasure doing business with you, Junior said. Tony Be Right Back flipped through it making sure everything was there. It was—even the cash.

THE PILLAR OF THE COMMUNITY

He became a part of the neighborhood. He was a fixture of the block. Junior at the Liquor Store. Standing there behind the counter with a toothpick in his mouth and his hands on his hips, staring off and out through the window. Surveying the cracks in the ceiling. The people. Watching the sky. Licking his lips. Observing the traffic. Watching over his domain. Chewing his toothpick. Considering the people milling around the Liquor Store he had stolen and opened on the site of his own mother's seized and demolished home. Each person nodding hello to him as they entered like he was the village lord. As if they knew him. As if he were their friend. He wasn't their friend. They didn't know him. He noticed how people react when you're in a position of power. Even a position as negligible as owning a Liquor Store. They might as well have knelt and kissed his hand. Usually he did recognize them, but mostly he stared back at them with a detached frown. He stood nodding and tonguing his toothpick, pretending to be listening to them as they spoke. He wondered if they had heard about how he had made his money. How he had gotten hold of the Liquor Store. Of course they had. Everybody heard everything in Centreville. Not everything—most things. What you let them hear. This was a good secret to know. He wondered if they knew about him having been in prison. Who were these people? Nobody. He wondered who the feds on surveillance were. Who Uncle Antonio's guys on surveillance were. Or the Italians on reconnaissance, trying to figure out what he was about, where his vulnerabilities were—trying to know this new enemy. A city of people looking at one another from the corners of their eyes. No, the Italians would stick out. You can sense the Italians around here. You can sense outsiders.

He found that people wanted to tell him about their wives, their probation officers, their knees, their kidneys, their hemorrhoids, their carbuncles. He discovered that he was becoming a lightning rod for these people's most private truths. Why me? he thought. They come to me, they confess their violations of the Lithiite Rules and Regulations into my ear. I have nothing to do with them. But I'm one of them. Whether I like it or not. I grew up here. This is where I live. I tried to leave. Look what happened. Tried to be Alejandro el Grande. What a fool. An impatient, overeager fool. With no wisdom. Expecting so much—the world—so soon.

He still felt foolish thinking about how young he had been.

These years were the good years. Fruitful years in which he saw himself all at once come to full flower. The war between the Irish and Italians created empty spaces and a distracted environment in which he moved and operated like a squirrel—a now-extinct, slow-moving rodentlike creature with a long, scaled tail and useless wings that hit its dead end as a species not long after the Visa Nuclear War—wandering around a minefield gathering nuts not so much avoiding harm due to its calculation or cunning but due to almost a happenstance, in fact seeming oblivious to the danger and not only not dying but flourishing, taking all the nuts left behind by those less fortunate others now dust.

From his cover as a business owner he began selling to loan sharks his capacity to inflict great violence. Worked as a collections agent, more or less. He'd stalk an indebted man for days along with Diego and Fernando then confront him in a Bar or some other public place and tell the man if he did not get his money right now he would rip out his teeth. If this did not work, he'd break into the man's home as he slept and rip out his teeth. Then a loan shark he worked for was slain by the Italians so Junior took over the abandoned business, stuffing the bodies of two others who showed interest in the trunks of their cars and leaving them out in Centreville with the keys in them for unknowing teenagers to make off with. Killed Stimulant dealers, bookmakers, and other criminals who seemed to be making substantial profits and took over their work. The deaths were blamed on the Italians as part of the war. He and Fernando and Diego executed one powerful bookmaker who ran a racket of nearly a dozen other Centreville bookies working below him. It was on a Sunday afternoon as he left his mother's home carrying a cheesecake. He called good-bye to her as he walked out the door, told her he'd call her tomorrow. As he got into his car and started it a bland Car Company Blue Sedan pulled up driven by Fernando from the backseat of which stepped Junior and Diego with machine guns, opening fire on the car as his mother watched from the bay window where she was watering her ficus. Then they sped off. The mother claimed she was in the kitchen when it happened and by the time she got to the window her son's murderers were gone.

To do business like this in Centreville was not easy. He was forced to pay Uncle Antonio a monthly tribute of $125,000. He was making more than four times this but it still made him sick. He had no choice. He was weaker than Uncle Antonio. This was a fact. He consoled himself by telling himself that it was only a temporary fact. He'd keep working. Eventually he'd find a chink in the armor. He was at times often incapacitated with envy toward him but he was willing to wait as long as it took for his opportunity. You can't expect to get everything you want at the moment you begin to want it. That's what did in most people like himself: not understanding this. He was objective and clinical. Recognized that as one of his strengths. Level-headed. He was living a life of crime and there were things that came along with that. He was entitled nothing. There were certain disciplines one had to grasp in order to not only survive in the realm of lawlessness but thrive as well. And he wanted not only that, not only to thrive. He wanted to rule. The most important discipline was patience. The second was moderation in all aspects. Most of those drawn to this life were drawn to it because they were impatient, indulgent, and incapable of self-restraint. They were sociopaths. But they were human beings. And human beings are all alike. Always have been, always will be. The only difference between one and another is in how much rational self-restraint they can demonstrate. That's why his competitors and contemporaries were always in and out of prison or disappearing or dying or scrambling around playing cat and mouse with the Visa FBI or somebody: because they lacked it. Maybe they were content with that in exchange for a small fortune, a couple decent homes, a bit of power. But he wasn't. A happy wife and nice things would never be enough for him. He wanted something else. The design in his will called for it. The design was crazy but he had it and was driven by the need to fulfill it. He had been studying martial arts. Checked a couple books out of Visa Library on the subject. What he discovered in his research was that one of the first things you learn in martial arts is not how to knock someone's head off. It's how to fall. Nothing with the exception of the imperialism of Alejandro el Grande ever made more sense.

He knew the greatness inside himself. How it trembled. Twitched. Called out to him at night. Dark nights of the soul—plenty of those. Tossing and turning in the modest apartment he could finally pay for easily. Doubting himself. Wondering if maybe he would always be a nobody. It didn't make sense to be doubting himself in the midst of all this recent success. But he did. Maybe it was all a fluke. Everyone hits the jackpot sometimes. You don't have to be anything special to do it. Just lucky. The way the wind blows. Wind blows some good fortune your way, wind can just as easily blow some bad fortune your way next. He'd move out of that shit apartment soon. Get a nice place. Every moment he spent hovering in mediocrity was an eternity in hell. His will roared furious impatient commands at him. But he restrained himself. Because he knew how to fall.

Ascent. Built community swimming pools and upgraded the equipment on Centreville playgrounds long neglected by the state. There were cases in which treasured family heirlooms or tools crucial to a man's job stolen out of the homes of innocent hardworking families were recovered not by going to the police who either were incapable or indifferent but only by going to Junior Alvarez. He was the only one who could get things like that done. He was said to financially support the wives and children of men murdered (their murderers rarely caught) or jailed for something they either did not do or could not help. Donated to youth sports and local branches of the Church of Kevin Lithis. Could be seen attending Seminar every Sunday at St. Jackie Kennedy's. He wore a suit, arrived early, passed out programs, help set up for coffee and doughnuts in the basement afterward. Took groups of boys on overnight church camping trips.

There was talk that Centreville had never been better. Junior

Alvarez kept the trash out. Junior Alvarez got things done. Junior Alvarez and his guys were on the wrong side of the law but was there a right side of the law in NoVA?

Nobody could run Centreville better than Centreville could. In Centreville they were family. They took care of their own in Centreville.

He actively fabricated a spiritual camaraderie, almost a father-son relationship, with Father Alfonso, the aged regional president there at St. Jackie Kennedy's. He'd bring him chocolate cake—the priest's lone vulnerability. They would sit for hours talking. One evening through mouthfuls of chocolate cake Father Alfonso was imparting onto Junior some piece of wisdom or moral example that Junior was pretending to be listening to though really he was just watching in disgust the bits of chewed cake falling out of the old man's blessed mouth and the icing clinging to the priest's little teeth, so eager was this gleaming, sanctified earthly minister of Holy God to deposit over and over a new forkload of gooey cake into the digestive tract of his body—the ineffable temple itself—that he was not even pausing to clean his mouth out with his heavenly tongue first before doing so, when he mentioned something he had been told in confidence in the stormy throes of a client's spiritual midnight. Father Alfonso stopped here as though surprised that what had just come out of his mouth had come out of his mouth. He seemed to be taking measure of whether he should say what he was about to say next. He stared at the cake of which he had alone in a matter of a couple minutes consumed more than half, his fork still digging out another chunk to deposit into his mouth and yet he was still chewing the previous load slowly and ponderously like a cow, Junior thought, a dumb filthy animal with no purpose but to provide milk and meat which in ancient times, he'd read, had been worshipped and protected as sacred by men held in as much respect and moral authority as this one, men who in their time were believed to be just as wise as this one was believed to be in his. You could see the warring going on in the man's ethics. He had all of a sudden somehow seemed to split into two Father Alfonsos now and it was like he couldn't determine which one was him and which one was his double. He glanced at Junior. Childish, guilt-ridden eyes. Broken eyes. How easily, how quickly, they had broken. Like they had wanted to break for years but had just been waiting for someone to make the suggestion.

—Junior, what I am going to tell you I am telling you in total confidence. I should probably not be telling you at all, because it violates the ethos and trust of the priesthood. But I feel a kinship with you I cannot explain nor understand. Junior, do I have your word what I am going to tell you will stay between us?

—Of course.

The priest still had gobs of soft brown icing stuck to his teeth and lips as he continued to wrestle with this. Then for the sake of whatever the moral lesson was he was so driven to impart, which was so meaningless to Junior that he would not be able to recall it in the immediate moments after its imparting, the priest came out with it. He dug into the cake with his fork and said, —There is a man in Centreville. A career criminal. Recently he had a kind of a spiritual conversion. Now he sees the wrongness of his life of illicit activities. However, those illicit activities have been very profitable for him. And for his family. His character is too weak and his family too dependent on the benefits of his violations of the Rules and Regulations to give them up completely and go straight. It's too hard. So this man, with my guidance, to at least partially atone for all his wrongdoings until he develops the strength of character and weans his family off the lifestyle they are accustomed to, has become an informant to the FBI. He's now actively feeding the FBI information from deep within the underworld about his enemies and associates while still committing crimes with them. And the FBI is using the information to build cases that will put people much worse than he is away forever. Without his information, this would not be possible.

Junior did not ask who it was, not wanting to appear too interested. In fact he hardly reacted at all beyond the expected mild excitement any layman would display hearing privileged tales of local gangsters. But in time he found out who it was, as he knew he would. Everyone knows everything in Centreville—it was not impossible. It was a loan shark who worked for a man who worked for a man who worked for Uncle Antonio. Though he'd never had much contact with this man—a forty-eight-year-old named Orlando Trieste, a Centreville father of three teenage girls—Junior now made sure to stay away from him. He avoided him like the virus. He made sure never to let Orlando Trieste see or know anything about Junior Alvarez. To keep the existence of Junior Alvarez out of the cognizance of Orlando Trieste completely. And he began watching Orlando Trieste from a distance. He stalked the rat. He studied the life of the rat as though the rat's life were the saga of a fictional character. He learned everything about the rat. He was unsure of what action to take in regard to the rat. He did not hate the rat. He felt no moral outrage. He felt nothing more than a scientist does crouched over a snake that can kill him, studying its habits precisely so it will not kill him. There was something there, some kind of fortune to excavate if the ground was dug correctly. He didn't know what. For now he just observed the rat.

Junior played cards with an alderman whom he met at St. Jackie Kennedy's. In a dramatic hand he won two dozen jobs for Centreville husbands and fathers laid off in the recent foundry closings working security on the alderman's reelection campaign. The alderman, who had been holding a flush, was so shocked by Junior's unlikely victory that he reacted by punching him in the face. A reflex of violence. He apologized right away, horrified by himself. As a result of his winning jobs for them, these men developed strong emotional loyalties toward Junior that they passed on to their friends, relatives, wives, children. They spread the word: Junior Alvarez is a hero. He's a champion of the people. Be like Junior, they would tell their kids. He has integrity and principles. He believes in helping his fellow man. In Centreville, if you wanted respect and to make your father proud of you, you wouldn't be a lawyer, you wouldn't be a doctor, you wouldn't go to Ivy League University. You'd go to work for Junior. If he'd have you.

He sold alcohol at steep discounts, further earning the affections of the Centreville Irish. To be able to do this he sent Diego and Fernando around to all the other Liquor Stores in the neighborhood. These two monolithic senseless men making themselves at home in the stores' back offices, carrying weapons, Diego studying the family photos arranged on the desk with disturbing interest as Fernando told the owner his prices were too low and would need to come up.

When Junior noticed a new parking lot being laid on the property of the Liquor Store nearest his own he arrived out of the blue one day preceded by his two unruly mammoths carrying a box in his arms. He loitered around by the Red Wine Companies holding the box, the owner behind the counter ringing up a customer and eyeing not Junior but the box. And when the customer left and the store was empty Fernando locked the door and flipped the CLOSED sign. Junior approached the owner.

—I don't like your parking lot.

—No? What don't you like about it?

Junior didn't answer. He didn't even act as though the man had spoken. He just turned his head and spat on the rug. Didn't even take his toothpick out first. The owner was eyeing the box. Glancing at Fernando and Diego, Fernando by the door and Diego wandering around. The owner knew who Junior was. He could see Junior's arms were strained, testifying to the weight of whatever he had in it.

—You know what I do to people? Junior said. The owner didn't say anything. —I rip their teeth out of their heads.

The man didn't say anything, just kept eyeing the box. After a short time he said even though he knew the answer, —What's in it?

Junior just spat again, with his toothpick still in his mouth, left.

The next day the construction of the lot was stopped and never resumed. The owner got a call soon after. —Junior says you and him are damn friends now.

Police officers and federal agents began appearing at his store.

He continued to keep a close but distant eye on the rat. He could not figure out how to capitalize on this man, this information only he knew. It was an unsolved equation of mathematics. There was one objective ultimate answer but no matter how he worked the numbers or changed his angle of perspective he could never arrive at it, even though it seemed to be there, just on the other side of what he was thinking about or looking at. He would think and think about it until he felt himself becoming frustrated and then he'd put the matter aside. He knew that getting frustrated would not yield any productive results. The frustration of being unable to arrive at the answer would only make it more difficult to arrive at the answer, thus frustrating him further, thus making it less likely that he would arrive at the answer, and all that frustration and unlikeliness would feed each other and both would just grow, forever and ever without end. So when he came to this threshold of frustration he'd use his immense capacity for self-restraint to put the entire matter aside in his mind and think about it no more, even though everything in him wanted him to continue brooding on it, knowing and believing and most of all understanding that the best inspiration and most prudent, clear-eyed judgment come when the mind is occupied by nothing.

He bought a Visa Gym location. Managed a few teenage amateur MMA fighters who trained there, taught them about self-restraint. Met NoVA police officers who worked out there. Also met cops through Manny. Cultivated friendships with them. He led them to believe via close study of their habits and personalities and then reflecting it back to them that he understood them like no one else did. By being associated with Junior Alvarez they found they earned a respect in Centreville—often where they were from—far greater than they had ever received as cops. Their families treated them differently, strangers nodded hello to them, held the door into Convenience Store for them. Sometimes even, imagine it, cooperated with them in investigations. No longer were they fixed with icy silent stares of loathing and mistrust at all times, the usual reaction a policeman could expect just standing in line at Bank on personal business in Centreville. They invited Junior to their homes for barbecues. He'd stand around with them with his feet far apart like they stood. Rolled his neck like they rolled theirs. Picked up the cocky, doubtful inflections in which they spoke. He'd become what they were, which were men who were fatally weak without absolute control. He'd laugh at their obscene jokes and pretend to drink Backyards—taking gulps but blocking his mouth with his tongue, dumping it out down the bathroom sink or in houseplants here and there—feigning drunkenness because they were drunk and in this way they would continue to feel comfortable with him, knowing the suspicious even neurotic natures of these men, how needful they were at all times for a sense of comfort to go along with their grand illusion of control. Like babies. They were babies, cops were. He could not stand them to such a degree that it was difficult for him to believe his face was able to contain his disdain. But the reason he suffered their company was because of what happened when the sun would go down. After several hours of gluttony and inebriation their judgment would have worsened and inevitably one would decide in the midst of telling a humorous anecdote—normally revolving around someone else's humiliation—or in the midst of a complaint—usually about women or the ninny state's passing of law after illogical law that only inhibit their ability as policemen to enforce the law, thus hampering them from restraining man from the chaos and horror which they believed he would break first chance he was given if not for the unappreciated work of overtaxed, undermanned cops—one would decide in the midst of an anecdote to mention as necessary detail to the anecdote, after first seeming to hesitate a moment to consider Junior's being there, some sensitive piece of information that should not have been leaked outside the circle of law enforcement. Such as where various bugs had been set around town for the purpose of acquiring damning evidence against members of the criminal underworld, one of which they did not know or were not able to admit to themselves was standing among them, like Joey, Kevin Lithis's disciple who in the end betrayed him by testifying against him in the child molestation trial in which Lithis was the victim of cultural conspiracy and guilty of nothing but was the mechanism by which man this time achieved his inevitable end of annihilating again and again as long as he should live the one sent to save him. That is why we call traitors and turncoats Joeys. Anyway Junior then avoided these bugged locations and anyone who spent any time there as though they were soaked in radioactive nuclear fallout. Junior gave his cop friends cash gifts at Gift Giving Holiday every year. He let them come into his Liquor Store and take whatever they wanted whenever they wanted it. Free of charge. He knew the bottomless need for gratification and sense of comfort that had to be fed and that was fed by being able to illegally park their car out front in a Visa No Parking Zone, swagger into the store knowing the unnerving air they introduced to any room, say something vaguely bullying and insulting to whoever was working behind the counter, force anyone in their way to step aside, take something off the shelf like it was the pantry of their home and walk out with it, everyone else who was not a cop like they were but an evil-born man on the brink of chaos standing in line pretending not to be watching him. Junior knew how important this routine was to a cop. It kept a cop happy to be able to do things like this. It made a cop feel in control of the world. But you should never want to feel in control of the world. Because the world cannot be controlled. If you believe that it can, you are under a delusion. A delusion is dangerous, it is poison. Because it is a vulnerability.

So let them feel in control of the world.

He gave their children toys at Gift Giving Holiday. Aluminum rings for their wives.

Aluminums: a very rare, very expensive rock mined in West Virginia and considered to be very beautiful, a symbol of status and regard. Most of the ones Junior handed out had been stolen.

He was said to rescue prostitutes, help them resurrect their lives, especially the ones who came from honest and hardworking Centreville families, white women who had fallen into the clutches of black pimps who then got them hooked on Stimulant or Painkiller. This was spoken of in the tone of awed myth, how Junior would show up alone and sometimes literally snatch the victimized white girl out of those black claws, assault the pimp at the risk of his own life, return her to her white family to be cleaned and loved.

He patrolled the streets of Centreville at night, it was said, looking for hoodlums and drug dealers. He'd punish them if he found them. Chase them out of the neighborhood for good so they could not harm the people, the children of Centreville, any longer.

It was said that he never carried a gun and that he did not allow his men to carry them either. Did not believe in them, it was said. Thought they posed too great a harm to innocent people and were a negative influence on youngsters, it was said.

Volunteered his time at Visa Homeless Shelter serving ladles of soup and counseling despondent men about business and life decisions. Put on a Gift Giving Holiday pageant each year in Park #12 which had been cleaned up by a team of volunteers he had organized and funded.

A Gift Giving Holiday pageant consists of reenacting the birth of Kevin Lithis, including as interludes and vignettes the performing of several of Lithis's more well-known Visa advertisements as collected in the Lithiite Rules and Regulations and so deeply ingrained in the world culture that even those who don't subscribe to the religion know them and can enjoy the pageant and be encouraged and inspired by its nonthreatening moral themes.

He was profiled in the local section of *Visa Times* as a citizen making a difference in an economic downturn.

He returned to City Hall where he went around to all the receptionists, cleaning women, maintenance men, and other support staff handing out five-thousand-dollar gift certificates to Day Spa. He had a meeting with the governor there, a son of the governor Junior had once met so many centuries ago it seemed. Sat with him in his office to discuss a bill passed by the Visa Legislature that would mandate a life sentence for the use of a machine gun in the commission of a felony, a bill that Junior strongly urged the governor to sign into law, being a concerned and socially conscious citizen who did not believe in guns.

He was said to have anonymously financed the new hockey rink on the roof of Visa Low Scores Elementary School, where he himself had gone to school once upon a time.

Stood next to the mayor at the ribbon cutting for the Second World War II veterans memorial that he helped finance and that was built in the small courtyard in front of City Hall where he used to eat on his lunch breaks when he worked as a janitor there.

He tipped off a rival about a truck carrying a load of aluminums scheduled to make a delivery, knowing that the rival would try to rob it and would use a machine gun—in fact Junior advised that he use one because the guards would be heavily armed and he even introduced him to a man who could sell him one—and knowing also that the truck would be filled not with aluminums but with police conducting a sting operation based on an anonymous tip that someone was planning to rob it and knowing one other thing which was that the governor had just signed into law a bill mandating a life sentence for the use of a machine gun in the commission of a felony.

Soon the rival was not a rival anymore.

He was spoken of with pride by the people of Centreville. He never killed anyone who did not deserve it, they said. Who wasn't an incurable scourge upon society and a threat to the children. Who wasn't trying to kill him first.

Like an iconic professional athlete, was how they spoke of him. It was not him they were speaking of but themselves. What he represented to them. The meaning he gave to their lives, to their city.

One morning around four A.M., his usual time for leaving his new spacious luxurious Reston condo two blocks from the Expensive Hotel and its front doors where he'd been humiliated nearly two decades earlier—though it felt like yesterday to him, the fear still just as strong, always humming within—to start his day, he opened the door of his car, got in, put on his seat belt, put the key into the ignition, started to turn it, stopped, took the key out, got out of the car, stepped back from it, studied it, took some more steps back from it, crossed the street, took out his phone, called Tony Be Right Back, made him get out of bed and come pick him up. As he waited he stared at the car, trying to figure out what felt wrong about it. As though if he were to stare hard enough he would be able to look through the metal exterior and beyond all the wiring into its deepest guts where the wrongness would reveal itself as plainly as someone waving to him. He called Visa A Tow Truck, had the car hauled off, later that day bought a new one with cash. A few weeks later as it sat in the A Tow Truck lot, the car exploded. Flames and mangled chunks of metal shot hundreds of feet into the air in a towering column of red-orange, filling the sky for kilometers with black smoke and a poisonous stink, blasting the glass out of the windows of all the other impounded cars. No one was hurt. The only one around was Hector, the owner's son, who had just come back from towing a Car Company Green Sedan and was now dozing drunk in the backseat of it, his feet sticking out the window, putting off for the third day in a row fixing the knob to the door of the office trailer which had fallen off. He was too work-averse to haul the car much farther than a few feet beyond the gate, which turned out to be fortunate because it put him at a safe distance from the blast. At the explosion he woke up, eased himself upright, brushed the pieces of broken glass off his face, stared out the car's broken windshield at the inferno and now the chain reaction as the gas tanks of the cars around it were exploding one by one. He thought he had done this. By yet again putting off fixing the door to doze drunk in the backseat of a towed car he had caused this to happen. Kevin Lithis punishing him for his chronic self-indulgence and sloth. He groaned, climbed out of the car, and slouched toward the trailer office. —Okay! he yelled at the flames, cars still going off like fireworks on the Fourteenth of April. —Okay! I'll fix the smucking door! Kevin Smucking Lithis!

A few days later a small amount of cash—$891—was found on the steps up to the now-repaired office door along with a note: SO SORRY!

It was unsigned.

One day a rumor. It appeared overnight on the streets of Centreville. The rumor was that Uncle Antonio had muscled Junior out. Junior was done. Uncle Antonio had shown up at the Liquor Store and put a gun in Junior's face. Junior started crying. Tears and snot running down his face. His voice a high-pitched meandering whine. He was on his knees before Uncle Antonio, the gun against his nose. He was begging for his life, certain he would die. In a panic he offered Uncle Antonio fellatio. If he let him live, he'd suck his cock. Uncle Antonio couldn't believe what he heard. Made him repeat himself. He did. Junior said, his eyes glassy and red and filled with fear, —I'll do anything. Let me live and I'll do anything you want. In one version of the rumor Uncle Antonio just to humiliate Junior and to display his dominion over him took him up on the offer. Either way, all versions of the rumor ended with Junior agreeing to step aside followed by the muscle accompanying Uncle Antonio brutally beating him there in his own office and leaving him for dead.

So Junior was out. Like so many others who had shown up out of nowhere to make a noisy run at the kingdom were beaten back into the oblivion they'd come from.

There were those who did not believe the rumor. People who had firsthand experience with Junior. They'd seen the force of his will. There was no way he would go so easily and so pathetically. But it seemed true: In the following days, Junior was seen in Centreville with a swollen lip, caked-over wounds crusted upon his face, left eye swollen nearly shut, a black absence in his teeth when he opened his mouth to speak. He looked like he'd been in a car wreck. He now walked hunched over, his head bowed like a subservient beast of burden. A noticeable limp. Another sad-sack Job, forgotten as all the others, just another one who was too weak thus weeded out.

So he was out. Junior was out. He was now just a humble local business owner working himself to the bone for scraps within the confines of the law. A harried, Sisyphean nobody scrambling just to stay afloat so that he might continue his harried, Sisyphean scrambling.

One version of the rumor said that when Uncle Antonio put the gun in his face, as if on command Junior defecated in his pants. Like the weak and harmless coward that was the kind of man he apparently had truly been all this time.

The feds stopped showing up at his store. Now he wandered the city, no one knowing or caring who he was. A man walking down the street. A man at a red light. A man in Hardware Store comparing toggle bolts.

Wore indistinctive Cheap Clothes Company, drove an eight-year-old Car Company Navy Blue Pickup Truck that looked like any other vehicle in the world, made the payments on time, paid the taxes, brought it in for inspections as required.

Reunited with Maria who now was a single mother of four. Three different fathers. Two of them ex-husbands. One ex-husband a Painkiller addict shot to death outside Bar on Union Mill Road over a gambling dispute stemming from one of the multiple squash games a day he played to justify his many chronic pains to the many doctors who wrote him his many Painkiller prescriptions. Another ex-husband sober but abusive and now a deadbeat but at least out of her and more important her children's lives. And the third father an ex-boyfriend who was dependable and kind but profoundly, depressingly boring. The kind of man with an unremarkable job he has no strong feelings toward but which he's worked for fifteen years, following the same routine of waking up, going to the job, coming home from it, eating whatever there is to eat, and falling asleep in the recliner in front of the TV, living in such a fog of ennui that he does not even recognize it as such. In fact he was a person so uninterested in life that now Maria sometimes privately marveled that he was able to get it up long enough to impregnate her.

Junior started coming over during the day on his way back and forth between the Liquor Store and his Garage or his Newsstand or one of the many other semisolvent businesses he owned. Brought things for the kids. Listened to Maria play the piano. One day he sat on the sofa and watched her play Visa Classical Music Piece #3 for him. He watched her become lost in the music. He studied every contour and glow in her face, as if to confine it forever to memory. When she was done he was near tears. He said over the final notes still lingering, —Among all the ugliness in this town, Maria, you are a pearl. Always have been, always will be. Pearls are unlikely and disobedient things. A grain of sand goes somewhere it shouldn't. It turns into a pearl. All the other grains of sand who stayed where they were supposed to, they stay sand— unremarkable grains of sand, billions and billions of them all alike, none of them worth a thing. Pearls are not supposed to happen. Yet they do. Just like you should never have happened, considering how rotten and soul-killing this goddamn town is. But somehow you did. You were disobedient enough to. And now you're more beautiful and precious than a million pearls.

Just being in the room with him electrified her. He bought her clothes, took her on vacations all over the world, gave her money for shopping and groceries like it was nothing. Surprised her. Challenged her. Became so furious with her at times that she, scarred from her past, braced herself for the violence that never came. Which she needed. She could not be with a man who would not hit her if she pushed him to that point. Her ex-husbands had each done different things to her that together had left her ruined. She did not like to be made love to anymore. She did not like to be kissed. She did not even like to be touched. She expected this to scare him off, remembering how he had been when they were young. It had scared off other men who would have been good for her and her children. When she sat him down to have the conversation she did not even dread anymore so much as proceeded toward like to a foul chore, she expected him to sit there listening, consciously fighting off the distaste creeping over his face as she spoke, then when he was done assuring her they would get past it, and she saying thank you, thank you so much for accepting me for how I am, and he saying of course because I love you for you, meaning the entirety and truth of you, both of them knowing deep down that the things they were saying were not true, that they would never get past it, that this marked the beginning of the end. She expected that then in weeks or even days she and Junior would be gone again from each other's lives. But Junior surprised her. As he always did. When she finished telling him, he seemed delighted. She was suspicious. Why did he of all people seem so glad to hear such a thing? But she decided she would not allow herself to think herself out of happiness. She allowed herself to accept his acceptance of her, to enjoy the apparent unconditionality of his love.

He purchased Visa Health Insurance Expensive Plans for her and her children, getting them off those wretched Cheap Plans they'd been on for years. Now they could go to the doctor more than once a year. Now they could get braces if and when they needed them. They could even go to a shrink if they felt like they had Depression or Anger or some other Visa Mental Illness. Put them up in a large new apartment with a dishwasher and new oven on the nice end of K Street. His help—she did not know where he got so much money, there was no end to it, there seemed to be a reserve far more vast than a man like him would have—allowed her to quit her job as a nail technician at Salon, which had hardly been denting her overhead and massive debt anyway, and spend more time with her kids. Rosana liked him, her oldest, who never liked anybody she dated. She looked like a younger version of her mother but prettier. Junior brought Rosana jewelry, talked to her, made her feel like the daughter she'd never felt like before, being the spawn of a drug addict she would've never believed she'd ever met if not for a single half-ripped photograph of a man she was told was her father holding an infant she was told was her, a man who was slain the night after the picture was taken because his love for his vices was greater than his love for her.

Junior had grown up from the juvenile delinquent Maria had once known. But there remained traces. He was still quiet—intensely at times. But his eyes were never quiet. They were always darting around or staring off as though seeing another dimension in the things everyone else just accepted as the decorative scenery of the terrarium in which they'd been dropped. He looked like anyone else in Centreville yet seemed incapable of saying or doing anything she could have anticipated. Or being in a mood she could have predicted. She was forever off balance, never sure where she stood with him. She went weeks believing he was leaving her followed by weeks in which she was unable to believe she'd ever thought he was leaving her. He never fell into routine. He'd be gone for days, he'd be home for days, never with any explanation. He never explained himself. She always felt like anything could happen. Not just to her but to the world, to mankind. With Junior Alvarez, at any given moment anything—*anything*—could happen next.

THE ATTEMPT

Following dozens of failed attempts to just walk up to the ghostlike Junior Alvarez on the street outside his Liquor Store and bash out his brains, Josefina used Little Josefina to smash her way in through the front display window of the closed Gun Store on Visa Highway 29 in Centreville, NoVA, ignoring the alarm bells, using a welding iron to burn through the steel bars on the window and getting inside in about twelve seconds. She came out with a bazooka, crouched down behind a trash can as a Visa City Bus came by, leaped onto the back of the bus, clung to it, rode the city bus a couple of kilometers up to the Visa Northern Virginia Parkway, leaped from the city bus to a recycling truck at nearly thirty-five kilometers an hour, and rode the recycling truck to somewhere in it must have been Herndon where she leaped into the bed of a rather shabby Car Company Pickup Truck as gracefully, as soundlessly, as a flea, lying on her back, watching the night sky zoom by above her with its forever stars and everywhere moon, possibly thinking about how we have been watching this very same moon for thousands maybe millions of years, maybe trying to wrap her head around the idea that even a thousand years ago in the moments of quiet before man's storm of self-decimation we probably did a lot of the same things we do now and were the same inside as we are now and we did these things and were this way all beneath this exact same moon, the very same one she was looking at right now, and that it looked exactly the same as it looked now except for not having all the infrastructure on it and that then as now maybe not everyone took the time to let the meaning of it sink in and to consider how not only unlikely, how not only like pearls, but how miraculous we are.

She bailed in Reston, unseen, unknown, a spirit in the night, somersaulting into an alley as the truck drove off and away and looking out, her squirrelly eyes scanning the proximity. She was sweaty, dirty. Holding her breath in order to hear better. The streets were quiet and wet. Streetlights reflected off the puddles. A middle-aged Lithiite priest happened by alone, talking loudly on his phone apparently with a state senator or congressman because he was warning that if NoVA passed a proposed resolution allowing homosexuals to marry one another then it could expect the regional corporate headquarters of the Holy Church of Kevin Lithis to withdraw all the funding it contributed to the state's Visa Homeless Shelters, which had been keeping them afloat and thus would cause their shuttering if withdrawn, sending all those people who depended on the shelters out into the street to fend for themselves, Lithis help them, the priest had been told by his superiors—very high-level, very holy (and mostly, secretly, very homosexual) senior Lithiite executives—to pass this on to whomever he was speaking to. Josefina crept out of the alley behind him, pouncing with a handkerchief soaked in Visa Pharmaceutical Company Liquid Anesthetic which she put over his mouth and nose, sedating him into quick unconsciousness, catching him when he collapsed. The phone dropped from the priest's hand into a puddle and died. Josefina dragged the priest into an alley and took off her clothes, standing there in her Visa Clothes Company sports bra and underwear as something dripped near her head from above and rats scurried in and out of the Dumpsters nearby. She squatted down and took off the priest's Expensive Clothes Company pants and blazer and shirt with 100 percent aluminum cuff links and put all this on, tying the priest's silk tie around her neck and buckling the priest's 100 percent aluminum Expensive Watch Company around her wrist. She tied up the unconscious priest and left him with an erection in his boxers and white crewneck undershirt and covered him up with some old soggy broken-down cardboard boxes that were there, and emerged from the alley just an ordinary and humble earthly spokesman and minister of the Visa Will of God.

The bazooka was in a large gym bag, along with Little Josefina. Josefina made her way through Reston Square on foot following her handheld GPS until it became jammed up by an automated security measure that directed GPS devices looking for the address she was looking for to a Portable Toilet Company Emptying Facility in Alexandria. She whispered, —Yes, yes, I know it's hot in there. I know. I'm sorry. But we're almost there. Remember it's for Jaime. It's all for Jaime.

Passing Expensive Hotel, two blocks from the luxury condo building, Josefina unzipped the gym bag and without breaking stride withdrew the bazooka and placed it on her shoulder, shoved in a mortar round.

She was now one block away from the address she at times thought she'd never discover. It had been so shrouded in a labyrinthine hell of misleading census records and false deeds of purchase and an unending succession of records of sale pinballing back and forth among innumerable incorporated groups and enterprises that seldom had a history or a future beyond that one transaction and whose owners were always men who did not exist. Or did exist but had no idea that their identities had been stolen. All of this by design to exhaust into submission anyone trying to discover where Junior Alvarez lived.

But here she was.

She knelt down on one knee. She was flush against the brick wall of a Bank branch, sighting her shot on the penthouse where the demon lived, the one who in the last several years as she'd observed his rise—like a predator stalking lethal prey that did not even know it was now the one being stalked—had become the manifestation of all her horrors and hatreds. The disease that would now at last be cut out of the body of mankind after years of pursuit, trying to pin him down long enough to eradicate him but always failing, failing, never failing with any other but always failing with Junior Alvarez. It was due to what she now believed was natural law's protecting and enabling of his life. For reasons she was not interested in discovering. Because what could be done with such knowledge? And because nothing could break her, not even natural law. So she pulled the trigger. Nothing happened. She pulled it again. She did not even hear the explosion. It did not have any colors or smells. It had nothing. It just felt cold, hollow. Like how death must feel.

In Bed

—What was that?

—What.

—That noise.

—Hmm?

—Someone's moving around in the kitchen. Someone's out there.

—I don't hear anything.

—Hear it?

—Probably one of the kids. Rosana maybe.

—What the smuck is she doing in my kitchen?

—I don't know, Junior. Opening the fridge it sounds like.

—Don't speak to me like that. It's a little late for people to be opening the fridge, don't you think? She should be in bed. She has school.

—Go out there and tell her yourself then. You probably want to anyway.

—What do you mean by that?

—Nothing. I just see the way you look at her.

—Who? Rosana?

—Do you have feelings for my daughter, Junior?

—Maria. Kevin smucking Lithis.

—She's nine years old, Junior.

—I know she's nine years old. That's not even the—

—Nine, Junior. At least just wait until she's grown. That's all I ask. Wait until she's old enough to make that sort of decision for herself.

—What you're saying is smucking out of line. For one thing you know I'm not interested in that kind of thing. Sex. And for another even if I was, what you're accusing me of is smucking disgusting. You're accusing me of some serious shit. She's your smucking daughter. It's Rosana. You're accusing me of being a kid smucker. Is that what you're saying? That I'm a pervert kid smucker?

—Shhhh. That's not what I'm saying.

—That's not what you're smucking saying? Then what the smuck are you saying? Maria, if you ever say anything like that to me again—

—What'll you do? Snap my neck?

—That's right.

—I know. I know you will. Fine. Do it. Because, Junior?

—What.

—Stay away from her.

— . . .

—Will you do that? Will you promise? To wait at least until she's grown and can make her own decisions for what's best for herself?

—I don't have to promise because it's not even—

—Will you promise? Do you promise?

—I promise. If it makes you happy, I promise.

—Thank you. Come here.

—What.

—Give me a kiss.

—Maria.

—Please? It's nice to be kissed sometimes.

—Fine. Lithis. Where are you? It's too dark.

—Here.

—Okay. Hold still.

— . . .

—There. All right?

—I love you.

—I love you too. Time to sleep.

— . . .

—What was that?

—What.

—That noise.

—The fridge.

—No, it was a different noise.

—I don't know.

—Kevin Lithis it sounded like an explosion. Hold on, I'm gonna take a look.

— . . .

—Kevin smucking Lithis.

—What is it?

—The Bank down the street blew up.

—What?

—The smucking Bank down the smucking street blew up. What are you, deaf?

The Subterranean

She dragged herself crying and deafened from the rubble on her elbows, both legs broken and useless, a couple teeth gone, flesh and priestly garb ripped up, some fingers bent in terrible unnatural ways, spitting blood, overall blackened like something lifted out of a collapsed mine. Through the night she went like a beaten alligator over broken glass and cigarette butts and human spit and piss, undetected by the passing cars, a trail of skin and blood on the concrete behind her, one eye shut, nose broken, something metal and jagged sticking into her just beneath the ribs. She came to a particular place in the road and leaned up behind a parked car gasping and clutching herself waiting for all traffic to clear then she slithered out into the street and unzipped her duffel bag that she still had around her torso and she withdrew a crowbar and whimpering from the pain she pried up the manhole cover by jamming the crowbar into one of the holes on the cover and putting all her weight on the other end of the crowbar, dislocated shoulders sending shrieking alarms of pain up to the top of her scalp and down her spine to her toenails and everywhere else, all through her, and the cover went toppling over with a loud heavy metal *tongalongalong*. She collapsed heaving air and crying and spitting blood then slithered over the hole and got her legs in holding herself up with her arms, breathing like a woman in labor and nodding as though saying yes to the pain, then she let herself drop and she fell ten feet or so and lay there in a heap at the bottom of the sewer, rats scurrying near her ears and head, a trickle of some kind of hot feculent liquid running beneath her. Then she rolled over and got out a mining light and put it on her head and continued. She crawled hundreds of feet, growling, spit gathering on her lips. —Come on, she said. —Come on you have to. Come on. She ended up in an abandoned subway tunnel and crawled along there until she came to a doorway. She crawled in and was in a fairly big room with a high ceiling. Some kind of former maintenance room. Clutter and cobwebs everywhere. Old public transportation maintenance equipment covered in dust. Trash. Old food wrappers. Beer bottles. Her light flashed over a human being. A man sitting in a chair with his back to her. —Please help me, she said. The man didn't answer. She got closer and said hello again. She pulled herself over to the man and got to the front of him and looked up at his face. His face was black. No eyes. She touched him and he was as hard as wood. She pushed him out of the chair and he toppled over, leaving his lower half still in the chair. She pushed this off as well. A patch of his leathered flesh remained stuck to the seat. As she pulled herself up to the chair she imagined the circumstances of his death. She sat on the chair and looked at her broken legs and the bones sticking up out of the skin at the shin. She could not feel that yet. But she knew it would not be long before she would not only feel it but would not be able to imagine ever not feeling it. She unzipped the bag and took Little Josefina out and placed her on the ground behind her and facing away saying, —Don't look, girl. She began taking medical equipment out of the bag—gauze, hypodermics, various bottles of pills and liquid, bandages, finger splints, needle and thread. She shook a Visa Pharmaceutical Company Antibiotic tablet out of a vial into her hand and swallowed it and injected herself with Visa Pharmaceutical Company Local Anesthetic then with the needle and thread sewed up her open flesh. She yanked out the metal shard from her side, screaming, no one hearing, stanched the heavy bleeding that followed, sewed that gash shut too. She wrapped her left hand in a bandage. It was now as big as her head.

When she was done she sat there in the chair staring at a spot on the wall illuminated by her miner's light gathering the will to drag herself to a hospital to set the dual comminuted compound fractures of her fibula and tibia knowing the gruesome pain that she did not now feel but could see moving her way like a hurricane. She wondered why she was doing this. To what end was she struggling? The eradication of evil so that it might be replaced by the prevalence of good? It was insane. She was alone in the world. Others accepted it for what it was and changed accordingly whereas she upheld an ideal and endeavored and suffered to protect it. Years and years of striving and nothing gained but wounds. No mending to her heartbreak. Others did the best they could then called it a day and crawled back inward and distracted themselves with simple pleasures content to let the evil fester so long as it did so somewhere they could not see it. This wasn't enough for her. She knew she was destined for something greater. She had no simple pleasures. There was right and there was wrong. This fact was inside her. These bones were this fact, poking out from her white and naked and broken. There was the world and there was Josefina Hernandez. She could rejoin it but she'd rather have the hurricane that was now almost here. She could almost hear it approaching. She'd rather have the satisfaction of hunting down the evil and murdering them one by one, crawling after them on her belly with both legs broken if that was how she had to do it. There was right and there was wrong. There was good and there was evil. NoVA was a land of compromise. And compromise was weakness. Compromise was that which robbed her of her son. She was not weak, she was strong. And she was right. She did not waver in this conviction.

I am the good, you are the ghastly.

You can take my child but not my soul, my joy but not my righteousness.

You have power. I have truth.

There is nothing more I need.

PROTECTION

After that, he moved to a new condo on the other side of Reston. One day while standing behind the counter watching a man about his age and build browsing the aisles of the Liquor Store with a smarmy grin on his face—not giving much commitment to his pretense, hardly even taking his eyes off Junior as he walked up and down the rows, making no effort to conceal the grin—it occurred to Junior what to do regarding Orlando Trieste. It had been months since he had even thought about him. But now here the answer was, delivered to him like a baby birthed whole, clean, and full-grown, set down on the counter wrapped in a blanket.

Now, as he rang up the man's bottle of Visa Liquor Company Fruit Liqueur, the man standing there on the other side of the counter with his hands in his pockets jingling his keys and loose change kind of leaned back on his heels with his feet set wide and body open to Junior as though about to pull out the linings of his pockets as though to prove his innocence of some sort of theft, the pink tip of a tongue sticking out between his teeth because he was still grinning that leering, sordid, taunting smirk, and standing upright so as to seem to peer down onto Junior even though he himself was the shorter man, Junior decided that the thing to do with Orlando Trieste was to kill Orlando Trieste and become Orlando Trieste. He'd kill him and sometime later approach the Visa FBI and offer his services as informant, knowing they'd now be in need of one. They would not know for sure that he was dead, as no body would be found, making it unclear whether he had in fact been killed as could be expected of an informant or was a coward who ran off with his own small life leaving behind his wife and children. He'd get him to one of Fernando's houses under a

160

pretense, tie him to a chair, and strangle him to death with a toaster cord. Bring the body to the Visa Funeral Home he bought late last year, stuff it into the casket of a client scheduled for cremation.

The man was now rocking on the heels of his shiny black shoes trying to peer down onto him with his tongue in his cheek as though cleaning his teeth with it, grinning like a man about to receive the worrisome sexual favor he'd paid for. —Heard Banks are exploding out in Reston, he said. Junior handed him his change. Didn't answer. The toothpick turning and bobbing in the corner of his mouth. He turned his head and spat. The man dropped the change into his pocket. —Know what? Know what we're going to do?

—...

—Nail you to the smucking wall.

—You wouldn't do that.

—No?

—You'd never pay full price for your Fruit Liqueur.

The man's grin disappeared. He snatched the bottle off the counter. —It's for my wife. He turned, headed out.

He could already see it. Trieste's life running out of his eyes. There would be no sound but the stomping of his feet on the concrete floor. Maybe the squeaking of the chair as he seized and fought against his own death. He could hear this sound like he could see the eyes. The sound, the apparition of the walls coming down and the sun coming up on a blue sky springtime valley, the world endless edge to edge, gravity disappearing, the feeling of unlimited possibility. Greatness. Empire. At last.

The man stopped at the door. He pounded the wall beside it with his fist. —Gonna nail you to this.

Junior watched him go, said nothing.

The next week Orlando Trieste went missing. He was never found. His wife and daughters changed their names and disappeared.

Junior approached the authorities. He told them, —My perspective is fresher than any other informants you have right now, as I am an outsider and lone wolf, unassociated with any of the gangs, Irish or otherwise. I have worked for the Italians in the past in the capacity of enforcer and collector. I am friendly with the

Italians. And they are friendly toward me. Because though I am Irish I am unaffiliated and have done good work for them.

They said, —What exactly are you offering us?

—The Italians.

His handler was Esteban "Dickey" Salazar. He was raised in the same Visa Housing Project as Junior Alvarez, one story up from him. A respectable man of humble origins who had great virtue and self-restraint but was held captive by the demands of his body which craved at all times and to an intense degree the pleasures of food and alcohol and flesh. He was bent on decimating the Italians. Junior knew this. Junior met him for the first time for lunch at Restaurant. He watched in fascination and disgust as Dickey when the food came stopped talking in midsentence and single-mindedly set forth consuming his hamburger as though he hadn't eaten for days. He did not even pause to wipe the grease from his chin. Juice dripped off his fingers down his wrists and forearms. He lifted his face from the thing clutched between his hands only long enough to chew and swallow at times when his mouth reached full capacity. He seemed irritated at even this short interruption. When he was done—everything on the plate consumed—he collapsed back in his chair in a cross-eyed euphoria and sighed, hands on his belly. Junior was wearing a wig and sunglasses, his hand on his ice water. It was the only thing he ordered and he had not taken one sip of it. After a few moments Dickey's euphoria seemed to dissipate. His eyes cleared. He sat up, called the waitress over for another Backyard, his third, ogled her, then turned his attention to Junior. In his eyes now something completely different. Junior recognized it but was unsure from where. It was alarming, almost frightening even to him. It was in Dickey's voice too when he spoke, the same thing, whatever it was, wherever it was from. But mostly it was the eyes that held it. It neither attracted nor repelled him. Rather it was as though the two met at a stalemate halfway across the table, suspended over it like two hawks colliding in midflight, their talons lanced through each other's ribs, beating their wings over the course of the small moment before beginning their joint descent, each unable to fly while bearing the weight of the other.

Then he realized where he'd seen it before, whatever it was in Dickey's eyes: the mirror.

It was the man's will.

Dickey kept him solvent. When his name came up on indictments, Dickey had it cut out. When Junior was suspected of murder, Dickey convinced his colleagues that the victim had settled his debts with Junior before his death and so Junior could be ruled out as a suspect. He tipped Junior about stings and bugs in order to keep him on the streets and continue providing him information on the Italians.

When Dickey wrecked his service vehicle while driving drunk on duty he brought it to Junior's Garage where it was fixed free of charge. Junior beat to death with a tire iron a low-level drug dealer who had killed one of Dickey's undercover colleagues in a botched sting.

Much of the information Junior provided about the Italians he made up on the spot.

He also told Dickey where weapons and drug dealers kept their storehouses. These weren't Italians but Irish. Centreville Irish. Then after the resultant raid Junior would arrive to tell them he heard about the raid and was sorry but could make sure they'd be warned in advance about such things in the future if they paid him for the service. He sold similar protection to anybody doing illegal business in NoVA. If they denied his offer he either brutalized them and chased them out of town and took over their business or he killed them and took over their business or he arranged their imprisonment by providing evidence on them to Dickey and took over their business. Protected loan sharks, pimps, bookmakers, legitimate business owners, drug ships in the Chesapeake Bay, weapons shipments heading to Ireland to arm the Second Irish Republican Army, a Lithiite force in bloody conflict with the Separatists over discrepant interpretations of the Rules and Regulations, weapons that were often used in acts of terrorism on Separatist civilians and children. Soon it seemed that everyone doing business illegal or otherwise not just in Centreville but in much of NoVA was under his thumb, working for him or paying him for something or another. He could not even keep track of who owed him what. He trusted their fear to keep them honest.

He gave Dickey gifts. Crates of Expensive Red Wine Company. Cases of Expensive Beer Company. Bottles of Expensive Scotch Distillery. Arranged free dinners for him and his wife at Expensive Restaurant locations all over the state. Put him in touch with prostitutes and other attractive, willing young women.

The money coming in was a lie. It was too much to believe in. He stashed it away in safe deposit boxes and around town in public places where if found it could not be traced to him. He took Maria on trips throughout the world where he hid quantities of cash in safe deposit boxes, Visa Self-Storage units, and other more creative locations: in the ceiling panels of Clothing Store dressing rooms, under home plate on high school baseball fields, atop caskets in recently interred graves. He knew from his study of history that one day he would have to rely on these hoardings and he was planning for that day. He thought of it as an alternative to a Visa Bank Retirement Plan. Investing in an invisible, secret infrastructure that one day he would have to call upon and rely on for the rest of his life which, as far as he knew, could be forever. Because what evidence was there against his living forever? What proof did he have that he would ever die?

He began to find himself anxious and uncomfortable at times. He woke up almost every night at least once, drenched in sweat, screaming. He had taken to keeping a towel on his nightstand next to his gun and sleeping without any clothes on because he got tired of changing into dry underwear and T-shirts in the dark half-asleep.

He was summoned to Uncle Antonio. He was to show up at one of his Fast Food Restaurants. To be killed. By his father.

The week before, he had taken control of all gambling in Northern Virginia. He'd done this in a methodical and gruesome sudden spree of murder in which thirteen high-powered bookmakers who had survived the gang wars were shot to death. One was massacred at his son's sixth birthday party at Visa Park #12 in front of thirty-seven friends and family. Cake and flittering scraps of shredded peenyata everywhere. The man's riddled body slumped sunward atop the picnic table that was stacked with blood-soaked gifts. No one came forward as a witness. Not even the man's wife.

Another was kidnapped in the parking lot of Grocery Store and never seen or heard from again. No one saw anything.

He now owned gambling. And Uncle Antonio would kill him for that.

He told Dickey everything he knew about Uncle Antonio. He verified rumors, revealed names. Agreed to wear a wire to the meeting at Uncle Antonio's at which he would be killed.

At the meeting, as Uncle Antonio held a gun to his head, agents burst in and saved Junior's life, hauled Uncle Antonio off, shooting to death one of his bodyguards who opened fire on them.

Uncle Antonio was charged with conspiracy, tax evasion, and, in time, dozens of other felonies including seven counts of murder. Bail was denied. Junior's information and the evidence gathered on the wire Junior wore—including Uncle Antonio near tears holding the gun to Junior's head asking Junior how he could have done this to him when he had invested so much in him, treated him like his own son for such a long time—were key to the prosecution's case that Uncle Antonio was a lifelong honcho of organized crime and needed to be locked away from society for life. Which is more or less what happened. He spent the next three decades in jail, released in a controversial act of compassion when he was in his nineties and infected with late-stage Visa Virus, given two months to live.

After less than a week of freedom, he was arrested in Centreville for trying to rob a Bank branch with a butter knife. His underwear soiled. Until the story broke in the media—a minor mention on *Visa Times*—neither the teller, the other customers, nor the police who arrested him recognized him.

VICTORY

In the morning the bodies were pushed off the pavement by the street sweepers. Hoses sprayed the blood into the gutters where it turned pink and mixed with the trash and trickled down into the drains to be washed out to sea, its pinkness gone. Standing above the heap of dead or jailed was a bland man of middle age who looked like a high school English teacher. English was an Information Revolution Era language. The man's name was Junior Alvarez. He stood behind the counter of his Liquor Store, toothpick in his mouth, looking out the window one slow winter afternoon in August. The snow falling hard from a deep gray endless sky. His tongue and jaw worked in ponderance. Toothpick bobbing and turning. He could feel the cold emanating off the glass. The store was empty. Outside it was just cold. The snow gathered around the windowpane. Its coldness insulated the store from all the sounds of the city.

And he realized something: He had done it. He'd become a prestigious man of power. He thought back over the last few years. It was like if it all were to be done over and over for all eternity, it would turn out like this only once. One time out of infinity. Here he was, having done what he had set out against all the laws of the universe to do. He was free. Exiled. He answered to no one now. He entered through the front door. Or the back door. Or whatever door he chose, it being up to him, any door being his door after all either way.

But he did not feel like he expected to. He still felt like he'd felt when he was a maintenance man. Like he hadn't done anything. Like he'd accomplished nothing at all.

After Dinner

After dinner they drove home through the city along Braddock Road. Maria looked at Junior who was glancing up at the rearview mirror. She turned in her seat to look out the rear window. Junior said, —Don't look.

Maria turned back around, facing forward. —I don't think they're following us.

—Correct. They're following *me*.

—They're just somebody driving in their car.

—No, they've been following me since we left the restaurant.

—Who do you think it is? Who'd be following us?

—Visa DEA.

—No.

—It's Visa DEA. They don't know how obvious they're making it either.

—What would they want to follow you for? You're not a drug dealer. You keep the drug dealers out. You do what they can't do or choose not to do. Go follow one of those smucking creeps bringing all that shit into our neighborhoods. Go follow one of those smucking creep drug dealers.

—Maria, don't talk about this sort of thing in the car, please. Bugs.

—Why do they think you're dealing drugs? You're not, right?

—Of course not.

This was not true. He kept the drug dealers out of Centreville via a mystique of grotesque savagery under a public pretense of moral righteousness but really it was not to protect the children and the city but to protect his own enterprise. He used to just shake down drug dealers but now was in control of distribution himself and thus secretly behind every illicit nonprescription Stimulant and Painkiller transaction in Centreville.

—Anyway it's too dark. It just looks like a car. I don't think they're following us.

—You can tell because of the headlights. See the headlights? Those are Visa Federal Government DEA cocksucking headlights.

—Well so what. You're not a drug dealer. We're not doing anything. We're driving home from dinner. A husband and wife.

They drove on in silence, Junior eyeing the rearview mirror. At a red light near Visa City Hall he adjusted it. He adjusted the side mirrors. He watched the Visa DEA agents following him as he drove.

Without warning he did first one very sharp U-turn then another, traffic blaring and skidding on all sides, Maria grabbing the handle above the door, tires squealing, Maria by instinct reaching her arm out in front of Junior to hold him back in his seat. They were behind the DEA car now, following it, the roles reversed. Maria could see the agitated silhouettes in the passenger seat turning around to look back at them, speaking into a radio or a phone. Junior followed the car down some side streets, circled a block four times, swerving through narrow alleys, running stop signs and traffic lights, holding on as the DEA car tried to shake them. Junior said as he just avoided running over a small boy on a bike, —Come on, you smuckers. Let's go, you smuckers. Somehow they came out on Visa Route 50 and the black car peeled off a ramp toward the Visa Angelina Jolie Beltway and Junior let them go. The driver flipped them the bird out the window. Junior waved at them. Maria let go of the handle above her door and watched the DEA car disappear. Junior made another U-turn, this one slow, calm. They headed home.

THE SON

The old man stood there in the middle of the store with his hands in the pockets of his faded old red parka, beard, blue eyes, a jovial flush to his cheeks, one blue eye half-closed, the other blue eye drifting off to look in a different direction, a warm smile on his face.

—Hi, Junior, it's me. Your father.

Junior stood there, looking back at him saying nothing. He turned his head, removed the toothpick from his mouth, and spat on the floor.

—Look at you. You look good, Junior. You've really done good for yourself. I always knew you would. Look at you. You look fantastic. Your own business. Making more money than Lithis. I always knew you'd make something of yourself. You and your brother. You boys got this town wrapped around your fingers. That's my boys. The Alvarez boys. Come here.

The old man stepped forward with his arms open but Junior put his hand out against his chest to stop him.

—You're not my father.

—I am.

—No, you're a drunk bum. And I don't know any drunk bums.

The old man stared at him. —Your own father who gave you his hardworking smart genes comes in here starving and freezing after so many years and you're going to deny him?

The door of the stockroom swung open and Fernando and Maria came through it. They halted behind Junior, and Fernando, seeing who it was who was standing there, blurted out, —Oh damn. It's his damn father.

The old man said, —See, Junior? Even they say it is.

169

Maria said, —Junior, you didn't tell me your father—

—He's not. This is just a drunk bum coming in here looking for money like every other one in Centreville.

—I'm not drunk.

—I can smell you from here. Liquor and vomit. Why don't you work for a living like the rest of us?

Fernando said, —I don't damn smell anything.

—Don't you have something to do? Junior said to him.

—I don't smell anything either, Maria said.

The old man turned to her and said, —His own flesh-and-blood father comes in off the street hasn't eaten for two days and he won't even give him just a little something to get some dinner for himself. That's all. His own father who gave him the genes to become so successful.

Junior didn't say anything, just stepped toward the old man, took him by the collar. He shoved him against the wall knocking over a rack of Red Wine Companies. The old man was so small and weak he was like a woman but he didn't blink or look away from Junior, his expression didn't change as Junior said inches from the old man's face smelling the old man's sweet alcoholic vomit breath, cigarette smoke stained in his parka, spit flying into the old man's face but the old man still not blinking his bloodshot eyes, —I don't know you, you drunk, you bum clown.

The old man just said quietly so only Junior could hear, —I never imagined you'd become such a highfalutin ungrateful son of a bitch.

Junior pushed the old man through the door and dragged him out onto the sidewalk. He was so limp and unresisting that it was like dragging an unconscious body. Gave him a shove. The old man stumbled a few steps. Junior chased after him, gave him a hard kick in the rear end, and took the Beepollen Shop cup with change in it from another bum standing nearby and threw it at the old man. Coins scattering everywhere catching the winter sun, the blue sky with no clouds, snow in gray chunks along the base of the street. A voice, Junior's, shouting, —Here's some money, you smucking clown! Go get something to eat, you smucking clown! Go feed yourself! Go eat! Go drink is more like it. Go drink yourself to death! He picked up a couple coins and pried open the man's mouth, shoved them in, held his jaw shut. The old man squealed and cried and twisted trying to get free but Junior held it tight. —Eat these, you drunk jackoff! Slapped his face. —Is this highfalutin enough for you? Slapped him again. —Is that? You no-good piece of shit! Go get hit by a bus! He shoved him. The old man staggered off and regurgitated the coins from his mouth into his hand, gagging and hacking. The coins were covered in thick spit. He was now squatting down and picking the rest up off the sidewalk. The other bum was heading over there to get his money back but Junior couldn't help himself and was feeling very good so he ran over there pushing the other bum out of the way and kicked at the old man's hands as he grabbed for the coins, stomping on his fingers, twisting his heel into the old man's grimy hands with uncut brown nails. The old man squealing from the pain. —Oink oink, you smucking pig! Junior yelled happily. —This is from a highfalutin lace-curtain mothersmucker, you smucking pig-clown shit-smelling piece of shit! He kicked the old man in the face. The old man cried out. Blood all over his nose and mouth. He kicked the old man in the ribs, in the chest, in the arms, knocked the old man's feet out from under him as he tried to get up, kicked him again in the ribs. Dull thuds and soon no more crying out. —Oink oink oink! Junior was yelling with glee now over and over. The old man was choking, trying to breathe. He rolled over and climbed onto all fours, choking, spitting. Junior pulled the man's pants down exposing his ass, not knowing why, just felt like it. Kicked it. He tore the old man's smoky filthy red parka off him and threw it into the street. The old man was sobbing and Junior was laughing and making oink oink noises. He spat on him and went inside and got his coat and left saying nothing except pointing at the broken bottles of Red Wine Company on the floor and saying clean it up. Nobody was looking at Junior or at one another. Everybody was looking at the floor, ashamed of themselves.

THE DAUGHTER

Rosana sat with her daddy in a booth at Ice Cream Shop. She was thirteen. Her ice cream was pink and tasted good. Her father watched her. He wasn't her real father. Just her mom's boyfriend. But he'd been her mom's boyfriend ever since she was little and she secretly called him her father in her mind. Her daddy. He had the look of a happy father now across the table watching her eat her ice cream, saying no thank you when she offered him some. She was glad to make him happy. Because she was happy too. Again. She used to be happy all the time. Even when she and her mom and sisters were poor and moving all the time. But ever since she turned thirteen things had changed. Her mother had become a liability to her. And she had become an alien to her mother. And it was like nothing she ever said to her mother or to anybody at all was heard. And she could never get comfortable: When she walked she felt like she was walking wrong, when she sat she felt like she was sitting in a way that was funny to other people. But right now, with her father, she was comfortable and felt like she was doing everything right and no one was laughing at her. She wanted to sit here with her father for the rest of her life and let him watch her with a happy look as she ate pink ice cream.

He leaned toward her, his elbows on the table, and said in a low quiet voice, —Rosana, I have something to talk to you about. It's a secret. Just between you and me. Can you keep a secret if I tell you one? She was thrilled by the way his voice was. She nodded, trying not to show it for some reason even though she wanted him to see it. —I'm prepared to remake you in my image. Would you like that? She just shrugged, licking the melting ice cream running down the side of the cone into the spaces between her fingers though inside she felt so happy about being let in on a secret with her father. —Would you like that, Rosie? If I were to remake you in my image?

She thought about it not understanding what he was saying exactly. She licked the spaces between her fingers and licked the side of the cone and licked pink ice cream off her upper lip. Maybe she looked stupid the way she did it and people were laughing at her but she didn't care. Because of the way her father's voice was. She nodded.

—I see greatness in you, Rosie. I do. You either have it or you don't. And you have it. Not everybody has it. It wouldn't make sense if they did, would it? A lot of people have the potential to have it. But not everybody wants to take it out and use it. These people are not brave enough to allow themselves to be great. Because it is too lonely and too frightening for them. Too hard. So they would rather be someone who does whatever the great people want them to do. That is how the world is designed, Rosie. This is nature. And it is very important for you to remember this all your life. There are the few great men and women and then there are the rabble. Do you know what rabble is? It means the mass of humanity, all slaving away and crawling all over each other for food and shelter and anything else an animal needs so it can go on being an animal. The great people make the decisions and run the show and enjoy their lives the most. The rabble just do their shitwork. So as to— You listening to me?

Rosana nodded, trying to look as serious as he looked.

—So as to facilitate their greatness. Of course no one can tell the rabble that, for obvious reasons. So we tell them things like: Family Is What's Most Important. Money Can't Buy Happiness. Blah blah blah. All those Visa Slogans. To make them feel good about being rabble. To ease their self-doubts. And soothe their rancor, their hatred of greatness. Do you know about the devil? A long time ago, there were people called Christians. They believed there was something called a devil who made them do evil things. Because he hated goodness. The rabble hate greatness for the same reason the devil hated goodness: because they know they will never have it. If you have greatness within you and you are not brave enough to take it out and use it, it just dies. Like a plant if you don't give it water and sunlight. And someone else who is brave enough and willful enough comes along and what do they do? They co-opt you. And now you're rabble. You work to facilitate their life. That's the only point of your life. And they make you believe what you need to. It's Not Whether You Win or Lose But How You Play the Game. That's something losers need to be told now and again because the losers will always outnumber the winners. And they feed off you. Like you're an animal or a beast or a slave or just a goddamn, I don't know, a goddamn screwdriver to them. The challenge of greatness is believing in your greatness, Rosie. That's the biggest and hardest part. When you walk into a room you must walk into a room as a great man, not as a normal man. That way everybody will know which one of the two you are. When eating ice cream you must believe, you must *know,* that it is a great man who is eating this ice cream. Humans are intuitive, Rosana. They sense things like this and react accordingly. It's in our nature. We're dogs. Do you know what dogs were? It doesn't matter. You have so much light within you, Rosie. I can see it bursting out of you. It's like you have a candle inside you and the light is shining out of your eyes, your ears, your nose, your mouth. I am offering to help you nourish that potential so that one day you can work alongside me and one day inherit the earth. Not having any sons or children of my own. Would you like that? Would you be honored by that? Pulling the strings? Calling shots that affect the lives of millions? Do you think, Rosie, that you can persevere and work hard and believe enough to become worthy of being my colleague and one day my successor? Do you believe that you can, Rosie? Do you *know* that? You have to *know* it, Rosie. You have to *know* it like you know your name is Rosana.

Rosana was confused by what he was saying and frightened by his intensity. She stared at her pink ice cream unable to look up at him, mad at herself because her face was red because she did not understand what he was saying and was afraid he could see this.

—Rosie? Do you know it like you know your name is Rosana?

Knowing what he wanted her to do if not what he was saying she nodded and said yes. But her father didn't acknowledge her response. She at last was able to peek up at him and found him staring off over her shoulder at something very far away, his chin in his hand, his blue eyes clear and watery and their pupils tiny, unfocused, a strange sad smile on his face. Like his body was here but the rest of him was on another planet.

She was lying awake in her bed in her bedroom that night. Her own bedroom in her own house as opposed to the bedroom in Junior's condo which she had to share with her brothers and sisters when they stayed there sometimes. She lay facedown, still thinking about the ice cream earlier that day and the exciting loving inclusive secrecy in her father's voice and she was no longer confused and ashamed for not understanding but happy and excited because she could imagine that maybe everything was good and not confusing and that Junior loved her enough to want to marry her mom finally. Meaning Rosana would be allowed to call her father her father out loud and always feel like what she was saying was heard and like she was walking correctly and sitting in a way that was not funny to other people. She heard footsteps creaking down the hallway and stopping outside her door then the door opening slowly a bar of light from the hall spilling in onto her face. Rosana sat up in bed wincing at the light. She started to speak but the figure that came into the room—a shadow, no one she knew or had ever met before—seemed to silence her. It seemed to take all the air out of her and replace it with silence. It closed the door and it was again pitch-dark and quiet and she could hear the shadow breathing in her silence, she could hear the shadow's heart beating in her silence, she could hear the shadow whisper in her silence, —Rosana . . . And coming to the bed and sitting down on the bed and the bed creaking and sagging in her silence. —How do you know my name? she said. —Shhhh. Rosana, you have to go to sleep, it's past your bedtime. And Rosana doing what the shadow said, lying down on her tummy and clenching her fists, so wet and hot and stiff, and trying to sleep, the shadow breathing loudly through its nose in her silence and stroking her back and head with its heavy thick hand and she could hear the shadow's heartbeat in her silence and feel the heartbeat through the fingers now going down her back and touching the elastic waistband of her pajamas and Rosana could feel cold air on her and her brain SURGING. Rosana holding her breath because the silence had to be kept. She tried to be silent and go to sleep as the heartbeat fingers in her silence were wet like hers but cold and trembling instead of hot and stiff. She tried to sleep as the shadow whispered, —Rosana . . . You are Rosana. . . . She heard breath close to her ear and she felt herself withering and she tried to sleep in her silence but saw out of the corner of her open eyes the shadow stand but stay bent whispering so loudly that it was like powerful wind, —Rosana . . . Rosana . . . Shhhhh . . .

She remembers on the nightstand was her froggy lamp that she still has and tonight, this night, years later too high on Painkiller in some apartment in New York, she remembers the smell of freshly brushed teeth, and that is all, that is it, that is when after such a long time of disobeying she finally obeys the winds in her silence and closes her eyes and feels herself give in to something almighty and this is when she stops remembering everything forever.

THE FRIEND

Fernando cursing and pacing the condo pounding his fist into his palm breathing heavily, his face red, the dishes in Junior's kitchen cabinets rattling Fernando was stomping so hard. —Damn bitch! Damn bitch! Junior watched him, smiling, shaking his head, standing in the kitchen. His own face still hot and red after that morning's intense advanced-stage total body workout which he had been in the middle of when Fernando showed up in the midst of a meltdown. Junior had entered a new phase of his life: health fanaticism. He obsessed over his diet, weighed himself multiple times a day, spent hundreds of thousands of dollars on equipment and products, had begun going every three months for kidney dialysis in order to clean his blood. Junior opened a can of Visa Food Company Tuna Fish, one of three he had been eating a day, eating nothing but this and Orange Juice for the last three and a half weeks after reading about the scientifically supported benefits of such a diet in *Visa Diet and Exercise Book #357–987–354.*

The reason Fernando was melting down was because he had just discovered what everyone but he had known for the better part of a decade: that Fernando's wife, the mother of his children, a third-grade teacher, a remarkably attractive woman with a host of self-destructive psychological issues, was a sex addict and compulsive liar who was having an affair with the physical education teacher at the school where she taught, Visa High Scores Elementary School–Haymarket. This morning one of the enforcers Fernando every now and then had follow her around and report back to him just in case something like this were to happen had come to Fernando with very pornographic video footage he had taken last night of Fernando's wife and her colleague on the colleague's desk surrounded by physical education equipment, at one point utilizing a jump rope in such a way that made it seem like it should be illegal to allow children to play with jump ropes.

—Junior, I want you and me to sit down this afternoon and discuss a method of what we need to damn do about this, violence-wise.

Junior laughed and shook his head as he ate a forkload of Tuna, swallowed and wiped his face with the towel, strapped his automated blood pressure monitor to his arm, and said as it inflated, —I'm sorry. I understand it hurts.

—Junior, did you damn know? Damn tell me the truth.

—Everybody knew.

Fernando made a shrieking noise as he pulled at his hair with his fists.

—It's humiliating, isn't it? But listen. Your humiliation is absolutely understandable in this situation. Your anxiety and humiliation are a natural response. Because, Fernando, you have to acknowledge the facts here: This is not an isolated incident. Giselle is scum of the earth. There have been lots of men. Lots. You have to acknowledge that. She makes a vow to you and takes your money and lives in your home as your wife and does this to you? You have to be tough and be honest with yourself, Fernando. From what you've told me in the past, she's into perverted things sexually. So with this in mind, Fernando, you have to be honest with yourself and let yourself see something. You have to let yourself see that this guy? This one particular guy of many, many, many? He most likely smucked Giselle in her ass, Fernando. Okay? Your wife. Smucked your wife in her ass. Smucked your children's mother in her ass. To understand the truth of this situation in its entirety, you need to let yourself understand that. Not just intellectually but emotionally too.

Fernando was bent over at the waist making a deranged guttural noise.

Junior was quiet, eating Tuna, drinking Orange Juice, watching him. —Stay with that. Stay with that emotion you're feeling. Fernando stayed doubled over and anguished, still making the strange noises. It was not apparent whether or not he was listening. Junior put the Tuna down and went over, put his hand on his back, and leaned down toward his face. —It hurts me to watch someone I love like a brother have something like this happen to him. You loved Giselle more than anything. You gave her the world. She made a vow to you. And the whole time you were honoring that vow she, well, she most certainly was not.

Fernando stood upright and collapsed onto the couch now, his face in his hands, his hair sticking up from where he had been pulling on it. Saying over and over, —That damn bitch. That smucking damn bitch.

Junior sat beside him, put his arm around his shoulders. —Correct. She is. So you can't blame her for doing what a bitch does. It's her nature. It's not her fault. It's your fault.

At this, Fernando froze and stared straight ahead. His eyes were glazed and unblinking. —It's my damn fault, he repeated. He said it like it had occurred to him not from Junior saying it but out of the torment of his own anguish. —It's my own damn fault. I should've been damn watching her closer. I shouldn't have let her have that damn job. She's a mother and she's supposed to keep my house and raise my damn children. She doesn't need no damn job. I can't damn believe it. I have to damn kill her. Yeah. And him damn too. And maybe myself and my damn kids too. I have to maybe damn kill everyone. As many as I damn can before they stop me.

—Now now now. Knock that off. You know who responds to this sort of situation like that? A loser. Don't be a loser. Be a winner.

—I'm killing everyone and my damn self.

—No, you aren't. Fernando, what Giselle did to you is an evil, evil thing. But think about it: You kill everyone and yourself, the final image we all have of you is as the poor piece of shit who let the world get the better of him. Twice. The first time was when he was too stupid to know his wife was running around for ten years smucking anything that moved. The second time when he reacted in this way you're suggesting you might act. You have to keep a cool head. Now's the time to regain control for once. What this should teach you is that you need to make changes in your life and in your general psychological outlook.

In Fernando's eyes the frenzy seemed to begin to alleviate.

—A man doesn't freak out and kill everyone. That's for kids.

And anyway I can't have it. It'd be anarchy if everyone did that. And you know what? You'll be dead or in jail and everyone here will be laughing at you more than they already are. They already have been for years and years. It's a critical time for you right now. Now's the time you need to show everyone that you're still a man.

Fernando sniffed and said, —Okay so what do I damn do then? I mean what do I damn do?

—Well, Fernando. I think there's really only one thing to do.

—Damn what.

—Turn the tables on her.

—Damn how? What do you damn mean? Like, damn specifically.

—Okay. This is going to be a sensitive thing for me to broach. So you have to understand it's not to insult you but to help you.

—Of damn course, Junior.

—It's going to sound pretty out there at first, Fernando. But you have to keep in mind who it's coming from. And you have to understand that it's the only way out of this mess and it's the only option you have at this point if you want to save face. Do you want to save face?

—Damn yeah.

—Do you want others to perceive you as a man and not a boy?

—Damn yes.

—Do you want to be someone people respect? Especially your children?

—Damn yes.

—Do you want to show her and everyone else that you're the one who's in charge?

—Damn yes.

—Because women have no use for any other kind of man. You understand that, don't you?

—Damn yes.

—Do you really though?

—Damn yes.

—I don't know, I'm not so sure you do.

—I damn do, Junior. I damn do.

—Do you want to know what you do here?

—Damn yes. Damn tell me.

—Okay. She wants to act like a whore, you treat her like one. Fernando did not understand. —You make some dough off her. Only thing a whore's good for.

—. . .

—What's going to happen next is this: She's going to come to you begging for forgiveness. She'll be crying, saying how she loves you and how sorry she is. She'll say she's going to seek professional treatment for her issues and blah blah blah. She'll be looking up at you with those beautiful vulnerable eyes of hers. And it's going to be tempting to forgive her. Your heart will be aching. You'll be thinking how beautiful she is, remembering the best times you've had together, wonder if you'll find anyone like her again. But what you need to do when you start feeling this way is think about her opening her mouth—that same mouth with which she's saying all this—so some piece of shit can stick his hard cock in it. How does that feel to think about? Stay with that feeling. Sit with it. Embrace it. Explore it. The same mouth, those same lips she made the eternal vow of marriage to you with, wrapped around some piece of shit's cock. That same tongue licking it. The same hand that wears your ring jerking on it. Think about her coming home afterward and kissing you with that mouth and kissing your children with that mouth. Maybe there's a little semen still in it when she does. Maybe there's some in her when she comes home from smucking him. Sleeping in your bed next to you while that smucking gym teacher's semen leaks out of her ass, onto your bed, your sheets. Her ass sore from him smucking it. Think about that. Concentrate on how that makes you feel. See her sneaking in after she gets home from smucking him and going into the bathroom, looking at herself in the mirror after she cleans herself up, laughing to herself for getting away with it, laughing at you for being too naïve to suspect anything. *Laughing*. And when you think about that and feel that emotion, you grab her by the back of the neck like I'm grabbing you right now but real hard, as hard as you can in order to put the fear of Lithis into her, to make her know without an inkling of doubt that you're a man, that who she has betrayed is a man. And you force her onto her knees. And you stand above her so her face is eye level with your crotch. And you shove her face into your crotch so she feels your big old dick against her face—and I've seen it, Fernando, and I'm telling you, it's a great big massive one you got there—and you tell her you're in charge and you make the decisions.

Fernando was quiet, listening.

—Okay. Listen. Tell you what. As your friend, as your brother who grew up with you and who in this time of need when it seems like you can't trust anyone is the only one you can trust? If it makes it easier? Make it me. Better your brother than some asshole, right? And you know me. You know me. You know I don't get any pleasure out of it. You know I can hardly stand it. But I'd do it for you, Fernando. Listen, everywhere south of Route 50? I'll give you the reins on Stimulant. That's tremendous, Fernando. A tremendous territory. And it's all yours. That's my payment. You have to take payment. That's my payment. I'm willing to do this for you, brother. To help my brother in his time of hurt. Because that's what brothers do for one another. And because I love you, brother.

—I damn love you too, Junior.

—Are you my brother, Fernando? Are we brothers?

—We're brothers, Junior, but I don't damn know. You're damn sure this is the right thing to do?

—Absolutely. One hundred percent. Call her over. The sooner we get it over with, the better. Where's the phone? I'll have you run out before she gets here and pick up some Stimulant from the warehouse. You know she can't say no to that junk and you told me it makes her wild and crazy, right? Here's the phone. Tell her you're ready to talk to her about what happened and want to discuss the children and that my place is a good neutral location to do that. Tell her you're only comfortable with a neutral location. Don't take no for answer.

—It's damn ringing.

—I want you to be a man, Fernando. I want you to show control. I want you to have power. I want you to be here for it too. It'll be therapeutic for you.

A couple hours later when it was noon and the day outside was yellow with cool breath tumbling through that hapless city and the sun had a hold on the browned sides of buses and brick snowbanks blackened by exhaust, two men were in the living room of a condo and a white blanket was spread out on the floor and a woman was nude on the blanket. Her hair fell down over her face. There were ashes still smoldering on the piece of foil on the coffee table. The room hazy with smoke wisps that themselves seemed like the elusive forms of ghostly beautiful women emerging then vanishing in the air among one another. Within her head was the fear of what she had been told while getting high. That if she did not do it, she would be divorced on the grounds of infidelity. If she did not do it, they would use their connections to arrange it that her children would be taken from her. One of them sat alone in a chair with his pants around his ankles watching while the other wore no clothes and was behind her, she murmuring nonsense names and phrases as though the voices of the smoke-women ghosts were jumping in and out of her in broken-up spats, fighting one another to be channeled by her, her eyes closed and opening only a little bit now and again as if not to look upon the man in the chair but only to reveal the flittering whites of her eyes to the same whiteness of the blanket so the two could see each other and know the other was white too. There was sweat and it was irrigated along the woman's spine and in the creases of all their knees and there were salty bodily scents too. The woman's skin was reddening first only in some places but then in other places, spreading so gently and slowly it was almost imperceptible. She said the name of the man in the chair who just stared at her with no expression while her eyes showed their fleeting whiteness to the blanket and the blanket showed its whiteness to her eyes. The man in the chair going up and down her with his own eyes which were not flittering or unblinking or white, watching her skin which soon was all red from her heels to the tip of her nose. Sometimes for brief moments of time he watched the other man, the man behind her, mere glances, as though trying to decide something or figure something out.

Making Pasta

Standing in his kitchen making pasta one night when there was a racket down in the lobby. Junior heard it through the bug he had down there, transmitted through the speakers installed in the walls and ceilings throughout his condo. Fighting, shouting, eventually a couple gunshots, then more shouting, then glass breaking. Heavy footsteps on the stairs. The woman who lives downstairs screaming, her deer barking, more shouting. The bugs he had in the stairwell picked this up. Junior glanced at his surveillance monitor showing the premises outside but there was nothing. He listened as whoever it was came running up the stairs closer and closer to his floor. He listened like it was the radio broadcasting the game in the background while he made dinner. He stirred the pasta and reached over to the underside of the spice rack and punched in the code on the keypad to disengage the security system and unlock the door, reached for the sawed-off double-barrel shotgun on the counter next to the Parmesan, one of six always kept within easy reach throughout the condo. Stood waiting at the stove holding the gun at his ribs as the door flew open and a big bearded man burst in with a large automatic pistol in each hand and he looked at Junior and raised the guns at which point the guy's head essentially just exploded all over the living room carpet, walls, and ceiling as if a small bomb had gone off inside it. The body dropped, dark arterial blood pumping out of the top of the neck where the head had been. Now it was silent but for the deer still barking downstairs and soft splattering of the final spurt of blood falling to the rug after it was pumped high into the air toward the ceiling. Junior put down the shotgun and strained the pasta in the sink and tasted the marinara, added a little thyme, stirred it, tasted it again. He then went over and peered down at the carcass. There was a sound as a chunk of face dripped off the ceiling. Gray cranial matter, parts of skull, and tufts of facial hair clumped together with blood creeping down the wall. Called Dickey. —Listen, please make sure no one responds to the many 911 calls no doubt currently being made in regard to this address at the moment. Understand? No no nothing happened, everyone's fine. False alarm. Just an overexcited Visa Chinese Food Restaurant deliveryman and then one of my guns went off while I was cleaning it. No big deal. Nothing here but a hole in my wall now that I have to patch up and some mediocre orange chicken.

He called Manny next and told him the same thing.

He dragged the carcass farther inside so he could close the door and reengaged the electrical locks and security system via another keypad located by the door beneath the ornate handcrafted key hook from Expensive Furniture Store that had the word WELCOME carved into it. Went back to the kitchen, put the pasta onto a plate, poured the marinara on it, filled the saucepan with warm water and squirted in some Citrus-Scented Dish Soap and left it in the sink. How did he make it all the way inside? Must have known where the cameras were. The doorman must have been in on it. Junior had him on the payroll. He was to let Junior know every time someone unrecognized set foot inside the lobby for any reason. Even Visa FedEx guys.

Someone had been paying the doorman more than he was.

He pulled a chair up beside the carcass, ate his pasta while staring at the carcass, considering it, slurping the long flat red-sauced noodles manufactured in the same NoVA Visa foundry that also produced Industrial Concrete Sealant and made mostly of thamine mononitrate, folic acid, and a dash of biogenetically engineered lab-grown wheat (since this is the upmarket, locally produced kind) through his lips, sauce all over his chin, oblivious to the similarity between the sauce and the deathful grue before him, thinking about how many people out there wanted him dead. There was no one in the entire state of Northern Virginia who would not benefit from his demise. But they did not know that. Only he knew that. That is one reason why they stayed so silent. Another was fear. And the herd instinct of man that propagated this fear and silence. That is what Junior knew was his genius and the key to his vitality.

Kill the doorman. Already happened, it sounds like. Well, that's what you get.

Thought about the Italians. It was probably the Italians. Late last year he'd lunched with them. Or what was left of them. A sad farcical parade of denial and stubborn clinging to the past in which they seemed to refuse to admit to themselves how much had changed and how much they were bleeding. It was like he'd found himself invited to the final Overeating Holiday of a tragic and dysfunctional family. He went under the pretense of cordiality, having done work for them in the past and being neutral in the gang war and the only Irishman they liked and trusted. But really he was there as a necessary tactic of self-preservation: Dickey's bosses were considering cutting Junior off as an informant. Dickey told Junior who did not totally believe him that it was due to the more often than not bogus nature of his information. But Dickey already had a strategy worked out. His colleagues at the Visa FBI were applying for a warrant to put a bug in the Chantilly Laundromat which served as the Italians' headquarters. To be granted the warrant they would need to show evidence that spoke to the benefits of a bug. If Junior could go to the Laundromat wearing a wire, have lunch, chitchat in a friendly, informal nature, and come back with something on the wire that was useful that Dickey could put on the list it would make it more difficult for Dickey's bosses to cut Junior off lest they risk losing the future admissibility of the bug in court.

At the lunch it was clear to Junior that the Italians wanted nothing more than to move in on him but had not so far because leadership kept either getting shot, arrested, or bludgeoned to death by someone using a baseball bat, they believed it was. And because they believed Junior's forces must be legion to have toppled Uncle Antonio. He must have every Irishman in Northern Virginia ready to kill for him, they believed. He must have allies of other ethnicities too. He sat there realizing this is what they believed. He fought a grin twitching on his face. He resisted the urge to reveal to them if only for the gratification of his ego which he never indulged and which thus ached for even his slightest stroke that he had done it all and continues to do it all alone, with the help of no one.

It became clear to him as he realized this is what they thought that he could in fact have *their* operations. They were sitting there before him packaged and ready for whenever he chose to take them. He could have them because of his greatest weapon, which as always was what they did not know: that he was solitary Alejandro el Grande, leader of a ragtag force, and they were the vast once-mighty-now-doomed Persians.

One of them mentioned offhand an upcoming initiation ceremony. Junior knew at that very moment that what was left of the Italians was done. Because he knew that he would get them to talk in greater detail about it and that the Visa Second American Federal Government would be there when it happened and would be watching and listening and recording it all and that now was the time for him to fulfill the next dictate of his will which was complete and iron control of the entirety of the Northern Virginia underworld.

Conquest. Imperialism. Empire.

And he was right. Over the following year the Italian leadership fell in a fantastic sudden montage of indictments and sentencings. They were replaced by a weak-willed and impatient new generation that exhibited none of the virtues or talent of their fathers.

And that was why it was the Italians. The Italians sent it, he thought. Like the bunch of blundering misguided orphaned children that they were.

It was true that often he wondered how long it would continue to hold up, all this elaborate psychological warfare, this house of cards he had built upon the quicksand foundation of others' failings and misunderstandings. The only thing keeping it all together was the silence and fear of the people: the victims of his extortions and the families of those he'd murdered. The true power lay in their hands. One day they would realize it, overcome their fear, begin to speak about their phantom emperor. That day would come. It was inevitable. He knew this. History proved this. It was important that he always knew this. The only thing he did not know was when that day would be.

And as it was against them, what he did not know was their greatest weapon against him.

He ate his spaghetti and considered the symbolism of the

carcass. The blood seeping into his clean white carpet. Staining his home. You can't clean it. You have to cut it out. Or run. Someday. Not yet. They were coming for him. The city, the new generation of Italians no matter how inept, the new generation of Irish, the new generation of everybody else, always a new generation, the Visa Second United States Federal Government, the Visa Constitution of the Second United States, all of creation didn't even know it yet but it wanted him dead. They wanted to put his head on a stake at the city gates. Didn't even know it yet. They'd figure it out. When that happened he would run off and stop existing and he would become Roberto Torres whose identity he had been painstakingly creating with forged federal documents and fraudulent bank accounts and fictional real estate and business transactions ever since he got out of prison. Roberto Torres was now waiting for him in safety deposit boxes in Atlanta, Orlando, Nebrasklahoma City, Prague, Tibet, Oslo. Roberto Torres the technology consultant from Edmonton, who paid his taxes every year and even insured his vehicles and health. Get a farm or a ranch. A boathouse. Raise game there. Be surrounded by animals. He wanted to walk among chickens, sprinkling feed. He wanted to be Roberto Torres and grow a beard and sit on a porch in the morning sipping beepollen in a rocking chair with Maria. In a rocking chair on a porch, Roberto Torres. On a wide-open hillside with the sky and trees and grass. As a hobby he'd write about the life of Junior Alvarez. A work of amateur history detailing the life of the legendary honcho of myth and the times in which he lived so as to commit himself to the memory of the ages. A long thick book detailing every thought and sight Junior Alvarez ever experienced and everything he ever did so that it would be remembered. As Alejandro el Grande is remembered. Who also conquered by bluffing.

He ate his pasta and watched the carcass and experienced anxiety thinking about how short Junior Alvarez came up when compared to Alejandro el Grande, historically speaking.

You have to cut it out or you have to run.

Soon. But not yet.

When he was done eating he started to call Fernando and Diego to tell them to come over and to bring a lot of Carpet Cleaner, some paint, a circular saw if they had one, and any coolers or suitcases they had. But he stopped himself because he couldn't know for sure that they had not been the ones who had sent the carcass. They had their motives. Everybody did. Especially Fernando after the thing with Giselle. So he put on a floral-print dress and a gray wig and small glasses and a bra stuffed with balled-up Visa Extra-Soft Toilet Paper and wrapped prayer beads around his fist and this little old Lithiite lady left the condo and stepped over the dead doorman in the lobby and went to Hardware Store then came back with a circular saw and a miter saw and set up the miter saw in the bathroom with dropcloths all over the floor and walls and went to work chopping the body up with the circular saw first then feeding the pieces to the miter saw and wrapping up the pieces in wax paper. She went around painstakingly picking every single tooth out of the soup of pulverized cranium, counting them to make sure she had them all. Cut off the fingers and toes and shredded them in the miter saw. She taped the pieces wrapped in wax paper with duct tape like sandwich subs then fit them all into two large suitcases along with a sandwich bag containing the teeth and put the suitcases by the door. Then she cut out the piece of stained carpet and cleaned up the walls. In truth she was excited about finally having an opportunity to use the Paint Sprayer System she bought from Wholesale Club. It featured on-demand piston-pump technology, professional-grade-forged aluminum spray gun with in-line filter, and reversible spray tip that provided a superior finish and cleared clogs with just a twist—all for the unheard-of low price of $8,999.99.

She drove around in the Car Company Blue Sedan scattering the packages along with the tools and dropcloths and carpet square among various Dumpsters, landfills, and predug holes in isolated spots in Visa Parks around NoVA. Then she drove the Car Company Blue Sedan back to Centreville, the colorless shapeless vehicle with no serial number and whose plates were registered in the name of the daughter of the former Deputy Superintendent of the NoVA Police Department, murdered (the daughter was) four years earlier by a kidnapper who was never caught, her little body found badly abused but otherwise perfectly preserved floating faceup under the icicles of a waterfront pier in the Towson Inner Harbor, her blond beautiful hair frozen in a solid chunk. The father—at the time putting together something good against the inexplicable recent wave of Stimulant and Painkiller flowing into the city of NoVA, connecting dots and making progress in tracing it back to its source, who had a place for the name of Junior Alvarez in his good human heart—quit law enforcement, took the rest of his family, changed all their names, and fled, leaving his house full of furniture, family photographs, and most everything they owned. The air-conditioning still on. Never seen again.

She left the car in a Visa A Tow Truck Lot in Centreville that she had the keys to and unofficially owned though she had Tony Be Right Back run it and kept all the paperwork for the franchise agreement in someone else's name. She removed the plates from the car and buried them in the hole near the back of the fence by a couple rusted autobodies that had been there since she was a boy and she marked the hole again with a trash barrel. The old lady walked to Maria's where her own car was parked.

Earlier that day Junior had gone to Maria's house and surprised them with a little fawn. A gift for her and the children. They had all sat around the living room for nearly an hour playing with the deer. The children were fascinated watching the creature on their living room floor. Rosana was happy. Rosana who had been so glum lately. She had developed a sneer. Quite an attitude. She could become distant, unreachable. She hadn't been around much lately. She'd appear at odd hours now and again at her mother's for food or money then disappear as soon as she got it and stay gone for days. Junior didn't like to think about who she was with, what she was doing. There seemed to be nothing he could do about it. It was infuriating to suddenly find himself so powerless. The whole thing upset and embarrassed him. She had begun calling her mother by her first name. The mask of irony that she now hid behind created a gulf between her and those around her, as Junior did not hesitate to point out to her. She was surrounding herself with questionable male company. She'd disappear for days and come home with new jewelry, new clothes, once a new car that Junior made her take back to whomever gave it to her. Her mother was beginning to resent her. Rosana often threatened to move out.

—With what money? You're fifteen years old, you don't have a job—

—I have money! Lots of it! You don't even know what I do to get it and you'll never know!

He'd stand there on the sidelines of these arguments, sometimes refereeing, sometimes taking sides, most often just waiting for them to be over.

The streets dark and deserted. Shards of trash sticking out from the snow like hands. Crunching beneath the soles of his boots.

A gunky filthy skeleton town full of human hands reaching out from the ground.

Peeling paint. Wood chewed and excreted. Man-made snowbanks strategically placed on curbs at either end of driveways so no one could park there. Parking spaces dug out of the snow and reserved with orange cones and lawn chairs and in some cases an old television, a kayak oar. Chain-link fences and abandoned construction projects. Holes of mud.

A block from Maria's a couple of kids standing around on the street. When they saw this old lady shuffling along toward them holding her purse they stiffened and watched her approach and muttered to one another, elbowed each other. The old lady walking, wincing against the ice on her eyes and face. One of them broke away from the others and approached her, his hood up, face way deep inside the blackness therein, no face, no body, no bones.
—Excuse me, do you have the time.

She kept walking.
—Excuse me. Hey.

The kid stepped in front of her. She noticed the gun. A silver gun shining in the night, reflecting the orange streetlight above their heads. The kid stuck the silver gun into the old lady's face and started to tell her something, probably to give him her purse or something, but before he could the old lady had grabbed the kid's hand and turned the gun on the kid with the kid's hand still on it squeezing the kid's hand over and over, making the kid shoot himself in the face and head and neck over and over BANGBANGBANG, the kid caught so off guard that he wasn't screaming, a semiautomatic with what turned out to be a fairly full clip because she made the kid shoot himself over and over dozens of times before the gun stopped firing and started clicking, clicking. The kid's hood was shredded to fragments, down feathers fluttering in the air down to earth with the weather, the head, face, and neck a pink-and-orange afterbirth. The echoes of the barrage still bouncing around kilometers away. Gunpowder hung sweet and wooden in the damp air. The others were running off. The old lady still held the kid's hand in her own, the kid hanging from her arm above the ground like they were frozen in some sort of dance. She let go of the kid and the gun and both dropped without sound upon the snow and began to be covered by the flakes falling atop them. The old lady ran the rest of the way to Maria's, got in her car, drove off toward Reston. Within minutes sirens began crying out over all that trash, all those holes, the green slime and construction materials half-buried in grimy snow coming down gray and weightless. She stayed off major roads. As she drove there were black DEA cars everywhere. They were parked along the side streets lying in wait for her. She saw them up the block as she approached. She realized this was all a massive, elaborately orchestrated setup. Law enforcement was so much more sophisticated and brilliant than she could ever hope to be. But she would not surrender. She hit a new level of consciousness as she prepared to die. But as she got closer the black DEA cars turned into red cars, blue cars, green cars. They turned into Car Company Sports Cars, Pickup Trucks, Sedans, SUVs. Just cars parked on the side of the street. Nobody in them.

She heard helicopters. She pulled over and parked in a No Parking Zone and panicked, considered giving herself up after all. She pulled a lead blanket over herself. She kept it in the backseat always anticipating such a night. She heard multiple helicopters. There were upward of four or five helicopters in the sky. She could heard them circling, each one with a unique frequency and pitch. No doubt different agencies manning them. FBI, State Police, DEA, CIA, Visa Irish Separatist militias seeking revenge toward her for trading four tons of weaponry to the Visa Irish Lithiite militias in exchange for a shipload of Stimulant and Painkiller. She waited in her car for the helicopters to pass. She felt their radars penetrating her. Her head ached from it, a scratching, cleaving pressure. A high ringing in her ears. She sat there under the blanket waiting for the helicopters to pass until something inside her said that there were no helicopters, there had never been any helicopters, what she was hearing was nothing.

She drove home sweating and shivering and parked in her designated spot in the garage beneath the building. As she took the elevator up to her condo she had the persistent sensation of a presence behind her. She kept turning. She'd count to three then whip her head around. Swatting behind herself with her hand. She said in the elevator more than once, —Hello? Who's in here? She looked up at the ceiling and considered that there could be somebody up there on the other side of the panels. She pushed around the walls looking for a soft spot where somebody had cut into to hide. Slapping at her neck because she felt flies crawling on it, her hand coming away wet and cold. She began to lose it, whatever it was, whatever was left of it. She heard people calling her name. She shrunk down into the corner, her heart beating through her skull.

When the elevator door opened she poked her head out and looked up and down the hall. Nobody. Inside she took off the dress, the wig. Here again was Junior Alvarez. He spent forty-five minutes splashing ice-cold water on his face and an hour running from room to room making sure all his artillery was loaded and ready and then three hours examining his rug, walls, and possessions in a methodical grid technique he'd learned from homicide detectives, looking for implanted microfiber surveillance devices and fingerprints, hairs, clothing fibers, or other trace evidence of somebody having been inside while he'd been gone. He sat up on his sofa all night in the dark wearing body armor and combat boots and night-vision goggles, police scanner on, a shotgun in each hand, two belts of shells across his chest and dozens of boxes filled with them on the coffee table, various handguns all over the place, his fraudulent retroactive diary prominently displayed on the kitchen table, staring at the door, listening to himself breathe and his heart pump, wondering what compelled people like him to live this way.

He felt the beginning of the end coming on like a roaring orange light down at the end of all being. It was undeniable.

THE FINAL DECADE

He had always wired himself for his meetings with Dickey. It was to have something to use in working out a deal once he was finally indicted due to Dickey's inevitable betrayal. But now, in this final decade of his reign, he was carrying a little digital recorder in his left pocket at all times everywhere he went with which to record every conversation he had no matter how mundane. He bought new pants in a slightly bigger size so as to be baggy enough to conceal the recorder. He turned the recorder on when he went to Beepollen Shop to get a cup of beepollen. He held the recorder up to the phone when he called for assistance after forgetting his Bank online ID. When he ordered takeout. When he was with Maria. When somebody in the next lane at a red light asked him where Cedar Street was. At the end of each day now he sat for hours in the dark alone analyzing all of the day's conversations, the ghostly voices trapped here, time caught, rewinding and replaying, slowing it down, turning it up, running it through audio software and adjusting the equalizer to bring out the high frequencies, then isolating the lows, looking for something in the background or undertone though he couldn't be sure what until it would reveal itself to him—some sign of wavering falsehood within the rhythm of syllables, a crumbling integrity or duplicity of motive within others or within the will of himself.

For seven straight hours once he sat in his condo listening to himself say hello to his FedEx guy out front and his FedEx guy say hello back.

Wherever he went he felt the electric air thick all around his skin for there were bugs. They put heat inside his head. Like a nightmare. One of those dreams where there is a presence and

194

this presence is malevolent and powerful but you cannot see the presence and you start running, your heart pounding your ribs, your breath held and not knowing you're holding your breath but your lungs are tearing.

A ringing noise. A steady high-pitched alarm in his skull at all times, wherever he went. Bugs. A magnetic reaction to the bugs.

For ten years he lived like this, holding on, but at all times he thought, I am on the brink of utter legal and economic and emotional collapse. He imagined any day now he would find himself running naked and whooping through a major intersection with a gun, befouled by his own mess.

I can't take it anymore and am very close to falling apart.

He was trapped. He was in prison. No parole. No way out. There was nobody bigger than he thus nobody to give the feds in exchange for himself. All his life he had lived with the design in his head of one day being free. To choose the door he entered through. And he had done all that was necessary to obtain that. And yet he had not obtained it. He was not free. Everyone else was. How had it happened? What circumstance had transpired that caused him to become incarcerated even though he had obtained the total freedom he had wanted? He knew. The circumstance of himself. He did it to himself. He was in a prison where all the words he spoke even in casual chitchat with the people closest to him—Maria, Fernando—were carefully measured and edited before he spoke them. He weighed each word so carefully. Taking into regard the multiple meanings of the word. The subtexts and implications. The different ways in which the word would be heard. How the word would sound being passed on to others second- and thirdhand. What fact—no matter how true or untrue—the word would reveal about Junior Alvarez, a word that would then go out into the world like a stumbling toddler to grow and grow. Each and every utterance became a digitally recorded act of autobiography. He found himself telling people things about himself that were not true. Not facts but fabricated hints regarding how he may think, about what his motivations might be, all speaking to his historical greatness and innocence of criminality. Alibis. The grooming of future character witnesses. He manufactured an entire body of observations and experiences about his life that he told to Maria in casual intimate conversation strictly for the sake of her one day after his arrest or after his death or unsolved disappearance repeating these things to investigators or to a journalist or producer, leading to his permanent place in the myth of history. Every good-bye was a public relations maneuver. He could not shake a hand without considering the legal and historical implications of the act. This was why he stopped shaking hands. This might explain why at the end he ceased engaging in unscripted conversation.

At the end, he sat there most of the time alone in his condo watching history documentaries on Public Television Channel staring out from somewhere deep behind his own eyes, silent. Like the victim of a catastrophic mishap.

He gained weight. Felt like sleeping all the time. Started drinking. Overeating. Masturbating.

It all began to wear him down. Like a long dull saw cutting into wood—slowly, steadily. It was clear that the world preferred to see him break.

At the end he was afraid he might.

There was the world and then there was Junior Alvarez. This was the dual nature of existence.

He listened through his high-powered hearing aids and bugs. He could hear his underlings turning on him in desolate prison cells, the feds flying over his home in high-altitude stealth surveillance planes. These sounded like horseflies on a quiet summer night. He could see them on an unlit high school football field in the middle of the night somewhere in the boonies in the western part of the state running Visa Close Range Engagement Drills, preparing to raid him, to take him down. He could hear the fabric of their black uniforms crinkle as they raised their arms to signal to one another with their hands, pointing to their eyes.

At the end it became clear, more than ever, that he did not belong in the world. Not in this way, not in this state of things. Meaning the way the world was. All this—all their lives, this entire past millennium, that epilogue to man's end—should never have happened.

He began to carry lip balm in his pocket at all times. The back pocket.

Wait until they put me in the back of the cruiser and are driving off then slip out of the handcuffs and jump out. Or reach up and grab one of their guns right off their hip, start shooting. Don't even give them a chance to realize what's happened, just bangbang, two quick shots, one in the side of each of their heads. Then I'm free.

THIRD ACT

Springtime in NoVA

Late September. The springtime—the perfect season in which to become somebody else and leave. Several things happened that indicated it was time.

The first was what happened to Tony Be Right Back. One night in the middle of Television Show he stood up and muttered to his wife, —Be right back. He walked out the door, responding when she kept asking where he was going, —Be right back. He drove off to the parking lot of his old Cab Company garage. In his glove compartment a .38 magnum. Early the next day the morning dispatcher arrived for his shift. Right away as he pulled into the parking lot he recognized Tony Be Right Back's Expensive Car Company from when he had been around the station recently showing it off to his old comrades. He could see the shape of Tony Be Right Back behind the wheel. Parked beside him, hoping to say hello. Looked over with a big smile at Tony Be Right Back. The smile disappeared when he saw Tony Be Right Back with his head back and turned sideways staring back at him through the window.

At the funeral Lora was inconsolable. —We never had kids, she kept saying. —I wanted to but Tony never gave me any. The doctor said it was a physical problem but I knew it was because of the way Tony was. I used to watch kids playing and hate Tony so much for being the way he is, for living in grief the way he did and so never giving me a baby. Junior put his arm around her and she stopped crying, looked at him. —No. She pushed him away. —No. Everyone stopped what they were doing and watched. She yelled at him, —You did this. You're a demon. A *demon*.

Dickey called Junior the next week alerting him that Lora had been in contact with the Attorney General about wanting to offer incriminating testimony about him. Junior was disappointed but not surprised. Nothing ever surprised him. He prided himself on that. He thanked Dickey and he and Fernando went to the new large home in Visa Ashburn that Tony Be Right Back had built with the money he'd made working for Junior and where Lora now lived alone with nothing in her life anymore but brand-new Expensive Furniture Company furniture, three Expensive Car Companies, a gardener, a live-in maid, and other such things that a week earlier were luxuries provided by her husband's success but now were just profane litter getting in her way as she drifted day and night from room to room, finding herself just as exiled in this opulent house as she would have been if she were a destitute, ill woman living in parks, working out of motel rooms. She was still not only unbathed but unchanged altogether out of the black dress she wore to the funeral which she did not remember buying sometime between claiming the body and burying it but she must have bought it, at some point in that nightmarish three days she must have driven to a store and walked into it and looked at black dresses and selected this one from the racks and tried it on and bought it, even if she had no recollection of that, because it was not in a store now but in her home, on her body, wasn't it?

Junior and Fernando strangled her with the cord from the brand-new, state-of-the-art, wall-sized fifty-thousand-dollar Television Company until her face became brown and her eyes filled with blood and she died. Though really she was already dead. And they removed her teeth, fingers, and toes, and chopped her body up first with an ax from the gardener's shed out back then with a millsaw in the garage. Her body was never found, her disappearance never officially explained due to lack of evidence. Officially, she'd just vanished.

Though we all know the truth.

Then one of Junior's biggest drug warehouses was raided, the distributor running it charged. He turned within hours of being arrested, answered the feds' every question about his boss, Junior Alvarez. As a result twenty-seven more of his distributors and dealers were charged and each turned just as easily as the first. That led to another fifty-eight being charged. Each turned with little resistance.

THE GOOD AND THE GHASTLY

One woman whose husband—the owner of a Centreville Visa Convenience Store—had disappeared after refusing to buy Junior's protection had begun stepping out onto her front walk each night and doing what no one used to have the audacity to do: telling everything she knew about Junior Alvarez. The first few nights there was no one out there to hear her. She just stood there alone speaking into the dusk like a prophet. Then a man passed by one night walking home from buying cigarettes. He stopped to listen. When he got back he told his wife about it. His wife mentioned it to her sister the next day who mentioned it to her husband. They all started going each night. By now others had heard and began going as well. Dozens. It became a thing. A Visa National News Event. Soon there were news vans everywhere, dozens of microwave antennae reaching into the sky for blocks like a weird attempt at conjuring extraterrestrials, a sudden gypsy flock of producers, cameramen, and correspondents camped out on the street waiting for the woman's appearances. They were not covering the woman or the spectacle of the crowd gathered to witness the woman but the attention they as news media were paying the spectacle of witnessing the woman. This fueled things. The woman's front walk became a site of massive nightly pilgrimage. People wanted to participate not in the experience of participating in a major newsworthy event but in the experience of participating in the coverage of the event which itself was the event. Soon each night once the woman was done telling again everything she knew about her husband's murderer and disappeared back inside, waiting after her were hundreds of others who had before been mere viewers of the coverage and were now ready to become part of it by telling everything they knew about the man who murdered their own brother, their own daughter, their own grandfather, their own uncle, their own friend. With all the byzantine, self-reflective layers, Junior Alvarez became a white-hot story, a whale. There was an ongoing investigative series on *Visa Times* about Junior Alvarez. Visa Special Reports about him on *Visa Television Channel Nightly News*. In an instant his fragile anonymity was blown. It had been invaluable. It had allowed him to deceive. And become mighty. And stay alive. Now he was more than famous. He was as part of the modern ether as the weather or a sex scandal. Which made him as good as dead. He tried to stop it. It was like trying to stop ocean waves from crashing. His best effort: He learned where the daughter of one of the reporters doing the *Visa Times* series went to school. A seven-year-old girl in second grade. He waited for her outside. Intercepted her as she made her way to the bus. He bent down and introduced himself as a friend of her father's. He was nice, smiling. Gave her an envelope to take home to her dad. Told her not to open it. She obeyed. She gave it to her dad, told him about the man. He opened it, read it. Went white. Inside was a note that said: I KILL LITTLE GIRLS.

But the reporter did not desist. The series did not end. Nothing changed.

The articles contained not only litanies of Junior Alvarez's crimes but details of his fortunes which he worked so hard to keep secret under a guise of humility. And they contained allegations of narcotic distribution, contradicting the image of himself he had allowed to develop and groomed so deliberately, leading to more indignant witnesses coming forward out of a need to rectify the sense of betrayal they felt in their hearts.

He waited again outside the girl's school with rope and duct tape and large, heavy-duty trash bags in his trunk. But she never came out. He tried to find where she'd been sent off to but could not.

Several of his underlings in protection and bookmaking, indignant about Junior's threat against a child, out-and-out crossed sides without even being charged with anything first, giving up all their illicit activities and extravagant visions of wealth and power and respect in favor of being merely decent people scrambling to balance the dissonant elements of their Sisyphean lives.

THE BOWLING ALLEY

Sitting with his legs crossed in a plastic booth wearing a wire as usual and waving smoke away from his face and watching a birthday party of seven or eight children tossing bowling balls down the lane if not at the pins then in the general direction of the pins, most balls looping into the air and landing with a loud thudcrack before careening into the gutter. Dickey ashed his cigar into his empty Backyard bottle—his fifth, Junior noticed—and said, —They're coming for you. Junior nodded and watched the small plume of smoke swirl back out of the mouth of the bottle rising up before the child off in the distance behind it. There was an empty basket between him and Dickey that had for a duration of about two minutes contained the large order of greasy onion rings Dickey ordered upon arriving and single-mindedly devoured in voracious handfuls as Junior, drinking and eating nothing, watched in disgust, typical for these meetings.

—They got you in their sights, Dickey said. Soggy fried remnants of food on his lips and in his teeth and still in his mouth. —All these guys, you're it for them. *It.* And there's nothing I can do. It's gotten too big for me. So now we both have some very big decisions to make. Junior said nothing and adjusted himself in his seat. Dickey took a long deep drink then said, —*You . . . are . . . the . . . holy . . . grail.* This is not city police. This is not a couple detectives and a deputy DA. These are state agencies. I'm talking *Visa.* I'm talking Visa State Attorney General, I'm talking the Visa DEA. It's gotten bigger than me. This is big league. This is it, baby. It's happening. It's real. There's nothing I can do. They're isolating me. Because they believe they know what they believe they know. I can see it in their eyes. I am a flawed man. I never claimed I

205

wasn't. But the things I have done for this state. *I took down the Italians.* He struck the table with his fist. —*By myself.* They tried to do it and they *failed. But I did it.* And *they*? They wake up in bed each morning and they're thinking about you even before their morning wood has gone down. Having dreamed all night about you. They think about you as they brush their teeth, as they shit. As they leave the house. They think about you as they drive in to work. Then they think about you all day. And all night. And when they undress for bed. And then it all starts again. You are the impetus for all their monthly quotas. Junior, they got your photo, okay? A big blown-up black-and-white picture of you hanging on a wall in a conference room in the AG's office right there in the middle of everything. This is a very highly populated, high-traffic room. And there's all sorts of smucking documents and leads and maps and handwritten scribbles on Post-its tacked all around the photo. They spread out all across the other walls, the ceiling.

—What am I doing in the photo?

—It's not important what you're doing in the photo.

—But what am I doing though.

—I don't know, you're just standing there. It's a street. Broad daylight. There's a blurred object in the foreground that I think is a parking meter. Someone's hand is coming into the frame from the right. A passerby. It was taken in front of the store. You're wearing sunglasses.

Junior nodded, watching the children bowl but observing Dickey in his peripheral vision—his body language, his facial expression. He was drunk. His eyes red. Arms folded on the table before his Backyard and bloated face hanging off his skull. He paused as the waitress brought the pitcher he'd asked for. He ogled her but in a forlorn, hopeless way. Did not resume speaking until he'd poured one and drank half of it. Junior just watched him through his peripheral vision in arcane disgust.

—There's digital footage. Scrolling in a loop on several televisions dispersed throughout the room. One in every corner. A few lining the walls. There is no night in the room. No darkness. Because of the glow. It's eerie. You walking, you standing, you going in and out of a building over and over and over, like you're stuck in a revolving door. You driving, you . . . Well, you get the idea. It's eerie. I don't like to go in there. They won't let me anyway. I had to disguise myself as the guy delivering lunch. I put on a fake beard, spoke in an accent. They act cordial toward me like nothing's amiss when in actuality they have put me on a smucking *island*. After what I did. *I took down the Italians. Me.* Not them. *Me.* Those mothersmuckers. All you hear when you're walking through that office—the smucking entire building—all you hear is this smucking chorus of voices all around you, all saying juniorjuniorjunior. In various volumes and alternating regional accents. All day long. Wherever you go you hear juniorjuniorjunior. Not dickeydickeydickey. Juniorjuniorjunior. Walk into the shitter and it's echoing off the walls and cuts off when they see me. They got so much shit on you, Junior. They're going to take you down. Big-time. They're going to be theatrical about it. They're gunning for national news. Prime time. They want a Visa National News Event. It's like they're producing a smucking *Visa Action Movie* at that place. It's nuts. They've got Bank people over there with your records, going through them with our guys. Every transaction you've ever made. They got girls who are saying they used to turn tricks for you, star in porn for you. They're offering them free facial reconstructions and belly augmentations and a couple billion dollars each including a lifetime of federal law enforcement protection in exchange for telling them what kind of jokes you laugh at and any deviant sexual proclivities you have. An entire floor of the building is full of IT guys digging through Visa Internet Server finding every Visa Search Engine query you've ever made, every e-mail you've ever sent or received, every *Visa Times* article you've ever read, every advertisement you've clicked on, every visit to Visa Porno Site you've made. Apparently you looked at Porno Site's pregnant women area a couple of times? That's fine, I enjoy that kind of thing myself. But that was the joke over there for a while. They loved that. Somebody took a black marker and wrote a speech bubble on your photo that said, I love 'em preggo! That was the joke. It spread to our office. We had to pretend to laugh at it every time someone said it. People would say it at random, in different contexts. They'd get in the elevator and go, I love 'em preggo! and everyone would pretend to laugh. One guy kept going around to everyone going, Knock knock. Who's there? I love 'em preggo! He'd even do the Who's there? part. The people at the Sandwich Shop our office has been going to for lunch are even saying it to each other now, even though they can't have any idea what it means, they've just heard us saying it. Anyway they're working in tandem with smucking Ivy League University–McLean psychiatrists to use all this information to create a map of your psyche. Every thought and interest you may have ever had. It's fascinating but also terrifying. And it's working, Junior. They got you smucking nailed. It's a physical— it's literally a smucking map of your mind, Junior, spread out all over the floor of the goddamn cafeteria. They look at it as they eat, talk about it, point things out to one another. They could get you now, today, at this moment, Junior, if they wanted. They have evidence that will lock you up for the rest of your life. But they want more. They want to whip out their cocks. Total, theatrical, fat-dicked wall-nailing is what they desire. They want everything they can get, all the murder charges they can, which they do have right now but not quite as solidly as they would like. Essentially, Junior, what I'm saying is you got the Visa Second American Federal Government living inside of you now. A foreign-owned private corporate faceless god. An omnipotent, omnipresent, omniscient power. You stand zero chance. Having that in you is like a virus that has been dormant but one of these days—any hour now, whenever they decide to tell it to—will flare up and destroy you. These are very talented people. They are pathological. Obsessive to a clinical degree. Their eye is all-seeing. Their arm is all-powerful and ever-living. It's a machine. Your machine can't compete with their machine. You do what they make you do. You go where they make you go. I don't know what you have done in this department but I hope for both of us that you haven't been procrastinating. I will just say that from my side I intend to remain very discreet. And I hope you do as well. You have a lot of information about me. As I do about you. In order to take down the Italians I've had to do certain things that probably won't look too good in an indictment. These are things I would have preferred not to do but I had to do them. Measures that were necessary in order to clean my city and my great state of this scourge. Am I proud of it? No. But it was right. And it worked. I put them away. They're gone. Rotting in prison. Paying for their crimes. As they should be.

Junior waved smoke out of his face, giving Dickey none of the information from his facial reaction that he knew Dickey was looking for. He watched a little girl carry a ball as big as she was up to the line and spread her feet and bend over and gently push the ball from between her fat, stubby legs. It moved slowly, silently. All around her the other children threw the balls as hard as they could and they just hit the floor with a crack and went into the gutter. Hers looked like it would never make it down the lane. But it made it. When it did the pins fell over one at a time until they were all down.

Dickey said, —I don't understand what you're smiling about. I don't understand what's so smucking funny. I have kids. I'm a hero to them.

The little girl pushed the ball again and she and Junior separately watched it careen down the lane and cause the pins—through fate, because of chance—to again one by one totter over until they all lay in a tornado-flattened scene quickly swept up by a mechanical arm that descended from above.

—Dickey, this girl's a hell of a bowler.

Dickey rubbed his eyes. —Junior, the words I am looking for to come out of your mouth right now are, do I need to be concerned here? Do I need to worry about the history and facts of our friendship? I consider you a friend, you know. We're both good guys. We're on the same side. We took them down, Junior, you and me. Right? Do I need to be taking drastic action? Should I be fleeing, panicking, surrendering, offering a deal, what? Junior, what I want to know is, what's going to happen to me?

Junior looked at Dickey with big eyes as though only just now realizing the man was sitting across the table and said, —Who gives a smuck about you?

Leaving NoVA

Dickey came to him a few weeks later as he was downtown at Visa Tysons Corner with Maria shopping for the first birthday of Maria's youngest's baby, her second. Dickey was dressed in identical clothing to Junior's only in a different color: button-down transcotext shirt, sand-colored wrinkle-free pants, both by Clothing Company. Dickey called to them as they were leaving, in back of the Visa Downtown Central Plaza mall, by the loading docks where his car was parked illegally in front of a Dumpster, directly below a blinking, alarming NO PARKING sign. He kind of jogged toward them, smiling, looking cheerful. He'd been drinking. Junior looked around, at the tops of the buildings. Dickey smiled at Maria who did not smile back and Junior told Maria to take the seemingly hundreds of shopping bags they had somehow acquired and wait in the car. Dickey was still smiling as he waited until Maria was in the car. He had his hand in his pocket and Junior was keeping an eye on the hand, his own hand around the gun in his own pocket. He was not going to jail. They watched Maria get into the car. Junior kept glancing around, nervous.

—They just arrested Manny and Diego. Both on charges based on evidence you knew existed but they did not. But now they know you knew. That's why they're telling them anything they want to know about you. Fernando, they don't know where he is. Yet. But he's toast too. They have a warrant for him. When they find him they'll take him to where they have Diego and Manny. Which is to a location that officially does not exist for the purposes of extracting information from them. They'll use any means necessary. Torture, to be frank. I've seen it. With the Italians. When they find him they'll let Fernando in on the news that you've been providing me incriminating information about him for thirty years all of which has systematically gone into his file and has made it possible to indict him. I tried my damndest, Junior. I tried so hard. You and Diego and Fernando. You are my family. We're from Centreville. We're blood. I came over as soon as I heard. First thing I thought of was you. Dickey was tearing up. His breath smelled like alcohol. It was not Dickey's breath but Junior's father's breath. Eyes glassy. His father's eyes. Junior's hand was greasy on the gun in his pocket. Maria was in the car over there putting on lipstick. Junior looked around at the tops of the buildings and behind him and listened to the bloodless voices and static of the city. Dickey said, —I'm not telling anybody shit. What about you?

—No.

—You'll help me, right?

—Yeah.

They shook hands and Junior went to the car and got in and started it. Dickey stood there drunk, watching. Junior glanced over at him as he backed out, sun reflecting rectangles on the windshield—hands and knuckles, turning on a wheel. He was saying something to Maria, Junior was, as he backed out and put it into gear and drove out. Maria looked at Junior with the tube of lipstick suspended before her mouth, lips still parted and cupped over her teeth like an old corpse, Dickey thought. Someone a thousand years old pulled well preserved out of mountain ice. She peered from beneath the visor at him, squinting, then back at Junior who stared straight ahead with no expression as they drove off.

He swung by the Parking Garage and swapped the car with an unremarkable, unregistered Car Company Green Sedan with stolen plates, not explaining why to Maria and Maria not asking questions. They drove it to Maria's house. Rosana, now grown, used to stay at Maria's between boyfriends and husbands and roommates, between legal and financial dramas and doomed attempts at sobriety. But she had not been seen or heard from in more than a year, since she had become pregnant while staying there and Junior coerced her into getting an abortion because there was a chance it was his.

Maria was scrambling through the house trying to decide what to bring with her and what to leave behind on this vacation. Which is where Junior told her they were going. —A couple weeks. Just you and me. We need a vacation. Go sit on a beach and enjoy ourselves for a while, travel from place to place. Two nights here, two nights there. When's the last time we had a vacation anyway? He stood in the living room pacing, holding his phone, staring at it, telling Maria to hurry, we need to leave in two minutes, we have a lot to do. Maria did not understand what the rush was. But she knew enough not to ask. Even though there was a sad dread within her as she was thinking, But what about the birthday party? —Just you and me. An exotic month-long getaway. Maybe two months. What do you think about that? Three even. Four. Who cares how many months. As long as we want. Don't worry about the kids, we'll call them once we get there, they'll understand. We'll leave the presents for the baby here. And we'll call during the party. We'll sing her "Happy Birthday" over the phone. They'll understand. But right now we just need to get there. Bring a swimsuit, Maria. Or we can get you one there. We'll buy you three or four. Whatever you need but don't have, we'll just buy it, Maria. Even if you don't need it and just want it, we'll buy it. Prepare for months and months of unlimited romance and leisure, Maria. We'll buy it all.

After Maria's, an empty warehouse in Oakton he officially did not own. Junior went into the bowels of it and pulled up a floorboard and used his hands to dig deep into the dirt beneath. He pulled out a metal box in which was $800,000. Then to the scrapyard in Alexandria he owned through his money launderer where he dug up $500,000 more in cash beneath an old Car Company rusted and dead under a tree that had fallen on it years ago. Then to some condos he owned around NoVA in the names of various babies who had died in infancy where he kept stashes of weapons and money and identification documents. Then north on the Visa Angelina Jolie Beltway to a rest stop in Visa Maryland, out back behind the Plaza inside which families and the elderly milled about with trays from one Fast Food Restaurant counter to the other. He removed the cover of a nonfunctioning air-conditioner unit back there and withdrew from inside it two bricks of cash wrapped in brown paper totaling more than $900,000 and replaced the shell of the air-conditioning unit and shoved the money down the front of his pants then returned to Maria. She was waiting in the car. She could not stop herself from laughing at this serious-faced middle-aged man waddling among the motorists toward her with ridiculous lumpy pants and all the excitement, luxury, and stability he had provided for her and her children all these years.

They picked up Fernando at a Gas Station in Laurel. He hadn't been arrested yet because they somehow hadn't found him even though he'd just been driving around for days in stolen cars, not knowing where else to go or what to do. They headed to the airport. Fernando driving. Maria was in the back clutching her purse to her chest. Fernando circled the car around and around the road spiraling around Visa NoVA International. Outside the terminal Fernando pulled up to the curb. He popped the trunk and got out to help them with their bags. They said farewell to him and he drove off to destroy the car and run.

Inside the terminal, in line for the ticket counter, Junior in a sweat, face white, skin crawling, feeling all the eyes of civilized humanity upon him, a sense of the totality of the world closing in on him. —I should have peed, Maria said. His eyes scanning back and forth, feeling small and huge at the same time. He thought about where he went wrong. What mistakes he had made in his life to get him to this unfortunate situation. This was like pulling the loosened thread of a sweater—it went all the way past the superficial recent tactical and strategical errors all the way back to the source, the essence of his being. I am a ghoul, he thought. I should never have happened. We should not even be here. All of us—humanity. This entire piece of history. We were supposed to have been decimated. To make room for the next species. Like how the dinosaurs were decimated to make room for us. That's the natural cycle. The earth gives creatures a certain amount of time at the top of the food chain and then it wipes them away so another kind can get a turn. But we endured our wiping away. Our decimation. A meteor wiped away the dinosaurs, as it was supposed to, and we were supposed to wipe ourselves away. But we endured. Man always endures. And so now the natural cycle's been upset. And now time's all smucked up. This millennium a goof. And what have I done with my life in this mistake of a millennium? I could have used it for good. But what difference would that have made? Where did I go wrong? I didn't go wrong, don't panic, this is expected. Stay calm. Everything's going as you planned it. So what's wrong? I could have taken a place in history among the great men. I still can. There's time. Plenty of time left. So many men were doubted in their time only to be vindicated later by the vast machine. Later though. We're dead by then. Can't enjoy it. What's the point? Make yourself happy now, smuck everything else. Because you die and that's it.

Maria said through her teeth, —I have to pee-eeeee.

He wore big sunglasses and a Pro Baseball Franchise NoVA hat. He pulled an identical pair of sunglasses from his bag, pushed them into her stomach. —Here, take these.

—I don't want them.

—Take them. Put them on.

—I'm not wearing them, Junior. I have sunglasses and plus I don't want to wear sunglasses at this moment.

—Take them. They're big. Yours hardly cover your eyeballs. These cover your whole face.

—I'm not wearing those. They're hideous and the same as yours. We'll look ridiculous.

—Fine, he said, —don't wear them. Go to jail because you don't want to look ridiculous. See if I give a shit.

He turned away bracing himself because he realized the slip he had just made. But she only said, —What did you say?

—Nothing.

—Did you say jail?

—Jail? What the hell are you talking about?

—I don't know, what did you say?

—Nothing, nothing, I said nothing. Smucking Lithis.

—Well you mumble and whisper all the time and then you get mad at me when I can't hear you.

—Go pee please.

She looked away and crossed her arms and exhaled through her nose, stayed where she was.

They paid for their tickets in cash. They were going to Visa Nampa. It was a nice upscale seaside resort town in Visa Idaho with Expensive Clothing Stores and Expensive Restaurants. That would satisfy Maria. But he chose Nampa because he was interested in Oregon. Oregon is a mythic land that some believe was a state in First America and now sits submerged by sand beneath the northern Visa Pacific Ocean somewhere. It is believed to be where the survivors of the Nuke War threw together a huge makeshift federal prison as a place to quarter all the mutants created by the radioactive nuclear fallout—in order to quarantine their genes and all the diseases and deformities they carried from the ensuing vast repopulation effort—and all the criminals that in the sudden vanishing of all law and government were free to terrorize the earth unbeholden to the order of civilization and consequence of justice. This was centuries before the sea level rose as an aftershock effect of the environmental devastation and engulfed the land. Scientists of questionable repute now ride around in submarines spending billions of dollars funded by eccentric trillionaires looking for evidence of Oregon. Junior was hoping to get aboard one, ride along on an expedition.

They went through security. Junior tried to be discreet with regard to how he was walking. He still had the cash shoved down his pants. His balls were sweating from the nerves. The sweat was soaking into the bricks of cash shoved down his pants which were too big because he bought them back when he was into heavy weight training which he had since lost the energy to pursue and so had lost considerable muscle mass. He feared as he approached the metal detectors that they would ask him to remove his belt and his pants would drop, revealing the cash. He wouldn't be able to run because his pants would be around his ankles. And he was unarmed. He tried to remain calm, placed his bag on the conveyor belt, started to step through the metal detector, when he felt a hand on his shoulder.

—Sir, please step aside and come with me. A security guard with glasses and traces of acne.

—Why?

The guard repeated himself.

—We don't have time, our flight's in six minutes.

The security guard repeated himself once again. Junior took Maria's arm and pulled her with him through the metal detector, pulled her in the direction of their gate. An alarm going off. The security guard yelled at them but they didn't stop so he waved over a couple of cops who had materialized down at the other end of the terminal. People watched the middle-aged couple hobbling away from the security guard who was in pursuit, yelling at them to stop. They looked like someone's parents. The cops weren't far behind, their guns drawn. Junior said to Maria, —Maria, I realize you've never run anything more than an errand in your life, but you better smucking run now. They ran through the crowd, hurdling bodies, shoving people out of the way, bags and limbs flailing, cutting off to the side and running through the chairs of waiting areas then back into the crowd, zigging and zagging for daylight, the cops not far behind at all now, the security guard who'd already taken himself out of the pursuit keeled over a hundred yards back and sucking air. Somehow they ended up back at the ticket counters and heading in the direction from which they had come. People were screaming. The bricks of cash had slid down to his knees and he ran with his hands on them, holding them there. Maria ran faster than he did. He couldn't believe that. He was laughing, running, pushing people out of the way, people parting for them and pulling aside their children. He yelled, —I'm an old man, Maria. I'm an old man running like this. They were almost to the automatic sliding door through which they had originally entered the airport. A cop's fingers grazed the back of his neck. His breath in Junior's ear. —Got you, mothersmucker, the cop said. At this point through this door stepped an obese and gray-haired man with a large long-range automatic military rifle in his arms and he turned his body and spread his feet and started firing without discrimination as Junior and Maria ran past him and out of the terminal, the bullets ripping away large handfuls of the head and face of that lead cop, the mouth still moving as the corpse still ran a few last steps then flopped first prostrate then prone. Bullets exploded through the bodies of innocent children and men and women. Dozens of dead and writhing. Fernando fired a few more rounds and ran out after Junior and Maria and got back into the car, then peeled off to the Interstate which led them out and away.

CHANGE

The subsequent years saw a remarkable cat-and-mouse game that spanned the continent and often stretched internationally. In the aftermath of Junior Alvarez, the blood in NoVA dried up and flaked off from the streets in the strong winds that came screaming off the river and down around the buildings. Junior Alvarez was a hero fugitive. Centreville kids checked *Visa Times* in a compulsive manner for new information regarding his whereabouts, which were subject to broad speculation, rarely confirmed by authorities. They imagined him cutting through the open road in a convertible, big middle finger up above his head waving back and forth at the cops and government behind him. Outsmarting them all. Doing it for Centreville. They still believed in the myth of Junior Alvarez. The righteous gangster who lived by an unbreakable code of ethics and who did good deeds and protected the lives of the innocent and patrolled the streets of Centreville as a dark angel safeguarding with stealth and shocking force the well-being of the people. In his freedom and transgression Junior Alvarez represented what they hoped to one day be: wealthy, free men of strong moral principle doing what they wanted to do with their lives, unbeholden to the servitude of harried, Sisyphean modern-day living.

They did not notice—nor did anybody notice—the reduction of drugs and significant drop in violent crime upon the departure of Junior Alvarez from the state of Visa NoVA, the slow but true revitalization of their cities and neighborhoods, and the new life that was breathed into the vacuum he left. The old ways broke down like eggshells. The murder rate halved then halved again. Strangers greeted one another in passing, smiling. Open parking spaces were no longer reason for assault. The home break-in rate quartered in the first half of the year. The divorce rate dwindled, as the percentage of Centreville men in prison fell by nearly twenty points over the next decade, the life expectancy of a Centreville man growing by seven, eight, nine years. Graduation rates at Low Scores High Schools were at unprecedented heights. One by one a new guard of local politicians was voted into office who did not expect kickbacks and did not accept bribes and did not believe in the principle of unquestioning loyalty to Centreville as they had grown up in the regime of Junior Alvarez and had seen the filth and the horror caused by this wretch and thought, Loyalty to *what?* They restructured the budget, took money that once found its way to bogus contracts with construction, electrical, and plumbing companies owned by men running them for Junior Alvarez who reaped the profits, and set it aside for education. It was put toward turning the Low Scores Elementary Schools into High Scores Elementary Schools. The nearly two billion dollars that for decades had been spent each year by the NoVA State Police to handle the crime resulting from the activities of Junior Alvarez and to investigate Junior Alvarez was no longer needed and so could instead be redirected into Visa GED and Job Training Programs for the men and women of the state. A day-care program was launched with some of the money formerly used to fund the state's battling of Junior Alvarez. With the government funds no longer allocated for the NoVA Police Department to use to entice informants who would then be ratted out by the upper brass and killed or intimidated into silence, Visa Low Funds Hospital–Centreville was essentially renovated in its entirety and restaffed, turning it into an infinitely more capable, respectable hospital than it had ever been. The renovations and restructurings earned the hospital an upgrade to Visa High Funds Hospital–Centreville. It was able to offer affordable, quality health care for families of Centreville where the parents worked minimum-wage jobs that did not provide their children with health insurance and could not afford even Visa Health Insurance Cheap Plans on their own. Lives were saved. Babies were born in this hospital, cured of their illnesses in this hospital, a new generation aglow with all the hope they carried within them, sent home snoozing and peaceful wrapped in blankets in the arms of their smiling mothers who were hopeful too because they could feel it radiating warm from within their babies, it was so strong, the mothers no longer feeling like the bottom feeders trolling along the trenches of their society which they'd felt like all their lives but forebears of a torch they were chosen to carry into yet another new dawn of the endless American future.

ROAD TRIP REVISITED

They traveled west out of NoVA. They stuck to interstates and rest stops. They spent days moving, driving in shifts, zigzagging west, north, south. Never east. No more than two hours did they ever once spend moving in the same direction. They were weightless objects flittering in the wind. They stood in rest station parking lots sucking Soda Companies through straws among the families on vacation, who were packed up like small tribes of refugees fleeing their burning homes. They obtained Lithiite clergy garments and disguised themselves as the ordained. They sat in bridge traffic in nervous silence, craning their necks to see what was holding them up. Junior carried cyanoacrylate ester and conventional black powder with him at all times which he used to check the exterior of the car and the outside doorknobs of their Expensive Hotel rooms for any friction ridge detail left by human fingers each time when returning. They rented storage facilities using false names and Visa Identification Numbers to store boxes of cash. They lived in a nudist resort in the guise of a threesome in a polyamorous marriage.

It was in South Bend, Indiana, that they decided to split up. Fernando bought a used car with cash and forged documentation while Junior and Maria enjoyed a lunch of soup and ginger ale at the Visa Diner across the street. They shook hands in that Diner's parking lot after Fernando drove his new vehicle over. Junior said, —I'll see you. Fernando said, —Take damn care. He kissed Maria on the cheek. It was like they would see one another later that week. Junior and Maria were behind Fernando in his new car on the connector road for nearly four kilometers before Fernando went north and they went south. They honked, stuck a hand out the window. Fernando went all the way north from there to Visa Canada where he was immediately arrested at the border. He was indicted then prosecuted on a staggering list of felony charges based on evidence that had been provided to the Visa Second United States Federal Government by Junior Alvarez over the last thirty years all of which he was found guilty of and for which he was sentenced to serve forty-seven years. He was sent to a Visa Federal Prison franchise in Connecticut where he met four or five of the nearly two dozen young men who were inmates there who'd grown up in Centreville as well, not knowing until it was too late that each of these young men years ago, when they were little boys, their fathers dead or imprisoned, had been separately approached by Junior Alvarez and given the opportunity to help their families. They were told by Junior Alvarez who approached them after school and bought them ice cream that he had chosen them for a very special job. They could be the man of their family and earn money working for him so that their families would never again worry about being evicted or experiencing the shame of Visa Repossession Agency employees coming to their home and taking all their things again. Their mommies, Junior told them gently over ice cream, would never have to worry about being able to buy groceries or paying doctor bills and thus their mommies would never cry anymore. And all they had to do in order to create this dream, all they had to do to make their mommies stop crying, was to become men. And how they could become men was by making money. And how they could make money was this: If by chance at any point in their lives they were to ever end up in prison, if this man were to then show up in the same prison with them—he would slide across the table to them a photograph of Fernando—they were to appropriate at first opportunity a sharp object and use it to poke a hole into his body through which his life might leave. And they were to do it as soon as possible. Out of loyalty to Centreville. As the men of their families. As Irish men. As long as they agreed to do this, Junior would pay them. And they did agree. And that's what happened to Fernando.

They went west. It was quiet. The sky was big. He'd never seen a sky so big. They drove up into mountains, alongside lakes. It was like another planet out here. He imagined it never changed, that it looked the same as it did in the first days after the Nuclear War. Lonesome droves of a near-dead species in its second dawn living under the stars in communities of tents patched together out of materials left behind by their dead fathers, cooking meals over fires, passing on the half-remembered myths and popular narratives of their history, conspiring to rebuild it all again. Driven only by will.

He had his arm around her as they drove. Drove for days without stopping except to refuel. Swallowed Visa Trucker Pills to stay awake. Traded in the car for a new one in a different color and year and drove. Exchanged it again and drove. The sun on their faces, the wind in their hair. Just drove. Imagine it. Put yourself into his flesh and be him. See after a lifetime in rusted Centreville the endless skies, the sun, the ancient mountains rising as they always have gray through the haze off in the fresh springtime distance. Nowhere to be and nothing to do but drive this road and drive this road and drive this road.

Feel the moment when he first realized they would never get him. It happened somewhere out there, along that road.

There was a town waiting for him out here. He knew it was. It was small. Unassuming. A place so honest that America could never keep it in mind long enough to give it a name. He could see it when he closed his eyes. There it was, an image of a town so clear it was like he had been to it before: One stoplight. One Bar. One Laundromat with a small apartment over it in which he and Maria would live. A Bus Station across the street into which dust-covered buses would pull in and out at dusk, picking up cowboys and depositing lost women. A Diner. Love affairs amid cigarettes and beer in Motel rooms. A heartache ghost town in which everyone was on the run from something. Where born-bad youth stalked the streets under the Gas Station lights of Friday night, high school virgins seeing them from across parking lots and yearning for the wildness of the night into which they might be stolen. It would be a place for all those who just cannot conform. Insurgents and artists and exiles. Those who never understand what everyone's laughing about or what everyone's standing in a mile-long line for with money in their hands and who spend their lives exacting revenge on this world for being so untruthful that it bred their fathers and abandoned their mothers. No one would ask questions. No one would speak words ever spoken before. Because they would be so used to the wind blowing through their forlorn town of damaged angels and bright-eyed refuse, pushing rolling things in one day and pushing them out the next. He'd live there among them, in this place out west on the moon at the bottom of the ocean, not so much accepted by them as ignored, free to walk among them like a feral cat listening to their voices and seeing their faces if only to make sure now and again that there were humans here on earth still so he would have his counterpart to stand against, something averse to his nature to compare himself to and thus affirm his existence.

Feel that if you can.

He drove and drove, looking for this town. They'd live there. A little room above the Laundromat was all they'd need. He went from town to town. None was the town.

Maria grew impatient. —Why are we just driving around the desert? Where are we going? Can we at least *go* somewhere?

The woman who'd rent it to him would ask no questions. Not even his name. No one would. It would be a town where no one ever asked you a thing.

—We're almost there.

They'd stay there for a day or for a decade or for several decades. When the morning came to move on, they would. They'd go somewhere else. It'd be easy.

It was somewhere out here in these mountains, tucked into a pass. Carved by hand over the millennium by survivors of the world's end. He'd know it when he saw it. As soon as they drove in over its limits. They'd drive in slowly and the people would turn to glance at them from the doorways as he and Maria passed. And they would just nod and point them in the direction they were already going. As if to say, That's right, keep going, just a little farther up ahead is where she is.

She wouldn't use paperwork. She'd accept a year's rent paid up front in cash. She wouldn't even give him her name. She'd just take the money and hand him the key and say, —You're safe now. There's none of it here. It all stayed back there behind you, wherever you left it.

He'd ask what.
—History.

The road ended at the coast late in the morning. Parked the car, got out. Walked down to the beach and looked out over the ocean. Maria stood with her shoes in her hand shading her eyes with the other one, grinning into the sun. High soulful waves crashing before them. —It's beautiful, she said. First thing she'd said to him in days. She'd been so angry with him for just driving around and around the desert without stopping to sleep in a Hotel or telling her where they were going or asking somebody for directions like a sensible human being and for making her miss the baby's birthday. He nodded, crossed his arms. Stepped back to keep his feet from getting wet. Looked up and down the shore. No one else in sight. Only them here at the end, at last, of America.

—Used to be a desert, he said. She didn't answer. She was furious. —A thousand years ago. Death Valley Desert. Under there somewhere is California.

— . . .

—California was where people like Stephen King and Bob Dylan and all those people lived. Kind of like their Newfoundland sort of place back then. Anyway that's why it's called the Death Valley Sea.

—Why do they call it something so horrible?

—Because.

—It's so blue and clear and beautiful. It's so full of life. It should be called the Life Valley Sea. Or just the Life Sea. The Sea of Life. Why don't they call it the Sea of Life instead of something so horrible?

—It's historical geography, Maria. It's science, truth.

—Well, that's stupid. It should be called what it is, not what it was. And it should be named by whoever has to look at it now, today, not by people who are dead and so don't have to listen to a beautiful blue ocean be called the Death Valley Sea.

—You don't understand history.

—I do too understand it.

—No, you don't. If you did, you wouldn't say such stupid smucking things all the time.

It was quiet. He could feel her stewing. Braced himself for the blowup.

It never came. Glanced over at her to see why not. She was taking off her pants. —What are you doing. Her underwear, her shirt. Everything. —Maria, what are you doing.

—What's it look like.

She was naked.

—Someone'll see you.

She stood there facing him, nude and furious. Her face defiant, daring him to speak, her body as pale as milk save for the dreadful *V* of scarlet blistering at the base of her neck that her shirt hadn't covered these days of driving beneath the sun. She looked like a child he had never seen before. It was death-defying being out here exposed without sunblock. They had a tub's worth in the car. He started to tell her to wait while he retrieved it but she said, ignoring her hair blown into her face by the salty-cool wind, —You told me you were taking me on vacation. I was looking forward to it so much. All I've been thinking about ever since we left home was how soon enough this would all be over and I would be swimming in the ocean. So smuck you. She turned and ambled into the water. He watched her. She flinched when it first washed over her feet, turning to foam over her ankles. He saw the flesh on the backs of her thighs turn tight and bumpy. The crystalline blue washing up over those thighs now and her rear as she waded farther out. She squealed like a child from the cold, holding her hands out as though expecting to fall, waves crashing before her. She turned her face away from them, screaming. When she was up to her belly she stopped and pinched her nose and submerged herself backward, coming up in a spray of mist and private delight. She started to swim. A wave came and crashed into her. When she came up from beneath it and wiped the salt water off her eyes and opened them, Junior was there in the water with her. He was grinning, gasping, and treading water. His eyes were excited, he was laughing harder than she had ever seen him laugh before. It was, she thought, the first true heartfelt laugh she had ever seen from him. So it made her laugh too. —Where did you come from? she said. He just laughed. Splashed her. She said, —Are you naked?

He got a funny grin on his face, disappeared beneath the

surface, and reemerged farther out. He turned onto his back and floated laughing. Then he turned over again and started swimming—neither gracefully nor quickly, more pummeling the water with ball-fisted forearms as if to punish it for its wetness than actual swimming. He went straight toward the horizon. It seemed like he would just go and go forever. When he stopped and turned to her she could barely see his little head bobbing silhouetted like a waterfowl but she could still hear him laughing.

—I'm naked! he shouted at the sky, splashing his arms like a drowning man. —I . . . am . . . *naked! NAKED! NAKED!* He started to sing it like opera: —*NAAAAAAA-KED!*

Who was this man? One minute he was the culmination of all those uptight darty-eyed decades of whispers and blunt mistrust, the next minute he was this. She found herself laughing and swimming out after him, swimming to this man, whoever this man was, finding herself once again drawn to this man as she had been drawn to him all her life, wondering why, always wondering why, always would.

Even with a thousand years of training in the oceans of the gods, even with all their breath blown at her back, she could never have gotten to him fast enough.

BILLBOARDS

Along interstates and highways throughout all states and nations Visa Billboards scanned each approaching car's license plate and—using that information to find the owner's name and Visa Identification Number in the Visa DMV database then locating on the Visa Server all the owner's e-mails and Search Engine history and Social Networking Application activity—displayed advertisements tailored specifically to each motorist's desires, fears, and insecurities no matter how secret or repressed. Each passing car saw a different Billboard. Except for the Junior Alvarez Billboard. This was shown to everyone. It bore a candid photograph of Junior Alvarez taken on a NoVA street on a sunny day at an unspecified point in the presumably fairly recent past. The photo was replaced with a new one each passing year. They updated the photo by adding wrinkles and other presumed effects of aging. The photo drizzled away into his old mug shot from when he was arrested in Indiana decades earlier and then into looped grainy surveillance footage from recent years of Junior Alvarez shortly before he fled, driving in a car, driving in a car, driving in a car. It reminded everyone of *Visa Zapruder Film II*. A Community Alert crawling along the bottom indicated that this man was wanted very urgently by the Visa FBI as he had been charged with twenty-nine counts of murder among lots of other federal crimes including extortion, racketeering, rape, narcotics distribution, and weapons trading, all of it on information provided by Diego Colon, the late Fernando Santana, and dozens of other former underlings and associates who all now hated themselves for holding on for so long to such unquestioning faith in him or maybe in anyone at all. Before Fernando was shanked—when he finally admitted to himself that all the things the damn prosecutors and guards were telling him, all that shit the other damn inmates were whispering to one another and giggling about everywhere he damn went about how damn Junior his best friend in the world, his brother, the closest person to him on this damn earth, the only other person he'd ever trusted, had been ratting on him for damn decades—Fernando before his death made efforts at putting up his own Billboards around major cities that said he would pay double whatever the FBI was offering if whoever caught Junior instead of handing him over to the authorities held on to him and kept him alive for whenever Fernando got out of prison so that he could do the honor of administering justice himself via a blast to his damn head with a shotgun. But Visa wouldn't allow him to post that on their Billboards as it happened to violate a surprisingly specific subsection in the terms of use.

The Billboards stated that Junior Alvarez was very dangerous if cornered and that he was now on the Visa FBI's Ten Most Wanted List, first appearing at number 10 then rising slowly but steadily up the charts to number 6. The billboards also indicated the number to call should one see driving through their town the man they sought so feverishly. Kids in Centreville printed pictures of the Billboards off their computers and hung them on their walls. A rogue clothing manufacturer in Centreville without Visa sanctioning sold T-shirts with a photograph of the Billboard on them. He also sold shirts that said, Run, Junior, Run! The Billboards also had a picture of Maria, whom they believed to be traveling with him or else decomposing in a ravine somewhere. Her family, her children, had not heard from her. They'd been waiting and waiting each day and all through every night for her to call not so they could tell her to turn Junior in but so they could tell her that Rosana, her firstborn, her body had been found in an apartment in New York.

Overdose.

Roberto and Lucinda Torres of Edmonton

Roberto and Lucinda Torres of Edmonton lived for two years at Expensive Hotels in and around Little Rock Beach, Visa Arkansas, a seaside vacation destination and retirement spot for the wealthy elite. Someone parked his car for him, someone carried his bags inside for him, someone opened the front door for him through which he entered.

Roberto reclined on chaise lounges poolside slavered in tar-black goo, waiting for Lucinda to come back from the small bar in the pool with their drinks, pink and slushy, his a virgin, he and all the other guests coated head to toe in the goo like life-sized clay sculptures set out to dry, all white teeth and white blinking eyes, the odorous substance caked mudlike in the wrinkles and creases of their aging flesh.

They watched the boats on the harbor, the gulls. Children swimming. They ate well.

Roberto sat on the porch drinking beepollen listening to the ocean whispers of morning, reading about himself on *Visa Times* as Lucinda was out shopping.

They befriended other couples their age. Joined them for dinner, bridge, outings on their boats, holidays. Aside from the falsity of their names and origins the friendships were genuine and enriching. One of their new friends lost his savings in an investment scam and Roberto despite the man's protests paid the mortgage on his house for the remainder of the year. One night while falling asleep in bed Lucinda told Roberto something interesting that the man's wife had told her that day on the boat while he and Roberto were at the bow fishing and discussing weather patterns: The woman was drunk on Expensive White Wine and told Lucinda not to tell anybody this but they weren't who they said they were, nor were they from where they said they were from. Her husband, she told Lucinda, was an FBI agent working undercover in pursuit of a fugitive who was believed to be somewhere in the area and was very dangerous if cornered. She and her husband were supposed to be blending in as a normal retired couple in order to find him. It was that night that Roberto and Lucinda Torres slipped out of Little Rock Beach for Gainesville.

Gainesville is a similar but less exclusive oceanside resort town 885 vkm (Visa kilometers) to the east on the southern coast of Visa Florida from where one can ride a ferry to the island of Visa Orlando to visit the Information Revolution Era ruins of Disney's World, once First America's financial and commercial epicenter and now a Visa National Park, originally built by heartbroken Founding Father Walt Disney as an unworldly tomb for his beloved pet mouse Mickey.

They left word in Little Rock Beach that there'd been a family emergency back in Edmonton and they'd be back soon. They were never seen again.

Ten years passed. Life on the road. On the run. They changed their names, culling them from books Junior read about First American cities lying forgotten in soggy sand-covered ruins at the bottom of the Sea of Life: They became the Sandiegos, the Losfelizes, the Chicos, the Sanfranciscos. Naming himself after them was a way of keeping close to him the fear he had lived with all his life and thus lived in epic stubborn desperate combat against, which was the fear that he would one day end up down there among them. So that he would feel that fear every time he spoke aloud his own name, ensuring that he would never allow himself to believe the battle was over because it never would be.

There were moments when Maria came to the brink of getting up and running out of the Expensive Restaurant or out of the Expensive Hotel room or wherever she happened to be at the moment the urge flushed through her and standing on the roadside waving down a passing motorist to take her north or east or south depending on where they happened to be or to an airport so she could cross the ocean back to Northern Virginia her home and go to the Attorney General's office there to tell them everything if it meant she'd be able to see her kids and grandbabies again for even just a few minutes, having been unallowed to contact them since leaving. Rosana especially. She missed Rosana so much and missed her every moment of every day with everything that was in her, dreamed of nothing but the day she'd see her again.

THE HUNTRESS

She missed him by four hours at a ski resort in the islands of Seattle. She smelled the trash he left in an Expensive Hotel in Spain. She lived like a creature of the plains, moving by night, sleeping in Visa Homeless Shelters. She fabricated stories about having been beaten by her husband. They let her use their beds and showers and eat canned soup and prepackaged sandwiches and packs of orange crackers with peanut butter between them. The volunteers begged her to stay long-term to start getting her feet back on the ground but her force of will overpowered this strong temptation. And so on she moved, a tough-willed old vigilante with cool green eyes and skin dried by thousands of kilometers of sun. She did not look old but shrunken and smoked. Like a venomous and silent sand reptile. Big nasty red scars from cheap crude stitching down the front of each shin. She looked like a rural Stimulanthead. As she aged she grew tired and the temptation to get off the road and give up the hunt consumed her more and more. She saw images of beaches before her and quiet side-street mornings, bathrobes, cups of beepollen, a new television, corners stacked with dust bunnies tumbling from beneath her trunks and shelves waiting for Little Josefina to gobble them up—a nice, quiet life in which to enjoy her remaining years. But whenever she saw this vision and felt this temptation, she next saw images of her late son transposed over them—Jaime, gone, gone for good now years and years and years—shattering those pleasant images and poisoning her with an anxiety the likes of which none can describe unless they have been her. She could not eat, she could not sleep, as long as her child was still underground without her and the man who had done it was still alive and wandering about in wealth and luxury having paid no retribution, no, she could not remain still nor could she enjoy her life. And so the vengeance beckoned her onward. She would die out here before she quit. Death in fury, not in tranquillity. Her body would have to fail her. Her convictions and sense of righteousness would endure all other things. She feared any other outcome. This fear was a threat to her will. It pushed her on and on.

Over the course of time she went to every state and almost every town of every state and then returned to every state and almost every town in it. She bribed and interrogated the franchisees of Restaurants and employees at Mortgage Lender and Bank. She used the computer expertise she had developed over the decades in her life as a vigilante to hack into and scour Visa DMV databases, looking for something in someone's eyes, a hint that their face was a mask, a truth behind false flesh calling out to her.

In a Motel room on the trashy outskirts of Little Rock Beach, she became lightheaded and lost consciousness and fell face first to the floor where she stayed for eight hours before coming to with no feeling in her limbs and unable to get a proper deep breath and the first thing she saw was a foggy shadow of Jaime before her—Jaime as a small child, three or four—when they went walking through the snow in Chantilly and there was a bird sitting on a telephone wire and Jaime began crying for the bird because it was so cold and Josefina said, —It's okay, Jaime, it's not cold. See all his feathers? He's warm, he's warm.

There was life. There was the world and there was Josefina Hernandez.

She followed the rhythms of her vindication which rumbled the earth below the shredded tires of her vehicles. When she needed new vehicles, she stole trucks and junked parts from Visa Scrap Yards fenced by metal wire and sentried by drooling deer the size of small black bears and put the parts together to create motorcycles which she then rode through the deserts and mall parking lots and mountains of stubborn, death-refusing America. When she saw a man being mugged on the midnight streets of Second Chicago—built on what was a thousand years earlier Rockford, Illinois—she withdrew a firearm from the holster hanging at her ribs and stood there at the mouth of the alley discharging bullets into the attackers as the victim shielded his face and shouted for forgiveness from Kevin Lithis. When Junior Alvarez's enforcer Diego Colon was released from the federal prison franchise in Roanoke after serving just seven years and given $200,000 by Visa with which to start his life anew in NoVA, Josefina was waiting for him in the room of his Centreville Visa Halfway House and she bashed in his skull with Little Josefina and removed his head at the neck using a bone saw and she carried the head in a knapsack to the Visa Union Mill Metro Station in the middle of the night where she stuck it on a steel fence post where all the people in all the commuter trains and all the morning traffic on the Interstate would see it staring at them in open-eyed horror as though still alive and awestruck at the finality of good's triumph over evil to which it had paid firsthand witness. She then donated the $200,000 anonymously to a fund for the education of the unfathered and unmothered children of the victims of Junior Alvarez and the Alvarez Gang through his reign of iniquity. She crouched on the crests of hilltops surveying through binoculars the towns below. Circled Visa Motels and Visa Hotels utilizing expensive listening devices inadvertently hearing the sex and secrets of the people inside. The method was abstract but the laws of logic held that one day she would guess right. For time was infinite but the locations in which her enemy might hide were not. The earth had edges. No one could fall off them.

The Memoir

He spent two years in Visa Newfoundland living under the name Geraldo Rivera and trying to break into Visa's film production sector as a producer. Why? Because he wanted to.

Acquired the requisite Visa Film Production Certification License. Wanted to make Historical Drama Movies about the lives of great men of history. He already knew the first three he would make. A trilogy. Alejandro el Grande, Bob Dylan, and Junior Alvarez. He acquired Visa sanctioning as a writer so that he could write the scripts himself. Acquiring Visa sanctioning as a writer included signing the contract that stated that he would not disparage Visa or any of its executives or subsidiaries in his work and also paying an extra fifty dollars on the application-processing fee.

Did the Newfoundland social scene with Maria. Dived headfirst into that Gomorrah of handshakes, brush-offs, and mutual masturbation. The brittle nature of the hierarchy was something he recognized from the underworld. Attended and hosted parties, he and Maria dressed in the flamboyant styles of the moment. Raised more than forty million dollars in private financing for the first film of the trilogy which would be about Alejandro. He even found his Alejandro—a kid who worked at Huge Retail Store in the capacity of gathering the carts abandoned by shoppers in the parking lot and who looked almost exactly like Felipe Gomez. The resemblance was uncanny. Junior wondered if this was a clandestine bastard child of the cinematic legend. Or if it was Gomez reincarnated. He believed in reincarnation.

The financiers turned shaky when a similar *Historical Drama Movie* bombed. Then his Alejandro bit the ear off a customer in

Housewares. Turned out he suffered from Visa Schizophrenia and Visa Bipolar Disorder. The psychopathology of his star made up the minds of the financiers and they pulled out and the project fell through.

He didn't care. By then he did not want to make movies anymore. He didn't want to be Geraldo Rivera (a name he located in one of his books about American history—a great civil rights leader in the Information Revolution Era who freed the slaves) anymore. And Maria had become addicted to Painkiller after taking it following a hip replacement and had also—perhaps or perhaps not related to the drug addiction—become involved in a new, expensive Newfoundland religion that Junior was almost certain was a cult. Not that there was any religion that wasn't, he believed. So one morning he woke up, told Maria to pack everything but the flamboyant outfits and her Painkillers and anything having to do with her cult, and they drove to the airport. With as little ceremony or emotion as leaving a restaurant they left their spacious, centrally located home and the identities and relationships they'd built for more than two years and grown accustomed to, just as they'd left so many others.

This was the year Tahiti resurfaced. Junior heard about it on *Visa Times*. An Airline plane flying over the Visa Pacific saw it down there one day on a flight from the Brazilian Islands to Alice Springs, the capital city of Australia, this island suddenly in the middle of the ocean that had not been there the day before. There were unprecedented remnants of Information Revolution Era civilization on it. Junior wanted to go see.

While waiting for their flight, Maria was in the bathroom going through withdrawal and he was sitting in the Beepollen Shop in the terminal. At the next table a man on his laptop looking at *Visa Times*. Junior could see the screen. A real-time news feed of retired federal agent Dickey Salazar back in NoVA, being dragged hog-tied and upside down from his $37 million West McLean home by his own former colleagues. He was thrashing around, screaming something. He'd aged a lot. As they carried him closer to the location of the News Channel camera—one of several drones fixed to poles on the street and as common in any public space as fire hydrants so as to broadcast breaking news in real time—it became clear what he was shouting over and over: —But I took down the Italians! I took down the Italians! His grim former colleagues put him into the back of a car, apologizing. He was still shouting it through the window as he was driven off to answer to charges of Visa Conspiracy to Commit Murder, Visa Aiding and Abetting a Fugitive, Visa Accomplice to Murder, Visa Perjury, Visa Obstruction of Justice, and dozens of other Visa Felonies relating to his relationship with Junior Alvarez, all of them from so many years ago—nine years into Dickey's life as a retired FBI special agent in which he must have grown to believe so many things about himself and to see himself in so many particular lights that having it all show up one day on his front porch must have seemed more incorrect than dreadful. A glitch, a case of mistaken identity.

It was the story of the month. *Visa Times* and Cable News Channel exploded in ways not seen in almost two weeks since the transsexual in Texas gave birth to eleven children. Junior followed the story from his travels. Dickey, out on bail, hired Public Relations Firm to handle the onslaught of media requests and help him turn the unwanted notoriety into unexpected fame and profit. Public Relations Firm hired a stylist, a personal trainer, a self-described branding guru, a speech coach, a personal motivational consultant, a therapist who did something on the interface of Western psychology and Zen Buddhism all mixed in with downhill skiing, and secured a contract with Publishing Company, who opened an account at Visa Book Packager to begin constructing the Visa Memoir. Dickey became a star. A fixture in *Gossip Magazine*. There were the Visa Television Channel Reality Show, the Visa Sex Tape, the high-profile but short-lived romances with inappropriate and famous women, the pregnancy rumors, the steadfast denials followed by the confirmation of the rumors followed by the exclusive first-look baby photos. There was the alcohol-induced meltdown in the parking lot of a Newfoundland Gas Station in which he shaved off his eyebrows and threw a stand-up ashtray through the window of a Visa Paparazzo's Car Company Sports Utility Vehicle resulting in a few more criminal charges. The Reality Show spin-off starred Dickey's unwell and financially strapped and now estranged wife staggering around back in NoVA in a stunned fugue state from all this, trying to keep it together amid the shock of her life being turned upside down overnight, a show that was an unexpected summertime hit. The Stimulanthead party girl from the Sex Tape somehow parlayed her fame to first become an anchor on Morning News Show and then to get appointed to a federal executive position at Visa, putting her technically eighth in line—eight heartbeats away—from the presidency of the Visa Second United States. With the help of the trainer and his staff of twenty-three including several unsanctioned and very unorthodox psychologists Dickey learned to control his appetites and shed twenty kilos and became the face of Diet Company, a lucrative opportunity that financed his legal defense and then some. Meanwhile the Texas transsexual was pregnant with another four children and Dickey was rumored to be the father. He earned $150 million that year.

The day he was found guilty on most counts was the same day the memoir was released. It was written by a team of three uncredited professional ghostwriters on staff at Book Packager working off four telephone conversations with Dickey and was mostly true. It covered his childhood in the slums of gritty Irish Lithiite Centreville alongside the infamous notorious Junior Alvarez, two willful men on opposite sides of the law doing whatever they had to do to pull themselves out of the poverty and shame and oppression and struggle of their grim origins. It covered Dickey's being recruited into the Visa FBI by a Visa Fraternity alum at Visa University–Northern Virginia and becoming a turncoat playing both sides, helping one of the FBI's most wanted men in history escape the clutches of justice in order to accomplish what he saw as the greater good: single-handedly breaking the big invincible Italian Mafia. It was a story of good and evil. So as to polarize and antagonize, two necessities if one wanted to succeed in the contemporary media market, it detailed not just how he single-handedly took down the Italians but also layed out in grotesque detail all his character flaws and shortcomings and all the mistakes and outright transgressions against civilization he had ever made. There were long, lyrical passages rhapsodizing the objects of his ravenous appetites against which he was helpless: food, alcohol, women. To appeal to female readers, Book Packager threw in a chapter about an international quest for spiritual, romantic, and gastronomical rejuvenation. Enthusiastic endorsements of certain

NoVA Restaurant locations to which he had never been but who had paid Book Packager to include embedded advertisements in the text. The cover itself while appearing at first glance to be a normal book cover was actually a piece of computer art that, when glanced upon at the right angle, suggested in 3-D (including a fairly graphic visual) that if you want up to eight hours of protection against your heavy menstrual flow without sacrificing comfort, freedom, and flexibility, you want to use new Visa Tampon Company Maxisport tampons. The litany of violations of the Rules and Regulations extended far beyond the realm of Dickey's work as an FBI agent. It went into the intimate details of his marriage including his poor wife's mental health issues and sexual dysfunctions. It went into his overeating, his failings as a Lithiite, the various ways he'd been dishonest on his taxes, all his romantic relationships from second grade on, and the various ways in which he'd contributed to their dissolutions including infidelity. Also covered: his struggle with Visa Depression, his nose picking, his annoying habit of talking back to news and advertisements on television, his feelings of intense, homicidal hatred mixed with sexual attraction to his own mother (the book stated that the attraction was acted upon when he was fourteen years old, leaving out no detail of the ensuing years-long incestuous affair that his mother could not deny, as she'd passed away years earlier. Thus despite the vehement denials of Dickey's siblings and invalid father it could never be known for sure whether or not it was true), how he once broke his younger son's watergun while playing with it and blamed it on his daughter. And so on. Anything repellent-salacious about himself that he could think of or Book Packager could imagine was included in the memoir, which was the star of Publishing Company's fall catalog that year.

At sentencing, the mother of a missing government witness who Dickey twenty years earlier exposed to Junior Alvarez in exchange for what turned out not to be the gun used by a midlevel Italian leg breaker in the murder of an FBI agent's brother was one of thirteen to deliver a Visa Victim Impact Statement. In a quiet, trembling voice Melinda Almeida stood before Dickey and expressed how the last time she had seen her son before he vanished forever they'd had a fight. He came over to visit and made a Food

Company Frozen Pizza. He left the oven on. She called him an idiot. He became hurt and angry and left. It was a stupid thing to do, she said, and she did not mean it, she was just in a bad mood. And the next day she called him to tell him she was sorry. But he didn't answer. Because he was already gone. Junior Alvarez had already murdered him. And now she had to live the rest of her life with the fact that the last thing she'd said to her son was to call him an idiot for leaving the oven on after heating a Frozen Pizza. And it was all because of what this man had done, this Dickey Salazar, this so-called FBI special agent who had been trusted with the well-being of the people.

He was sentenced to time served, thirty years' probation, four hundred hours' community service, a $3,000 fine, and court costs ($420). The first printing of the memoir sold out in four days. To celebrate, Publishing Company threw a party for Dickey in a ballroom at Expensive Hotel in Reston, the same one where Junior Alvarez was humiliated as a young man, located three blocks from the courthouse where Melinda Almeida gave her Victim Impact Statement.

He was a frequent guest on Morning Talk Show, Afternoon Talk Show, and Late-Night Talk Show, the polarizing effect of his brand and image—more viewers and culture pundits followed his every move so as to feel infuriated at his life and his success and his voice and what he symbolized than did those who were fans— giving the programs dependably high ratings and news coverage whenever he was on. This led to more sales of the book, which plateaued around the three and a half million mark but continue to hold steady to this day.

You probably remember all this. How could you not? How you couldn't turn on the television or look at *Visa Times* without seeing Dickey's increasingly browned and chiseled face, his ultrawhite teeth bared in a broad smile as he sat for an interview or was shown live leaving a courthouse while the anchor informed us of some new revelation of the saga. You probably remember the things you felt as you consumed the story. Titillation combined with disgust—at him for what he symbolized, at yourself for consuming the story of what he symbolized—a sense of both the nauseous indignation and the reassuring comfort that comes with belonging to your culture.

THE GOOD AND THE GHASTLY

Remember how influenced we were by the story? How Visa established Carlos Guerra as our president that year partly (some would say mostly) because of the board's emotional reaction to the rhetoric of his vast Dickey Salazar–inspired Visa FBI ethics reform agenda that he ran on even though he lacked executive experience and familiarity with even basic political philosophy and would prove to be one of the most disastrous, divisive presidents of the era? Do you remember the movie? The record-breaking opening weekend? Dickey Salazar at the premiere before the flashbulbs, a gorgeous sprite on each arm, leaning in with a grin to confess to the television interviewer covering the event live that they had had three-way sex in the limousine en route? Remember the stars, the night, the glinting of all those lights off their teeth and shiny shards in their gowns and off their eyes, big and hungry with the sex of money and fame? You must remember the clip they played at Visa Awards Show that year in the litany of the nominees in the moments before the film was handed the award for Movie of the Year, its ninth trophy that night. It was the scene in which Manuel Rio, playing Dickey in what would become his landmark role, tells Junior about a government witness who has been feeding Dickey's colleagues information that could ruin Junior. Junior over the next few days looks all over Centreville for the witness but can't find him. No one's seen him, no one knows where he is. He seems to have disappeared. Then Dickey one day at the office hears that the witness has reappeared—he's been picked up by the police on an old domestic warrant. Dickey shows up at the station, flashes his badge, talks to them, gets the man released, offers him a ride home. From the car he calls Junior. Tells him who he has, where he's bringing him. The witness in the backseat becomes awash in panic, tries to leap from the moving car but he's locked in. We feel his fear. He's crying, sweating, begging Dickey to let him out. But he's helpless. We feel his helplessness. It's tangible, visceral. Dickey pulls into one of Junior's Parking Garages, drives up to the fourth floor. Diego and Fernando are there waiting. Fernando's holding a tire iron. Junior (Julio Garza in an Award Show–winning role) stands in the shadows behind them, silent, obscured by the darkness, slapping his palm not threateningly but absently with a pair of rusted pliers, the hat he wears in the film cocked over one eye. You can see now probably the face of the violent idiot Diego as he opens the rear door to pull out the witness who's pushed himself against the opposite door kicking and screaming excuses and negotiations and apologies and for forgiveness from Kevin Lithis. Diego's half grin like someone anticipating the punch line of a joke. The greasy remnants of a recently devoured meal on his lips, cheeks, and chin and stuck in his rotten teeth. Remember the screams echoing off the naked concrete walls as Dickey drove off the way he came, trying with all he had in him not to look in the rearview mirror, not to feel or think, the impossible admixture of contradicting emotions evident, the moral war that was surely conflagrating within him with such furious carnage that it seemed to come out of his soul and off his face and through the screen where it turned into a cloud that floated out over the audience and settled wrenching and lonely upon each one of us as though only for us, bestowing the tuckets and bloody-mudded odors of his private war onto each one of us, because each of us was a king worthy of that?

And then the sudden cut to the woman meanwhile alone at her kitchen table with the telephone before her, the actress Rosalita Paulo. Remember that long shot of her sitting there in her dark quiet kitchen, her back to us, practicing three times, four times, what she'd say to him before picking up the phone and dialing and sighing with the phone to her ear as it rang? And the phone just ringing, ringing, ringing? Remember how loud the ringing began to seem, how harsh, how intolerable, several in the audience at each showing of the film across the world having to plug their ears and turn away in their seats, even some getting up and leaving the theater entirely just to escape that punishing unforgiving sound? And it dawning over Rosalita Paulo's face (we know it does even though we never see her face, only see her from behind but we still can see her face, we can see it even more clearly than if it were filling the entire screen in close-up) with each successive unanswered ring that she will have to live the rest of her life from this moment forward with that final word sitting on her tongue like a piece of rotting flesh that can be neither spat out nor swallowed nor washed away with water.

Remember?

THE GOOD AND THE GHASTLY

The scandal and the book.

Dickey became rich and happy. He moved to Santa Fe, bought a boat and a beautiful home on the water there, spent the remainder of his days doing whatever he felt like doing, whenever he felt like doing it. At night he sat at the Bar on the beach watching the harbor, eating and drinking and telling Junior Alvarez and Manuel Rio stories to gawking vacationers and fawning summer waitresses. And there was no shortage of women. They blew in and out of town on regular cycles always young and beautiful and interested in sleeping with a rich and famous man.

All he'd ever wanted was to eat food, drink alcohol, fornicate, and bring down the Italians.

He got it.

Junior avoided the movie and did his best to avoid the news stories but he did read the book. It was a matter of succumbing to a curiosity that started off as mild but soon grew to overwhelm him. It was titled *Visa Memoir #5–467–984*. He stole it from a Bookstore in the Spanish territory of Visa London, unwilling to give Dickey any of his money. He read it on a five-day cruise that took him and Maria around various watery locales of historic import including the spot—according to the tour guide who Junior decided to believe even though he'd noted several inaccuracies in his little lessons delivered to the group over the loudspeaker from the bow—where Scotland once was. Junior knew a little about the obscure, ancient island. He already knew before the tour guide said it that in the Information Revolution Era there lived a tribe of people there completely untouched by the modern civilization of their time. Their language contained no word for *time* or *money* or *success* or *hurry*. Or *will*. Thus they lived simple, satisfied lives of harmony, peace, and happiness. The ship then hovered over a particularly unremarkable spot on the water. The engine cut off. Just water and air and tourists and sun. The tour guide informed them that this was the spot, now obviously long submerged, where an enormous creature called the Loch Ness Monster was found beached on the shore of its namesake salina in the aftermath of the Nuclear War. This was after centuries of legend about the elusive beast had gone unfounded, its existence shrugged off by the most authoritative and modern minds of science as myth resulting from optical illusion, vivid imagination, and often outright hoaxing. Those who believed it was real were dismissed as quacks and fringe-dwelling oddballs and even con men. But now there it was, as the quacks and oddballs and con men insisted it would be, real and dead, stretched out on the shore for hundreds of feet, its tail disappearing into the ashen sea, a centuries-old monolithic water dragon with slick black skin and sand crusted in its cleavages and eyes open as though it did not know it was dead let alone no longer secluded at the depths. It was almost a dissatisfaction how sad and final the word on the matter was. There it was, the legend, the recluse, morphing before the eyes of the believers out of its mythhood and into the old landscape of the ordinary humdrum world they knew all too well which is why they had been so captivated by the legend of the creature in the first place. Junior reflected on what this meant for man and what man really knew and what he never would and how smart man really was or how smart he was not and how smart man will or will not ever be.

While he was on the deck of the ship reading the book, people would come up and point to it in his hands. They'd have a look on their faces like his reading the book made him a long-lost cousin. He could not take the book out in public without dozens of people coming up one after another like participants in some kind of prank and pointing to it in his hands with this look on their faces of the lost and alone seeking connection to a greater, more meaningful whole. They would ask him, —Where are you in it? A jerk of panic the first time he was asked that. But then he realized what they meant. First he'd oblige them with the sort of answer they expected but after a while he grew impatient. They were like pigeons. It was a violation of his personal right to privacy. Every man has the right to be left alone, he believed. Even outlaws and exiles. After a while when he was reading and would feel one of them approaching, their shadow creeping from above the upper crest of the page, knowing without having to look at them the unsure but excited aspect they carried as they anticipated the pleasure of joining with him in this cultural experience, he'd just look up and stare at them with menace until they became uneasy or even frightened and went away.

There was a part in the book in which Dickey alleged that

Junior, long believed by the people of Centreville to be an antidrug crusader, was after all not just the main distributor of narcotics in the neighborhood and the city but also such a hopeless drug addict himself that the whole time he was allowing the people to believe in his noble antidrug code of ethics and the myth of the principled hoodlum he was in actuality keeping an IV line into his chest open through which he had one of the several attractive Centreville boys he kept around him for the purposes of debauched gratification steadily feed him Painkiller around the clock. They'd follow him wherever he went and whenever he'd pull up his shirt to reveal the plastic nub hanging out of the flesh just below his right nipple like the penis of a twin self-aborted in utero they'd be ready with a loaded syringe to inject the contents into it. Dickey alleged that Junior had Visa Münchhausen Syndrome: that he psychologically and physically made himself ill in order to procure prescription drugs from doctors for the purpose of abusing them. He did this by doing things such as sitting out on his balcony in the middle of winter soaking wet wearing only his underwear to catch a cold that would hopefully if all went well turn into pneumonia. He had even gone so far, Dickey wrote, as to inject his own stool into the IV line with the intention of inducing sepsis.

While Junior was on the deck of the ship reading all this about himself, disgusted by the magnitude of the lie and the easy triumph of lie over truth, betrayed not only by that triumph but by a sense of violation, his face hot and hands sweating and heart pounding at the base of his skull, short of breath, thoughts racing, blinking because the words were turning blurry before his eyes and doubling and moving around on the page, a bourgeois middle-aged American woman leaned down and tapped him on the shoulder, a look on her face like they had once known each other.

—Where are you in it?

He looked up at her and just threw the book overboard. She let out an anguished cry like it was her child he had tossed and lunged against the rail with her arms extended out toward it as it disappeared into the white foam of the ship's wake. It was as though if not for the rail she would have dove in after it. She was groaning strangely, sadly. Junior stood, started to walk off to leave her to her mourning. But she reached out and stopped him with a firm almost manlike grip on his arm. —It's okay, she said. He tried to pull his arm away but she squeezed tighter. Disconcerting, the hand strength of this woman. It spoke to something irrational and extreme within her. She held him there while she used her free hand to pull her own copy of the book from her purse and foisted it upon him.

—Take it.

—I don't want it, he said. He wouldn't touch it. She took his hand by the wrist and tried to make his hand accept the book. This set him off into a rage. He started yelling, —I said I don't smucking want it! Get your smucking hands off me! She wouldn't. He pushed her face away, still yelling, —I don't want it! She maintained her grip, even while he pushed her face, twisting her head completely around toward the water.

—Take it! she was crying, his palm over her mouth shoving her head away. It caused a scene. People were trying to intervene. They were separated at last.

—I don't smucking want it! I don't smucking want it! he was still shouting as Maria appeared and apologized to the woman now trying to foist the book into the hands of the man who had separated them. Maria placated the situation, took Junior belowdecks to get a glass of water and calm down.

Once back on land he approached several attorneys all of whom told him the same thing: He could do little in regard to a libel suit because he was a man without a country. He'd have to turn himself in to the government of the Second United States if he wanted to proceed with libel action. Or get a new country. The citizenship application process would take years. And any country he'd actually want to live in had an extradition treaty with the Second United States through the Visa Globalization Network so they'd turn him over as soon as he stepped foot into the Visa Citizenship Office. He never considered that living outside the law, being free of the conventions and compromises placed on men by the societal contract, meant that others who remained burdened by such things were free to slander him in their memoirs. It almost made him rethink his entire life philosophy. Maybe living like this—seeking complete and true independence and individuality—had not been worth it. Maybe rejecting everything that everyone else just accepted without thinking about it had been a mistake. Maybe it wasn't even that—maybe they *did* think about it and that's why they accepted it. Making him in fact not the smart one but the stupid one. Which is maybe what you are if you believe that you think about things no one else does. Yes, it was not the years of running from Expensive Hotel to Expensive Hotel, entering each one through the front door of course—now somehow feeling enslaved by that, by the very thing he had lived his life in the monomaniacal pursuit of obtaining—and years of running from country to country, years of changing names and suffering constant paranoid delusions and dread and often maddening isolation, of believing he saw in the innocent passing of vehicles outside his rooms patterns consistent with surveillance details, of never meeting or even seeing from across a crowded city street another human being— Maria included—without believing that this person was here to bring about his arrest or death—it was not the decade of living like this loaded with his captured dreams hanging around his neck like the carcass of a monstrous bird but the lies written about him, the attempt at tarnishing his name for commercial exploitation and personal satisfaction, his name, his legacy, the only thing we leave behind once our lives are done—the only thing he could say he was convinced was ever truly important—and the acceptance of this crude bludgeoning as truth by those who would ultimately make the judgment upon that legacy, that is, us, the people, us meaningless Sisyphean people of convention and commonality who make up civilized humanity and so filled him with disgust whenever he thought of us—it was the memoir that caused him to consider for the first time giving up, turning himself in, paying for his violations of the laws of the Visa Second American Federal Government and the Lithiite Rules and Regulations and making up for all he had done against the social game of man—which was all civilization and its rules were, he believed: a game, just a silly game, illusory and meaningless—not so that he then might find whatever redemption there was for a man like him but so that he might sue into living death all those responsible for the defamation of his character.

He obsessed over the matter for days. He'd wake up with his jaw sore, tense from brooding about it all night even as he slept. He made up his mind then changed it half a dozen times over the next three days in Ireland where he and Maria went to find the remains of Cork, the village where Junior believed his father originated before fleeing to NoVA as a young man during the Lithiite-Separatist conflicts sixty years earlier—acts of war and terror stemming from the matter of whether the church's leader had to be a direct genealogical descendant of Kevin Lithis or not, a man nobody could prove had ever lived, a disagreement that resulted in the death and disfiguring of tens of thousands of not just soldiers but innocent children and women and men as well. Maria ran out of patience with his waffling and thinking out loud and told him to just decide one way or the other because she was sick of hearing about it. One night in Belfast while eating pad thai and sushimi—the traditional Irish dish—the food mixed with the ambience of his origins and the general falling feeling of total freedom and he realized that at last now he truly had all he had ever wanted. It all came together in a perfect way that night in his own little place carved onto the grand stanchion of history.

That was the one and only time he considered giving up.

THE TASK FORCE

The Visa Federal Joint Task Force consisted of representatives from the various law enforcement sectors. It was dedicated to the bringing to justice of Junior Alvarez. Visa's financial sector allowed it to offer citizens a reward of one billion dollars in exchange for information leading to Alvarez's capture. As a result, the Joint Task Force spent a lot of time examining photographs taken by security cameras or cell phone cameras all across the world of white-haired men who sometimes bore only the vaguest resemblance to Junior Alvarez. They studied Visa Professional Baseball telecasts tipped by frantic e-mails from viewers that the man behind the dugout two rows back who you could see only when they cut to a shot of the on-deck hitter was Junior Alvarez. Blond women in Department Stores and street markets in Visa Central America who if one squinted while crossing one's eyes just so could be Maria. Shaky pixilated video taken by cameraphone of an older couple in the Spanish territory of Visa London. A white-haired man diving naked from lush blue waterfalls of New Mexico. Though they privately confirmed three, four sightings a year, the Visa FBI told the media all the sightings were unconfirmed.

There was a particular chief of the Joint Task Force named Miguel Aybar who for the four years of his time in the position lived on airplanes and in Hotel rooms, zigzagging across the world chasing ghosts. Miguel Aybar went to Uruguay to look at the crispy remains of an American found bisected on train tracks. Maggots in the eyes, black flies buzzing in a thick cloud around the head. He went to the desert in the Visa Russian territory of Dakota to a little hut there that was the Visa Police Station, two gas pumps outside, sodas and fleshy objects they called hot dogs available for purchase inside, upstairs rooms available for rent by the hour, downstairs in the basement a jail, the region's only Visa FedEx Location situated in the rear. There he interviewed a frail white-haired man found stuck half dead in an air vent at Bank who the cops informed Aybar was known to them as the Senior Bank Robber who had been pulling strings of Bank robberies all over their desert region for the last four years and now that they had him and got a look at him they believed he was that gangster guy they were looking for. They told Aybar he could have him for a hefty sum of money and weaponry, an offer that he declined. Aybar spent in total five weeks' worth of time in federal prisons interviewing inmates who confessed to the guards late at night in fits of detoxification from Stimulant or Painkiller or alcohol addiction either that they were Junior Alvarez or that they knew where he could be found. The search for Alvarez consumed Miguel Aybar body and soul. He became obsessed. In year three while pursuing a lead in Vietnam he received word from a lawyer claiming to represent his wife. This man claimed Aybar's wife had just filed for divorce on the grounds of abandonment. That was the moment Aybar realized he had not spoken to his wife in almost an entire year. He destroyed the message and chose to believe the lawyer was lying or mistaken and went to Ireland to a Visa Pub in Lithiite Belfast which still smoldered from its burning at the hands of Separatists the night before. Junior Alvarez had been seen playing darts in this Pub the previous morning.

Miguel Aybar had copies of Alvarez's fingerprints from his arrest fifty years earlier sent to every Funeral Home and Medical Examiner's Office in the country and to as many as possible throughout the world to compare with any John Does they had.

It was interesting for Miguel Aybar to learn that Junior Alvarez, now one of the Visa FBI's Five Most Wanted, was living in the walls of a man's home in a little village in Visa India that Aybar had never heard of called Visa Bombay. Aybar was interrupted while smashing the man's walls with a hammer by a phone call from headquarters ordering him to haul ass to Africa because Junior Alvarez was in the village of Mogadishu living among a tribe there as a sort of godlike Kurtz figure who they believed possessed powers of healing. Colonel Walter Kurtz was a Visa Founding Father of the First United States, a key general in the Visa Revolutionary War who lived among the Native Americans learning their bloody and ruthless techniques of warfare—including scalping—that the colonists would use to achieve unlikely victory over their tyrannical British oppressors.

Four, five times Aybar looked into the decayed eyes of Junior Alvarez's corpse in some exotic country or another.

He broke through the door of an Expensive Hotel room in the tropical Montreal Kwabeck territory of Visa Upstate New York tipped off by a maid that Junior Alvarez was there. He found the beepollen percolator still gurgling and the bathroom mirror still fogged from a recent shower. There was a digital camera on the nightstand with pictures of beautiful white beaches and snowy mountain lakes, peaks of foggy southwestern mountains, vast earthly tapestries and far-off rich greens against fat white cloud skies. These were pictures of freedom, life as seen through the eyes of a free man, a man liberated of all that burdens us: laws, financial concerns, conscience. Miguel Aybar found himself standing there in the room scrolling through the photos again and again, alarmed to find himself so overcome with envy toward the immensity and might of this man's will that his knees became weak and he had to sit on the edge of the bed until his head stopped spinning and his stomach stopped flipping and his breath came back.

Aybar became a man who stood above gurneys in Visa Medical Examiners' Offices while small odd men pulled back sheets, proudly revealing the corpse of Junior Alvarez, now number two on the FBI's Five Most Wanted List behind only perennial number one Jason Anderson, the radical Seussian construction heir turned self-described holy warrior who had read certain passages in *The Lorax*, the Seussian religion's holy text, and took them to mean that God wanted him to direct his followers to do things such as blow themselves up in crowded shopping malls and hijack Second American Visa Airline airplanes and crash them into the Third World Trade Center, killing thousands and thousands of men and women and children, including themselves.

Junior Alvarez died several times a month. His death was all around Miguel Aybar. It was forced down into his belly through his mouth. It was in the blue skies with the green trees shimmering before it: Junior Alvarez dead, Junior Alvarez dead, Junior Alvarez dead.

But Junior Alvarez was not dead.

Bob Dylan

After seeing a new documentary about him on Public Television Channel featuring scholars of history, religion, and art discussing the man's life and work he began walking the streets of foreign cities humming the songs of Bob Dylan: "Imagine," "Auld Lang Syne," "(I Can't Get No) Satisfaction," "Beat It," "Amazing Grace," "Even Flow," "Sgt. Pepper's Lonely Hearts Club Band," and so on. His lifelong obsession rekindled. Wandering around the markets with Maria peering upon the indigenous objects laid out on tables for their inspection and purchase as tourists, small native children running amok through dirty fish puddles on sunpatch streets. Standing in the shadow of grand ruins jutting forth from unexpected swaths of green land—golden arches, swooshes, crosses, and other ancient Information Revolution Era religious symbols—as if the claw of the past tore through its tomb and reached for the life in heaven that its makers abandoned it for. Standing there in a windbreaker humming "Like a Rolling Stone" as Maria took photographs. All his life he had felt such a kinship to that song and could never understand why. For the last three weeks he'd been mutter-singing it as they waited for planes, as they strolled through city streets. He'd whistle it as he tied his shoes in hotel rooms. Maria finally had to ask him to please give it a rest. He kept secret from her that he had long believed himself to be Bob Dylan. A reincarnation. Junior once believed that he was Alejandro reincarnated but starting from as long back as before Newfoundland he'd seen that that had been incorrect—it was Bob Dylan who was the reincarnation of Alejandro el Grande. And he himself was the reincarnation of Bob Dylan. The reincarnation of a reincarnation. Before him there had been others. And the cycle would not end with him. Alejandro had existed and would continue to exist in all eras in which there was a man whose will was big enough and strong enough to host his spirit.

—Bob Dylan was ruthless, Junior told her as they wandered the markets. —He was a throat cutter. He was the meanest son of a bitch you'd ever meet. The most ambitious. He wasn't afraid to size you up and let you know you came up short. He knew what he wanted. Supremacy. Not financial supremacy or market supremacy but supremacy over himself. He decided very early on that nothing less than that was acceptable and he proceeded from there. For the rest of his life he was relentless in the pursuit of the designs he had in his head. In his case, particular sounds. He never settled. Never believed in making the best of a job or a life he had not chosen and carved out with his own hands. He never tolerated for one second living a life that had been chosen for him. Know what he did once? He was a worldwide superstar. Bigger and richer than he ever imagined he would be. Money, women, everything. But suddenly he had all these people—his entire generation and then some—pressuring him to do this or do that, expecting certain things from him, trying to fit him into their opinions or into the landscape of their lives, trying to make money off him, trying to tell him what to do, what to say, what kind of sounds to make, even though he heard his own particular sounds in his head that he lived in pursuit of. So you know what he did? Did he grin and bear it? No, he drove his motorcycle off a cliff. Of course he jumped off first. But he let them all think he died. They all moved on to other things to try and fit into their opinions and landscapes. Eight years later, when he suddenly reappeared, resurrected from the dead, no one really noticed except the few who wanted to hear the sounds he chased in his head. He had his life back. His life. The way he wanted to live it. Bob Dylan wasn't a musician. Bob Dylan was a mean, ruthless, conquering son of a bitch. It would have been the same if he had decided to go into, I don't know, concrete. We'd still be talking about his concrete. If he had designs in his will regarding concrete he would have done anything to stay devoted to them. He would have intimidated the hell out of anybody who threatened his pursuit of those designs. And that is why Bob Dylan is brilliant and why his legacy endures. Because he refused to have it any other way. To live any way other than how he wanted. And by doing that he willed himself into history. Everyone else, all those people who wanted to fit him into their landscapes? They disappeared. All those other musicians who were more talented than he was? They disappeared. Them and their work. Of all those musicians with beautiful voices only Bob Dylan, a singer who couldn't sing, remained. No one really knows a thousand years later that he even had contemporaries. Know why? Know why we still sing his songs like "All You Need Is Love" and "Ode to Joy" and "The Tambourine Man" and don't even know the names of the songs of his contemporaries? Because those contemporaries were just musicians. Musicians come and go. Bob Dylan wasn't a musician. Bob Dylan was something else.

There were no remaining photographs of Dylan's face but Junior believed the man must have had his face. While overlooking grand bluffs over white seacoasts in the Visa Mediterranean he wondered if Bob Dylan had ever laid his own Bob Dylan eyes on those seas. He reclined on white beaches eating lobster in the shade with Maria, Maria sipping lightly alcoholic rum drinks, he sipping virgins, both slathered head to toe in thick black goo, wondering if Bob Dylan had ever reclined on white beaches such as this with lobster and shade and drinks and a woman. What would Bob Dylan do if he were on the run from civilization? If he were in exile like a banished king? The only other man who could understand the feeling of having the whole world against you. Bob Dylan would understand that Junior turning himself in—as unthinkable as it was—would not even be enough. It would not quench their thirst. They would want to account for all—beyond the realm of the criminal. They wanted to lick his blood from the webbing of their fingers. He even said to himself, I am Bob Dylan. He never died because like Alejandro el Grande he never lived at all but rather was a spirit that blows through all time landing into vessels of which I am but the latest. His successor. This he knew to be true. He held these truths to be self-evident. Escaping the past by journeying backward and naked as though the rest had not happened. Leaving his life and the evidence of its effort there in the earth undisturbed, to be found by others. Or to be ignored. It didn't matter. The point was to be vital. All forces pull us toward invitality. Fight them.

He danced with Maria in elegant ballrooms all over the world. In exotic cities he slept beside her in Expensive Hotel rooms, windows overlooking Information Revolution Era ruins, the ornate remains of how things were before we decided to annihilate them. He smoked cigars on the back porches of private dining rooms and read books about the Information Revolution Era and thought about writing his own book, one greater than any of those he read, a comprehensive, impressionistic volume on the life of Bob Dylan. It would focus on the man's later years in which he reseized the vitality of which they tried to strip him. The work would be the mark of legacy for all three vessels of the will: Alejandro, Bob Dylan, Junior Alvarez.

That holy trinity.

INCONTINENCE

Visa Topeka National Park 3411 A.W. He stood in line at the Beepollen Shop adjacent to the multistory gift-shop-cum-hotel. A toothful man wandered up and down the line selling Topeka National Park T-shirts, can coolies, key chains, and other such doodads. The line went out the door into the ash fields out there. Acres of hardened gray concealing deep beneath it a thousand years of vanquished First American civilization. Decades-long archaeological excavations were marked off-limits by yellow tape. Two years earlier they'd pulled out the first one, a female, a plaster casting of an entire female who died in her home sitting on her couch like a cat with her legs curled beneath her, a remote control in her hand, a person who in the centuries after her death dissolved in the petrified ash coating, leaving as evidence of her life the empty shape where her body had been and the things she had owned and the home she lived in and nothing else.

Children ran over the ash fields, their arms spread out like the wings of airplanes.

They believed they'd uncovered an ancient small residential neighborhood. The things—the cars, the buildings—had not dissolved as the people had but were preserved almost perfectly by the ash. There seemed to be a stretch of road piled with smashed vehicles. They'd uncovered something called Chili's.

Fathers with high shorts and socks pulled up over the shins leaned in a dutiful, grave way to examine the placards on wooden posts explaining that archaeologists believe that buried beneath the ash fields was the best and most perfectly preserved specimen of Information Revolution Era humanity ever discovered, an entire ancient town frozen in its time exactly as it was a

257

thousand years ago on any given unremarkable midday instant, caught naked and whole at the moment of its swift and sudden destruction. Food half eaten on plates, people for a thousand years heading out to their apartment complex parking lot to run errands. A man had been excavated half risen from his toilet to peer out his bathroom window, likely alarmed by a heinous unmistakable noise coming in the distance from every direction. A wad of toilet paper remained perfectly preserved where it had been clutched by his now disintegrated hand. It was still filthy in the intermediation between the wipe and the dropping of it into the toilet bowl which also remained. As soon as it became exposed to the present-day air, the paper in one brief moment like a magic trick just vanished before the scientists' eyes, getting right with the time that had so long passed it by. The scientists who saw it in that instant before it vanished were intrigued to notice that the ancient filth was brown rather than the deep gray of our present-day filth. A by-product of the matter's aging, they hypothesized.

He'd been in line for a long time. He'd just wanted a cup of beepollen while waiting for their trolley tour of the park which they had tickets for. Maria was sitting on a bench nearby waiting for him. He'd already twice asked the woman behind him to hold his place while he went to use the restroom. Fifteen or sixteen times he'd gone today. Only actually urinated four of those times. Weak trickles that did not make sense considering the urgency with which he'd had to go.

It was summertime. He'd come here for history, to see the ash people, the ancient city of Topeka which he'd found so exciting when he read about it on *Visa Times*. To convince Maria to leave the mountaintop idyll of a cabin in Colorado and come here he told her about the multistory gift shop. He wanted to peer into the plaster faces of the people of ash. Their open eyes, their lips curled in midutterance, extinguished as they were without warning, unaware that this conversation they were engaged in regardless of its inanity or profundity was their last. He wanted to consider the nature of historic American man presented in unromantic coldhearted candor.

There was an ironic cheer from his section of the line when it crossed the threshold of the gift shop door and into the air-conditioning. He blended in, a quiet old codger. The man in front of him turned all of a sudden and said, —Seen the Topekans?

Four different people sitting at tables were on their laptops reading stories about him on *Visa Times*. There'd been an unconfirmed sighting in Austria this morning. His picture from years and years ago staring out from beside the scant text, this wanted fugitive standing feet away watching them look at him in such improbable and hokey environs.

—Not yet.

—Poor sons of bitches, the man said. He stared soberly at Junior. Junior nodded. —What I want to know is, if we evolved from monkeys, why don't these people they're pulling out of there have tails? Has anyone asked those Palinists that? They look just like us. That could be us they're pulling out of there. Evolution my ass.

—It will be, Junior said.

—What do you mean by that?

—What do you think.

Short pause. —You think it'll happen again?

—Of course it will.

—Wow. Lithis. That's twisted. That's really just— You should be more optimistic. The man was shaking his head, looking at the floor, almost seeming to become more angry the more he thought about it. —You can't say that. You can't just go around thinking like that. Kevin Lithis what a twisted way of looking at the world.

Junior was slightly embarrassed about the quality of the photograph. It was so out of date. A bad picture regardless. Thought about having Maria take a newer, better one, one he was more comfortable with, and sending it in as a replacement.

The man had turned around again to face the front. He was still shaking his head like that, repeating again and again, —You can't say that . . .

He felt a hot trickle of piss on his upper thigh.

He knew the picture. He had never seen it before but he remembered the day it was taken by a security camera. The Visa State Lottery Office on West Ox Road in Fairfax. Once upon a time, about a hundred years earlier, he'd been in there to collect the winnings of a lottery ticket. A low-life Centreville Painkillerhead named Juan Ramirez had actually by the Visa Grace of Kevin Lithis drawn the winning numbers on a multibillion-dollar jackpot. Juan was getting blotto around town all day in celebration, showing off the winning ticket to everybody he saw. Junior heard about it. So he and Fernando and Diego drove around until they found him at a Bar and kidnapped him. Brought him to his Garage. Fernando and Diego held him down and pried his mouth open while Junior took hold of his front tooth with a pair of pliers and told him he was going to start pulling until they were all scattered around the floor like marbles and then he was going to bite out his eyeballs and then his tongue and then he would bite off his scrotum and then his penis, stuffing each thing one at a time as he bit it off into his anus, and the only thing that could stop him from doing this he explained was Juan telling the Lottery Commission the truth when he went in tomorrow to claim the prize: that back when Juan had been on his way to purchase the would-be winning ticket he'd stopped in at the Liquor Store to say hello to his good friends Junior, Diego, and Fernando, and while there he made a deal with them to split any winnings four ways. Junior tugged a little on the tooth and asked Juan if he had the story correct, if Juan agreed that this recollection of events was what the truth was. Juan did.

The next day they all went along with Juan to the Lottery Office. Fernando drove.

The three-million-dollar annuity gave Junior a legitimate income for years, providing a means of preventing the DEA and Visa State Police and other law enforcement entities with whom he did not have connections from indicting him on money laundering or tax evasion or other such charges, which, he had read in prison, was how after decades of failure they had finally pinned Tony Soprano back in Information Revolution Era New Jersey.

The man turned back around, but only halfway, more turning his head to say over his shoulder with disgust in his voice, —You know what? You're *wrong*. It *won't* happen again. Because we're not like those people. They lived a thousand years ago. They weren't even Lithiites. You think we haven't advanced at all since them? For one thing we have Kevin Lithis and his slogans and his Rules and Regulations. And we have *history*. That's the *point* of history. *To learn from our mistakes so we don't make them again.*

Now he could see that the people on the laptops were reading news about other occurrences in distant parts of the world on this day in the thirty-fifth century: nationalism and religion and sex and money and bigotry and imperialism and anger and hurt and fear and self-deceit and state-of-the-art weaponry that made it easier to kill one's enemies and harder to be held accountable for it or suffer any consequences of it—politically, emotionally, spiritually—with further technological advancements being made to make it even easier and even easier and even easier as they stood there reading about it.

He did not argue. What was the point? He knew who was wrong and who was right and who had evolved and who hadn't and he just wanted his smucking cup of beepollen so he could get on the smucking trolley to take the goddamn trolley tour.

THE STENCHES

Maria began waking up in bed in the middle of the night to find Junior gone. She'd go downstairs and have the night concierge bring the car around, and she'd drive around town until she found him terrified and distraught on a playground or at a bus stop, once in a freezer in the frozen-food aisle of a twenty-four-hour Grocery Store. He was nude and blue, surrounded by silent store employees staring at him like he was a confusing piece of art in a museum. At last he agreed to come out but only after seeing Maria on the other side of the frosted-glass doors and hearing Maria's voice calling to him through the desert wind sounds that blew in his skull.

His right shoulder became arthritic. The cartilage in his knees and hips ground away until it was bone on bone. It became too painful to fly or to climb stairs. They had to take boats and trains, request Expensive Hotel rooms on the first floor.

She found three lumps in her breast while showering in China. Didn't tell him.

They became cranky and impatient with the size of the text on Restaurant menus. She had to shout for him to hear her. They were always tired. He'd smell awful, horrific odors that she did not. They were so pungent and rancid to Junior that once he was convinced someone had died in the room next door and called the front desk who sent somebody up to check.

Four, five times he called her a name she had never heard before and accused her of having drilled into the hotel room through the floor using the mindpowers she had developed through years of evolution as a subterranean extraterrestrial of some sort.

They asked if there were any menus with bigger type. Junior ordered mountains of food then forgot that he ordered them and ordered it all again the next time the waitress came around not believing her when she sweetly and gently told the little elderly man he'd already ordered it. When the food came Junior was certain that he did not order all this food but when asked what he did order he could not remember the answer to that question, even though it was right there, sitting right on the tip of his tongue.

IN THE GARDEN

It became the season for losing. He felt himself going the way of all the earth.

He'd been bracing himself for this night, this season. He'd always been aware as an observant and philosophical participant in human history that it hovered ever foreboding like storm clouds in all our horizons breathing its hot breeze through the leaves and our hair: death. Now he could see it coming. Now he watched his bone density lose away and his hearing and his seeing and his general tolerance for others lose away and his ability to sleep lose away. What would be taken next? His mind? His will?

Tonight in a room in an Expensive Hotel somewhere or another where a man parked his car for him and a man carried his bags for him and a man opened the front door for him as he entered through it—*the front door*—nowadays not even really aware of the men and what they did or what he did not do or what was being done for him or that he was entering through the front door any more than he was aware of there being ground beneath his feet or air going in and out of his lungs. He had not slept in three days. How could he when he felt death coming? All night tonight he stayed up first staring at his own gray shriveled visage in the mirror then with jealousy watching Maria who still had her sleep. She lay there on the bed on her back, hands folded atop her thin belly like a virgin awaiting a vampire, eyes closed, duvet bunched at her feet, starched white sheet folded back at her waist, lips parted as though in expectation of a kiss, body gaunt and long-looking, lumps in breasts now terribly drastic, visible even through the fabric of her cotton nightgown which was darkened around the underarms, clavicle, and groin with musky dank perspiration that as well condensed on her forehead and hairline and trickled down into her ears and hair. Doll's hair, Junior thought. Always strands of it found all over the floor and shower drain and curtains and bedding. In what had become routine before moving on from an Expensive Hotel Junior now had to go around with a vacuum cleaner he now traveled with, kept in the trunk of whatever car they were driving, and purify the rooms of all the hairs prior to checking out.

Maria's voice had become raspy. Painful for her to speak. She communicated mostly through writing. He had started hoarding the free pens and notepads from the Expensive Hotel room desks for her to use. Now and then he'd feel something on his lap and look down and there'd be a piece of stationery that said only, I Love You.

Face and skin dulling even beneath its liquidy mask. Deadening. Junior knew death, had seen so much of death, had made a life of it. He knew it when he saw it. He knew the stink of it.

He was not sure what town or country this was that he was in tonight. But he had slowly lost his sleep in its entirety over the last five, six months. He'd begun experiencing spells of amnesia and dementia followed by an unrelenting panic about it. He sweated and sat there all night tonight in this Expensive Hotel room, seventy-two hours without sleep, air-conditioning off in the dead of summer because that machine made such a roaring noise and he didn't like not being able to hear anything outside. He chewed the skin around his fingernails ripping chunks of the white calcified flesh away and swallowing it. Listened to the noises outside. TV off, fan off too, lights off. Maria off. Everything off. Except for me, he thought. The world after me more than ever now. It's a hornet's nest, the world is. And I've kicked it. Boy have I kicked it. Kicked the living hell out of it. I have done this simply by living. By being who I am.

Eyes in the wall, cameras behind the mirror, a two-way mirror, or in the mirror. That's why he'd begun hanging bath towels over all mirrors upon initial entry of an Expensive Hotel room. Surveillance equipment in the screws holding the mirror on the wall and in the carbon monoxide detectors behind the bed— microfiber supertech tools built with new science so far beyond his comprehension. This sent an unending deep terror through him. It thrived on the insecurity that it created. A racket of fear. Every mammalian scurry and stick-breaking. Bugs and birds chirping. Every far-off highway whistle. Machine gun with full clip propped up on the side of the room's desk always. He thought, We have to get out of here. Where will we go? Another Expensive Hotel in another city in which we will be strangers and alone, another year of lies and suspicion and nights without air-conditioning like this one, death nonetheless still approaching just as it does now? No—change. The need for change is undeniable. But what kind?

A crusted bucket at the side of Maria's bed which she woke up now and again in order to turn over the side of the bed and wretch greenly into before falling back to sleep—all without sound. Living a vow of silence they had taken in their lives as outlaw monks.

Junior getting up now to go to the window and peek out of it at the spot off in the distant unseen black hills where among the blackness and odd red blipping light of the aerial tower there he sees yes a young man staggering down singing the words How does it feel, how does it feel, to be on your own? His father, his daddy, coming home from Bar in the early-morning hours while all the other daddies walk past him in the opposite direction on their way to work. As it was every morning when Junior was a boy, before he disappeared and before Junior stole the car that sent him away. Junior'd be woken in the middle of the night by an absence in the room. He'd go to the window just as he is at this window now and he would sit there watching for his father, listening for the drunken warble of his bellowing. It was always that song. And here he is, coming home at last after all these years: his father. And it feels good to be this little boy again. This son. A child with a father and his whole life ahead of him. So much vitality yet so much strength to acquire. So much to experience for the first time. Everything ahead of him and nothing behind him. It feels better to be this child than to be what he is: an old man. An old man with nothing ahead of him and everything behind him.

I'd give it all, I'd give whatever it takes, anything to be a child again.

He put his chin on his forearm and his forehead against the glass as his father dissolved away into the blackness of the hills that he could not even see. The final resonation of the sad drunken brouhaha more a taunt than singing fading into silence. He stared out with unblinking watery eyes. It looked like he was listening intently to something at the deepest undertones beneath the silence. He was still. Eyes darting. He was not even breathing. Every weak withered muscle in his doomed tired body was tensed. He tried to figure out the next move but found himself thinking instead about his life. All the things behind him.

He had no appetite nowadays. The thought of food repulsed him. When even water entered his mouth his throat just dried up and constricted like a slug doused in salt. Fizzling salival juices burned the hinges of his jaw. An urge to retch. Maria no longer had her appetite either. But she could sleep. How he was jealous of her.

If I could, I would sleep for days. I'd wake up feeling young again. Nothing behind me, everything ahead of me.

He'd gone to such outrageous lengths just to become the man he wanted to be. He had lived his life with the philosophy of living it in such a way that when a night such as this very one came in which he could hear the dingdong approaching he would look back at all the things behind him and feel no regrets. And here that moment was and when he looked behind himself he was shocked to find nothing but the nagging mosquito whine of regret in his ear. He swatted it away.

I should not be here, he thought. I should not be running around like this. I am an elderly man who should be cared for by those whom I have benefited. I am of an age and point of mental and physical degradation where I need rest and to be cared for. If I had children of my own. If I had a home. I need a home. A real home. That's what we need. That's the change. That's the right move. The right thing to do. In the morning I will take Maria and acquire for us a home. We will rest in it. We'll give her children a call. They will come. They will bring the grandbabies. They will care for us.

When it was morning he went over to wake her so they could go and acquire a home in which to rest and be cared for. He kissed her forehead. That's how he normally woke her. Her forehead was cold and hard. He touched her face but the flesh did not seem to move against the pressing of his fingers. He said her name first softly then with force and she did not answer. He pulled her hand from where it was folded upon her belly but it was like she was resisting him. He used his fingers to open her eyes and look into them but there was no mind behind her eyes. They stared up and through him in bland horror. He put his ear to her mouth but he couldn't hear anything. He stood there for a long time just staring at her and staring at nothing and listening to himself breathe. Then he reached down and began undoing the buttons of the nightgown. He slid his hand inside. Felt her flesh. It felt like cold wood. He put his hand over her hard left breast, feeling those inhuman chunks in them as hard as pebbles. He stared off at himself reflected like a hologram in the window, seeing himself as a black sinister thing perched over the comatose virgin Maria, mother to dead children.

He was feeling for a heartbeat. There was not one.

He stood there thinking. Then he took his hand out of her nightgown and pulled the hem up over her thighs, her waist, rolling it over her stomach, raising her up off the bed enough so that he might roll the nightgown up over her spine and sharp delicate birdlike shoulders. He lifted her body up off the mattress. It was light, almost weightless. And he pulled the nightgown over her head, letting her body fall back down on the bed naked and still and, taking one last look at her face, he pulled the sheet and the bedding over her face forever. He undressed. Stood there naked. He held the nightgown before himself as though it were a holy but rent ephod. Pulled the rank garment over his own head, down over his own body. Strands of loose blond hair clung to his face. Picked them off. The fabric smelled of her. It always would. He put on his wig, his glasses, gathered his things and put on her coat, left her there.

Downstairs the old lady was not noticed among the other guests wandering toward the café for the free breakfast buffet.

She left the hotel through the back door.

RECKONINGS

By the next week the old lady was far, far away. She bought a home with cash. It was in your neighborhood, across the street from you. The house had a porch and a rocking chair in which she sat one morning saying her prayers as you passed by on your way to work.

And now the old lady works. Night and day, in the spring following the brutality of winter, in the basement of her home, the top two floors empty with thick cobwebs spanning the doorways and corners of ceilings and thick dust like atomic fallout coating the floors, no footprints in them, virginal and perfect all.

She is engaged in the final, greatest, most unlikely act of her will.

The windows of the home are boarded-up first with thick sheets of plywood she's nailed to the interior window frames with hundreds of large nails shot from a high-powered Tool Company nail gun. Then when she was not satisfied that this was enough to secure her home and work, she welded large sheets of lead over them.

Her frail skin and huge eyes are yellowed from jaundice. Teeth missing from neglect. Ghastly breath. Unbathed with a greasy pallor. A hunchback from so many long hours spent bent over her workbench. She has not eaten except for rats she catches down here in the basement when she knows her body requires sustenance. Talks to herself, mutters, spits. Slaps her face to stay awake. Flies in her hair and ears that sometimes she catches and eats believing them to be sources of protein. Her stomach distended with the unused digestive acids dripping from its lining, eating away that membrane with a painful burn that she does not feel due to the hard coating of scar tissue that has developed. Muttering to herself as she pads around without patience toward some tool or material she needs, —No more, no more, no more, no more . . . Sitting at the workbench with a single bulb burning over her head, eyes having adjusted to the near total darkness in which she now lives her life. Working, working—like a nocturnal vermin, working. So much to do, such a tremendous undertaking. Thousands and thousands of small tasks to do over and over until they are done right. Sometimes she sits here at her workbench for four, five days on end, legs going numb and blood clotting behind the knees. Thin, almost transparent flesh wraps her bones. Hands jittery, arthritic, blue veins popping out from beneath her flesh, forcing now and then a live squealing rat into her mouth and biting into it though it's so hard and dry in her mouth, going down her throat in a wet-furry unmoving mass that she coughs and gags on but finally works it down through her chest where it sits in her sternum and is broken down over weeks by enzymes that carry it off pieces at a time into her blood until it is all gone at which point she eats another. She has lost all concept of time—a cheap kitchen timer reminds her when it is time to eat. So easy to get wrapped up in her work and forget. But if she doesn't eat, she cannot work.

She does not know how long she has been here working on the final act of her will. She knows only that she must continue. If she has ever known anything it is that she must finish. Nor does she remember anyone named Maria. Or Tony Be Right Back. Or Alejandro el Grande—any of those ghostly names that have made up her life—though they have each visited her here in the tomb over and over, one at a time, standing there and staring at her, even her victims, with toeless feet and fingerless hands and toothless gums and smelling like the river water that filled their throats, all of them saying over and over, —No more, no more . . . until she said it back to them, in that way acknowledging them, at which point they fizzled away like her father did.

One morning while the old lady was sitting on the porch, watching you leave your home on your way to attend to your life, the men taking her garbage, an oblivious police cruiser drifting past the number-two most-wanted man in the world, she thought to herself, Now I have a home. Now I can rest. But what about my name? What about my legacy? If I only had children of my own. To be a father to. A brood of sons to carry on my name and legacy. This line of thinking traveled further like a crack spreading in glass: It was as though inviting in this small, harmless-seeming thought led to a black influx of big, horrible thoughts swarming in behind it. And the regret that in the Expensive Hotel room had been a slight mosquito buzz in her ear that was easily shooed away now without warning grew louder, so loud it began to consume not just her hearing but all of her senses and consciousness.

She thought, If I had been born into a more nourishing, more positive set of circumstances with better role models in a more economically vibrant time.

If I had had a stronger, better man for a father he would not have left and I would not have stolen the car. If I had not stolen the car, I would not have gone to juvenile detention. If I had not gone to juvenile detention, they would not have ordered me to be taken in through the back door. If they had not taken me in through the back door, I would not have been so afraid and humiliated and enraged that day when I went to deliver the gun for Uncle Antonio. And if I had not felt that way I would not have lived my life ever since that moment for the sole purpose of never being made to feel that way again, that feeling of being sized up and turned away for not being good enough.

If I could live my life over, I would live it differently. I say that with remorseless honesty and cruel regret. It is an act of masochism to say it. But I say it. I would live it differently. I would commit no crimes. I would work hard in school. I would overcome the challenges of my upbringing the proper way, the way my brother did to become a Visa Second United States Senator: with hard work and focus and hope and positivity. With goodness. I would be dedicated to virtue and wisdom and justice. I would be humble. I would maintain the strength of my will but couple it with patience so as to control it rather than allowing it to control me as I can see I have allowed it to all my life under the delusion that the opposite was true. I would scorn Alejandro el Grande. Tear up every book I saw about him. Scream over every mention of his name, drowning it out from being heard by the world. If I could become young again, that is what I would do. Lithis, make me a child again, with everything ahead of me and nothing behind me. Forgive me. Start me over. I give you my solemn vow that if given this chance when this night comes around again, instead of hiding in a basement alone with the windows covered in metal I will be in the warm home of one of my sons, playing with my grandchildren after dinner, my son and his wife sipping beepollen and looking on in adoration. When this night comes again I will be watching the lives and names and legacies of my sons and grandchildren growing beyond mine which I can see now is the only thing in the world that matters, the only reason we are alive.

It was here that the regret she had lived her life with the purpose of never experiencing suddenly overwhelmed her like the force of an ocean just as beastly and indifferent as she had been to others all her life. It rose from a buzz to a roar. How wrong, how utterly wrong, she had been. The roar increased the more she admitted to herself that though she had lived her life with this moment in mind when she would be alone to do as she pleased, free of all burdens, and though she had achieved that, all she knew now was that she did not want it. In fact she could not even remember now what had driven her to pursue such a life with ruthlessness and lack of conscience. What had been so terrifying to her about the obligations of selflessness and morality and virtue that she had been willing to delve to such blackness in order to escape them? What had been so alluring about her own will that she went to such lengths to satisfy it? She was a scourge upon mankind. She saw this now. What could she do? She had to atone for it. She had to rectify it. But how? There was no penance for this.

After reaching a new intensity that was so awful she thought it would kill her, all at once the roaring stopped and it was quiet. She stood up from her chair and stood there on the porch, still, heart pounding. She had to rewind time, she realized. That was the only way to atone. She had to rewind it. All the way. To before her father left, to before she stole the car. She had to start her life over again and live it the way she now vowed she would. This time she would be one of the good ones. Her task was clear. She had to go back. She had to start over. She had to do it all again. She had to do it right this time. She could do anything she wanted using only the force of her will, as she had demonstrated throughout her life, so why not start over? She looked down at her hands and saw that they were covered with blood. It was stained in the flesh. She wiped them on her bathrobe but it did not come off. All the lives she had taken screamed at her from inside her skull. This was what had been the mosquito buzz and now the roaring: a dissonant concord of anguished death-shrieks. She dropped to her knees and began scraping her blood-blackened hands on the splintered wood of the porch, nearly in tears. She added her own shrieking. She kept doing it even as you stood there at the bottom of the stairs holding your silly tissues out toward her, believing you, you of all people, could do anything to help her.

What a horrid trick, a nasty game of chance, was life. A coin-toss of perspective. But she was still here and she could still fix it all and as a student of history—her life could be interpreted as that of a student of history—she knew the one way to do it.

It was that day that she decided to do what worked so well the first time to reset the history of this massive, wayward human empire.

It has taken months of work, years of work. The world has gone on but she has not. The time has lost itself. The months and years have gone by so fast. They have not been months and years but seconds and minutes. She's been acquiring the materials from Scrap Yards, construction sites, Hardware Store, Waste Disposal Centers, Visa Department of Defense research laboratories at Ivy League University–McLean, into which she breaks late at night. She's been unable to step back to examine her progress. It has not been possible because she's been so consumed by the work. She's known only that she is so close and is creating something total and infinite and if she were to step back and try to understand the enormity of her accomplishment the depths and intricacies of it would only exhaust her. No, she must ride this rhythm, no time to stop, no time to think. Consideration is death. She does not know how she's known how to build it. It is as though the blueprints have been embedded into her instincts and she has been guided by a force that's been elaborately entwined for all time within each of her genetic ancestors and now her.

And now she's finished. The work is exquisite—the body smooth and shiny, no seams or other evidence of lazy work and shortcuts, a massive, multiton thing that looks like a harmless water heater. But therein lies true might. She imagines the shell somehow surviving the blast. She imagines it being found by survivors, or dug out of the ash one thousand years from now by future races—her future ancestors. Or her future self. Perhaps her future self—would that be the third Junior Alvarez? Who knows how many there have been?—will find it and know right away what it is despite not knowing how he knows, it being entwined within him too. The only thing left to do now is install the enriched plutonium pit. Her hands tremble as she unlocks the safe she's stored it in. What does she feel? Not the sentiment of finality. Not the animal quiver of approaching annihilation but wonder at the beauty of the thing she has made. She is too exhausted to feel much of anything else. She has no thoughts—no memories or wishes or even regrets anymore. The safe's combination is tattooed crudely on the back of her hand with the ink of a ballpoint pen. Dementia has set in to a near total degree as have the other disintegrating effects of aging. Her lungs burn. She has to will off sleep, death. Just for these final moments more. Her fingers have long become unresponsive brittle tubes of limp skin and bone, foreign appendages somehow attached to her hands. She lifts the cylinder. Her spine rages beneath her flesh. Muscles cramp and whither all over.

She removes the pit. It seems to weigh forty-five kilos. The tendons in her wrist pop like the snipping of cargo binding. Shaking so much with fear and excitement as she carries it over to the bomb that she fears she will not be able to get it in properly, that she will drop it halfway in and it will break something crucial and she will not know how to fix it because she does not know how she built it the first time.

Outside cars drive up and down the street. It is the last time they will drive up and down the street. Birds chirp. It is the last time they will chirp. The city and the world going about its tick tock way with no idea that obliteration's coming. Could all the people out there have guessed in a million years that they were about to become people of the ash fields? That it was all over? All they have done with their lives done, erased, just stick etchings on ocean sand?

The old lady, struggling to steady the pit, sweat pouring from her skin and the remaining few of her little square brown teeth sinking deep into her lip, ripping that scabbed cracked flesh.

Now as she extends the pit toward the bomb like she is offering something to the deities her small weak arms must do all the work. Though she wills them up, her arms go down. Lithis, she just needs to find the last remaining bit of life inside her.

Head down, back arched, grunting a tight desperate prayer, arms failing and more tendons popping this time not only in her wrist but in her shoulders, and the muscles in her neck and legs and ribs, disks slipping in her chicken-bone spine, horrific ripping pain all up and down, a body in revolt against itself. The pit slides maybe by miracle into the proper place. A whirring noise and a red light indicate that the deed has been accomplished. Countdown begins.

She collapses forward facedown onto the bomb then losing consciousness rolls off it onto the floor like a sack of mud, head thunking and arms splayed in an unnatural manner, wig falling off her head to reveal a hideous little white spotted scalp. She rolls onto her back and closes her eyes and waits for annihilation. It won't hurt. They'll all feel nothing. Just like the first time.

After several minutes nothing has happened. No annihilation. No rewinding the clock. No second chance. She opens her eyes, exhales. Her breath comes out in a cold foggy mist. She sees against the wall a shadow cast from the single bulb flickering over the workbench. It is the shadow of the bomb. She does not understand the shadow. Something is wrong with the shadow. It is raggedy, distorted, and monstrous. She lifts her head enough to see the bomb. It has changed. No longer the polished ideal of painstaking work and expert design, no longer even a bomb, now just a tangled sloppy mound of pieces of things discarded by people: rusted bicycle chains, dirty bottles, old computer components and hardware, the innards of obsolete televisions, automobile parts, rotted broken panels of wood with bent nails sticking out of them, and so on, all seemingly just tossed atop one another with no care or design. This is what she's worked like a beast on for years? This is the result? Just a pile of trash?

And it is in this dejection and confusion at the failing of her will—which has never failed before—that she spends her final moments of consciousness before giving in to the bottomless exhaustion, allowing its salty black waves to wash over and take her out and below.

She does not wake even as the intruder enters. Loudly and with great effort using a diamond-bladed slab saw to cut out a small hole from the concrete floor. The intruder climbs through it. It is a woman, more or less. She is covered in filth from crawling through the hundreds of yards of shit and piss in the underground city sewage system in order to sneak up to the house undetected. The intruder has a miner's light strapped to her head and she too is demented and furious-willed and withered from age and from struggle and from the isolation of evil though hers is a greater isolation because it is the isolation of victimhood. Head shrunken, no hair left but a few thin clumps. An awful bug-eyed scowling creature no bigger than a child. She looks like something pulled out of a drain. She has lived ninety-seven hard years and now here she is at the end of her life. It is a miracle she has made it here. She stands there looking at the pile of garbage against the wall, a bag of sugar spilled over it as though to mock it. She sways involuntarily, coughs up blood, dry old heart thumping. The miner's light shines upon the old lady lying there on the floor. Rats scurry away as the intruder approaches. She stands over her looking down at her, breathing heavily from either fatigue or the intensity of the moment. This damp basement has in an instant morphed into the sacred delubrum of ceremony as she pulls from the handmade leather sheath hanging on her back the cast-iron hand vac—rusted, old brown blood caked on it. She stands there over the old lady with the hand vac raised over her head, dripping sweat onto the old lady with such propensity it could be her will itself turning into water and breaching the limits of her body's capacity to contain it. Or it could be all the pain inside her that is turning to water. It has built up and built up and never went anywhere, just had more pain added to it, until it ran out of space. And now that moment has come. It is out of space. It must come out.

The old lady opens her eyes at the sensation of the water on her forehead and sees this awful thing ruined by the rectitude of grief standing above her with something raised over her head. They stare at each other. In the old lady's eyes looking up at the intruder there is not recognition but there is some kind of glimmer, as though she knows who this is and why she is here. Her lips part to speak. Thick white paste stretching between them like gum. The intruder does not give her the chance. Without warning or relish or any sense of history she uses the final remnant of her life to bring that hand vac down upon the skull of Junior Alvarez, crushing it with such simplicity that in an instant it is as though the skull never even was a skull or anything at all other than a mess of biological spillage. And the brains of Junior Alvarez splatter about the basement in a black pool, blood and goop and bile and all manner of filth bubbling up into what remains of the oral cavity of Junior Alvarez, that one-time child and all-time demon, and spilling out of his nose and down his chin, his body seizing. And the intruder raises the hand vac dripping with Junior Alvarez's cerebral fluid with teeth stuck in it, a large piece of scalp hanging off it jiggling like a sunfish, and she brings it down again and again and again until there is no longer the sound of cracking and splitting but only the muffled dinging of cast-iron on concrete.

The intruder's body then begins to shut down. It is like the dinging has cued that to happen. She drops the hand vac. She is heaving and crying though no tears are coming out because all the pain in her has already turned to water and gone. Now there is nothing left. She is weightless, unburdened. She is unable to see or hear. She's just thinking about her son.

She's on her knees beside the corpse as though in grief over it. She looks at him dead. She's the last one alive. She has outlasted him, if just by three breaths. For now her heart slows and she breathes out long and hard and her heart stops and she falls over onto her side next to the body of Junior Alvarez in such a way that her head lies at his feet and what's left of his head lies at hers and that is the way they stay forever and ever.

THE END

Printed in the United States
By Bookmasters